SAVING
SPARROW

BIRDS OF BOSTON: BOOK THREE

S. E. EMORY

—BIRDS OF BOSTON SERIES—

Chasing Phoenix — Leo & Everett

Finding Raven — Colette & Gage

Meant to Fly — Millie & Ski

Saving Sparrow — Natasha & Hale

Before you go on this journey with Hale and Natasha, please be
aware there are some themes that may be triggering to some readers.
These themes include explicit sexual scenes, explicit language, mentions of miscarriage, memories of childhood sexual abuse, thoughts
of suicide, flashbacks of suicide, eating disorders, violence/threats
of violence, weaponry including knives, guns, scenes of gore/bodily
dismemberment.
Please read with caution if any of the above could be potentially
triggering.
-S

Authors Note

The poems in this book were written many years ago by Maegan
Parada.

A young girl surviving in a world full of demons.

I love you, Mae Mae.

Never settle.

For the ones who found hell in their heaven and survived by making a haven of hell.

Hallow Bones | Anna Graves

Broken | Noelle Johnson

Love The Way You Lie | Eminem, Rihanna

Iris | Grace Davies

Angels Like You | Miley Cyrus

You're the One | Luca Fogale

Fall Into Me | Forest Blakk

I Can Love You Like That | John Michael Montgomery

Love Is The Answer | Natalie Taylor

Coal | Dylan Gossett

Surrender | Natalie Taylor

Hold On | Chord Overstreet

Last Man Standing | Livingston

In The Stars | Benson Boone

The Night We Met | Lord Huron

Love Me Back | Max McNown

"When the sparrow sings its final refrain,
The hush is felt nowhere more deeply than in the heart of man."

-Don Williams

hale

The suffocating hand of my failure tightens over my throat with the eleventh anniversary of her death.

Each second of the day drug into the next, my mind occupied, numbed to the workday, but now her loss rushes in and the breath in my lungs abandons me completely. The grief steals the focus I can't afford to lose and in my line of work, being distracted loses lives.

In previous years, I've taken this day off and gone home, but not this year. This year the pile of paperwork piled high upon my desk. Just too many tasks to complete and boxes to check. I thought being a federal agent working in the sex trafficking division would be all about swooping in and saving the day, but it's more than that.

More mindless tasks.

More cases.

More paperwork.

More missing men, women, and children.

More failures.

But what eats at me the most, if I couldn't save my own flesh and blood, what makes me think I could save any of them?

The spring air of Boston hits my lungs like a fucking ice bath as I step onto the rooftop of the Copley Plaza. My sister obsessed over the history of this hotel; it was the only thing I never understood about her. Then she came home, and it was the only thing I *did* understand. The peace, the quiet. Like stepping into a glass box, the solidarity of being atop this historic hotel softens the city below.

I keep my head down as I make my way toward the edge, admiring all the bird shit covering the rooftop of the luxurious Boston landmark. Ironic, huh? Despite its prestige, it's still covered in shit.

A sniffle breaks my trance, and I look up. I'm always up here alone. How did—

Perching on the ledge of the rooftop, a woman stands a single step away from falling to her death. Am I imagining her? Have I finally lost my fucking mind? Is she a ghost?

She could be, with her pale skin, lithe body, and platinum blonde hair that almost looks translucent. The contrast of her against the dark night shining like a beacon, lighting my way to the edge. The warm night air thickens, but the breeze has a bite of winter, the wretched season refusing to let go. She must be freezing this late at night, exposed to the elements in such scant clothing. Her white silk slip flutters as I look around to see if anyone else accompanies her but it's just my ghost and me.

"Shh. It will be okay. You won't suffer long," her angelic voice fills my ears, like a siren song. My involuntary steps take me toward her. Foolish of me, I'd hate to scare her. Realizing my mistake, I take a step back.

"Miss?" I say quietly.

She doesn't jump with fright but instead keeps her head tilted forward, looking at something in her folded hands. Her hair blows, carrying a soft lavender scent.

Lavender. Like home.

"Ma'am?" I inquire again when she doesn't respond.

"Leave me," she says.

"I can't do that." My thudding heart pulls me one small step closer.

"Do you think birds know how lucky they are?" A sigh of relief escapes me at her response. At least she said *something*, but what the hell is she talking about? My minds on high alert, ready for her to jump. Every instinct telling me to reach out and pull her into me, keep her safe, save her. But the special agent in me knows that any sudden movement I make toward her could literally send her over the edge.

"You should step down from there and we can talk about the birds."

"This one was lucky," she whispers, most likely not meant for me to hear but I'm hyper focused on everything about her right now.

"Which one? Can you come show me?" My feet remain planted on the concrete rooftop, but my muscles shake with tension. Filled with eagerness to grab her if she makes a move to go forward. Like a rubber band stretched and ready to shoot, I'm prepared to lunge for her if she sways.

I won't lose her.

She looks over her shoulder and her eyes strike me like a kick to the chest, filling me with such vibrant sorrow that I physically react with a step backwards. Their rich brown stands out, a stark contrast to her pale skin and halo of long, shimmering hair. Despite her softness, her eyes hold an edge, warning me away as much as they call me close.

It's at this moment, I know without a shadow of a doubt that if she jumps, I'm going over with her.

"What's your name?" I ask.

"Does it matter?" She looks forward again, breaking away from the hold I try to keep her in.

"Matters to me." I take a single step toward her and as if she could hear the near silent scuff of my shoe, she scoots slightly forward, hanging her toes over the edge.

"What's your name?" she asks with a timidness that tells me she might not be brave enough to take that final and everlasting step.

"I asked first." I don't move forward, but slightly to the side, positioning myself behind her. Easier for me to grab her if needed.

"Sparrow."

"Sparrow?" I repeat and she nods her head.

Birds. Sparrow.

What's with the birds? "Why do you think birds are lucky?"

The white noise of the traffic and the occasional honk below fill the air as her silence stretches on. *Come on talk to me, little sparrow. Keep talking to me.*

If she's talking, she won't be jumping.

"They are free to go wherever their heart and wings take them."

Fuck it. I move up in one swift step to stand on the ledge next to her. My body sways slightly and my arms stretch out momentarily to balance myself, her now worried gaze finding mine.

"You should get down. I don't want you to—"

"What? Fall?" I interrupt her. The delicate skin covering her pulse flutters faster and images of my tongue running over her flesh flash through my mind. "What if I wanted to fall? Would you stop me?"

No answer, instead she looks back down into her hands at the small bird cradled there.

But not just any bird—a sparrow.

The bird sits there, only the head moving slightly.

"I think her wing is broken," she sniffles as single tear lands on her hand. "She'll never fly again. Her life's over. Death would be a mercy."

I'm not sure what compels me but moving slowly, I take her chin between my fingers and turn her those haunting eyes to me. Those eyes I'd jump off a building for, just so that they would be the last thing I'd see on this fucked up planet. "You don't need wings to fly."

It's not that I want to die tonight, but I've been an apathetic asshole for eleven years. After losing the other half of my soul, I never thought I could feel again, let alone feel an innate, confounding connection to someone. Just like the way I felt when I looked into this woman's eyes. It's unexplainable and terrifying how desperate I am to keep her here with me.

She pulls her face from my hand and looks back at the small sparrow. "You're crazy. Of course you do."

"Come with me and I'll show you how to fly from the ground," I whisper in her ear with a small smirk on my face.

Her head whips toward me and she sways with the disequilibrium the motion caused. *Shit!* I act quickly; instinct taking over. My arms wrap around her waist and pull her off the ledge. We both stumble onto the rooftop, somehow staying on our feet as she wiggles out of my hold. My body the only force between her and that ledge.

She'll have to get through me if she wants to fly.

"You had no right," she fires at me with a spark in her eyes.

A small laugh escapes me as I shake my head at her. Now that she's safe, I feel an anger build inside. Anger at her, at myself. "You'll have to excuse me, but I don't give a shit about your opinion of what I can and can't do. I'm not the one that was up on a ledge, ready to jump. You think maybe me showing up on this night, at this time, was fate? Maybe you weren't meant to die tonight?"

"It's none of your business." Her expressive eyes soften, shimmering with unshed tears. I get the feeling that she's the type of girl who can get anything she wants with those eyes. But her death won't be one of those things.

"What's your name? Your real name?" My authoritative tone doesn't make her falter and something akin to pride sparks inside me.

"None of your business," she bites back, full of malice. She's as stubborn as a wild horse. I'm a fool for thinking of this woman as some fragile, broken thing. But if I know anything, it's that horses are gentle by nature, vicious by nurture and I would bet she's no different.

My posture relaxes a bit, and I sit on the ledge, still blocking her exit ticket off the planet but coming across as less intimidating, hoping she will drop her defenses just a touch.

"The bird's wing can heal." I let my gaze drop from her eyes to her hands, giving in first to give her some sense of control.

She steps closer and I tense, readying to grab hold of her again, but she kneels in front of me, taking up a position of submission and my mouth waters at the sight.

"Do you think her life will be the same when it does? When she heals, I mean." She holds the small creature in one hand and gently strokes its head with her pinky finger. With her statement, I get the feeling we aren't talking about the sparrow in her hands, but the one in her heart.

"No, I think her life will be vastly different. Different doesn't always mean bad though. But if she dies, she'll never know what awaits her on the other side of healing."

My sister's smile illuminates inside my memories, the smile I'll never see again. She could have a family by now. She could be a veterinarian like she always dreamed. She could have been completely different than the girl they turned her into, but she couldn't see the beautiful future that awaited her on the other side of healing. She couldn't see it and I didn't show it to her.

"Was your life better after healing?" she asks with a convicting gaze that fills me with guilt.

"I haven't earned the right to heal. I deserve the pain I go through each day. It's my penance for the hell I've caused," I confess as I keep my stare trained on my feet, my arms resting on my knees. The weight in my chest lifts slightly with the admission and my head falls into my hands.

I don't have to be looking at her to know she has shifted from the floor to stand before me. I've always been aware of my surroundings, better than most. It's been ingrained into me for years. But I've never been so aware of anyone the way I am right now with her. It's as if she alters the space around me instead of simply existing in it. Before I can look up at her, her hand grips my jaw, and she lifts my gaze to hers.

"I don't think the heart can heal like a broken wing can. The heart needs company and tonight, I don't want to be alone."

She turns and walks away from me, her body moving like a dancer—elegant and fluid. I'm hypnotized by the sway of her small hips, the way her back moves as she turns her head to look over her slim shoulder at me expectantly, like I should be following her.

I think I'd follow her to the depths of hell if I could die with my lips on her skin. I stand and match her pace as she leads me down the stairwell and into a hallway.

When I reach the door she disappeared through a moment before, a small push opens it and again, I follow her inside. I don't know what she wants from me, but after my confession to her, one I haven't told anyone before, I feel a connection to her that controls me beyond any logical thought.

Should I have walked into a room with a woman ready to take her life? Probably not. Should I let her use me to numb her own mind? Definitely not. But do I want to run my tongue over her body, find out if her skin tastes like lavender, feel her shimmering hair as it runs through my fingers, get lost in the warmth of her sorrow because it balances out the cold that has grown in my own heart? Fuck yes, I do.

"I don't even know your real name," I say as she puts a towel in the bathroom sink and gently sets the small bird down into it. She walks over to me and pushes my suit jacket down my arms. She may be a head shorter than I am, but she could drop me to my knees with one look.

"Natasha," she whispers before her lips meet mine.

hale

I shouldn't be doing this.

I should *not* be doing this.

But holy hell, this woman intoxicates me. She has completely taken control. I'm a fucking puppet on her strings as she manipulates me, and I happily move to her will. She clearly knows how to work her body and her tongue. Like the siren I know she is, she'll give me those eyes, and I will fall in her wake.

Slowly, she removes each strap of the slip from her shoulders and lets it fall before she lays back on the bed. The rich, golden sheets make her look like royalty and her naked body makes me want to hit my knees and bow to her.

"Fuck," I whisper as I run my hand down my face. I'm about to fall into my ruin. *Walk away, Knight.*

But how could I? I'm only human after all. The thin, old wood floors vibrate with my footsteps as I make my way toward her. Most women I have been with are shy about their body, wanting to stay under the covers or only comfortable when the lights are low, but not her.

Lights illuminate every corner of the room, and she stretches out on the bed, her arms raised above her head, one knee bent, her toes pointed and running up and down her other leg. Her skin looks as if it were merely a thin piece of silk draping over her prominent bones. There doesn't seem to be an ounce of fat on her body.

She's stunning but it makes me wonder... does her skin naturally cling so closely to her bones or does she sacrifice her health to make it so? Either way, she's beyond anything I've ever seen. Not even the sunsets from atop the hills of my home could compare. She works her body like a siren trained to be the exact picture of what a man needs and wants.

I slowly unbutton my shirt and let it fall to the floor. Sliding out my wallet from my back pocket, I take out the single condom and hold it between my teeth. As I work the buckle of my belt, her gaze travels up and down my body. A slow perusal I appreciate since I work fucking hard to keep in shape.

When I stand before her, fully naked, I fist my cock in my hand and stroke it once before sliding on our protection, allowing her to watch the movement and when she bites her bottom lip, I descend upon her. Falling between her legs, she instantly feels like home which baffles me since I just met the damn woman. Her warm thighs latch around my torso as I grab her hands in mine, threading our fingers and keeping them hostage above her head. "Where did you come from?"

Her lips brush mine, silencing my question. They explore me, mirroring the way I'm seeking to learn her body in return. I kiss her jaw, and travel down to her neck, then the other side. I want to map every area on her body, memorize her so that I can feel her when my sorrow creeps in.

"What do I—" A moan escapes her lips, interrupting her question. Her warm, supply breast fills my mouth and bite down gently, enough to feel her skin between my teeth, but not so hard it would leave a mark. "Call you," she finishes, and a smile breaks out across my face. Such focus. That just won't do. If she can still form a complete sentence, then I'm not doing my job properly.

"Call me Knight."

"Knight," she moans out as I trail my fingers over her pussy and find that sensitive area that will drive her mad. Circling her clit over and over, I tease her opening with the tip of my cock. Her nipples harden to stiff peaks as I suck on each of her breasts in turn, pulling and tugging at the soft tissue. Her body tenses under me, curling up tighter until she begins to shake, and I know I've got her. But she doesn't release like her body tells me it wants to.

The slow, tortuous pace I push into her with forces a moan from both of us. The little whimpers and pants that leave her lips with each thrust and the way her pussy pulses around me tells me she's experiencing as much pleasure as I am, but she's holding back. My hips pause, letting her mind focus on what my fingers are trying desperately to pull from her.

"Knight. I–I."

There we go. Incomplete thoughts leave her as her body tenses further, but she *still* doesn't let go.

"Do you feel my fingers, Natasha? Focus on how I touch you, how I make you feel. Don't think of anything else. Now be a good girl and come for me."

Her whole body shakes underneath me, her thighs gripping my waist like a fucking vice. Above her head, our fingers intertwine, and her nails dig into the back of my hand. My other hand continues to work her clit until she's a writhing mess beneath me. "I want you to come on my cock. Show me what you're made of and make a fucking mess of me."

"I–I can't," she whimpers as her body coils like a spring, and I begin to move slowly in and out of her. The warmth of her thighs around me, her palm in mine, her pussy around my cock drives me to blissful insanity. My gaze meets those sad whiskey eyes, "Yes, you can. Me and you. Just me and you."

As if my words finally gave her permission to feel something, she cries out and coats my cock and fingers in her sweet release. Her body vibrates all around me, moving of its own accord with no amount of control. She shatters under me in more ways than one as I bring her to her full potential.

"God, you are *fucking* incredible. Such a good girl," I praise her, and she whimpers as I bring my lips to hers. When she finally calms down, I plan to stay right here and soak in all that she is, but she flips my plans upside down as her small body sets mine off balance and she rolls us.

"My turn," she teases as she fists my cock and hovers over it. My hands glide up her thighs and rest on her small waist. I pull down slightly, encouraging her to slide down onto me but she resists. Does she regret this? Does she want to stop? Fuck, it would be the most difficult thing I've had to do but I could if she changed her mind.

Those brown eyes sparkle with mischief, and a small smirk tugs up the corner of her swollen lips when she slowly sinks herself onto me and it's the best torture I've ever endured. "Fuck," I whisper as I fall to my ruin, like I knew I would.

Her heat slowly envelopes me and my body shakes at the feel of her. Everything in me wants to ravage her, to go faster, further. But she keeps it slow.

Lifting slowly, she repeats the movement, and I let out a low growl. My grip tightens on her waist, and I see the question in her eyes. Am I going to let her have control or am I going to take it from her?

She might not be used to men who relinquish control, but I've never been afraid to be dominated. She can have whatever she wants from me. My body, my release, my praise. I release my grip on her and bring my hands to hers where she has them resting on my chest. Taking one hand, I guide it up and around my throat, her eyes blowing wide at my suggestion. Taking her other hand, I intertwine our fingers, lifting them above my head and showing her the position of power she wants to take but hesitates to test.

Pulled forward slightly, her sensitive clit rubs against my abs and her grip tightens, causing my head to rush from the slow of oxygen to my brain.

"You're in control, baby. Take what you want, I'll give it," I whisper in her ear, and she begins grinding against me. The movement of her hips like a fucking conductor leading an orchestra. Her moans are a sweet music our bodies create together.

She doesn't hesitate to pull her orgasm to the front as she continues to tighten around me. Her hand causes a delicious pressure in my head that makes me feel high and finally when she gives me herself for the second time, I follow right after. Her small frame falls onto my chest, a welcomed weight against my heart. In a praising kiss, I take the breath from her that she stole from me moments ago.

Even when tonight leaves us, she has forever left her mark on me. She's the little bit of heaven in the hell I've created.

The steady beating of her heart tells me minutes have passed as I count each beat. Some people don't know how it feels to have your heart still beat inside you when one half of it has been ripped from your chest, when you lose a part of your soul and question how you could ever go on. I wonder if she knows that pain. I do, and that's why I find comfort in the rhythm of her heart against mine.

After catching her breath, she looks up at me, her chin resting against my sternum. "Did I hurt you?"

A deep chuckle rumbles through me at the absurdity of that idea and she rolls off of me, tucking herself away again.

"You could never hurt me," I say as my body rolls toward hers. She evades my grasp when I attempt to pull her into me, and I don't fucking like it

"Please don't," she says as she slips out of bed and heads toward the bathroom and I chase after her.

"Don't what?"

The door begins to close but I stop it with my hand and grab her chin between my fingers, pulling those deep brown eyes back to mine. "Don't you dare slam that door in my face. What did I do?"

"Don't be nice to me."

Despite the break in her voice, her bold stare stays locked on mine, unwilling to bend. Fuck, those eyes don't lie, she's strong. A wild animal pacing beneath the surface, waiting for permission to be set free. The question stands then, why's she holding back? What... or who has beaten her down so much she doesn't even recognize her own nature?

"Why not?" Our chests collide, as I pull her into me. Our lips brushing as I place a small kiss to the corner of her mouth.

"I don't belong to you."

A growl vibrates in my chest. The fuck? I've never met a woman who belonged to me more. Even in a single night, I know she's mine. It's crazy, but I never claimed to be sane. She's got me utterly fucked up with a single touch. "Tonight, you do."

Her eyes burn, the fight in her surfacing. But as she assesses me, she must find some truth because the door opens completely, allowing me into the grand bathroom with ornate fixtures and a claw foot tub in the center.

The white tile floor chills my bare feet. If I'm cold, she must be freezing. I'd bet my last dollar she weighs no more than a hundred pounds soaking wet. Not an ounce of fat on her to keep her warm.

Turning the hot water on and then the cold, I find the perfect temperature and let the bath begin to fill. I find some sweet vanilla bath gel and watch as it streams out of the bottle and into the warm water, creating small bubbles. I may not know all about this shit, but I've been drug to my fair share of local artisan shops filled with bath gels, bath bombs, and soaking crystals, all kinds of girly shit and because I loved my sister, I let her talk my ear off about all the items because to see her smile was worth it.

"Come here." My hand reaches out to Natasha, and she takes it, climbing in.

"Too hot?" I ask as she submerges her foot.

"It's perfect," she replies as she sinks her lithe body all the way in, goosebumps breaking out over her shoulders. "It's really perfect," she moans, closing her eyes and relaxing fully into the tub.

I let her soak a minute while I go and put my dress slacks back on. I don't bother with my briefs because I know I'll be naked in her bed again after this bath, but I also feel a bit weird waiting there in my birthday suit.

When I return, she opens her eyes and her brows dip as she gazes down at my pants. "Aren't you going to get in?"

"I don't like baths. But I'll wash you... if you want." I round the tub and pull up a little wooden stool sitting next to the shower. Praying it doesn't break beneath my weight.

Her head nods slightly as she hands me a bottle. The lavender scent of her shampoo fills the room as it pools in my hand. I rub my palms together to warm it up and get it to a nice lather before massaging her scalp.

Her shoulders fall and her head gets heavier in my hands as she re-laxes. "I have great faith in fools - self-confidence my friends will call it." She whispers melodically as she gently runs her hands through the water, swirling the bubbles around her raised knee. I recognize the line, and it makes my lips mimic her own small smile.

"Marginalia. Edgar Allan Poe." The warm water trickles over her head as I begin rinsing her hair.

She giggles and wipes at her face, my lack of grace accidentally getting some of the water in her eyes. "Correct. Are you a fan of poetry, Mr. Knight?"

"A thing of beauty is a joy forever," I say in a gentlemanly tone.

"Oh, come on, that's too easy." She collects some bubbles in her hands, and I fear she may blow them on me, but she doesn't. "Keats."

"Correct."

"And this maiden she lived with no other thought ~ Than to love and be loved by me."

"Poe again," I say.

A somberness fills the space, radiating off her in a palpable wave. What happened to this woman? What can make someone so beautiful want to take flight off a rooftop? Why's Poe her favorite poet? I want to know everything about my little sparrow, my ghost from the rooftop, my mystery woman who has already begun to snip the threads of my undoing.

The lavender scent of her makes me heady as I lean in, whispering in her ear the opening lyrics from one of my favorite Eminem songs. As soon as I finish, she spins her head to look at me. A smile on her face and—fuck, it's so beautiful. It's the first time she's smiled, and she might as well have tattooed it on the inside of my fucking skull because I'll never forget it.

"That's a song. Not a poem." Her soft laughter fills the bathroom, echoing off the walls. Bubbles land in my lap as she blows them onto my pants. My brow raises and my hand aches to punish her for the bratty behavior. But I don't, not yet.

"Excuse you, Ma'am. Lyrics *are* poetry. Now name the artist or lose the game."

She rolls her eyes, knowing I'm right. "Eminem."

What. A. Brat.

"Correct. You win."

The small wooden stool creaks as I stand and grab her a towel then help her out, wrapping the white, soft linen around her shoulders. "What do I win?" she asks as she shivers slightly.

"What do you want?"

"A truth," she says, holding my gaze.

"Then I get one in return," I say as I begin to dry her legs off with a separate towel so that she doesn't have to relinquish the one warming her upper half.

"I guess that's only fair, you also won."

Once dry, she walks out of the bathroom, dropping the towel as she walks away and yet again, I'm chasing after her.

As she lays in the bed, I slip my pants off and climb in behind her. My arms wrap around her and her body molds into mine.

"What were you doing on that roof?" she asks, and I am grateful to be behind her, out of sight. I don't want to look at those eyes as I give her this piece of me.

"I knew someone once who loved this hotel. She would come up to the rooftop all the time. It was her safe space. The staff here loved her so they allowed her access when they shouldn't have but she had a way of batting her lashes and getting whatever she wanted." I smile at the memory of my sister using that to her advantage on more than one occasion. And it usually always ended with me being the one to cave. "I go up there every so often to remember her."

"What happened to her?" she asks, her tone laced with an undertone of sadness.

"She died."

I've spoken those words a million times and they never get easier to say. Grief never seems to leave us, does it? Sometimes it loosens its noose, sometimes it strangles us, and it seems impossible to survive the pain.

"I'm sorry," Natasha says as she turns in my arms.

"Don't apologize. It wasn't your fault." I run my thumb under her eye, along her cheekbone, feeling the soft skin there like velvet. "What were you doing on that roof?"

Her gaze dips between us. "I wanted control of something. My life seemed to be the only thing accessible tonight."

Not for the first time tonight, I wonder who this woman is and what happened to her. "Why don't you have control over your own life, Natasha?" My tone cuts sharp as my control slips. The already over-protective instincts that run through my veins amplify in her presence. Old habits die hard as I feel the intense need to protect Natasha. Even from herself.

"It's been such a long night. Can I answer your question in the morning?" Her amber eyes shine with tears that are being held back and just like with my sister, I can't say no.

"In the morning," I relent.

"I promise."

He told me it was my fault,

I said I know,

I said goodbye.

I don't know why I do the things I do,

I guess I just do them,

Don't ask why,

Don't ask how.

Just say I love you

And

Goodbye

-MP

hale

Five Months Later | September

I promise.

The memory of her lie wakes me from sleep. The last whisper she left me with before I woke in the morning to an empty bed and no sign of the ghost who has now haunts my days and nights. Not only did she leave me with more questions than answers and a boner from hell, but she also left me with that fucking bird.

Even though that night drives me mad with unanswered questions, I don't regret it. Something about her shifted something in me, making it a bit easier to breathe. A little easier to get through my days. I wish I could find her. Hell, I don't even need to be in her life if she doesn't want me to be, I just want to know she's okay.

That night she was ready to end her life. Did something change? Is she a little better now too? Has she decided that she wants to see what's on the other side of healing or maybe she's somewhere in a grave?

Is she truly my ghost now?

A knock sounds at my door, and I jerk upright. Another night I've slept in my office chair and my neck has a kink from hell. I make a mental note to go back to my apartment today before I begin to smell. Looking down at my white button up, I notice but don't honestly give two shits that it's a bit wrinkled. Two days in the same suit are noticeable, three's a disgrace. My Ma would whoop my ass if she knew I wore a wrinkled shirt with a questionable stain on the front pocket.

"Come in," I call, attempting to fix my tie.

Anderson walks in with a manila folder tucked under his arm. "We got the photos of the twins you requested, as well as the information on the people they have been spending time with while in Boston."

"Thanks Anderson," I say as I take the envelope. Anderson's one of our hackers, not as good as Eros but legal told me I can't demand Eros be on the clock 24/7. *Fucking bullshit.*

Walking past him, I go to flip the envelope open, but people trickle in the front door, nodding their greetings toward the boss... i.e. me and I fulfill my mandated pleasant and welcoming boss duties by returning the nods, waves, and smiles. All said things distracting me from opening the file resting in my hands and nagging at my brain.

"Hey boss?" Anderson calls out and I pause to look over my shoulder.

"Yeah?"

"Field team three found the two missing sisters from two months ago." He hands me the other manila folder tucked under his arm.

"Why wasn't I informed?"

"They completed their mission early this morning around three am, Sir. They haven't even written their full report yet, I wanted to give you a heads up so you could prepare."

My back teeth start grinding, only making my pounding headache worse. Prepare? How the fuck do I prepare to read a report about two teen girls who were sold into the trafficking rings two months ago and now, based on Anderson's tone, were not found alive. Answer? I can't. But I will. I'll continue to put myself through this torture because if I can get there in time once, it makes up for the fuck ton of times I didn't.

"Thanks for the heads up. Go home, Anderson. Get some sleep and hug your wife and daughter."

"Have a good night, Sir. Get some rest yourself," he says as he looks me up and down, noticing, as I assume everyone else will that I've yet again slept here.

As he turns away, I run my hand down my face, groaning because I won't beat the incoming day team to the break room and all the good coffee will be gone. I'll be left with the fucking knock off K-cups instead of the Starbucks flavored ones.

Tucking the Alessi file under my arm, I open the girls' file. A knife lodges right into my fucking heart when their matching blue eyes and bright smiles remind me that their parents will never see those features again.

At least they went together...

The faces of these girls will haunt me. Welcome to the party. It's a real riot inside my head.

When I finally make it back to my desk after the morning huddle and the girls' report from team three, I'm on coffee number two and I have about eighty-six emails to sort through. Man, sometimes I miss being a SEAL. Being the boots on the ground, making a difference. I'm useless here running this unit, but Boston's one of the most critical points for these operations. These victims move in through our shipping ports and because it's a large city, there are plenty of places to hide and plenty of "inventory to choose from" as one of the top traffickers we caught last year worded it.

And speaking of top traffickers, my mind closes all its tabs but keeps the Alessi one open. Finally cracking open that file.

The Alessi brothers are in my city and they need to be my focus. Their father, Dante, runs the largest human trafficking ring on the west coast for two decades.

His two boys, Rafael and Enzo Alessi, also known as The Devils of Seattle, don't come to Boston often but they make an occasional appearance. But the visits have increased and last time they were in town, I wasn't the unit chief.

If they are thinking of expanding, they're going to be met with a whole lot of trouble. I won't bow down to their money like the other officials do. Because unlike them, I'm not in this position for the money, I'm in it for revenge.

I flip through the photos, most of which are of Enzo since Rafael tends to keep out of the public eye and to himself. The picture of nonchalance, Enzo waves or blows a kiss at what is supposed to be our undercover camera taking his photo. What a fucking menace.

Honestly, if he wasn't a sick fuck, we might get along. I shake my head at the notion, but my world stops when I turn to the next photo and find a familiar blonde tucked between both the twins. Enzo with his arm wrapped around her shoulder and Rafael with his hand holding hers.

"What the fuck?" My chair lets out an awful whine as I stand, flipping quickly to the back of the report.

My heart violently knocks at my sternum, as if it's trying to escape and run to her. Images of her underneath me flash through my mind, those vividly haunted eyes begging me for... *something*. I wasn't sure what for exactly. If I could have had more time with her, I know I would have figured out exactly what she needed from me.

My finger runs down the short list of names the twins have associated with while here, till I come across a name I recognize.

Natasha.

Do you know how many Natasha's there or in Boston? Around one hundred and sixty inside city limits. None, however, were *my* Natasha.

A full name, *finally*. Natasha Parker Baldwin.

"Gotcha, little sparrow," I say as I run my thumb over her photo, remembering the feel of her velvet skin.

What the hell's she doing with the twins? Did she know who I was a couple months ago? Was our night together a set up?

As soon as the thought enters my mind, I push it aside. It couldn't have been. The pain in her eyes was real, the numbness in her voice a vibrant warning sign. But that doesn't mean it wasn't a ruse. She knew exactly how to work her body... she's the one who led me to her room...

I don't belong to you. That's what she had told me. Was it because she belonged to them? Is she one of their girls? Is that why she wanted to jump?

My brain switches over to detective mode as question after question runs through my mind like fucking Usain Bolt. I continue to read about her and her family, cataloging and storing all the information away.

Wealthy, from a small Oregon town. An heiress to a massively large hotel chain similar in prestige to the Copley. Someone with the status she has wouldn't be one of their products and even if they owned her, the twins wouldn't be all over her like they are in these photos.

I focus on a particularly dangerous photo of Enzo tilting her sweet face up as he smiles down at her. Her hands clench into small fists and her body leans away from him. In all ways she screams no, but he still has his hands on her.

Rage rolls through me as I slam the folder closed and text my favorite hacker.

Get your ass in here. Now.

Eros

> Do you know what time it is you fucking twat.

> Yes. Time for sleeping beauty to wake and get to work.

> Do I need to come give you a true love's kiss to wake your ass up?

> You can kiss my ass. I'm not scheduled to come in till noon.

> How did you know I'm into that? Have you been reading my diary? It's urgent.

> You're an idiot.

A short fifteen minutes later, Gage strolls into my office without knocking, per usual. I smirk because that asshole can never resist me when I call.

"The Alessi twins are in town," I say, leaning back in my chair. Gage casually strolls over to my office window, looking down at all the people bustling around, his Americano in hand. I swear he doesn't drink anything besides coffee. Probably why he's always such a joy, the dehydrated asshole.

I've never understood the obsessive way he is about his coffee, bitter as fuck. Although one could say the same for the man currently sipping from his ceramic mug and standing at my window as if he runs this place.

"Why are they in Boston?" he asks after taking a sip.

"Fuck if I know. But they are and we have our eye on them. We need you to dig around, see what you can find. We need to know why they are in our city."

See if you can find out why Natasha's with them sits on the tip of my tongue, but I keep that to myself. I can't let Gage sniff out my personal interest in her like the fucking hound he is.

Natasha's my secret and I'm not ready to share.

"Do you know where they are staying?" he asks as he comes over and falls into the chair across from my government issued metal desk, kicking his expensive leather oxfords atop my desk because he knows it pisses me right the fuck off. The man's cleaner than a murder weapon, I wouldn't be surprised if he fucking Clorox wipes his shoes after walking on the streets of Boston but still, disgusting. I knock his feet down and he chuckles.

Dick.

"Yeah, the Copley." I slide the folder toward him. I'll let him flip through and then find some way to ask him to investigate my pretty blonde bombshell. I study his face as he shuffles through the folder. Gage wears a face of stone, but his micro expressions give him away. At least to someone like me, someone trained to read them.

It's the lift of his left brow that tells me if he's caught off guard or surprised, the narrowing of his eyes if he's upset, the smallest dimple between his brows and clench of his jaw if he's pissed and finally the clenching of his fists if he's losing control over his carefully constructed facade. I don't know all of his past, but I've done my research. I have to if I'm going to work this closely with someone.

I know his dad resides in federal prison for possession and distribution of child pornography, aiding in child trafficking across state lines and illegal laundering of funds.

I also know that Agent Eros here put his own father in prison, and I can't help but wonder how deep his father's sins go. With how closed off he is, it wouldn't surprise me if he were one of his father's victims. Gage doesn't allow people close to him, emotionally or physically.

When he lifts his left brow slightly after he flips to the picture with Natasha, I know he knows something. "What? Why do you have that look on your face?"

He continues to stare at the photo as if it's a puzzle he can't solve. "This girl in the photo, the blonde. What do you know about her?"

"What do you know about her?" I respond with a bit more defensiveness than I meant to. Fuck. I'm already getting worked up over her.

Keep it together, Knight.

"I asked first," he challenges.

"I'm the boss," I fire back as I steeple my hands together on the desk and lean in. But my intimidation tactic fails, like it always does with this bullheaded agent of mine. I bite the bullet and let him have this win.

"Dick," I mutter and get up to get another look at her.

As I come around to stand behind him, her stunning features come back into my field of vision and for a quick moment I forget who she's associated with, but then I see Enzo's hands on her and I grip the back of Eros's chair, my knuckles whitening.

My jaw tenses and I repeat everything I read about her. "Natasha Baldwin. Heiress of the Baldwin empire on the west coast. Good 'ol Daddy Baldwin owns a series of hotels down the coast. And if she's involved with the Alessis, we can only assume her father is too. We honestly don't know much more about her. No record. Currently works at a dance studio as a ballet instructor. Grew up in a small town on the outskirts of Portland but recently moved to Boston. As far as we can tell she's clean. Which begs the question, why are the twins interested in her?"

Here's what I also know about her. She tastes like lavender and her smell drives me wild. Her skin reminds me of velvet, her body's smooth except for the moments when I run my hands down her side and the protrusions of her bones interrupt her beautiful curves. She's a fiery little thing with a vulnerable side that I feel a compulsive need to protect. She loves poetry and warm water running down her chest. She longs for control, but something keeps her from taking it. She left me in the middle of the night, the only night I've slept fully in eleven goddamn years. And last I saw of her—she wanted to jump off a fucking building.

But I don't say any of that.

"I'll figure it out," Gage says as he stands and heads for the door.

"Let me know what you find out." My feet carry me back to my own chair and I fall into it. What happened to you, little sparrow? Do you need me to save you... again? Do you even want to be saved?

Chapter Four

natasha

Present | October

"Hit me, babe! Don't be a little bitch!" Sabrina's shouts blend with the drums of My Name is Human by Highly Suspect as it blares through the speakers. The sweat pouring down my back and brow keep me focused. Drawing my senses to each bead that trickles down my skin like fingers gently tracing my spine.

My fist flies, landing a right hook to her cheek and she smiles as she whips her head back to me. Her scarlet red braids flying out behind her.

"Atta girl."

Joe's Gym has become my haven since I began training with Sabrina. Gage Eros, my high school boyfriend's best friend and my now FBI stalker insisted I learn how to defend myself. I thought he was crazy but the more I came, the more I fell in love with the rush of being in this headspace. When the pain from the hit comes, everything clears from my mind.

Sabrina and Gage are two of the best fighters I have ever watched... not that I've seen many, but they have a talent in the ring. The way they float on the canvas, taunting each other in a hypnotizing dance. Will I ever be on that level? No, not even close but now I have the confidence to take someone down if needed, and in my new world, that's a skill that may save my life one day.

B's fist slams into my side and I crumple to the mats, pain radiating through my chest that could rival a bullet to the heart. *Damn, she hits like a train.*

Landing on my hands and knees, I pant out my exhaustion. "Get up, babe. Come on. You get hit, you get back up stronger than before," she taunts as she bounces around me.

"Screw you," I slur out, trying to catch my breath as her hand slaps down hard on my ass. "Hey—"

"Come on, baby. If you're going to stay in that position, you better be ready to get railed like a bitch. Are you their bitch?"

"No," I whisper.

She circles around me again and gives a slap to the back of my head.

"What? I didn't hear you," she sing-songs. "Are you their bitch, Natasha?"

The shear exhaustion in my muscles makes me want to quit, but the memories force me to push my body past its limits and stand, putting my hands up to guard my face as B smiles and comes at me again. My eyes follow her movements as she circles me, jabbing at me.

"Baby." Another jab. "Baby." Another one to the other side of my ribs but I keep my elbows tucked and my hands up. "Baby." Another one that I block with my forearms, and she smiles again. Her small body moves in close, readying to hit me, but she doesn't, instead she spins around and gets me in a headlock, wrapping her legs around my waist.

"Bitch," she whispers in my ear before she flings us both backward. She takes the brunt of the hit as we slam down, her on her back and me atop her.

"I'm—no one's—bitch." I struggle to get the words out as I maneuver myself out of her hold. Finally freeing myself, I face her. Hands up again and ready. My chest heaves, the pressure from my sports bra constricting the movement, and my vision fades in and out, but I won't let her have control of this fight.

Men want women with long hair, Natasha, you will not cut it.

You will maintain a size two. If you can't on your own, I will ensure your meals are cut.

Unbutton the top three buttons, Natasha. Sex is the way to a man's heart. Everett is no different.

You will provide an heir; there is no other option. You are good for nothing else.

What kind of woman can't even carry a child. I knew there was something wrong with you.

I have brokered a deal. Finally, I will have my heir, and you will give him to me.

"Hit me!" I scream at Sabrina with a tear rolling down my cheek as their words filter into my mind.

B stands there, hands raised, bouncing on her feet but she doesn't come closer.

"Come on!" I cry out as more tears fall.

Her hands and her face fall. "You win."

"No. Don't give up on me, B. I need this. Put your hands up. Hit me... *please.*" My best friend walks up to me, wrapping her arms around my neck as she pulls me into her, our foreheads resting together.

"When you break like this, you win. You win, babe." She continues to hold me as I collect myself.

Over the months I have been training, B has been there for every breakdown. In this ring, I don't fight her, I fight myself. She taught me that vulnerability takes more strength than throwing up my defenses.

Every time we spar, she pushes me to the point of nearly shattering, like a glass vase with a million tiny cracks, barely holding onto its shape. Each time she pushes me to this point, I get a little closer to the other side of healing. I get a little closer to seeing what's on the other side of choosing to live. Like Knight told me.

"You good?" B pulls back and lets her emerald eyes roam my face.

"Yeah. Thanks."

"Who are you?" she says with a spunk that leaks into my own psyche.

"Not theirs."

"Not theirs," she repeats our mantra, and I let the air leave my lungs in a rush.

"Let's go get some pizza. We need to replenish all the calories we worked off." She laughs but when I try to join her the devil inside my mind breathes to life.

Just one slice.

"Pizza sounds great." My small smile masks my unease while I begin to unwrap my hands. "I'm going to take a quick shower. Meet you outside?"

As B makes her way to the little office room slash studio apartment on the second level, I head to the downstairs girl's locker room. It's empty late at night. The gym closes at nine, but B always lets me stay over and now as 9:30 rolls around, I soak in the solace an empty gym brings. Being alone has always been my safe space.

As a child I was forced to attend parties and large events filled with people who saw me as a broodmare or future trophy wife. At only fourteen, my parents arranged a marriage with a wonderful man, well boy at the time. But even as a teenager Everett was kind. Unlike any of the other middle school boys. He had a softness about him. His words and actions held a promise of safety.

But he fell in love with someone else.

My desperation to keep him made me do awful things. No... I chose to act that way. I realize that now. I can't blame my behavior on my situation. I was cruel. That's my mistake to own. But either way, life happened. Everett and I never married, and I wasn't able to give my father what he wanted out of the arrangement.

A male heir to his empire.

Because God forbid a woman rule.

Eventually I did get pregnant but... well, I lost her. The fear I felt when my father sold me to two powerful men still hums through my body at times. "Two men filling you up gives me double the chance" is what he told me when I found out I would be married off to the Alessi twins. And even though I can only marry one, both would be fucking me until I gave my father and the twins a male heir to their empires.

The one son to combine the families and inherit billions.

I strip off my damp sports bra and spandex shorts, then turn the shower to hot, all the way hot.

Cold showers only, Natasha. You will ruin your skin and hair with that temperature.

I turn up the heat a little more as a silent fuck you to my mother. The memory of her finding me in a hot shower and turning it ice cold while I was still in it sends shivers up my body.

"Screw you, mother," I mumble as I step into the molten water. I quickly rinse my hair and scrub down my body. The softness of my hips and the bones becoming less prominent immediately sends a signal to my stomach and it turns, readying to vomit. My eyes close and I take a deep breath, telling myself that it's okay to build muscle, it's okay to have some fat on your body.

When I'm finished, I squeeze the excess water from my hair, turn off the water and wrap myself in a towel. As soon as I get to the full-length mirror, I drop the towel and look at my body, now lightly covered in bruises. My hips are wider than they used to be and there's a cushion on my stomach that wasn't there a few months ago. As I lift my arms, I see that the muscle flaps when I wiggle it.

"What beautiful colors you have painted on your body, principessa."

Enzo's words echo through the locker room, making me jump. "Jesus," I say as I quickly pick up the towel and turn to find him leaning against the lockers.

"Nah, baby. He doesn't like to keep me company," he says as he stalks toward me and pulls the towel from my hands. I grit my teeth and hold my head high as he tilts his head and narrows his deep brown eyes as they roam my body. I get a sense that I should feel uncomfortable standing naked and being assessed by this man... but I'm not. My body's simply skin and bones. A vessel. Nothing more. Not in the eyes of these men, and not in my eyes anymore.

Men can see me naked all they want; it doesn't bother me anymore. But what would I do if they wanted to look into my heart? Would I be so brave?

"Such a shame, that body would draw in some dirty, dirty bastards." His rough thumb and finger grip my chin as he turns my head to look back into the mirror and his malicious eyes assess me through our reflection. "Could you imagine the monsters we could bring in with a prize like you?"

I jerk my chin out of his hand and grab the towel from the floor. "What do you want, Enzo?"

"Raf formally requests your presence at Divino." He folds his arm across his waist and bends forward in a formal bow.

"Nothing with you two is a request." His dark gaze follows my white lace panties as I shimmy them up my legs. His dark irises are filled with an appreciation, not a sinister hunger like other eyes have gazed upon me with.

"Look at you learning." Leaning up to his full height, which towers over my 5'6" frame, a small smirk graces his deviously handsome face. Both the Italian twins were not only blessed with intelligence but also ruggedly handsome looks. Like two lurking lions, looks that draw you in but claws that would rip you to shreds.

I roll my eyes and turn my back to him to grab the dress out of my backpack but then in an instant his body presses into my back, his hand coming up to wrap around my throat and I go still, holding my breath as if that would help.

"Don't roll your eyes at me and never turn your back on the devil, principessa." His hand tightens, cutting off my air and I begin to panic but then remember what B taught me. It's my panic that they want. *Take a breath, take control.*

"Hey big boy, why don't you pick on someone your own size?" Enzo releases me and my breath returns to my lungs as B walks in.

He turns, stalking toward her, but she stands her ground as he comes within inches of her.

She smaller than I am at only five feet, but her attitude and balls are bigger than I've ever seen.

"You want to fight me, piccola diavoletta?" he seethes, and fear makes my chest tight.

The bravest girl I know slowly trails her finger up the mafia prince's white button up, following the trail with her eyes until she reaches his gold chain hanging around his neck. She hooks her finger under it and pulls, bringing the devil himself right down to her so they are face to face. "I would, baby, but that would be considered animal abuse."

She pushes past him, in what would be a shoulder check but because of their height difference it's more like her shoulder against his ribs, and stands between us, hip cocked and looking at her nails like she isn't facing down an *actual* animal.

I slip my gray silk dress on as Enzo continues to stare down B like she's his last meal.

There are those hungry eyes.

The last time someone looked at me like that, I left them in the early morning hours with a half dead bird...

"If you're going to look at me like that, love, you better be ready to fuck me or kill me," B says with a salacious tone that has me questioning what team I bat for.

He steps up to her again and puts his finger under her chin as he tilts it up. "How bout I do both, baby."

She swats his hand away, then knees him in the dick and when he leans forward to clutch his balls, she throws her knee up again, straight into his nose. "Sounds like a fun night. How 'bout we skip the boring, sweaty fuck and you get out of my gym before I kill you for putting your paws on something that isn't yours?"

Enzo groans as he stands and starts to back away, blood pours from his nose but he doesn't even try to stop it as it continues to drip down his face. His teeth are coated in red as he smiles, "You're mine, piccola diavoletta."

"Keep dreaming, doll." Her long red hair flips over her shoulder as she turns and walks up to me, her eyes roaming over my throat.

Assessing the delicate little lamb for injuries left by the big bad wolf. Little does she know, my injuries run much deeper.

"Stop being a mother hen. I'm fine." I throw my black blazer over my dress and smooth out my blonde hair that has started to dry in its natural wave. "How are you so brave against that psychopath?"

"I've dealt with worse than Enzo Alessi, plus I get the feeling he's all bark, no bite. Trust me on this one." She waves me off dismissively as we both head toward the exit. I think I'll choose to *not* trust her on this one. I have no doubt in my mind that Enzo Alessi is in fact all bite.

"Sorry I can't get pizza tonight. My presence is requested by Rafael," I say, lowering my tone to mock Enzo and B laughs.

"No worries, babe. I'll see you tomorrow. Be safe, don't do anything I wouldn't do!"

"That's not a long list, B."

She winks and pulls the garage door to the gym down as I turn to see Enzo wiping the blood off his face with a white handkerchief.

"What's so important about me joining Rafael tonight? And isn't ten a little late for dinner?" I ask as I step into the open door awaiting me and scoot into the back of the black Mercedes.

"Raf's meeting with an important contact in Boston. He wants his future wife on his arm. Simple as that." He ignores my curiosity about it being so late and smirks as he slides in next to me.

"Great," I say sarcastically.

"Cheer up, principessa. If all goes well tonight, there's a possibility we can stay in Boston."

My body perks up at this. There had been talk of them moving me to Seattle, but when I told Raf that I wanted to stay in Boston, he said he would see what he could do. I thought it a bullshit answer to placate me but is he actually trying?

"Who are we meeting?"

"The FBI's very own Unit Chief of the Human Trafficking division here in Boston. If we are to stay here, we don't need him breathing down our necks. So be a good girl and you might get to stay in this shit city like you wanted."

You turned me into a monster,
Into a whore,
You tricked me,
You played with my heart,
And I hate you for that,
You treat me like trash,
I'm done,
With the crying
The fighting,
The name calling,
The hurting,
I'm done with you.

-MP

natasha

As we drive downtown, I admire the night and as they typically do, my thoughts drift to Knight. He saved me from that rooftop, gave me the most intimate and heartbreaking night I've ever experienced, took care of me, and held me after. He was kind and gentle. I knew that he looked beyond my body. A familiar brokenness haunted him, one that I recognized in myself and for the first time I felt an instant connection with someone.

With Everett, my first love, we had known each other since we were little. He was my comfort and my safe space, of course I always felt connected to him and thought he would be my forever. But he wasn't meant to be mine, his heart belonged to another. When she took him from me, I became a raging tornado of grief at the idea of losing him. God, I was awful. But I was desperate. I lost the one person who saw me for who I wanted to be, who protected my heart when my body no longer felt like mine.

And worse than that, when my father found out I had lost Everett... my *training* began again, and I went numb.

I lost everything when I lost Everett, but then Knight looked at me on that rooftop and he saw straight into my heart.

And he didn't run.

I did.

I had to. I felt so fucking safe in his arms, and it terrified me. How, in a single night, could I already feel so utterly dependent and attached to this stranger? I knew if I woke up in his arms that morning, I would never let him go and it would cost me... or him.

But one day, like everyone else, he would have left me. It's better that I left him while my heart was still capable of walking away.

It doesn't matter anymore though, not only because I belong to the twins, but I never got his real name. Even if I wanted to, I wouldn't be able to find him.

The dark cabin of the Mercedes hides the tear that falls down my cheek and I wish I could say why I'm crying, but I don't know anymore. Sometimes the tears fall, and I hate it. I hate that as they drip down my face, people finally see the weakness leaking from my body.

Enzo's hand falls to my thigh, drawing my full attention to him. "Natasha, you will do as you're told tonight, without argument or questions. Do you understand?" My body stiffens at his grasp, but I don't remove it. What's the point?

"What will be asked of me?" I can't help the raise of my brow and the sarcasm that drips from my lips. I may have given up on myself a long time ago but that doesn't mean I'm going to let him or anyone else take from me what I will not freely give. If they want me, I will put up a fight, no matter what it costs.

Because now I have something to fight for. What that something is, I'm not sure yet. But Knight sparked something inside me. A small glimmer of light that I feel the need to chase. To run toward. To fall into and I'll never get the chance if I don't fight for it.

"You'll see." He winks and a devilish grin crosses his face, making the dimples on his cheeks pop out. Damn bastard's too pretty, like a poisonous flower.

The car pulls up to Divino and he comes around and opens my door. "What a gentleman," I say with a sweet smile as he takes my hand and helps me out of the car.

"Nah, principessa. Just don't want you trying to make a run for it."

"In these shoes? Please." I flip my long hair over my shoulder and walk into the restaurant with practiced and perfected confidence. Despite the fear in my heart over what I'm about to be asked to do, I maintain my mask of indifference.

The dimly lit Italian restaurant would be perfect for a romantic dinner, but that's far from what this is. The tables are spread out evenly, covered in white linens with a single candle as the centerpiece. All around are expensive meals, even more expensive wines, and what I would assume are exorbitant escorts on the arms of most of these men. Even this late at night, the restaurant overflows with hungry guests. The demons who run the night need to eat too, I guess.

The dark-haired waitress gives come fuck me eyes to Enzo who hasn't even given her a second glance as he walks at my side, his hand resting on my lower back. His other hand hides away into the pocket of his black dress slacks. He didn't even change his shirt, yet he gives zero fucks that all these people can see the blood splattered on the soft cotton. They don't even know if it's his or not, yet I don't think it would matter. Not like they would say anything to *the* Enzo Alessi. Because despite the twins not being from Boston, in the wealthy circles, their names are synonymous with the boogeyman.

We round a small corner, and I see Rafael stand to greet us and then right after him, another man stands and my heart drops.

No.

My feet come to an abrupt halt and my chest caves in as all the air in my lungs release into the air. The overwhelming need to turn and leave sparks chills to race across my skin.

He's an FBI Agent? No... He's the Unit Chief... *fuck my life.*

His wavy, dirty blond hair now brushes the nape of his neck, but his beard, the same one I ran my hands through while he slept, is the same length, short and clean cut. His Neptune eyes look at me, but not like they did on that rooftop. Not like they did in that bed. Not like they did in that bathtub. Now they look at me with mistrust. With hurt and I...

Enzo nudges me forward, interrupting my thoughts as I'm forced to take a step toward this man who makes my brain fuzzy and my fight or flight instincts kick in.

Rafael takes me around the waist and places a kiss to my cheek. "Agent Knight, may I introduce my fiancée, Natasha Baldwin. Divine, isn't she?"

Knight takes my hand, placing a soft kiss to the back of it, his eyes never leaving mine. "It's a pleasure, Natasha." The way he says my name ignites a fire inside me and I can't decide if I want it to be the only word he ever says or if I want him to never utter it from his perfect lips again.

Rafael guides me to the chair he pulled out for me, and Agent Knight sits after.

Enzo leans down behind me, then a moment later, his breath tickles my neck, but his eyes remain on the man sitting across from me. "Behave."

Before anyone can say a word, the waiter in his white shirt and black apron comes up and pours water into the tall narrow glasses that adorn the tabletop. "May I offer our signature wines this evening, we have—"

"A bottle of your finest red, please," Rafael says, and the waiter nods and leaves. "Agent Knight, shall we begin?" he says as he gently lays the cloth napkin in his lap and looks to mine, cuing me to follow.

The agent's jaw clenches, his back teeth grinding together as his eyes slowly and reluctantly leave mine. "Of course. As you were the one who requested this meeting. I'll let you begin."

The waiter returns, making a show of uncorking the bottle and then begins to pour us each a glass, starting with me, then Rafael. When he gets to the brooding agent's glass, he places his hand over the top and shakes his head. Refusing the wine.

Raf releases a small laugh as the waiter leaves. "Do you think it poisoned, Hale? You watched the man uncork it himself."

Hale. Hale Knight. I catalog his full name in my brain under the tab–to avoid at all costs or you might lose your heart.

"I don't drink," he grits as he holds Raf's eyes with a hard set to his brow, clearly bothered by the show my fiancé displays.

"Fair enough. I'll get straight to it then. Were you close with the previous man who held your position, Agent Knight?"

"Not particularly. Why?"

"Just curious." Raf grabs the menu and places it in front of me.

My eyes run down the list of overpriced menu items, but I already know what I will be getting. Still, I take this moment to appear distracted while I intently listen to the conversation next to me.

"Agent Riggins and my father had an arrangement. One of our finest girls, for his... confidentiality." The waiter comes back and before he can speak, Raf does. "Filet mignon with the red wine sauce."

The waiter looks at me now. "Caesar Salad—"

"She'll have the lobster and truffle tagliolini," Raf interrupts me, and I swear I feel myself having heart palpitations.

"I—" I go to protest but am silenced by the look in Raf's eyes. The look that tells me to shut my mouth, so I bite my tongue. It's fine. I can eat the lobster. I'll avoid the pasta.

Hale orders the same as me, well what Rafael ordered for me, and I look at him when he says it. His eyes are narrowed on me, as if trying to solve a problem that he can't see clearly. The glass sits warm in my hand, the red wine settling slowly as I swirl it first, then bring it to my lips. Trying to calm the nerves racing through my body.

"Back to the matter," Raf announces as he hands the waiter our menus. "I am interested in offering you the same deal that my father had with Agent Riggins."

"And what kind of deal is that exactly?" Hale places his elbows on the table with a smirk. Clearly not caring about higher society rules regarding table manners.

"My finest girl for your ability to divert attention away from the Alessi name in Boston. As you know, we are focused on the west coast, however, over many years we have been slowly filtering into your city. Our business is expanding. We do not need your cooperation; however, both our lives would be easier with it. You keep our name off the records, you keep your nose out of our dealings in Boston and in exchange, our finest girl and every so often we will throw you one of our larger clients. To keep suspicion low, of course."

A jealous, raging wench wakes inside me at the thought of Hale with another woman but I flick that bitch in the forehead and remind her that he. Is. Not. Ours.

Hale contemplates in silence, bringing his thumb to run across his bottom lip over and over again and I'm hypnotized by the action. His eyes flick to mine for a moment, then back to Raf. A glimmer shines in them, like a cat preparing to play with its dinner. "Let me get this straight. You want to offer me your finest girl and in exchange, I will keep your name out of our reports and investigations."

"To put it simply, yes," Raf confirms as he takes a sip of his wine, leaning back slightly like he isn't offering up an innocent girl.

"Then let me put it simply for you. There's no woman on this God-forsaken *fucking* planet that could make me corrupt not only myself but my unit as well." Hale stands, throwing his napkin down, his silverware clatters and my body jumps. "Go fuck yourself, Mr. Alessi."

"Please don't insult me. Call me Rafael. And I think, Agent Knight, that I have in my possession the *only* woman who would make you reconsider."

Hale pauses as Raf looks at me with a lifted brow. "She is our most divine selection at the moment."

My eyes look from Rafael and then up to Hale as my mouth falls open. His eyes widen as they look at me then narrow as if he's upset with... me?

"You sick fuck." Hale slams his hand down on the table, rattling the silverware and candle. "She's not for sale. She's—"

"She is ours to do with as we please. And if it's not you who takes us up on our offer, we will find another. You are not the only man with power in this city, Agent." Rafael's tone leaves no room for negotiation as he sits up a little taller, filling the room with his presence.

Hale's eyes rage with war, stuck between protecting me and protecting his own morals. And the moment his gaze lands on me, I see who has won the war. I shake my head at him, a silent plea. I'm not worth it. He can't. The pressure in my chest builds to an almost unbearable level.

I need air.

"Excuse me," I say as I stand and excuse myself to the bathroom' racing toward the restroom before Rafael can stop me and when I burst through the doors and splash the cool water onto my face, I feel a moment's relief.

Knight's one of the good ones. He cannot put his career and his own morality on the line for someone like me. I'm not worth that kind of sacrifice.

"Natasha." His deep, gravelly timber fills the space, my ears, my heart. Oh God, my name on his lips is like a symphony to my soul, it soothes and corrupts all at once.

Turning from the mirror, he stands in his black suit, white wrinkled shirt and thin black tie that could be tightened a touch, but he looks effortlessly handsome, just as he did the first time I met him. He leans against the door, blocking anyone else from entering and I notice his arm reach around, flipping the lock.

"Hale," I whisper as my hand comes up to cover my mouth and my eyes drop. I can't look at him long. I'll crumble, and I need to remain standing tonight.

"God." He strides toward me without hesitation and grabs my face in his hands. Inches from my face, his breath hits my lips, and it takes everything in me not to kiss him. "Tell me it's not true. Tell me you don't belong to them. Please." His voice wavers as he begs me.

My eyes bore holes into his chest, the rapid rising and falling matching my own. "Don't make me lie to you."

He releases me and steps back, his chest expanding and a hardness overcoming his demeanor. "Why did he call you his fiancée?"

"Because that's what I am." I can't meet his eyes, so I let them drop to the cold black tile floor.

"Was that night on the rooftop—was that a ploy to draw me into you? Make me undeniably obsessed so that when this offer was propositioned, Rafael would know without a doubt I couldn't refuse? Was it all fake?"

That night was the most honest form of who I have ever been, yet he believes it was all a lie.

"It was real." I reach out to him, but he backs away.

"Then walk away. If they don't own you, leave with me tonight." My gaze flies to him as those eyes beg me and I want to give in, but I can't. He must know who these men are, the power they hold.

"It's not that simple. You don't know what you are asking of me."

His head tilts up slightly as he looks down on me and his nostrils flare slightly. "I may not know what the hell's happening right now, or who you really are but what I do know is that if your life's on the table, I'm making the deal, no matter what it costs me."

"Are you insane?" I whisper at him, my anger at this entire situation pouring from me, as I come up to him and bring my hands to his rugged face. "Hale, please, I'm begging you. You cannot make a deal with Rafael. It will only end in tragedy."

"I became insane, with long intervals of horrible sanity," he whispers as he runs his thumb under my eye, along my cheekbone and then behind my ear and I find myself leaning into him. My traitorous body craves something my heart can never have.

"Poe," I whisper as I close my eyes and soak in his touch.

"Correct."

hale

What in God's name is wrong with me? How does one woman, who I spent a single night with, make me throw out everything I believe in, make me corrupt my morals and risk not only my career but my life?

There's no logical explanation, no words to define what raced through my mind as soon as Rafael mentioned offering her to another man, everything else went out the window. I couldn't allow that to happen, and I would risk everything to save her.

I don't know if what she says is true, if all of it was real. A part of me believes her but another part of me knows those eyes have probably claimed many victims. Maybe I'm her latest. And what a fucking coincidence that the same woman who infiltrated my fucked-up psyche and infected my brain happens to be the same one Rafael brings to leverage a deal out of me?

My stomach twists and my mind wars with my heart at the idea of making this deal, but the organ in my chest wins. *Am I about to do this?* What the hell am I saying, my decision was made the moment I looked at her in that gray silk dress and black leather jacket.

"Hale?" Her angelic voice calls and when she says my name in that way... fuck. It makes me want to hit my knees and beg for any morsel of love she could give me.

"I'm coming," I say as I follow her out of the bathroom. A few stares of disapproval shoot my way as I exit the women's bathroom.

Natasha's a beautiful enigma. One moment one goddess stands before me, the sparrow I met on the rooftop. The next, someone entirely different.

My instincts cry out to me, telling me that deep down she's a soul that's barely surviving. However, her being on that rooftop and being here now, part of this deal seems too coincidental. Maybe she wasn't in on the plan. Maybe they sent her to that rooftop with the goal of seducing me, but she never knew about the arrangement she would be part of months later. Maybe I'm simply telling myself this to comfort the unease in my heart at the idea of her manipulating it like putty in her hands.

Making it back to the table, our food waits for us, and we both sit. Rafael eyes us like he knows exactly what happened in that bathroom. I'm not stupid and neither is he. I knew he wouldn't believe the lie I spilled about having to make a call at the same time she excused herself to the restroom, but I honestly don't give a fuck what he thinks.

"Eat, Natasha," he says without looking at her.

When I look up from my own plate to hers, she's fiddling with the fork, moving the food around in a way that makes it look like she has taken some bites.

She forks a piece of lobster and glides it off the prongs with her teeth. Fuck, I've never wanted to be a utensil before but there's a first time for everything.

"I assume the deal is on by the way you are eye-fucking my fiancée, Agent Knight." Rafael's sarcastic comment pulls my attention away from her and back to his smug ass face.

"I will not tamper with evidence. If you're sloppy enough to leave it behind, it's your own fault. I will divert attention away from your name but will not remove it entirely. There will be no limit on how many names you give me. When I ask for one, I'm given one. When I ask for a top buyer, I'm given one. And lastly, Natasha stays in Boston."

I slip a bite of lobster into my mouth as I hold Rafael's stare. I may be making this deal, but I won't roll over like a dog.

He takes a sip of wine, licking his lips and leans forward. "I would never ask you to tamper with evidence. My brother and I don't leave any behind and if any of our men are foolish enough to do so they will be handled by us before your men could ever get to them. I would never expect you to remove our name, that would draw too much suspicion. I am happy with the diversion. I will give names as I see fit. That is not a demand you can make but trust me when I say we are after the same thing, Agent *Knight*. The names I give you will be sufficient. And Natasha will split her time between us. I still have appearances to keep back in Seattle so she will be with my brother and I when necessary but anytime she is not with us, she will be yours."

My tongue runs over my top teeth at his counteroffer. I don't like it. I don't like having no control of the names I receive, but that I can compromise on. I hate her being with them for any length of time, let alone all the way in Seattle where I can't easily reach her. Despite Rafael's reputation, there's something in his tone that settles me. I'm not sure I understand this odd feeling between us, but my instincts are never wrong, and they are currently telling me that he's a man of his word.

"Who will be there to look out for her when she's with you?"

"We will. She is ours, and we protect what's ours." He takes a bite of his steak, relaxing back in his chair again.

"Can I say something?" Natasha chimes in and I notice she still hasn't eaten much on her plate. Must be her nerves. Lord knows I'm fucking nervous and I'm not the one being traded like a fucking Pokémon card.

"You may," Rafael says as he gives her his attention.

"Could I bring someone with me? For when I am meant to be with you and Enzo."

"Who did you have in mind, Natasha?" The way he says her name, so formal and with that slight Italian accent grinds my fucking gears. I hate her name on anyone's lips but my own, but if I am to share her–God, thinking that makes my body revolt–but it holds true, if I'm to share her, I need to get used to it.

"Sabrina Shae."

"The owner of the boxing ring you frequent?" Rafael asks with a lift to his brow, clearly not expecting that answer.

"Yes."

Rafael's quiet for a moment, contemplating as he eats the bloody steak off his plate. "I can accept that." He looks up at me and tilts his head. "Agent, are the terms acceptable?"

No. None of this is acceptable. But what choice do I have?

"Fine," I relent and catch the smallest smile slip from Natasha's lips as she continues to fiddle with her food.

"Eat, Natasha," Rafael commands again. His demand riles me to the point I lose my own appetite, and I can't seem to find that damn cat that's supposed to hold my tongue.

"Leave her be. How do you expect her to eat in this situation? You are selling her off like fucking cattle."

"Then what a spoiled little calf she is, Agent. I will remind you only once, when she is mine, I will demand of her what I wish. You may take the same pleasure."

"Oh, for fucks sake." Natasha drops her fork, the clang ringing out in the restaurant. "While you boys fight over what I should and shouldn't eat, I'm going to find Enzo who might eat *me*." She stands and slams her napkin down on the table then mumbles out, "I deserve something out of this fucked up situation."

"Natasha," I growl but she ignores me as she walks away. "Damn woman." I shake my head and Rafael chuckles.

"Don't worry, Agent. No matter how much she begs, Enzo wouldn't touch her that way." He watches her walk away also, but it isn't anger or lust I see in his eyes. I can't place the emotion, and it makes me curious.

"I've seen the photos, doesn't seem that way to me." Taking a sip of my water to cool the fire inside me at the thought of him touching her the way only my hands should, Rafael waves me off dismissively.

"That's all for show. We would not be intimate with her." He emphasizes the last word to reassure me, but it only confuses me.

"But she's your fiancé?"

"Per the contract, yes. But there is only one woman who has ever held our attention and it's not Natasha." As he finishes his plate, the waiter comes around and collects our dishes and I find myself feeling abnormally comfortable with Rafael. As if we were two old friends chatting over life... *fucking disgusting*.

"What exactly does the contract say?" I question and to my utter surprise, he answers.

"I'm going to take a guess here, Agent, and say that you and I have more in common than you think. Whether you choose to believe me or not, I frankly don't give a fuck. But know that we will always protect that woman. She is innocent and we don't deal in innocent lives. Plus, we grew up in the same circle as Natasha. She is more of a sister to us than a wife."

A sister? I contemplate what his words as I narrow my eyes at him, trying to and failing to read his micro expressions. Bastard's harder to read than Eros.

"And the contract?"

"Can I trust you to keep a secret, Hale?" He leans back and finishes off his wine.

The second use of my first name catches me off guard, but I play along. "You can trust me to do what's best for her."

He nods as he accepts that answer. "Natasha was part of a contract between my father and her own. Her father, having only ever had a daughter, is in desperate need of a male heir. The misogynistic bastard doesn't believe a woman, even one as brilliant as her, could ever run his empire. When Natasha..." he pauses as he looks to the front door and if I wasn't mistaken, I swear I could see a sadness in his eyes as he speaks of her, "she... failed to provide an heir and because of that, she was given to us."

My fingers ball into tight fists. What the hell does he mean *failed to provide an heir*?

Before I can ask, he continues, "Our father is as desperate to continue the Alessi name. If she gets pregnant, everyone gets what they want, and the chances are better with two dogs in the race."

Murderous rage coils inside me as my fists clench and I do my best to to rein in the control that slips from my fingers. What the fuck kind of sick son of a bitch sells their own daughter as a fucking broodmare?

"I recognize that look in your eyes, Agent." Rafael leans back in his chair, sipping his wine. "My my, how the angel has fallen. Are you witnessing a side of yourself you don't recognize?"

I release my breath and close my eyes as I collect myself. "I fell a long time ago, Rafael. And I've been trying to stitch my wings back together ever since."

Rafael stands and straightens the lapels of his designer suit. "Stick with us, Agent, and I believe you will find your wings repaired in no time... or not. Sometimes being a devil is much more satisfying."

With that he walks off, leaving me with more questions than answers and I wonder if he's right. Will Natasha be the reason my wings heal, or will she be the one I completely lose them for?

natasha

"Wait, so you're going to fuck this agent dude and the twins? You go girl." Sabrina wraps her hands, preparing to spar with me as I wrap my own. It's been exactly one week since the dinner at Divino with Hale and Rafael, but I have yet to hear from either.

I know the twins are watching me, but I don't know why it's taken Hale so long to reach out. I mean I'm supposed to "belong to him" so why hasn't he come for me?

A little, broken piece of me is disappointed. I hoped he would be as excited about seeing me as I was him, especially now that he has permission to do whatever he pleases with me.

Am I sick for getting excited at that? Maybe...

But it's my nature, drawn to the things I can't have.

"First off, I'm not sleeping with the twins and second... I don't know about Hale. He seemed different from the first time I met him."

Of course, as soon as I could, I talked B's ear off and told her all about my one-night stand with Hale, leaving out the whole rooftop thing.

"Yeah, but you want to." She winks at me.

"Want to *what*?"

"Screw his brains out."

"Whose brains are we screwing? I've got a screwdriver in the car." Enzo comes up, hanging his large tattooed arms over the ropes of the boxing ring. Sabrina rolls her eyes and turns away from him to start stretching.

"Not that kind of screwing, you psycho," I say, beginning my own stretches.

"Well, I'm down for the other kind too. Tell me who. Guy? Girl? Doesn't matter to me."

"Enzo!" I scold and he laughs as he throws his hands up in mock defense.

"Kidding! It does matter to me. I'm a proper gentleman. I like to wine and dine, you know give 'em the whole nine yards before I give 'em nine inches." He winks at B, and I snap my fingers in front of his face.

"Enzo. Why are you here?"

"Right. I brought you a present. You're welcome."

Just as he says that Agent Knight walks through the gym doors, his hands tucked casually into his dress pants pockets as he looks around the gym. When his eyes land on me, a small smirk graces his face and his eyes soften.

"Agent," I say with a small, shy smile.

"Natasha."

"Well," Enzo claps Hale on the back and gives him a goofy grin, "I'll leave you two love birds to get to know each other." Then he walks away leaving Hale with a disgusted snarl left on his lip as he keeps his eyes trained on the Italian twin.

"What's all this about?" I ask as I slide under the ropes and walk up to him. He can't hide the way his eyes drop down my body, taking me in. My sports bra and biker shorts hug my body, and I know he appreciates the view. I wonder if he's thinking back on the last time he touched my body, I know I am.

"I figured we needed to work out what this arrangement consists of. Are you free?"

I look back at B who watches Hale and I. "Umm. I was about to get a workout in. Can we meet after?"

His hand runs down the back of his head and to the nape of his neck. "Yeah. Sure."

"Okay."

"Okay," he says, shy all of a sudden. "I'll just... wait?"

I nod and hop back into the ring. B and I run through a quick session and the entire time I feel his blue eyes on me. I can't help but wonder what he's thinking. The urge to look at him is next to impossible to resist but by some miracle, I do. When B and I finish, I practically sprint to the showers, needing his heating gaze off me before I combust.

My skin flushes with heat, whether it's from the workout or the heat of Hale's gaze, I'm not entirely sure. The warm water trickles down my body for only a few minutes before I turn the knob off and get dressed. My black bodysuit clings tightly against my chest and stomach. My cheetah-print mid-length skirt flutters when I walk, giving my edgy outfit a girlish touch. Completing the look, I throw on my black leather jacket and check myself one last time in the mirror.

My style has always been feminine, but I love to add edgy elements. Growing up, my mother never let me, so now I relish in the disobedience I feel every time I slip into something she would disapprove of.

When I exit, Hale paces back and forth, talking on the phone in a stern tone that sends flutters all the way from my chest to my toes. He must hear the click of my heels on the stone floor because his head lifts when I come up the stairs from the women's locker room.

"Gotta go," he says as he hangs up, eyeing me like he's ready to pounce.

"You didn't have to hang up, I could have waited."

"Trust me, even the most boring thing you could say would have been far more interesting than that conversation. Are you hungry?"

I feel my lips twist up in a sideways smile and nod.

"Ever been to Luis's?" he asks as we exit the gym. I reply with simple no, and he smiles, "The best subs in Boston. You okay with walking or do you want me to get a cab?"

"I'm fine with walking."

It's a bit chilly on this October day, but it doesn't bother me much. Coming from Oregon, I'm used to the colder weather. We are silent on the walk, the tension between us thickening. The suffocating wave of it threatens to pull me under—a feeling I hope will fade as we begin our arrangement.

It's funny, when I met this man on the rooftop, I felt like I'd known him my entire life. His company was comfortable and easy to breathe in. But walking with him now, it's like there's a palpable force between us that I want to shatter.

"So… it's… nice weather." *God, Natasha. What a stupid statement.* I internally cringe and Hale chuckles.

"Are we actually going to talk about the weather?" He turns his head with a grin on his lips.

"No." I blush and dip my head, looking at my black patent leather heels as the sidewalk passes underneath.

"What's on your mind?" he asks. "No bullshit. The truth."

"This is awkward…" I blurt out and stop walking.

He does the same and turns toward me without saying anything, but he holds out his hand, cuing me to take it. His fingers interlace with mine and then he pulls me forward, continuing our walk.

"Better?" he asks as we walk hand in hand down the street. As my hand warms in his, the strangest feeling comes over me, and yes… it *is* better. His touch soothing my nerves.

"Yes."

Finally, we arrive at Luis's where we order and snatch a table. It's a small mom and pop style sandwich shop. Only five tables line the wall across from the ordering counter and the walls are lined with pictures of the shop dating all the way back to the 50s.

"How would you like this arrangement to go?" Hale asks, taking a sip of his water.

"What do you mean?"

"I'm not going to force anything on you, Natasha. If you don't want to see me, we don't have to speak. I only entered this deal because I didn't want you being sold off to another man. If you don't want to see me at all, I'm okay with that."

I'm a little surprised at his statement, but then again, I shouldn't be. Hale's a good man, I've known this since the first moment I looked into his eyes. "Do you not want to see me?"

An elderly man brings us our sandwiches in little green baskets, and I open mine, picking all the insides off the bread.

His eyes trail down to my sandwich and then back up to me. "I do. Want to see you, that is."

"Well, I want to see you too."

Hale scoffs and shakes his head. "Fuck, this is the weirdest shit I've ever had to discuss."

I smile and decide to take the lead. I'm not given many opportunities to do so but I can tell that Hale straddles a line he can't decide which side I want him on. He wants to give me control but knows that neither of us has much of that in this whole situation.

"How about this, I'll stay at my place, you at yours, and we can go on dates."

"Dates?" he mumbles with a mouth full of sandwich. His widened eyes tell me he wasn't expecting for me to propose us dating.

"Do you want to date me, Agent Knight?" I say flirtatiously.

"Yes," he rushes out without hesitation. "But..." A moment of concern crosses his face; the same untrusting expression I saw him wear at Divino. His hard eyes burn into my soul, "Can I trust you? Is all this part of some plan the twins have?"

My heart flutters and not in a good way. I understand where he's coming from, it all does seem to fit together almost too perfectly. Our night together months ago, then the dinner and the deal that I'm part of. But it's not part of any plan… feels more like fate playing a wicked trick on us.

"It lies not in our power to love or hate. For will in us is overruled by fate, when two are stripped, long ere the course begin. We wish that one should love, the other win." I echo the poem that comes to mind as he questions my intentions. When he questions why we have met once again. His eyes narrow as the wheels turn in his head.

Finally, he shakes his head, drawing a blank. "I don't know that one."

"Christopher Marlowe," I say, and he nods. "You can trust that I don't want to hurt you, Hale. I don't know how any of this will turn out. But I'm not malicious or part of any grand scheme. I'm a woman trying to survive in a world full of devils." I reach my hand out and lay it over his, hoping he believes me because of all the people on this planet, he's the one I can't stand to hurt. He's the one I need in my corner because I'm so damn tired of fighting alone.

"Hell is empty, and all the devils are here," he says, pulling his eyes from our joined hands to collide with my own desperate gaze.

"Shakespeare," I whisper.

"Correct."

hale

"**Y**ou have a *date* with Natasha Baldwin? Are you a fucking dumbass?" Gage snarls and by that, I mean *literally* snarls. His lip pulls up like a rabid dog. "Don't answer that. You are a fucking dumbass. Natasha's nothing but bad news. A bitch in high school, a manipulative snake after and now she's associated with the Alessis."

The coffee slips down my throat, the bitter aftertaste causing me to shake my head a touch. "I'm aware of her new associations, Gage. But what was I supposed to do? Let them sell her off to some scumbag?"

Gage's brow peaks.

"Don't answer that." I point my finger at his face in warning, and he smacks it away.

With the deal I made, I knew I couldn't keep him in the dark. One, he's too smart to let their name slip from the reports and two... I needed a little bro support, but I now find I'll be sorely lacking in that regard.

"Look. You made a deal with two fucking dipshits, rich and pow-erful dipshits but still. Now you have to honor the deal. What are the terms exactly?"

"Simple really." I take another horrendous sip of my coffee and Gage notices, taking the cup from me, walking over to the counter of Henry Leo's and ordering something new. When he comes back, I'm handed a light brown mixture with a little heart in the milk. "What's this?"

"A latte. You seem like the frilly type."

"Asshole," I mumble before taking a sip of the smooth, sweet concoction. "I'll be damned. That's delicious."

"Knew you were a pussy." My dickhead of a best friend smirks.

A short woman with dark curly hair walks up with a plate of muffins in hand, smacking Gage across the back of his head.

"A man who loves a latte is not a pussy, Gage. Everett loves lattes."

"My point exactly, Leo," Gage retorts and I shake my head, feeling a kindred spirit with Everett, Gages other best friend who also seems to get as much shit as I do.

The woman in the little black apron rolls her eyes and sets two muffins down. "On the house. I'm Leo by the way."

Her small hand extends out and I take it, shaking it once.

"Hale Knight. I'm Gage's friend."

"My boss," said friend corrects before biting into the muffin.

"Friend."

"Boss."

Leo stops our back and forth with a giggle before she places her hand on her hip. "It's okay Hale, the more shit he gives you, the more he loves you. I better get back to it, but it was nice to meet you, Gage's boss... and friend." She winks at Gage who rolls his eyes.

"She's cute," I remark, and Gage's already grumpy ass face turns murderous.

"She's taken and the closest thing I have to a sister so... Fuck. No."

My hands go up in surrender. "I wasn't going to make a move, calm yourself. I have Natasha, remember? How do you know her?"

"We went to high school together. She's married to my Everett." He finishes off his muffin as I take a bite of my own and good God, this blueberry muffin is heavenly. The sweet vanilla with the tart fresh blueberries should be downright illegal.

"Fuck that's good."

"Family recipe or something like that," Gage mumbles before taking a sip of his coffee. "Anyway, the deal?"

"Ah, yeah. The deal." I take one more bite before brushing the crumbs from my hands and swallowing the muffin, chasing it down with the delicious latte. "In exchange for keeping the Alessi name out of most of our reports and turning a blind eye to their dealings, I get Natasha when and wherever I want. Apart from when she's required to be with the twins for some appearance's sake. Apparently, she's engaged to one of them. We also get a few names thrown at us, clients of theirs to bust."

"The deal seems a bit one sided don't you think?"

"What do you mean?"

Gage takes another sip then looks toward the counter, watching Leo chat with Colette, Gages girlfriend. His eyes soften a little when they look at her and I recognize that look because it's the same one my dad has when he admires Ma.

"Well, you get the girl and names of their top clients, and they get... what? For us to ignore their presence here? They don't cause much stir when they are here anyway so either they are planning something big, that you've now agreed to ignore..."

"Or..."

"Or this deal is more about Natasha than the trafficking rings."

My teeth dig into the side of my cheek as I contemplate what tumbles around in that big super nerd brain of his. "Natasha seems to be the center of all of this."

"Exactly where she likes to be, the center of everyone's attention," Gage snarks and my eyes narrow on him.

"If you could dial back the dick face attitude, I'd appreciate it. I think there's more to her than you know."

"Yeah, Everett used to say the same thing but in my twenty years of knowing her, I've yet to see it."

"Maybe you're looking at the wrong side of her. Everyone has sides they don't like about themselves and shit they've done in their past they aren't proud of. Doesn't mean they should be labeled as such for the rest of their lives. Don't you think people can change?"

Gage pulls a coin from his pocket and flips it through his knuckles. "I don't think people can change, what you've done will always be a part of who you are, but I guess that doesn't mean one day your light can't outshine your darkness."

"If I could guess, I'd say Natasha has been left in the dark so long, she doesn't even see her light anymore."

Gages eyes meet mine for a moment, a seriousness in them I rarely see. But just as quickly, he rolls them again and sighs, "Whatever you say, Shakespeare."

Chapter Nine

natasha

Thwack, thwack... thwack, thwack.

The sound of fists hitting a bag echoes throughout the gym as I slide up the large garage door and slip inside. Rounding the boxing ring and entering the area with all the bags, I expect to see B but instead find Gage. *Shit.*

I should have known it wouldn't be Sabrina this early, hell would freeze over if the woman awoke before nine in the morning.

Gage roundhouse kicks the bag before collapsing forward, his hands resting on his knees as he catches his breath.

"Been here long?" I ask as he spots me.

He doesn't respond, only steps past me to where his water bottle rests on a bench, then chugs it.

"Okay, never mind." Turning my back toward him, I set my bag down and pull out my own water bottle and wraps.

"You warmed up?" His voice startles me, making me jump a little, I expected him to ignore me the whole time like he usually does.

"No. I just got here, obviously."

He squirts some water over his head and shakes his hair out, the droplets fly, sprinkling my shirt and legs.

"Oh, so fucking gross!" I shriek and he shoots me a closed lipped smile.

Wait? Did he actually smile?

"Get in the ring, Natasha. I've been waiting for this day for a long fucking time."

The canvas bounces slightly as his body leaps onto it. The lights above illuminate his sweaty skin, and I take in all his tattoos. He's covered, even more than when we were in high school. I knew he started getting tatted at a young age, but his collection has grown. The only ink free skin is his face and even that has a small C imprinted below the outer corner of his left eye, right where a tear would fall.

He's a beautiful man, if only his attitude wasn't horrendous. Doesn't mean I can't appreciate the muscles that ripple beneath all that ink.

"In the ring, Natasha," he barks and I jump to attention. The canvas cools my skin as I roll into the ring and stand tall.

"But I haven't warmed up yet."

His hands come up, palms facing me. "Let's go. Start with a one-two, then a one-two-three, then I want to see a one-two-four. Can you keep up?" He smirks and I want nothing more for him to drop those hands and feel my four.

"I got it."

We run through the combo and by the time he blocks my right hook, I've got a light sweat going and my heart rate has picked up.

"I thought you didn't box with women?"

"I'll make an exception for you. I've been waiting to put you on your ass for years."

"Such a gentleman." My eyes roll and I barely remember to throw my hands up before he makes a jab right at my face.

"Whoever told you I was one, lied."

"Clearly," I say before blocking another hit.

"What do you know about the deal between the twins and Hale?" he asks before making a weak hit toward my ribs that I sidestep.

"What? Nothing."

Another jab. "Liar."

Another sidestep. "I swear. I know what he knows."

A kick this time. "Is Hale in danger?"

Another sidestep. "Worried about your boss?"

"Worried about you and the trouble that seems to follow you like a shadow. The Alessis are dangerous and you associating with them means the people I care about could be in danger. It's my job to protect them, so fess up. What are you and those devils up to?"

My hands drop at his endless hatred toward me. We are adults, all that's in the past is in the past. Although, that's not true, is it? I seem to carry who my past self with me like... well, exactly like he described. A shadow.

Maybe he has some shadows too.

His fist collides with the back of my forearm as I barely get my hands up to block in time.

"Gage, let it go."

"I want to know one thing first," Gage pauses, dropping his hands. "Why did you hate Leo and I in high school? We never did anything to you."

My teeth clench at the sudden change in subject and I close my eyes. Maybe this is what's followed him for so long. He deserves an answer, I'm use not sure I can give him one. "I'm sorry, Gage. I have no excuse."

Another jab, but he's too fast for me to sidestep. The hit takes my breath away as it lands. His fist connecting shocks me, but it's not painful. Not as hard as Sabrina hits me and that's how I know Gage is pulling his punches.

"Not good enough." His gaze never leaving mine as he reads my movements.

He wants to know why I targeted him and Leo. I can't admit it. I'd rather him think me a vile bitch than know the truth.

"I don't know," I grunt as I block another kick, my body bending to the side as I almost collapse from the impact.

Another jab. "Bullshit. Be honest for once in your damn life."

"Gage, stop!" I yell as he comes at me, combo after combo. But to my utter surprise, as soon as I tell him to stop his attack, he does. Our chests heave as we glare at one another.

"Come at me," he says, raising his fists to block his face and bouncing on the balls of his feet.

"What?"

"Hit me." He motions with his fingers in a taunting way, challenging me forward.

I throw a jab, and he blocks it.

"Come on, Natasha. Why were you such a bitch all those years?"

"Just. Who. I. Am," I say with each combo I throw at him, but he blocks them all, batting my hands away.

"Liar. Why did you make my life and Leo's life a living hell? All because we were close to Everett?"

"Shut up," I grit out as I throw out my leg, trying to catch him in the ribs but he pushes it away.

"Ah, there it is. Everett's the key, huh? Were you so insecure you thought we would take his attention away?"

A burning in my chest tells me I'm close to breaking and I hate it. He doesn't know what I had to go through every time my period came. He doesn't know the men my father would bring in. He doesn't know the threats not only I faced... but also the ones made to eliminate any distractions that were swaying Everett's attention from me, including him and Leo. He doesn't know that if Leo hadn't left Everett, she would have been killed or worse... sold to Dante Alessi. His desperation to have an heir from Everett's family meant he would do anything, including killing or selling Gage and Leo. They were disposable to him, like most humans.

"You don't know shit, Gage!" I yell. *Please let it go.*

"Come on, Natasha. Spill your secrets on the canvas. Why did you hate us so much?"

I never hated them. I *envied* them. Their freedom, their friendships, their love.

"Stop it."

"Why did you hate us?" Another hit. Another block.

I stay silent this time, solely focused on hitting him one time. Hard enough to shut him up. Combo after combo, I relentlessly pursue him in an attempt to land one single hit.

"Why did you hate us?" he demands again as I kick at him. I throw jab after jab, kick after kick and still he doesn't relent. He's after my soul, and I can't hold onto it much longer.

"Why?" he finally shouts.

"Because I hated myself!" My throat burns as I scream at him, tears running down my face. "I hated who I was! Okay? Who I was forced to be! How I never hated you at all! I hated how no matter what I did, it was never enough! I hated how I was drowning and nobody saw, and even more, I hated that nobody would have cared."

My chest collapses, as does his and our hands drop.

"I know exactly how that feels. But you're wrong about one thing."

The wrap on my hand collects my tears as I swipe them away. "What?"

"We would have cared. You should have come to us."

"Should haves and could haves don't matter now, Gage," I say as I catch my breath, he comes closer and looks down at me with an honesty in his eyes that makes me feel incredibly vulnerable. My stomach turns, threatening vomit as I wait for him to decide my fate following my confession. What will he think of me now? Could it possibly be worse than what he thought before?

"You're right. It's already set in stone." His leg kicks out, hooking my knee and dropping me flat on my back. The breath is swept from my lungs and my head spins not only from the exertion of our fight but from the hit my head took against the canvas. "My advice? Buy a fucking sledgehammer."

hale

Our first official date and I'm sweating fucking bullets. Why am I so nervous? I've fucked this woman before, and I wasn't nervous then? Okay, I was a little but nothing like this.

My comb runs through my hair, pushing it back off my face as I check my appearance one more time in the mirror. I'm taking Natasha to my favorite sushi restaurant tonight. We agreed to do small dates, but this woman is a fucking heiress... small won't do for her. Or maybe she wants small? Maybe she's tired of big, extravagant things? Fuck.

I should cancel the reservation.

No... she'll like it.

Cancel it.

Shit. Pulling my phone from my pocket, I dial Gage's number, and he picks up on the third ring.

"What?"

"Should I take Natasha somewhere nice, or should I do something simpler for our first date?"

Silence.

"Gage?"

"Why the fuck are you asking me?"

My hand runs through my hair, and I grip the back of my neck. Should I even wear a tie? Maybe more casual is the way to go... well I guess that would depend on where we're going. I need answers.

"Because you have a girlfriend, you should know this shit!"

"For fucks sake. Colette says what she wants, I make it happen. What does Natasha want to do?"

My feet halt. "I didn't ask..."

"Mistake number one. I'm going to text you Leo's number. She'll know what to do."

"Leo from the coffee shop?"

"The one and only. She's always planning shit for her and Everett to do." My heart slows a fraction, and I take a deep breath.

"Thanks man, I owe you."

"Sure." With that the line goes dead. Per usual, Gage skips the goodbye.

When I get the text with Leo's number, I call it right away.

"Hello?" she answers and a little boy's giggle fills the background.

"Hello, ma'am. This is Hale Knight, Gage's friend from the coffee shop. I don't mean to bother you, but he gave me your number. I need... help."

A moment of silence and then her voice rings through again as I put my phone on speaker and begin unbuttoning my shirt. I decided a button up and tie would be too formal, even for sushi.

"Sure. Um, what can I do for you?" She doesn't question my intentions first, instead immediately ready to help. No wonder Gage speaks so highly of Leo.

"I'm taking this girl on a date, and I don't know where to take her. Gage told me you do a lot of planning. Thought maybe you would have a good idea."

Slipping a dark navy Henley over my head, I check the mirror and then unbutton my dress slacks.

"Well, I think if you're taking a girl out you need to show her something that means a lot to you. We don't get to know people through words, but through actions so take her somewhere where you can show her a piece of yourself."

"That's...Actually not—"

"Rune! Don't you dare jump off that!" Leo's stern command makes me smirk because she sounds exactly like my Ma and I'm pretty damn sure my mother has said those exact words to my sister before. She was always the wild one, not me like most people would think.

"Ev, don't encourage him! I'm sorry, I have to go. Just be you, Hale. If she's meant to be yours, you'll fit together like two puzzle pieces."

"Thanks Leo," I say as I slide on my Wranglers and button them.

"Anytime. We should triple date sometime! Good luck!"

The line goes dead before I can even comment on the utterly bad idea a triple date would be between us. Now I'm left with where to take Natasha. My first thought might not be the best but then again, Leo did say to show her a piece of myself, and I can't think of anywhere that fits me more...

Here we go, I guess.

***

Fifteen minutes later, I'm waiting outside Natasha's apartment, the Boston breeze carrying scents of street food mixed with the warm aromas of the neighboring coffee shop connected to her apartment complex.

Not two minutes after I arrived, she emerges and takes my breath away. Her hair in a slick ponytail, the tips of the golden strands brushing her mid-back. She's in a pair of matching leggings and a light, dusty pink crop top that brings out the warm tones in her whiskey eyes. A black leather jacket wraps around her sexy figure, a tempting package begging for me to tear it open.

"Where are we headed?" she asks, stepping out in front of me. My eyes trace down her body, roaming her face, landing on her lips. God, do I remember how they tasted.

I want to taste them again.

"Hale?"

Fuck. I got lost.

"Right. It's a surprise." I swear I see a spark in her eyes that does some crazy shit to my heart. "Do you like animals?"

We begin walking, hands clasped, and I can only hope she says yes, or this date's going to end in epic failure.

"I've never been around them before."

"You didn't grow up with any?" I couldn't imagine a life without at least one furry creature in my home.

"No. My mother and father never let me have one. I wanted a puppy when I was young but alas, it never happened. We weren't home a lot—always traveling—so it probably wouldn't have been fair to them anyway."

"I get that. What kind of traveling did you do?"

We pass a food cart and the sweet fragrance of cinnamon pretzels wafts through the air. Ma's favorite. I make a mental note to bring her one next time I visit. Stopping at the vendor, I order one and look at Natasha. "Want one?"

"Uhh, no. That's okay. I already ate."

After I pay, the man hands me a twisted pretzel on a stick coated in the glittering flecks of mouthwatering cinnamon sugar and I eagerly bite into it, burning the shit out of my tongue.

"Fuck," I swear, pulling air into my mouth in a desperate attempt to cool my tongue.

"I think it's hot," she giggles, and I glare at her.

"No shit."

"Here, let me take it." She grabs the twist off the stick, pulling it apart before reassembling it piece by piece into a pretzel shish-kabob.

"Thanks."

She licks her fingers, but before she can get to the last one, I seize her wrist and pull her pinky into my mouth, sucking off the butter, cinnamon and sugar. Her eyes blow wide and her lips part. My body inches closer to hers and before I pull her in for a kiss, some asshole with a death wish bumps into her.

"Hey dipshit! Watch where you're going!" I shout and the guy mumbles something in another language before scurrying off.

Her sweet smile calms my mind a fraction as she takes my hand, leading me the direction we were walking. I offer her a piece of the pretzel, but she denies it again.

"So, *Agent* Hale, how did you get into this field? Isn't it competitive?"

"It is but I was set up for success from my time in the military."

Her hand grips mine a little tighter as I slide one more piece of pretzel off the stick with my teeth.

"You were in the military?"

"Navy," I mumble with a mouthful. "Then I got out, was recruited by the FBI and here I am. Worked my way up the ladder in a relatively short time."

"And do you like your work?"

Do I? No. Sometimes.

I toss the empty pretzel stick in a trash can and contemplate how to answer her question. It's a simple yes or no question but why do both answers seem wrong.

"I... used to. Sometimes I still do, when we make a save or catch the bad guy. But those days seem to be few and far between lately. The trafficking rings are growing, and our numbers are dwindling. Plus, it seems more and more of our agents are going dark, turning in their badges, losing their battle with the horrific PTSD that haunts us—them."

"I think you do noble work. You're making a difference, even if it doesn't feel that way." Her small hand grips mine tighter and I flick my eyes to meet her gaze.

"Am I? Look at you."

Her gaze drop and I see her chest expand with a deep breath. "Exactly. Look at me. You saved me. I'm here with you."

"For how long?"

I stop in front of our destination and face her. Taking both her hands in mine, I bring them to my lips and kiss each knuckle. "How long before I must turn you over to them? How long before you are no longer mine to protect? How long, Natasha?"

Her eyes glass over with worry. "I don't know. But why don't we enjoy the time we do have?"

The agent in me wants to push more, to see if I can get her talking, figure out what she knows. But I don't. While I have her, I'll show her peace and happiness. Well, I guess that depends on if she likes dogs...

"Natasha, welcome to my favorite place in the city."

Turning my body so she can see, she reads the sign above the door, and I take in her reaction. "Boston Humane Society?"

She doesn't seem repulsed so that's a good sign. Maybe a little apprehensive but that's okay. I can work with that.

"I volunteer here when I have some free time. Helps me relax. You ready to get a little messy? It's grooming day."

Her eyes meet mine and when I expect to see disgust, I'm sorely mistaken. They light up with a playfulness that shocks me to my core. "Let's go."

She pulls me inside and I'm greeted by Frank, the front desk attendant. "Hale! Long time no see, man. Ready to get dirty?"

"Always, Frank. And I brought a friend today."

Frank's eyes land on Natasha and he gives her his most welcoming smile. "Welcome, pretty lady. You know what you're in for?"

"I was told it was grooming day," she responds, looking at me as I nod.

"You'd be right. Hale here likes to help with the big dogs, you up for it?"

She simply nods and Frank presses a button, opening the door for us to walk through.

"Gracie, Benny, and Toto need bathing today," he says as we follow him back to the kennels.

"We'll take Benny and Toto first," I say. "Gracie will take the both of us."

Frank chuckles, knowing exactly why Gracie will take two sets of hands. "Sounds good. You know what to do."

"Why will Gracie take us both?" Natasha questions and Frank and I look at each other, both trying to hold back our laughs.

"You'll see."

natasha

Toto shakes his head, followed by his body as I scrub behind his ears with a towel, drying his black fur. The Labrador covers me in not only soap and water but tiny black hairs as well. My Doc's are most likely ruined and I'm not sure I'll ever get the smell of wet dog out of my hair but... I also don't care.

My cheeks hurt from smiling and as I watch Hale across from me, scrubbing at Benny the Pit Bull's large head and talking to him like he's a baby, I realize for the first time in a long time I've completely forgotten about everything except the present moment I'm in.

My mind never shuts down, jumping from one topic to another, keeping me in a constant state of stress but with Hale and these dogs, my mind freely enjoys the moment..

My heart pounded a little faster when I realized we would spend our time bathing giant dogs. I'd never done it before, and I wouldn't be lying if I said I felt a little intimidated but Hale walked me through every step and the way Toto looks at me, those deep brown, almost black eyes... he looks at me like I'm the sun his world revolves around. He doesn't know about my past, the things I've done, he loves me. His tail wags a mile a minute and I can't help but shower him in scratches.

"Ready for Gracie?" Hale calls Toto and Benny down, looping the leashes around their necks to guide them back to their kennels.

"As ready as I'll ever be."

"Be right back." He smirks.

I could be jumping the gun, but I think this is the best date I've ever been on. Everett took me on a few in high school but mostly to the movies or dinner. Nothing this intimate. And even though we haven't even kissed, this is without a doubt the most intimate date I've been on. I've seen Hale in a few different lights so far. His cold, hard side that he shows as an Agent, like the night he made our deal. And the soft and tender side, like the night on the rooftop. But now I'm getting the carefree, silly side. My favorite so far? This one. The one bathes shelter dogs and doesn't care that I smell like wet dog.

A loud ruckus echoes down the hallway and not a moment later, Hale's shout follows. "Gracie! Calm down!"

A booming bark fills the space as the door flies open and the biggest dog I have ever seen drags Hale in.

"That is not a dog! That's a horse!" I shriek as Gracie almost plows into me, only stopped by the tug of the leash. It takes Hale's whole body, but he manages to stop her before I'm trampled.

"Natasha, meet Gracie the Great Dane. Gracie... Shit!" Gracie lunges, her mouth slobbering all over my stomach. Drool coats my exposed skin, and I throw my hands up in disgust. "Meet Natasha."

Gracie finally sits and I meet Hale's gaze. He's out of breath from battling the giant dog and me... well I struggle to hold back laughter and then fail.

Both of us burst out laughing as Gracie sits between us, tongue lolling out of her mouth as she pants.

When we finally catch our breath, I grab Gracie's face in my hands and massage below her ears, her tongue shoots out and licks my face as my mouth drops open— a colossal mistake that allows her tongue to land in my mouth. I sputter out, trying to spit away the French kiss I received from this mess of an animal.

"Well, that's not fair, she got a kiss on this date before I did," Hale protests, earning a laugh from me.

"I have to say, Gracie could give you a run for your money."

"I'll have to prove myself then." Hale's dangerous blue eyes meet mine and heat a touch. Enough to let me know that he's now thinking about kissing the shit out of me. He clears his throat a moment later. "Now you see why Gracie takes two. I'll hold her, you wash. She gets a bit excited by water."

Hale leads Gracie to the center of the floor to ceiling tiled room and positions the giant dog directly over the center drain hole. I turn on the hose and wet down Gracie's black and white coat. She stands from her sitting position and begins wagging her tail, forcing her entire back side to sway. When I scrub her hips and she looks back at me appreciatively, her massive tongue hanging out of the side of her mouth.

"That feel good, Gracie?" I say, moving up her body. The soap mixes with fur and soon my hands are drenched in stiff little hairs that stick to about every surface I touch.

"You can rub me down like that." Hale smirks and winks as I grab for the hose.

"I bet you would like that," I say, rinsing Gracie thoroughly. She shakes her head, and I freeze, knowing exactly what's coming.

"Gracie... no. Don't!" Hale shouts before her entire body shakes—soap, water and slobber fly, covering us. The not so graceful Great Dane sits nice and pretty, looking nothing short of proud of herself and Hale and I both glare at her.

"You're a mess, Gracie," Hale chides as he shakes his head.

"And so are you," I say, pointing the hose at him.

"Natasha..." he warns. "Don't you da—"

Pulling back the lever, I let the water fly and soak Hale's shirt. He drops Gracie's leash as he lunges forward and captures me around the waist. Gracie jumps around the large, tiled washing room and barks as I try desperately to escape the large arms encircling me.

Somehow, he manages to get the hose from my hands and opens fire right over the top of my head. Soaking me from head to toe. One arm pulls me close to his chest, his warmth seeping into me as he holds the hose over our heads, showering us in a cool drizzle of water.

"Have you ever been kissed in the rain?"

"This isn't rain," I correct as my gaze falls to his lips.

"Just answer the question, woman."

My arms wrap around his firm torso. "No," I whisper as I rise on my tippy toes.

His arm moves from my waist and wraps around my shoulder, his hand snaking around to grip my jaw as he continues to let the hose water rain down lightly over us. When his lips meet mine, they're wet and soft. But the payment they demand is my heart, a heavy price for a single kiss.

One I can't help but pay.

hale

Natasha and I have met up a handful of times over the last two weeks. A small dinner here or a lunch date there. Her schedule's open outside of the dance classes she teaches, but my schedule seems to collide with hers more often than I'd like.

We haven't kissed since our date at the Humane Society. I can tell I might have gone too far by pushing her for something she wasn't ready to give yet.

But I want to see more of her. Fuck, do I want to. I'm determined to make it happen in some way. Even if I must sleep outside her apartment door so I can greet her each morning with a cup of coffee and walk her to the dance studio.

And that's exactly how I find myself standing outside her apartment, coffee in hand as I pace the sidewalk, waiting for her to grace me with her presence.

I'm a fucking fool.

Damn, I knew after our first date together I would have it bad for her. And as always, my instincts were right. I'm utterly obsessed with Natasha Baldwin.

I'm still not completely sure that she isn't part of some kind of plan with the twins, her words are pretty, and her eyes tell me to believe her, but I've never been the type to trust something that seems too perfect.

Everything meant to kill is always wrapped with a pretty bow and this woman's no different.

The door attendant's been eyeing me, two seconds away from calling the police, but then he opens the door, and Natasha comes out in a light pink puffy jacket, cream-colored sweatpants, and a pair of tan boots with fur lining the insides. Her head looks up from her phone when she nearly crashes into me. "Oh my—"

Her eyes meet mine, and I shake my head, clearing the big, goofy grin plastered on my face from seeing her. "Hi."

"Hi," she says with a bit of apprehension. "Did we have a date?"

"No. I—" A sudden clenching of my chest makes me a bit nauseated. Why am I nervous? "I wanted to see you. I brought coffee?"

Stretching out my hand, she eyes my offering before taking it. "Thank you. I would love to do something, but I have a class."

"I have the morning off. Can I come?" My feet trail her as she starts to walk toward the studio. I'm a damn lost puppy dog looking for its home and my mind and heart seem to think they've found it.

"To my dance class?"

I nod.

"My twinkle toes dance class that consists of ten tiny humans who would absolutely fawn over you."

Her attempt at warning me off fails, I fucking love kids. "I love tiny humans." I smile, and she giggles. God, that sound lights me up like a fucking firework. My dick apparently thinks it's a great sound too as he jumps with excitement. For fucks sake, all she did was giggle.

"Well, okay then."

The short walk to the studio flies by, we don't even have time to finish our coffees before she unlocks the door and flips all the lights on. She connects her phone to the sound system and puts on a classical playlist.

My eyes refuse to leave her body as she slips off her sweatpants and unzips the puffy jacket to reveal her stunning body encased in a black leotard, pink tights, and a short black skirt. Her ass peeks out from under the thin material of the skirt as she bends forward to stretch. Of course, her ass faces me and of course I eat that shit up, letting my eyes travel over every inch of her.

"Fuck me."

"What was that?" Her head lifts to where I sit on the back wall.

Shit, did I say that aloud?

I clear my throat, "Nothing..."

The door opens and I adjust myself in my pants, trying to hide the raging boner I've popped, especially now that a crowd of tiny humans' race inside, their parents giving Natasha a quick wave. She smiles and gives the children a few moments to take their own coats and pants off.

There are seven little girls and three boys, all around the ages of five to seven and they all give her their full attention when she claps her hands twice. "Alright, my shining stars, time to stretch. Follow along."

She stands at the front of the class, assessing the children behind her in the full wall of mirrors. They mimic her every move, as much under her spell as I am.

When they finish, she turns toward them and smiles at me. "Today, we are going to learn a new sequence. You can all partner up for a duet. And lucky for you, I've brought along a friend of mine to assist me."

She motions toward me and my face falls.

"Oh no..." I begin to protest, but the children erupt in laughter and their little eyes fill with excitement that I can't resist. *Dammit.*

I stand, take off my jacket, and walk to the front of the class. I guess my Henley and jeans will have to do since I didn't prepare to dance this morning. "You owe me," I whisper as I come to stand next to her.

She walks the children through the first couple of steps, calling the male roles the nutcrackers and the female roles the swans.

"Our nutcrackers," she looks at me and I step behind her, "will hold our swans around the waist like so." Taking my hands in hers, she guides them to the dip of her waist. My fingers slide over the soft, silky material of her leotard. Small enough I can almost touch my thumbs together at the small of her back.

"Then our swans will relevé, pirouette and arabesque." She rises on her toes as her arms come up gracefully, spins in a circle and then extends out one leg as I stand there supporting her. Her toned muscles tighten under my hands, and I know she doesn't need me here; she could do this easily without me but fuck, she would have a hell of a time getting me to let go.

Her body lowers, but my hands stay glued to her abdomen. She clears her throat and looks down at my hands, giving me a small smile. "You can let go now," she whispers.

Can I?

Before I run my hands all over her body in front of ten tiny, innocent humans, I release her.

"Right."

All the little ones practice the move over and over as she goes around, correcting posture and praising. I notice that even when she corrects, her gentle tone turns each critique into a compliment. Saying things like "focus on tightening these muscles here, but your arabesque is perfect" or "keep your toes pointed as you lift but your arms are so graceful."

I can't help but admire how encouraging and kind she teaches the children. A natural nurturer and leader. She'd be an amazing mother.

Fuck, slow your shit, Hale.

The class ends and the parents come by, gathering their little humans and thanking Natasha. She reminds each one about hydrating after practice and stretching when they get home.

When she turns back to me after everyone has left, a blush creeps up her chest and cheeks. "Why are you looking at me like that?"

I know exactly how I'm looking at her—like I want to scoop her up, run away with her, marry her and fuck her till her belly's swollen with my children, but instead of saying that I simply tilt my head and run my thumb over my bottom lip. "Like what?"

"Like I could get pregnant from your eyes alone," she says as she takes a drink of water.

"What would be the fun in that?" I step toward her, those heart-crippling eyes unsure but brave at the same time. That look draws out of me a primal need to own her as much as she owns me.

I want her to feel as captivated as I do, as obsessed as I am. And it isn't a physical attraction alone. Over the weeks we have been going on our little dates, I've come to appreciate and crave her mind, her wit, her charm and even her vulnerability that she keeps locked away. The secrets I can see she wants to share but won't, her raw, unfiltered pain that she thinks she's hiding, but is strikingly transparent in her eyes at the briefest of seconds. I devour those small moments as if they were my last meal.

I close the space between us, and our bodies connect, my hand reaching up to brush her cheek and her eyes close on an exhale. Her skin, so fucking soft under my rough, calloused thumb.

"Stay with me tonight," I whisper.

"I can't." She steps away from me and my heart drops.

Fuck, I moved too fast. Natasha's a wild animal; she needs gentle coaxing to comfortability with small movements and even smaller acts of service. I learned the first night I was with her that she bolts at the first notion of something deeper.

Even after the dates we've been on, I can tell she's still holding back. Maybe it's the deal with the twins, but my gut tells me it's something more.

"Actually, I'm meeting with Sabrina after this for lunch. I should go."

Gathering her things quickly, she goes to the door and holds it open, encouraging me to leave.

"Natasha," I plead.

"Don't. I... I need to go." She scurries off and my head falls.

Way to go, dipshit.

natasha

It's close to Thanksgiving and I haven't spoken to Hale since I left him at the ballet studio. He's reached out a few times, texted and called, but I've ignored all of them. I did check in with him before I left with the twins for Seattle. Just to let him know I would be gone for the week, and he told me to call if I needed him.

My heart froze solid when he suggested I stay with him. He's getting too attached, and I know I encouraged it by suggesting we go on these little dates but I... well I don't know what I wanted when I did that. I guess I wanted to be near him.

But I've been ghosting him because, well... Hale Knight would be heartbreakingly easy to fall in love with, and I cannot under any circumstances fall for him.

Too late...

Shut. Up.

Right now, with the mess I'm in with the twins and my father, I can't let him close. Not only for the sake of my tortured heart... but more importantly, his.

The only person I can get close to is Sabrina who thankfully agreed to spend time with me in Seattle. At least I won't be alone amongst the monsters, and I know she can hold her own.

Speaking of my red-headed firecracker of a best friend, she sits across from me, twirling a knife in her hands like she's some menacing assassin. It's laughable with her size and boisterous personality, but I know she would only hurt someone if they attacked first.

"Are you sure you're willing to come with me? You'll be spending Thanksgiving in Seattle, away from your family."

She waves me off then tucks the knife into some kind of holster at her back. She slides out of the car and drags a suitcase larger than herself to the private jet awaiting our arrival. "Please, the only family I have is Gage and that grumpy bastard doesn't do shit for the holidays anyway. Plus, it's been a long time since I've been to Seattle. It'll be fun."

"I can definitely make it fun for you." Enzo walks up behind her, unashamedly checking out her ass as he reaches out to take her suitcase. "Let me get that for you, piccola diavoletta."

A small game of tug of war ensues as B glares at him. "Go fetch your finance's suitcase, you ass."

The smiling twin lets go and B stumbles backward but remains on her feet as she flips her long red hair over her shoulder and lets out a huff.

Rafael comes up behind all of us and swoops my suitcase away with ease. "I've got hers. Please Sabrina, don't be so difficult."

"Don't be a sexist pig and I won't be difficult," she fires back, and I snicker under my breath as we all walk toward the jet. "I'm perfectly capable of carrying my own luggage."

"It's not sexism, it's being a gentleman," Rafael says and B rolls her eyes. "And now you're being a brat."

I catch up to where B and Enzo walk next to each other, Raf a few feet ahead. B sticks her tongue out at Raf behind his back. In a split second, Enzo reaches out and grabs hold of her tongue, and we all come to halt.

I would love to say I know what's going to happen, but it seems with Sabrina Shae and Enzo Alessi, I honestly have no clue. The two individually are psychotic on an unexplainable level, but together?

The fiery little redhead turns her body toward Enzo and opens her mouth wider, sticking her tongue further out as he towers over her, glaring daggers at her. "Stick your tongue out at my brother again and I'll cut it out. That bratty mouth will still feel good with half a tongue, baby."

My gaze searches for help from Rafael but I'm disappointed when he continues walking, ignoring the whole ordeal.

Looks like it's up to me...

I raise my hand to pull B back, but she steps closer to Enzo, her body pressing into his as she tilts her head back. Her eyes close as she lets out a sex-filled moan and he swiftly releases her tongue as if it burned him.

"Oh god, how did you know I was into that?"

With her closeness, she knees him in the balls faster than I can blink and when he leans forward she takes her small hand and pushes his head to the side, away from her.

"God I'm so fucking turned on," he laughs out as she struts away, grabbing her suitcase and walking ahead of all of us.

Where the hell did this woman come from? It's like she isn't intimidated in the slightest by these violent men.

We file into the plane and Raf and Enzo go straight to the back while B and I find two seats across from each other. She places headphones over her ears and eases into the extravagant, soft leather seats.

B's past is her own, something she keeps from everyone, including me and despite my curiosity surrounding what made this tiny thing so fearless and defiant, I haven't asked. I know from experience how vital to one's sanity it is to keep your secrets. But the easy way she carries herself around these devils tells me she must have grown up in hell. God help the person who breaks Sabrina Shae's sanity.

"Ma'am, can I get you something to drink?" The flight attendant approaches in her tiny little suit with too short of a skirt and red little necktie.

"No. I'm fine. Thank you," I say, keeping my spine straight. Unlike B, I can't relax. My mind races with the unknown. I've been with the twins for months now and although Enzo has a crude mouth, neither of them have harmed me. My father has been in business with the Alessi family since I was young, but I can count on one hand the encounters I've had with the twins in all those years.

But Dante Alessi, their father? Last I saw him I was ten and he was the monster of my nightmares. He's the biggest unknown, one I'm not sure I could prepare for even if I knew how.

I do remember he was a man that exuded power. He didn't need to use words or weapons to make your chest freeze with fear—a trait he passed down to his sons.

My mother taught me how to read men, how to judge their wants and needs and how to adjust my own character to manipulate them into getting what I wanted. But I've never met two men like the twins. They're immune to manipulation. Their eyes may show an appreciation for my body, but they wouldn't hand over their hearts so easily. Maybe they've already handed the beating organs to another?

Honestly, growing up I believed it to be a superpower, something that made me unique and special. Now I realize how cruel it made me because not only did I use it on men, I used it on my friends as well. I used it on innocent girls in high school, bullied them to feel that power, to feel special.

Now I feel sick.

Sick of my actions.

I think often about my daughter... what if she would have been one of those girls I tormented? What if she had turned out like me?

"Natasha. A word please," Raf beckons me from the back of the plane, pulling me from thoughts of Aurora, the little girl I lost.

I learned from a young age to pick and choose my battles, and survival often comes down to which battle you choose to fight and which you choose to lose. Picking a fight with Raf on a plane that will soon be 10,000 feet in the air is a battle I'll take an L for.

As I step into the small room in the back, I recognize it's a small office with a desk and reclining chair in the corner which Enzo currently lounges in. His tall frame looks more than a bit awkward in the short chair.

"There are some areas of discussion we need to go over before we land in Seattle," Raf says coldly, drawing my attention back to him. I nod and he links his fingers together on the small desk already littered with paperwork and a glass of whiskey.

"When we arrive, we'll be staying with my father for the holidays. You will be staying with me, in my room."

My eyes meet his and I want to protest but stay silent.

"I'll take the couch. But the men in my father's house are ruthless. They will not hesitate to take what and who they want. I need you to be on your guard, always stay with Sabrina or one of us."

"But I'm not one of the girls... they can't—"

"They can, principessa, and they will," Enzo chimes in, eyes closed, hands relaxed behind his head. "But not if they know you're ours."

"Natasha, in our world, the only rules those men follow are my father's and he doesn't have many, especially when it comes to women. A public claiming is the only way to ensure your safety, but I won't put you through that."

"Can I stay in the room with Sabrina?"

"Ah yes, that bratty little thing. Damn, am I going to love staking my claim over her," Enzo chuckles like he's made a joke to himself.

What the hell kind of world am I walking into? I'm a hotel heiress from small-town Oregon and here I am with two men talking about the "public claiming" of women.

"I'm sorry, I think I've slipped into an alternate universe... Maybe this isn't the best idea for me to come. What if I stay at your place?"

Raf shakes his head. "It won't be allowed, Natasha. In the simplest of terms, our father purchased you and he will want to know that his investment is producing results. It's a role we must play to placate him until his reign ends. When it does, you'll be free. You have my word."

Free? I don't even know the meaning of the word. My chest caves in as I release a breath. Is he messing with my mind or does he mean to let me out of this arrangement? "What do you mean? My father will never allow that. He wants his heir."

"The how is not your concern. We will handle both of our fathers. We simply need you to do as we say until the deal is done."

The calm collected brother stands from his desk and comes to loom over me. He runs his finger along my cheekbone, as Hale did at the studio. "You have to trust us."

How can I trust devils such as the Alessi twins? They're certifiable psychopaths. They're the dogs that Dante Alessi sends after the most dangerous criminals when they don't play by his rules. They're the boogeymen in the dark, the ghouls in ghost stories—the men my father has threatened me with since I was sixteen. But as his thumb runs over my skin, I see a gentleness in this devil that I'm not sure anyone else sees.

"Why?" I whisper. I didn't mean to, but it slipped out and I don't know if I'm asking why he's being gentle with me or why I'm in this situation in the first place.

"We don't deal in innocent lives, Natasha. Our fathers made a mistake when they brought you into the deal. They unleashed their dogs, not realizing it was their blood that we've been hunting."

He steps away and I'm left with a sense of overwhelming relief because despite their reputation, I seem to fall under their protection and there's nothing like the devil's protection.

"Principessa," Enzo singsongs, interrupting my confused thoughts. His deep eyes study me from across the tiny room. "Can we have a little chit-chat?"

"Do I have a choice?"

He stands in front of me now, taking the spot his brother left. If they weren't dressed differently, Raf in a full three-piece suit and Enzo in slacks and a button-up, I wouldn't be able to tell them apart. "I want to make this clear, you will always have a choice with us. But if your life is in danger, I will remove your choice and ask for forgiveness later. Understood?"

"I don't understand any of this. You are literal human traffickers. You buy, sell, and distribute innocent men, women and children, yet you talk about innocent lives and..." I run out of breath as everything in my mind comes spilling out of my mouth.

"Our father deals in innocent lives. We hunt and kill the monsters who don't pay."

"But you're still part of the business," I snap. "Two wrongs don't make a right. I'm supposed to believe you have my best interest at heart?"

My mind reaches out to find anything I can use to demonize these two men. But looking back at my time spent with them, they haven't hurt me or forced me to do anything that I didn't want to do. They're abrasive and dangerous, but maybe they aren't as monstrous as I had always believed.

"For now. We are. That is our burden to carry. And sure, two wrongs may not make a right, but it sure as hell feels good when wrong things happen to bad people, don't you think?" He tilts his head, studying me. "But let's have a little talk about you and Agent Knight, that's a whole lot of wrong that I want to explore..."

Shit.

"How did you meet him?" he continues, relaxing back from me a hair.

"At Divino, you know this." I break eye contact—my first mistake. Enzo smiles.

"I'll ask again. How did you meet him?" He sits back down, but in Raf's chair this time, and I take the seat he vacated. I fiddle with the ends of my sweater sleeves as his gaze bores into me and he kicks his feet atop the desk, basking as if he overthrew God himself. "Tick tock, you, my dear, are ten thousand feet in the air with no escape and I've got nothing but time."

"I met him a couple months before I was given to you two. I haven't seen him since."

"What did you two do?" he asks as he leans forward sharply, his feet coming down and a dangerous curiosity in his eyes—as if he's excited by the opportunity to use this information against me or Hale.

"It's none of your business, Enzo." I stand and leave, his dark laughter following me out the door. To my shock, he doesn't follow or chase. He stays back in the office and when a flight attendant slips past me, it doesn't take a rocket scientist to know what mile high festivities he's about to partake in.

When I get back to my chair, B's asleep or at least she looks like she is with her head resting against the window as she hugs a pillow to her chest.

I assume a similar position and close my eyes, but I don't fall asleep. Instead, I listen to the low whir of the engine and the clink of glasses as the stewardess prepares another drink for Rafael. The solid thud and slight vibration under my feet tells me Enzo left the back office a little bit ago. Finally, soft whispers between the brothers fill the cabin the rest of the way.

The familiar drop in my stomach alerts me to the descent of the plane and I open my eyes. B still snoozes and Enzo sits in the chair across the aisle from her, whiskey in hand as he stares at her.

Rafael comes from inside the cockpit and sits across from his brother, crossing his leg over his knee and I notice his white-knuckled grip on the arm rests.

"Are you afraid of flying?" I couldn't hide the amusement and surprise in my question if I tried, however Rafael doesn't seem to appreciate my observation.

"Flying does not bother me, Natasha," he grits out before setting his gaze above his brother's head.

"It's the landing part that makes him shit his pants," Enzo chuckles as he takes a sip from his glass.

"I do not shit my pants, *cazzone*."

"Then why do you keep an extra pair in the closet?" Enzo fires back with a smirk.

"For when your favorite flight attendant rides me like a bitch in heat and gets her sweet little come all over my Armani trousers."

The water I sipped flies out of my mouth as Rafael delivers the insult with a straight face. Enzo bursts out laughing and the flight attendant, the one who happened to walk by for that little exchange, blushes.

"Prepare for landing," the pilot calls and I hold back a laugh as the great Rafael Alessi goes pale as a ghost when the wheels touch down, bounce, and then settle on the asphalt. As soon as we have wheels on the ground, he gets up, straightens his lapels and makes his way back into the cockpit. I finally let out my giggle at the whole ordeal, unable to contain myself any longer.

Sleeping beauty jerks awake as soon as she hears the seatbelt light ding, and I raise my brow at her. "You slept through that entire landing?"

"Girl, you don't even want to know the things I've had to sleep through," she says as she fixes her hair and wipes the drool from her chin. As if she could sense Enzo looking at her, she levels him with a glare. "Take a picture, it'll last longer."

"Oh, I have." Enzo stands and exits the plane as B and I stare at one another.

"Did he just—" she stutters out.

"Yeah. But is it honestly that surprising?"

"I hope he at least got my good side."

"Do you have a bad side?" I cover the laugh that escaped me with my hand as we exit the plane and walk toward the waiting car.

"A downright dangerous one, my dear." She winks, linking her arm with mine and off we go, into the lair of the beasts.

natasha

The car ride from Sea-Tac Airport to the grand mansion on the outskirts of Seattle could be classified as the most uncomfortable ride I've had the displeasure of taking. Raf spent most of his time on his iPad, doing some sort of work. Enzo and Sabrina bickered the entire time, him mostly flirting and her brushing off any advances the man made. And me, I sat there looking out at the beautiful trees and traced water droplets as they rolled down my window.

As the driver pulls down a white gravel road with tall pines lining each side, I admire the stunning property. The open space and luscious fields would normally bring me peace, but the anticipation of what's waiting at the end of the long drive clouds my mind and my chest tightens.

When the driver pulls around a large stone fountain, the home comes into view—a grand two story, white brick mansion with a black roof and vines crawling up the side makes my breath catch in my throat. The golden light illuminating through the windows gives it an inviting appearance but I know that demons lurk inside.

The driver stops and Rafael doesn't wait as he opens the door and hustles into the mansion. Enzo lingers as he waits for us to get out.

"I will take your luggage to your rooms, ladies," the driver says as Enzo ushers us inside.

"Welcome to home, hell, home."

"Home, hell, home?" B mimics as she steps in front of us, confidently striding into the mansion as if it were her own home.

"Well, I wouldn't call it sweet," Enzo replies as he steps to her side and pushes a book sitting on the entry table to the side, messing up the otherwise perfect décor.

I'm accustomed to extravagant décor. Coming from money, my dad was not shy when it came to splurging on lavish things including our home, cars, and clothes but this home marvels anything I've seen. The walls are a soft cream color with ornate crown molding incredibly detailed with filigree. Two wide staircases on either side of the entryway lead up to the second level which overlooks the first, a black iron railing skirts the entire second floor. The cream-colored furniture accented with deep, dark wood screams luxury.

"This is..." I look at Sabrina who observes the room but not in awe. The look on her face is... sad. Her jaw tight, her brows turned down. As if stepping inside this house brings back a haunting memory.

Her eyes meet mine and she perks up, clearing her throat. "This place is amazing! Where's my room and who do I have to marry to stay forever?" She spins in a circle, places her hands on her hips, and looks at me as if waiting for approval on her feigned performance.

I'm a bit confused and when I narrow my eyes at her, looking for something more behind her act, I'm interrupted by the bulldozer of a man who walks past me.

"You would be staying with me, piccola diavoletta, and I will gladly volunteer," Enzo chimes as he gives her a wink.

"And where is your room?"

"The basement."

Sabrina's brows tug in as she tilts her head. "The basement? Really?"

"Really. I was always a little too loud for daddy dearest. My night-time activities tend to interrupt his beauty sleep. But I never minded, I could make them scream as loud as I wanted."

"Did the ghosts of this place scream with fright when they saw your ugly ass face in their territory?" B follows Enzo as he walks toward the back of the house and I'm left standing in the entryway, unable to get my feet to move. I look around and realize Rafael's nowhere in sight and I'm all alone.

"Miss Baldwin, I presume?" A tall, built man with graying brown hair and hazel eyes comes out from behind the left staircase. His suit slightly wrinkled, tie loose but I can tell he isn't part of the help. Probably one of the twins' or Dante's men.

"Yes. And you are?"

He steps up to me, only an arm's length away and I take a small step back to keep the distance. I didn't mean to but something about him forces my body to retreat.

"Lorenzo. I'm Mr. Alessi's right hand."

Lorenzo. Mark that name down as one, batshit crazy, and two, someone to avoid.

"Was your flight comfortable?" He steps in again. I step back and he smirks like a cat toying with their food.

"It was fine," I grit out. Trying not to show fear while all I want to do is turn and run. The look in his eyes tells me he wants to do more than talk and I wonder who else Dante offered me to.

"Why don't I show you to your room? You don't want to be lingering in these halls all by yourself."

"I'll find it on my—"

"Lorenzo," Raf calls from behind and I sigh, relief washing over me like a tidal wave.

"Rafael. You seem to have lost something. I was making sure it was put back in its rightful place."

Its. Like I'm a lost toy.

"Thank you for your hospitality, Lorenzo. I was under the impression my father would not be arriving until this evening?"

"We left early, he wanted to be here to greet his sons and future daughter-in-law." Lorenzo steps back as Raf comes up to my side and pulls me in by my waist. My body willingly snuggles into him and my hand even rests on his chest.

"Then where is he?"

"He had a last-minute call come up. He should be down shortly. Why don't you all get settled and I'll go see who else the cat dragged in, hmm?"

"Enzo will be more than happy to see you after so long, Lorenzo. How's the hand? Still missing those fingers?"

Lorenzo's lip curls as he turns and stomps away and my shoulders drop.

"I see you have already made a friend, Natasha. I apologize, no one was supposed to be home yet. I won't make that mistake again."

"It's okay," I whisper as Raf turns me in his arms, the lapels of his designer jacket brushing up against my sweater.

"Lorenzo is dangerous. The worst dog my father owns. He's been by my father's side since we were born, in fact, that's where Enzo gets his name. Sometimes I think a little bit of Lorenzo's psychotic tendencies leaked into my brother that way as well."

"What happened to his hand?" The curiosity in me has been building ever since Raf made that comment and how it triggered Lorenzo so easily. There could be something there I could use if I needed to.

"Last time we saw Lorenzo a few months back, he made a threat toward my brother, and he took what was due. Three fingers from his left hand. Father was upset but the hierarchy protected Enzo from retaliation and Lorenzo was furious. He hates that despite his loyalty and age, Enzo and I still outrank him, and we always will."

Raf lets my waist go and grabs my hand as he leads me up the right side of the staircase. "What was the threat he made?"

"It's of no concern. It will not come to fruition."

I want to ask more as he leads me down the hallway, but I leave it be. When Raf opens the last door on the right, placing the last three fingers on the touchpad, I'm led into a beautifully dark, all black room. Black walls, black bedding, black curtains. Everything dark and sleek, reminding me so much of the twin who still has my hand in his.

"This will be where you will stay. The door is coded, and your fingerprints have already been uploaded to allow access. You will lay your left middle, fourth, and pinky finger together on the touchpad and it will unlock."

I release his hand and walk toward the balcony that overlooks the front lawn and beyond that, a stunning body of water.

Raf approaches from behind and his body heat warms me against the chill of the breeze. "The Puget Sound. Sometimes you will see pods of orcas breach the water. It's one of my favorite views. Although the one from my home is better."

"It's breathtaking," I whisper and then step away feeling a bit overwhelmed by all that transpired today. My stomach growls and I wince as Raf's eyes drop down to my body.

"Did you not eat on the plane?"

"No. I wasn't hungry."

"Breakfast this morning then was the last you ate?"

"I might have skipped that as well," I say with a shyness I wasn't expecting. Shame gnaws away at my stomach. As much as I try, I still can't overcome the thoughts that plague my mind when I think about food and its association with my figure. I've restricted myself for so long, I don't know any other way.

Raf shakes his head, running his hand down his face. "Natasha, must I force feed you? How do you expect to get strong when you don't feed your body what it needs?"

I let out a small laugh then curl my lips in as he levels me with a glare. But I can't help it, the image of Rafael Alessi spoon feeding me provokes my laughter. "I will eat at dinner. Don't worry yourself. I was nervous today."

He grunts, walking toward a set of French doors that look like they lead into a closet. "I've already had Lorinda stock everything you will need for your stay this week. If there is anything missing, let me know. You can dress in anything on the left side for this evening, these are approved dresses."

"Approved dresses? Now I don't even have control over my attire?"

He rolls his eyes then faces me fully as he fixes his tie. "Natasha, I have selected dresses that are acceptable to my father without being too revealing. I cannot have his men tempted from scandalous attire. Which I happen to know is something you favor."

Scandalous attire was all I had been allowed to dress in. Ever since I began to develop as a woman, my mother dressed me in the most revealing and barely acceptable clothes for my age. She always taught me to use my body like a weapon, to lure men in to get what I want. I've never known any other way to dress. Even as an adult, I'm not comfortable in anything unless it clings to me. The way loose clothing hangs and brushes against my skin irritates me. But Raf's right, I don't want these men looking at me like I'm a piece of meat, even though to them, that's all women are.

"Fine. I will wear what you select."

He goes straight into the closet, spending less than a minute selecting my attire and when he comes out, he lays a midnight blue gown across the end of the bed. The silky fabric will cling to my body, but the neckline sits high, the sleeves long. The back opens low and drapes down to mid back. It's elegant, sexy but modest at the same time. The shoes he comes out with next are a silver pair of heels and then he lays a set of simple diamond studs on the dresser.

"This should do fine. Hair down and curled." Rafael picks up his phone and dials a number then exits the room.

Stuff me in a box and call me fucking Barbie.

natasha

"You look hot as hell," Sabrina comments as I step out of Rafael's room into the hallway where she and Enzo had been waiting for me. My eyes practically exit my skull at the dress option she has chosen.

"Why do I have to be modest, and she looks like a siren ready to steal your soul?" I ask Enzo as he leans back against the wall, his tie loose but at least he's in a full suit.

"She can defend herself. You're still learning. Plus, no one comes for what's mine. They know I'm fucking crazy enough to pluck their eyeballs from their skull with my salad fork."

"And I'm not yours?" I snide back at him and choose to ignore the salad fork comment... But I know I'll never look at one the same again.

"As far as the men see it, you belong to Raf, and they will test his boundaries simply so he can prove he's capable of doing what needs to be done to take over for our father when the time comes."

"They don't test yours?" Sabrina chimes in and stares at Enzo, hand on her hip.

"Nah. I'd have to have boundaries for them to test first, plus I'm not meant to rule, only break the rules." Enzo twists a curl of Sabrina's red hair around his finger and brings it to his nose, inhaling her scent.

"Paws off, you hound." She pushes at his chest and turns on her heel. We trail behind Enzo on the way to the dining room, our arms linked and I'm incredibly grateful she came with me.

"Where did you get that dress? I need one for myself. Although I think I would want mine in red." I let my eyes travel up and down her body, taking in how gorgeous the dress is. The royal blue velvet material clings to all of B's curves and her hips look ravenous as the corset top tapers at her waist, the rouging of the fabric right at the hips makes them look fuller than they are. From there, the material tapers at her knees before flaring out slightly again to create the mermaid look. A high slit in the skirt comes all the way to mid-thigh. Her bust popping out from the corset and the neckline lined in matching blue lace and jewels.

"It was in Enzo's closet. I guess he had ordered it for me for the occasion. It's a little scary how well he knew my style and measurements, but who am I to complain. A poor, gym owner dressed in jewels. Like a real-life Cinderella story here."

"I think you may have your princes crossed."

Her long, curled red hair flips over her shoulder as she fixes herself. I never thought I'd see the day Sabrina Shae dressed to the nines but here I am, gazing upon her gorgeous figure and feminine make-up. At the gym, her face always sweaty with not even a swipe of Chapstick on her lips. I've always figured her to lean more on the tom-boy side than the girly side but call me corrected. Either way, she should do her make up more often like this. Her eyes are done in a simple cat eye, and her lips are painted blood red, matching her hair. She's stunning.

Right before we enter the dining room, which I assume overflows with the most dangerous men in Seattle, Raf meets us, and I link my arm through his. "You look nice, Natasha. The dress fits perfectly."

"Thank you. I would say you clean up well, but I don't know that I've ever seen you... dirty."

He gives a small smile. "Those are the men you must always worry about, Natasha."

"I do," I whisper and find that my honesty surprises even myself. My heart pounds and my chest constricts but when Raf pulls me closer, an unexpected ease washes over me.

The butler opens the doors, and we step into a long rectangular room with a table that could seat forty people in the center. A large crystal chandelier hangs high above and there are candles lit all along the table creating a soft glow. It's a magnificent sight that I would appreciate more if all the men surrounding the table didn't stop all conversation and set their evil stares upon me.

Making eye contact with each one, their leering gazes make my body shiver with unease. An instinct of danger makes my hairs rise. The air thickens with mistrust between me and them, them and Raf.

Enzo leans in, his breath a tickle on my ear, "Remember your role, principessa. You are to be Raf's queen. Act like it."

With that, I straighten my spine and lift my chin slightly. He's right. Even if I am the least powerful person in here, I must play the part. Easy, I've been playing a part all my life. I can alter my role to fit the crowd I'm in; these men are no different from the vile men my father frequents. I can do this.

Raf leads me in and the crowd of men part to reveal Dante sitting at the head of the table.

"My sons, I am so happy you were able to join the family for the holidays." He stands and Raf lets my arm go as Dante embraces his son in a hug, then he does the same to Enzo. B and I scoot slightly back and closer together.

The twins are almost identical to their father and Dante himself has not changed much since I saw him last, maybe a few more gray hairs lining his temples and a few more lines crowding his dark eyes.

The rumors I've heard say that Dante has become a recluse, rarely leaving his home and when he does, he brings at least twenty guards with him and only travels via his own plane or cars. But you wouldn't be able to tell he's a paranoid psychopath because he's as boisterous and put together as I remember him. His personality has always been one people are drawn to; he's the type of man you want to be acquainted with because somehow that makes you feel more important.

But I know how truly vile Dante Alessi is.

"Please, sit." He motions toward the chairs and at his command every person in the room finds their seat.

I sit across from Lorenzo and his eyes eat at me. I want to cower, instead, I steal my spine and try my hardest to remain unaffected.

Dinner comes and small conversations fill the space, but I keep silent. Occasionally, Raf will lay his hand on my leg, a reassuring gesture, but I don't speak unless spoken to.

After everyone has finished, classical music filters through the room and the double doors open as women flood the dining room. All dressed up in gowns more revealing than my own. The men grab at the women and even though they don't protest, I can see the reluctance and fear in their eyes.

I remain close to Sabrina, but I've lost the twins—they must have been called elsewhere. We stand and drink from our glass champagne flutes as our eyes stay alert to anything dangerous.

As a woman passes by, she slips on her gown and spills her champagne all over Sabrina's gown, profusely apologizing after.

"Oh sweetie, it's fine. Not like I paid for it." B winks at the girl as she blushes and hurries off. "I'm going to clean this up. Come with me."

We walk out of the dining room turned ballroom and stop outside the bathroom down the hall and to the right. The halls are empty as everyone's attention remains on the women inside and I find the silence comforting. "You go in. I'll wait here. I need a moment," I tell B as she gives me a concerned look but then goes into the bathroom, shutting the door. My mask drops as the click of the door echoes in the empty hall.

Not two minutes pass before a hand wraps around my elbow and I'm pulled into a dark alcove, I try to scream but a hand clamps down around my mouth and the large figure pushes me into the wall, my back arches from something poking it and my chest collides with his.

"Shh shh now. Wouldn't want anyone to hear us." The smell of whiskey and cigarettes fill my nose and makes me want to gag. Lorenzo's face nears mine and then his tongue darts out and licks up my neck. I try to scream again but his hand wraps around my throat, cutting off my plea.

"I said shut it," he grits out as his hips press forward, a hard length digging into my hip. My stomach turns but I swallow my repulsion down, like old times.

"Rafael thinks he can keep you all to himself and his shit-for-brains of a brother, but Dante promised all of us a turn. Doesn't matter how used up your pussy is, I bet it will still be nice and wet for me, won't it, little heiress."

His hand digs tighter into my throat as I try to pull away, my hands tug and pull at his wrist, but he doesn't budge. Probably used to women fighting when he's got them in this position. "Don't act like you don't like this. Your daddy told me how he had you trained real good and well. I bet you're soaking for me. Like a bitch salivating at the mouth for the treat her master gives, no matter who the master is. Am I right? Oh, pretty pretty please tell me I'm right."

"Natasha?" B's calls for me, but she can't see me in the small alcove that Lorenzo has hidden us in. I can't scream because of the force of his hand around my throat. My vision swirls in and out from the lack of oxygen. I pray that he doesn't get his hands on her too.

Just before I black out, I see a tattooed hand grab Lorenzo's throat and my breath burns as it returns to my lungs. My hands find my throat as I begin to cough, trying my best to catch my breath.

"Loreeeeenzooo," Enzo singsongs in a cynical tune and I've never been happier to hear such a daunting sound. "Looks like you touched something that wasn't yours," he tuts as he easily handles Lorenzo, dragging him by the throat to the ballroom.

B comes up to me, helping me stand to my full height as we follow. "Are you okay?" she whispers, and I nod. Her small hands rub soothing circles over my back, and my mind returns to my body.

Walking into the ballroom, the crowd of men and women notice the grip Enzo has on the slimy piece of trash and they immediately form a circle. Enzo tosses him into the center, and he scrambles to his feet, coughing like I did.

"What is going on, Enzo?" Dante says as he steps into the center, hands in his front pockets.

"Your *dog* touched something that doesn't belong to him."

"She was offered to all of us by your father." Lorenzo grits out with a scuffed voice.

Rafael calmly walks into the circle, hands relaxed into the pockets of his dress-slacks. He looks at me with a furrowed brow as I clench my throat in my hands. His finger curls in a beckoning motion and I comply without question.

"Let me see." His deep brown eyes trace down my face to my throat and I remove my hand, letting him inspect the damage. "Did he touch you anywhere else?" His neutral tone, neither angry nor nice, demonstrates his refined control and patience.

I nod. "He... licked my neck." My body cringes at the coolness on my skin where his salvia remains. It makes me want to drown myself in a bathtub full of bleach.

He hums and then looks at his father. "Natasha belongs to Enzo and I."

"Has she been claimed?" Dante asks, just as calm. As if discussing if they remembered to buy sugar and eggs for the cookies we plan on fucking baking tonight.

"She has and I will not provide proof because I am Rafael *fucking* Alessi and I do not need to. My word will be obeyed." He proclaims with a cold, calculated edge, tucking me in closer to his side.

The entire room falls into silence as his father considers what's transpired. I look at Sabrina whose eyes are as hard and determined as Enzo's, both glaring at my attacker. She looks ready to skin him alive alongside Enzo.

"If you have claimed Natasha, then the offense stands. What will you do about it?" Dante's quiet declaration resounds through the entire room as if he were speaking through a microphone. This must be what Enzo meant when he said Raf had to prove what happens when someone tests his boundaries.

"He has not provided proof—"

"He's my heir. No proof is needed." Dante stops Lorenzo's plea with a sharp tone and raised hand.

As Lorenzo accepts whatever comes next, he straightens to his full height, facing down Rafael. "If she is yours, you carry out the punishment, boy. Or do you let your rabid dog fight all your battles?" He nods toward Enzo as a challenging smirk graces his face.

He must think he's embarrassed Rafael, but from the grin and head shake that the man protecting me provides, I assume Lorenzo's plan to humiliate and challenge him was futile.

"Enzo is my blood, and I am his. Therefore, he can spill the blood owed to me. Besides, my rabid dog hasn't been let out in a while. He's practically drooling. What kind of brother would I be if I denied him his fun?"

"Pus–"

Lorenzo doesn't get to finish his insult because Enzo's forehead flies into his nose. A small cut drips blood down his forehead but he's unfazed, smiling and laughing sadistically. Lorenzo grabs his nose as it sprays blood all over the floor as he howls in pain. The psychotic twin, who I'm eternally grateful to now, pounds his fists into him one after the other until Lorenzo sputters on his back, trying but failing to fight any longer.

Enzo pulls him up and sets him on his knees as the bloody faced man almost falls forward but somehow keeps upright. "What did you say he did to you again, principessa?"

"Uh... lick me..." I reluctantly reply, afraid of what this means for Lorenzo. I mean, does he deserve everything coming to him? Yes. But still, the thought of it coming because of my words makes my stomach twist and I look up at Raf.

"Watch. This is our world, Natasha."

My eyes reluctantly trail back to the gory scene as Enzo takes out a knife and pulls Lorenzo's tongue out as far as it will stretch then before he can even realize what's happening, Enzo slices the knife, severing Lorenzo's tongue off. He falls back, screaming and holding his hands to his mouth.

Enzo looks to Raf now, "What else, brother?"

"From the bruises painting her throat, I would say he had attempted to rid her of breath."

"You know," Enzo taps the bloody knife to his forehead as if thinking, "I think you're right." He points the knife toward his brother now. "Such a smart man you are."

Grabbing Lorenzo's left hand, he lays it palm down on the hard floor, presses his knee onto his elbow and begins severing his hand at the wrist.

Lorenzo's screams echo off the walls as he thrashes on the floor.

"Slippery little shit, hold still will ya," Enzo grits out as he continues to hack away and finally Lorenzo's body goes still as he passes out from the pain. "That's better."

Enzo finishes the job and stands, his white button up splattered in crimson red and the knife dripping blood slowly onto his shoes. "Shit... was it the left hand, or right?" he questions, looking at me.

"The—the left," I sputter out even though I'm not sure. But I don't want to watch him take the other hand.

"Well then." Enzo spins in a circle, addressing the crowd. "Does anyone have any questions as to who Natasha Baldwin fucking belongs to?" he says calmly as he crosses his arms over his chest with a smug smirk.

Two men come in and drag Lorenzo away, taking him to who knows where while the crowd remains silent. "I'll take your silence as submission. Anyone fucking looks at her, I take your eyes. You touch her, I'll add your hand to my collection atop my shelf." He pauses, waving his knife around as he looks at some random man. His voice turning jovial. "They make great ring holders once rigormortis sets in. Just remember to mold it to you liking before that happens…" His tone darkens at the flip of a switch, and he dips his chin to look out at the crowd again. "You think about her, and I'll fucking lobotomize you. Are we clear?"

Silence again.

Then Enzo looks all the way to his right where Sabrina stands and holds up his knife, pointing the bloody steel right at her. "And that one is mine," he growls. "Anyone touches her, I will take you to the basement and personally see to your endless misery."

Sabrina's eyes go wide and her jaw drops.

"Bloody fucking pig made a mess and now I have to miss dessert, dammit," Enzo mumbles as he walks away and Sabrina walks around the large pool of blood in the center of the floor to reach me. Raf takes my chin in between his fingers and tilts my head. He stares into my eyes, promising me with those dark irises, "No one will harm you in this house."

A clap sounds and Raf releases me as all our eyes go to Dante. "Who wants strawberry cheesecake?"

"Are you okay?" Sabrina whispers as she rubs her hands up my arms.

"No," I say. "But I have to be."

I wanted everyone to know who I was,

They did,

They still did,

But not in a good way,

They say I'm a whore,

That I sleep around.

It hurts.

-MP

natasha

T he week with the twins went by quickly after the ballroom show and most of the men kept clear of Sabrina and me. After that horrendously gory dinner, she hasn't left my side. She's even ditched rooming with Enzo, though I doubt that would have lasted long anyway, and has camped out in my bed since.

She's been quiet since that night and one thing Sabrina Shae is not, is quiet. I'm not sure if that night shocked her like it did me or if there's more to the story. I brought it up once, asking if she was okay. She shrugged and said she was "peachy."

Enzo has haunted B and I, like a shadow, only leaving us at night when we were securely locked in our room.

As much as I wish Enzo were the only shadow following us, Dante Alessi lurked too. Lingering around us with his mischievous eyes that constantly roved over my body. Raf and Enzo did their best to divert him but there's only so much they can do to their own father in his own house.

At one point, we candidly talked about what he expects from me; I already knew most of it, but the message came through loud and clear. Deliver a male heir to both the Alessi and Baldwin families, one child to join two large and influential corporations. At the end of the year, if I am not pregnant with a boy, I'll be disposed of, and the twins will be given a new bride. If a son's provided, I'll marry Rafael to continue giving him more children and until our marriage, Enzo's free to have sex with me to increase the chances of a child.

Great.

Way to make a woman feel special.

Sabrina falls into the soft reclining seats of the Alessi private jet we have boarded. I decided not to tell her all the details of my situation, even though I consider her my one and only friend, entrusting someone with every detail of my life seems pointless and overwhelming. Even not being fully transparent with one another, I still know her better than she thinks. Which is why I have a feeling something is wrong.

"You okay?" I ask as I pull out my headphones and she does the same. Her eyes grow wide with concern, brows dipping down a little. She peers at me through her lashes and the slip of her mask disappears.

"Oh nothing. I'm great." She shrugs but I don't believe a word she says. "I'm fine!" she huffs.

My hand reaches out, lightly lying against her knee. "By chance does this have anything to do with Enzo and you?"

She shakes her head, but I see the blush stain her pale cheeks. "No."

"Well, know if that 'no' ever turns into a 'yes', I don't mind. He doesn't belong to me."

"Who doesn't belong to who because you are definitely mine. I almost killed a guy for you." Enzo leans his forearms against the back of my seat and looks down at me with the flirty grin I've come to find comforting.

"I'm sure you've murdered men for much less," I joke.

"That hurts, principessa. I'm wounded. I'm a good fucking person, you know that. I'm like a fucking teddy bear on the inside. And murder's defined as unlawful and premeditated, all my kills are lawful and almost none of them are premeditated. They just happen. A shame really."

Just when I expect a sarcastic comment from B, she turns her head toward the window. He looks at her with a stone-cold face and walks away. My wild best friend makes eye contact with me and a hardness washes over her face. "Okay, what is going on with you two?"

Before she can answer, a flight attendant comes by and drops off two glasses of champagne. We both reach forward and happily take the fizzy drink.

"Nothing," she says before taking a small sip.

"B, I recognize a queen of deception when I see one. Talk to me. Please. You've done so much for me, let me be there for you."

Her eyes assess me and she downs the entire glass. "I forgot who Enzo was. That's all."

"You forgot who he was?" I ask, a little confused because how on Earth could she forget.

"Yes." She doesn't elaborate and I respect her wish to keep her secrets.

***

"Natasha! Come down already, you're going to be late!" Mom's voice echoes through the house as I put the finishing touches on my makeup. I hate wearing so much, it suffocates my skin but if I'm not flawless then I'll surely hear about it, and I don't have that kind of energy today. Nightmares kept me awake through the night and the bags under my eyes are so big I could charge as much as an Hermes.

"Coming!" I shout out as I slip into my red bottom heels.

I rush down the stairs and stand before my parents, both of their eyes running over my outfit choice. Daddy huffs and walks away, but mom steps up and unbuttons one of the little white snaps on my white collared shirt. "You have to use what only a woman can, Natasha. Show a little cleavage and you'll have men wanting more."

"Everett and I have been dating since seventh grade, Mom. I'm set to marry him. I don't need other men looking at me."

But despite my protest, she continues to fluff and primp, making me her own Barbie doll.

"Everett will want what other men want. If you get complacent and comfortable with your appearance, he will leave you, and we can't have that."

I roll my eyes because I know Everett isn't like that and head for the door, but she stops me again.

"Oh, and Natasha? That girl, the town whore's daughter. What's her name?"

"Leora, I think."

"Leora. Remember our eyes are everywhere, Natasha and I've seen the way Everett looks at her. She'll take him from you and if she does, you know what will happen."

"Yes mom, you will find another husband for me, one that 'isn't as kind'. You know it's not a bad thing that Everett doesn't want to knock me up yet. We're seniors. Give us time."

"Keep her away, or your dad will take care of her. Nobody would miss her." She turns, her heels clicking on our marble floors as she heads down the hall.

Leora is a sweet girl, much too docile for this town, in my opinion. People here are cutthroat. If you're not the top dog, you're nothing. My parents and Everett's parents run this town and the people they have on their payroll are just as powerful, the town doctor, the judge, the head of the police. No one is safe in Aurora, Oregon. But it's home and luckily, if I do what's expected of me, I'm safe too.

If I can keep Everett's interest in me.

***

"Babe, wakey wakey." A small shake at my shoulder has me slowly coming back to reality. God, what an awful dream, scratch that... memory. I remember that day so clearly. The first day of senior year and the day I officially lost Everett.

He was my best friend for so long, and then my boyfriend, the one I gave all my firsts too, but he was never mine. And it took all the stages of grief for me to realize that I was never in love with him. I was in love with the safety he could provide. But that doesn't mean the loss wasn't real, or the pain wasn't justified. I'm happy for him and his family, but that doesn't lessen my own hurt. I've learned that two truths can occur at the same time. I can feel the pain of losing Everett, and I can be happy he's found his soulmate.

"We've landed," B gently soothes as I fully awaken.

"What?"

"Now who's sleeping through landings? Huh?" She smirks at me, and I sit up straighter. Did I sleep through not only the plane ride but the landing as well? What the hell was in that champagne?

"Rafael and his cray-cray twin already got off the plane. They're talking to that hottie with a badge."

"Hale?"

"Sure. Come on."

When we come down the steps, Hale stands tall in his cheap suit, shirt wrinkled and tie loosely hung around his neck. But still, he's as handsome as ever. His unkempt dirty blond hair and neatly trimmed beard give him a rugged yet sophisticated look.

"Agent Knight," I say as I step up to him, unsure if I should hug him, shake his hand, or maybe a crisp high five?

How do you greet the man you've been bargained to? Who also knows you wanted to off yourself a few months ago and then fucked you till you saw heaven right after? And then took you on the sweetest of dates only for you to freak out and reject him when he tried to make a move?

"Natasha." He nods his head.

A head nod.

Okay, I guess that's how.

I nod back.

"Can someone say awkward..." B whispers next to me but not quite low enough as Hale narrows his eyes on her.

"Sorry." She bows her head and tries to hold back a laugh.

"Agent, I emailed you the official terms of our agreement, I am still waiting for your signature. I will be in touch about when we will next require Natasha's presence. Sabrina, the NDA you signed prior to leaving still holds," Rafael scolds her as if she's about to blab to the whole world what happened in Seattle.

"Don't you worry your little black heart, Rafael. My lips are sealed." She pats his chest, and he immediately brushes the spot off as if she left a mark on him. Enzo leans in and whispers something in her ear and her face goes white. Her eyes darken, and she spins, leaving all of us wondering what the hell Enzo said to her.

I shoot daggers at him, ready to defend my friend but he winks at me and gets in the car.

"Ready?" Hale comes up next to me and takes my suitcase from my hand and I nod.

We walk in silence the fifty yards that separate the tarmac from the private lot where the cars wait and a small tingling begins in my stomach due to the proximity to him, not only that but the idea of being alone with him again.

I know what my heart wants. The giddy little thing wants to fall in love with this kind man, wants to let herself be swept off her feet and ride into the sunset. But my brain knows better. His angel wings could never survive the fires of my hell.

And don't even get me started on the whole self-sabotaging thing. I know I do it well. It's the next best thing I'm good at next to sex. But I'm being honest with myself. The girl Knight met on that rooftop, his Sparrow, she can fall in love, she can be saved, she can have the happily ever after. But she isn't real.

Natasha Baldwin is a vile bitch who pushes away anyone that could hurt her, could leave her, could pretend that she's the one. Natasha Baldwin protects the soft heart that Knight wants to fall in love with.

I know who I am.

I know what I've done and how I've treated people.

I'm the villain in many people's lives, and that has allowed me to be the hero in my own. Sometimes you must sacrifice others to save yourself, but I think I'm starting to realize that I'm tired of being the villain.

The sound of a car unlocking pulls me from my thoughts and I look up to find Hale putting my suitcase in the back of an old, beat-up truck. The blue and white striped pick-up looks straight out of a country music video and my steps halt. Did he put my Louis Vuitton in the bed of a fucking Ford?

"You have got to be kidding me." My jaw drops at the offense.

"Sorry we can't all be daddy's princess. Get in the truck."

I snap my jaw closed and pull the old silver handle as the door horrendously creaks. I slide into the cracked and worn leather bench seat. The smell of mud and animals fills the cab and my nose scrunches up.

"You drive this thing in the city?"

"Her name is Rosey. And no, I mostly walk but when I go home, I take Rosey. Those fancy electric cars wouldn't make it out where we're going."

"Excuse you? We're going to Boston." I gawk in horror as the man takes an actual tool, that I don't know the name of, and uses it to pinch some wire and start the truck. "I'm going to die today. Can this thing even get us where we're going? The twins will murder you if I die and I will haunt you if it's in a Ford truck that smells like animal shit."

"Please, Natasha. Rosey here has been faithfully getting my family and I from point A to point B since 1990. Although, your judgmental tone may offend her. She can be temperamental like that."

"And where exactly is point B?"

"My home. An hour outside Boston. But first I need to stop and pick up something at my apartment."

"And why, may I ask, are we not going back to Boston? I thought you were here to give me a ride?" The truck jolts forward and I'm a little surprised it, in fact, *can* move.

"The Alessis warned me that you are a sought-after individual. They asked me to keep you out of the city until they have things settled with their father. Apparently, your Seattle trip caused quite a stir."

"Fucking Enzo," I murmur, gazing out the chipped windshield at the city in the not so far distance.

"Hopefully it won't be too long."

"Hopefully."

I can't believe this. I found a city I love and now I'm being pulled from it again. I'm like a rag doll being torn in half by two children who can't share.

Thirty minutes later, we pull into the city and I thank some higher being because I have a headache from all the noise the old Ford made, and I need a break. It only takes a few minutes to reach Hale's apartment. The building doesn't have a door man which is a little odd but it's clean inside.

The apartment itself resembles the man. A little disheveled but still put together somehow. The furniture isn't brand new and shiny, but it's good quality and although I expected a bachelor pad, but the warm, intimate decor surprises me, with art prints hung on the walls, some books lining shelves and even a plant.

"Just stay here, I'll be right back."

"Sure thing, boss," I snide and he rolls his eyes.

I do a little snooping and find that he has many poetry books and even some old records and an antique Victrola. I run my fingers along the spines of the books, then down the records and finally over the record currently on the wheel.

I scoff, "Eminem, of course." My memories travel back to when he quoted the famous rapper while he was bathing me, and I smile. I want that again…

No. Natasha. Keep your distance, keep your heart.

He's taking much longer than I thought and I need to pee after that bumpy ride, so I head down the hall in search of a bathroom but overhear him talking to someone. I shouldn't snoop. I shouldn't do a lot of things, and I did intend to turn around but then his whispered voice catches my attention.

"I'm bringing a friend home, Ma. Just wanted to give you a heads up. She needs a place to lay low."

A few moments of distant mumbles fill the space before Hale begins talking again. "No, we've gone on a few dates but..." A small groan comes from him. "Fine, nosey woman, we had sex once. I fucked up, I made a mistake, so don't get your hopes up."

My heart sinks. That night saved me, yet he saw it as a mistake.

"No, Ma. She's... she's broken like Ivy was. I can't do that again."

Who's Ivy? Must be an ex-girlfriend, maybe even ex-wife.

Well, I guess Hale has a type, the *broken* type. Hit the nail on the head there didn't you, Agent.

See heart, I told you so.

natasha

The hour drive goes agonizingly slow as the death trap—I mean Rosey– tops out at 55 miles per hour. And to make things even worse, a silence fills the cab thick enough to cut with a knife. It's torture. How could I feel utterly tethered to this man months ago, and now I feel completely isolated with the same one?

Probably because he sees you for what you truly are, a broken, pathetic girl who will amount to nothing but being some man's prize mare.

"Natasha, I... My parents they... Fuck." His brows pull in, a small frown on his face. Fields of farmland surround us as he pulls over on the side of the narrow two-lane road. He turns slightly toward me so he can look at me. I can see his mind worrying through his blue eyes. I can see the love he has for his parents. "My parents are going to adore you. But I don't want them to attach themselves to you."

Like you did?

I withdraw slightly and clench my back teeth, but don't say anything. What would I even say to that?

"I'm sorry, I know that sounds strange, but they've been through so much and when they give their love, they completely empty themselves into that person. I just... I don't know what I'm asking exactly, I don't want them to get hurt if you..." His head falls for a moment, then picks back up, looks out the front windshield again as he puts the truck back in drive.

"Just say it, Hale. I'm not a glass doll. I can handle what you actually want to say," I snark at him, unable to hold back my attitude.

He lets out a large sigh and digs his thumb and finger into his eyes. "Fine. Don't make them fall for you and then leave them so suddenly. It will break them."

"I won't get attached, Hale. I can promise you that."

"It's not you I'm worried about," he whispers as he checks his side mirror and pulls back onto the worn-down paved road. Not a mile further, he turns onto a dirt road, and we drive under a wooden arch with the words "Revival Ranch" carved into the dark wood. I look ahead but see nothing but grassy fields surrounded by white fencing for what looks like miles. Not a house or building in sight.

Large metal containers of hay are in the center of each divided field, and I see cows and horses, donkeys and even some hoofed animals I don't recognize.

Great. He's brought me to a farm. This only confirms I will not be getting attached. In fact, the sooner I can get back to the city, the better.

The truck bounces, forcing me to throw my hands out to catch myself on the dash. "Jesus. Could you slow down a little, I'd like to arrive without brain damage."

The asshole chuckles, but I do notice the truck slow slightly. After ten minutes down this pothole-filled dirt road, the trees part to reveal a two-story white farmhouse with a wrap-around porch, deep brown shutters and a red door. Black lanterns line the porch along with four rocking chairs, two on each side of the front door. Behind it, a large red barn with pastures extending beyond. Next to that a brick building that looks to be from the 1800's and a closed porch off the side of it.

"Wow." I let out on an exhale, not meaning to comment on it at all, but the sight took my breath away.

"Home, sweet, home."

The truck pulls to a stop on the side of the house, next to another pickup truck, although this one a little newer. Hale gets out, slamming his door shut and I open my own and step out onto the muddy ground.

The screen door squeaks open and a short, heavier set woman with blonde hair peppered with silver comes out and next to her a large, German Shepherd. A white, pin-stripe apron covers her jeans and light purple button up. Her hair thrown atop her head, held in place with a silver clip. She approaches Hale as he pulls my suitcase out of the bed and the wrinkles surrounding her eyes and mouth only deepen when she smiles at him.

"Hale, oh honey. I'm glad you made it safe. Jennings's tractor broke down on Lackey Road, I'm surprised you were able to get through."

Hale slings his large arm around the woman's shoulders and pulls her in for a hug. "He must have gotten it up and running, Ma. We didn't pass his tractor."

Hale kneels, scratching behind the dog's ears, receiving appreciative licks on the face in return. "Hey Max, you been taking care of Ma for me?"

The dog huffs and spins before sitting right at the woman's feet.

"Good to hear. He's supposed to come help us with a few things around the ranch next week and he needs that tractor."

Hale stands and places a kiss on her forehead. "I'll call him, make sure he's got it running, okay?"

My arms wrap around my chest, as I stand there and take in the warm welcome. Their love is heartbreakingly obvious. I can see it in their smallest movements, the way she clings to her son to the way he looks at her with care tells me that they have an unconditional love.

"Ma, this is Natasha." He lifts his hand and motions to me.

Her hand comes up to cover her mouth as her eyes widen a moment and then soften, a small smile pulling up her lips. "Oh my, you are a mighty beautiful thing, aren't you?"

"Thank—"

Before I can finish, her arms wrap around me and her warm embrace makes my heart skip a beat. She pulls back before I can return her hug, her warm hands now holding my cheeks. "Oh, sorry dear, I'm a hugger. Hope I didn't overstep."

Her dark brown eyes meet mine and there a softness and understanding in them warms my untrusting heart.

"No, you're fine. I just—I haven't been hugged like that in... well, ever I guess."

Her brows scrunch in and her head tilts, as if she can read my entire story from my eyes alone. She nods but doesn't show me pity. "You mean to tell me; you've been in the company of my son and haven't been truly hugged? Shame on him." She leans in so only her and I can hear, "Remind me to withhold his dessert tonight. You can have his." She winks and pulls away, walking toward the house again.

"Well come now, dinner's ready. Gotta get it while it's hot." She disappears through the screen door, and I look at Hale who holds my suitcase in one hand, keeping it from touching the muddy ground.

"Come on, Natasha." He nods his head toward the door as Max nudges my hand with his cold wet nose. "Ma may live in the north, but she's from the south. I'm sure she has an entire feast prepared for us."

The wooden steps wobble a little as I follow, and when I step through the screen door, I'm hit with a warm, sweet scent that fills the space. The home opens into a large living room with a fireplace straight to the back, directly across from the front door. It's not lit currently but I can only imagine how inviting it must feel when it is. To the left a large kitchen with white cabinetry and butcher-block countertops. Six barstools surround a large island, and a large rustic rectangular table sits off to the right of the kitchen.

The living room has a large gray L-shaped sofa with quilted pillows and throws. An array of mismatched rugs adorns the old hardwood floors and the entire space feels incredibly inviting.

I move further into the farmhouse as an older man comes down the stairs. "Is that Hale already?"

"Yes, hun, they didn't get delayed like I thought they would," Hale's mom, who I still haven't gotten the name of yet, replies.

"Well, then. That's good, Jennings must'a gotten that ol' tractor up and going again. I told that bastard he needs to invest in a new one, but the stubborn man won't listen to me," the older man grumbles. He wears a dark pair of jeans with stains on the thigh area and a flannel button up.

"Your brother is as stubborn as you, honey."

Mr. Knight lets out a huff as he rounds the kitchen island and places a kiss on his wife's forehead and then embraces Hale in a hug. "Good to see you, son. Did you bring that girl you told Ma about?"

Hale nods his head in my direction, my feet still rooted next to the front door. My eyes lock with the older man's and see where Hale gets his blue eyes, Mr. Knight's are as Neptune blue as his son's.

"Well, don't just stand there, come on in, sweetie. Don't be shy."

I step toward the family, huddled in the kitchen and Hale steps back to let me take his spot.

"I'm sorry. I didn't get your names," I say politely.

"Oh, silly me, I'm sorry, child. I'm Grace." She rests her hand on my arm and gives me a warm smile before looking at her husband. "And this is James."

"It's nice to meet you." I nod.

"Well, let's eat before it gets cold. I hope you like fried chicken, I think I made enough to feed a whole defensive line."

My heart begins to pound at the thought of the word fried... *all that fat.*

Swallowing down the dry lump in my throat, I head toward the table along with everyone else. I assess the food quickly, looking for anything not fried or coated in butter, and begin to breathe harder when I see there isn't anything that wouldn't add inches to my waistline.

Fried chicken, mashed potatoes, collard greens in a butter sauce, rolls, corn on the cob, also slathered in butter.

"I—you know. I'm pretty tired. I think I'd like to retire for the night. If you don't mind."

"Natasha." Hale looks at me with his brows furrowed, and I can't tell if it's concern or irritation in his eyes. "You haven't eaten all day."

"I had a big breakfast," I lie.

"Rafael said you refused breakfast also."

Grace's head bounces back and forth between us and then her eyes soften as they land on me again. "Hale, let her be. She's had a long day." The kind, southern woman stands and straightens her apron. "How bout I show you to your room and I'll bring something up later?"

"Thank you," I say as I turn for my suitcase. James and his son murmur behind us but I can't focus enough to make out what they're saying. My stomach revolts at the thought of all that food on the table.

I follow Hale's mother up the stairs with my suitcase but then stop and turn when the bag tugs free from my hand. Hale stands there with his hand clasped around the handle of my bag. He lean's close to my ear and his breath tickles my hair as he whispers, "Ma would whoop my ass if she saw I wasn't being the gentleman she raised…"

I don't reply as I let him take it and we all ascend the stairs. Grace opens a door at the end of the hall, and I step into the simple room. A white and pink quilt covers the bed, a white dresser and bed frame with two nightstands bracketing it.

A warm light illuminates the room as Grace clicks on one of the lamps and turns to face me. Hale stands in the doorway, unsure what to do until his mother clears her throat. "Hale, go keep your father company downstairs. I'll be right there."

He nods and heads out.

She steps up to me, looking at me like she knows all my secrets. Hell, maybe she does. I've been thrown about so much lately, I've lost track of which mask I'm wearing.

"What would you like me to make for you, dear?"

"No please, I'll be fine," I protest as I step around her.

"You must eat, child." Her warm, soft hand lays on my forearm. She seems incredibly genuine, but a quiet dread creeps into my mind. Like fog covering a beautiful lake, I can't help but wonder what's hiding below the surface.

"I'll run to the store in the morning. Please, don't worry about me."

"The closest market is forty-five minutes away. I keep a stocked pantry. Please, what is it that you would like?"

"Can I look in the morning?" I pull back from her and see the hurt in her eyes at my refusal. I can tell, after only knowing her a few moments that she's a woman who only lives to care for others but like Hale warned, I won't get close to her. I won't let her get close to me.

"How about I bring you up some yogurt and fruit after dinner? Hmm?"

My stomach growls at the idea and I practically drool. "Yes. That sounds nice. Thank you." I nod and she returns the gesture.

When the door closes, I release a sigh of relief and fall onto the bed. I only allow myself to rest for a few moments before I begin to look around. The room's small but welcoming, its white walls have a pink plaid wallpaper on the upper half, separated by molding in the middle. There's a large painting of a beautiful garden with lavender climbing up the gray brick walls of what looks like an old building. It's the only thing on the wall, making it the focus of the entire room.

I open the drawers of a dark wood dresser to find soft linen shirts and pants, knitted sweaters and some warm knit socks. Some jean jackets and cotton dresses hang in the closet with an assortment of women's cowboy boots, some nicer than others. I'm not sure who owns these clothes, but I hope they won't mind me invading their space.

I unpack my suitcase and open one of my favorite poetry books to begin reciting the poems. Most I can do from memory at this point but seeing the words printed on the page is a therapy that can never be matched.

I'm not sure how much time passes before a knock raps against the door.

"Come in," I call, and the door slowly creaks open.

Grace comes in with a plate of fruit and a pinkish colored yogurt. "I hope strawberry is okay."

"Yes, my favorite actually." I sit up in bed and take the plate from her. She wipes her hands down her apron and then sits next to me on the bed, the mattress dips with her weight.

"Is the room to your liking?" She looks around it with sadness in her eyes.

"Yes. Is it okay if I wear the clothes? They seem to be more appropriate than what I brought. I didn't know I was coming to an actual ranch," I laugh a little and she dips her head with a soft laugh as well.

"Yes, dear. Wear whatever you like. You two look to be about the same size. And it's not like she will be using them any longer I suppose."

"Who?"

"Our daughter, Hale's sister." She pats her hands on her lap and then stands. "Well, the bathroom is through that door there, it's a jack and jill that connects to Hale's room. Our room is downstairs, if you need anything at all, please don't hesitate to ask."

"Thank you, Grace."

She waves her hand in dismissal. "Please, call me Ma. No one calls me Grace, not even the neighbors. I'm Ma to everyone 'round here."

I don't know if I'll be able to do that, but I can at least smile. As I do, she leans forward and places a kiss on my forehead and my eyes grow wide. "Sweet dreams, Natasha."

hale

The morning sun streams through my window, and I let out a groan at the devastating fact I have to get up and begin this day. I have three days before I must return to work, three days to get the princess of Boston settled into ranch life. She didn't shy away from the dogs at the Humane Society but she's always full of surprises. I've also gotten a bit of a cold shoulder from her since I picked her up from the airport. Not sure what that's about.

I'm a fucking idiot for thinking her and I could simply fall in love and ride off into the sunset. Just like my parents, I'm a person who loves easily, but time has taught me to also love cautiously. She can't drag me around like a safety blanket and then when it comes time to get close throw me in the trash.

I'll still protect her, keep her safe. But I need to know if I'm putting my heart on the line along with my body.

I roll to my side, then push up and lay my feet on the warm hardwood. Dad must have the wood burning stove going this morning to heat the floors. It's only then that I notice my feet were not warmed by the weight that heats my feet through the night... where is my fucking dog?

"Max?" I call, but no answer.

The Wranglers I put on are much more comfortable than my dress slacks and I smile a little at being home. It's always chilly here in the morning and I'll have to go feed with dad before breakfast so I also throw on my old Ford hoodie that has half the front pocket torn off from when a certain sassy horse got a hold of it.

Growing up on this ranch, I know the routine like the back of my hand. Caring for the animals, taking care of the house, trying, and clearly failing to look out for my wild sister was my entire life once. A life lived long ago but never forgotten. I step out of my door at the same time Natasha does... along with my fucking dog.

Sucker.

But as soon as I spot what she's wearing, anger burns through my body and my teeth practically crack from how hard I clench my jaw. "Why are you wearing those clothes?"

My sister's clothes. They haven't been worn since she left. They still smelled like her last time I was here and now that soft honeysuckle scent will be replaced with Natasha's intoxicating lavender aroma.

"I–Your mom, she told me it was okay. I didn't—"

I turn and walk away from her, running a hand down the nape of my neck, trying to calm myself before I say something I'll regret.

Her feet softly tap against the hardwood as she comes up behind me and wraps her hand around my bicep, halting my steps at the top of the stairs. "Hale. What's wrong? They're just clothes."

"They're not—" A groan escapes me at my inability to talk about her still. My throat tightens and I close my eyes, the familiar burn of tears threatening to fall. "It doesn't matter. Leave 'em on, take 'em off. Doesn't matter to me."

"It clearly does. Hale—"

I pull my arm from her hand and jog downstairs to find Ma already cooking, homemade biscuits and bacon with eggs. Her usual morning breakfast. Max goes straight out the back doggie door for his own morning ritual. He'll make his rounds around the pastures before coming in for his own breakfast and our leftovers.

"Good morning you two, did y'all sleep well?"

"Yes, thank you," Natasha replies as she sits on one of the stools at the counter, accepting the cup of coffee Ma hands her.

"Do you like cream? Sugar?"

"Just black, thank you." She sips from the ceramic mug, and I try not to watch the roll of her throat as it swallows. What a pretty sight on such an infuriating woman.

"Hale?"

"Huh? Yeah. Cream."

The old woman shoves at my shoulder. "Honey, I know how you drink your coffee. I asked if you were feeding this morning?"

"Oh uh. Yeah. Dad up yet?"

"He's with the birds." She hands me my coffee in a to-go cup, and I take a sip of the warm coffee.

"He'll take the north side; you take the south. Also, we moved Gambit to the east pasture. He's still on the same supplements."

"Why's Gambit in the east pasture?" My heart drops, anywhere but the east pasture.

"It's his time, honey."

Not the fucking east pasture. Damn, I guess I didn't realize how many years it's been. I guess the time for him to retire to our best pasture, to live out his days spoiled as hell has finally come.

"He'll be happy to see you," Ma says before reaching up on her toes and placing a kiss on my cheek.

Gambit was the first horse I rehabbed by myself. I looked over his medical notes, came up with his rehab plan and executed all his care. He came to us off the racetrack, a wild card who ended up breaking his hind leg. They wanted to put him down, but we brought him in. He was only two years old at the time, I was twelve and we bonded immediately. He was never re-homed like many of our animals, and I think my parents never did that because they knew what he meant to me.

"I'm going to get going," I say as I head toward the door. "Ma, Natasha will need a to-go cup as well."

Nat's eyes widen as she chokes on her coffee, catching the little spittle on the back of her sleeve. I snarl my lip as she pulls her hand away and I see the black coffee stain on the light pink knit.

"You stay here; you work here. Those are the rules. I'm going to teach you to feed the North lot today, tomorrow we'll take the South and then you'll be able to pull your weight."

She slides off the stool, coming up to the front door where I'm pulling my boots on. "You want me to... work the farm? Do I look like a ranch hand to you?"

"Right now, you look like a spoiled, entitled princess."

"Why are you being a jerk to me?" she says, slipping on the boots I tossed in front of her. Also my sister's boots that Ma keeps by the front door as if she's ever going to return. She's wearing her sweater and pajamas, might as well complete the outfit.

"Let's go," I say as I slam open the screen door. Honestly, I don't know why I'm being a dick. I know I am, but she's so fucking aggravating right now. I saw her soul that night on the rooftop and on our first date. She's lyrical and captivating and she has a depth to her no one would expect. She can look into your soul and calm your demons. She felt like home that night, but right now? Now she feels like a distant memory, and I hate it. I hate that she's so far, putting up her walls faster than I can break them down.

Or maybe it's me putting up walls? I don't even know anymore. All I know is I want the woman who was in my bed at the hotel, who laughed as a Great Dane slobbered all over her face, as she danced and taught those little humans.

She speed-walks through the mud as I lead her to the red barn out back. Once inside, I load up the small trailer attached to the 4x4 with bales of alfalfa. "These are a bit heavy, but I think you're strong enough. You'll load the trailer with six bales, one for each pasture on the North lot. Three to the east, three to the west."

She takes in what I'm doing, like she's studying for a test. I expected a protest but receive none. I toss some gloves at her, and they hit her chest, then she catches them before they fall. "Why don't you try and load this last one."

She comes up to it and I show her where to grab the two strings and the best way to lift it. She struggles at first but then once she gets her legs under her, she lifts it well enough to get it into the trailer.

"I'm impressed."

"I'm stronger than I look," she pants, already out of breath from one bale and I let out a small laugh as I shake my head at her.

"Next is the grain and supplements for the horses. Easiest way to do it is to put the six buckets in the back of the 4x4, here." I show her how to line up the buckets. "Then fill."

I walk her over to the grain bins and give her a scoop. "It's pretty easy. They are labeled A, B, and F. A is for our horses who are maintaining weight, B for horses who need to gain weight, and F for our older horses who need additional supplements. Fill two buckets with each type of grain."

She begins filling the buckets, scoop after scoop and I step back to assess her work. She's already building up a sweat and I can't help but admire her determination and willingness to learn and help out. *Is it that you're admiring or the way her skin looks when she's hot and sweaty?*

Shaking the images that have now infected my mind, images of her naked on my bed, sweat beading down between her breasts and over her navel... "What now?"

Her sharp tone breaks the moment, and I push off the wooden beam I leaned against, walking toward her.

"You're doing so good." As I say the words, I can't help but imagine praising her in another way and clearly, she does too as a pink tint travels up her cheeks.

I step away before I do something reckless like take that blonde braid, wrap it around my fist and make her scream for the heavens in my own parents' fucking barn.

Focus, Knight.

"Next, the specialty horses. These guys need a little extra help. Their buckets are labeled with their name, here." I open the cabinet next to the grain bins and show her the seven horses we have that are on extra supplements. "There's a list here with who gets what and again, everything is labeled with letters. So here is A," I grab the glucosamine supplement and show her the A scribbled on the top with permanent marker. "And then you can see from the chart that Gambit, Maverick, and Mamma get this supplement so add it to their grain after you fill it. These guys all get F grain."

I help her with the supplements because I'm not that big of a dick and we quickly get it done, stacking those seven buckets on top of the other six and then the seventh in between her feet as she climbs into the 4x4.

"Now we feed."

I pull out of the barn and begin driving the half mile that separates the barn from the pastures. The cool wind blows in, and from the corner of my eye, I catch Natasha wrap the sweater around her more. She didn't dress for this, and I should have given her a coat, but my frustration at her wearing those clothes kept me from thinking clearly.

When I pull up to the pasture, we hop out and I pull off my hoodie and hand it to her. "Here."

"I'm fine." She pushes it back.

"I can tell you're cold, would you please take the sweatshirt?"

"I said I'm fine." She crosses her arms and cocks her hip, spitting fire at me with not just words but eyes as well.

"Woman, you're as stubborn as an ass. Take the damn sweatshirt before I come over there and put it on you myself." I continue to hold the hoodie in front of me as her eyes give in and she comes toward me. Taking it and hooking it over her head.

When she has it settled onto her body, she looks around, taking in the beautiful sunrise and pastures of the ranch. "These are the ones we passed on the way in?"

"Yeah. These are mostly for our hoofed animals. Horses are in A, B, and F. A and B are here." I point to the first two pastures on the west side. "And then F is this one here. It's the closest and has the best amenities for our older horses." I unlock the pasture gate, then step back into the 4x4 and drive it through.

"You can leave the gate open? They won't run out?"

"Nah, they know there's no place better." I give her a small grin. All the anger I felt toward her earlier melting away at seeing her natural curiosity for my favorite place on this Earth.

I show her how to kick out the bale and cut the ties. "Then I like to shake out the alfalfa a bit to make it easier for them." I start taking leaf by leaf and shaking it out and she does the same.

"Now you repeat for all six pastures. You'll empty the A and B grain into the galvanized containers. The F grain is specific to each horse so we will empty those into their stalls. There are gates connecting each field, so you don't have to go back to the main road until you have to hop over to the other three.

"So, all get the hay and A, B get grain?" she confirms and I nod.

"That seems easy enough."

"Yeah, the North side is easy. Just wait till we have to feed the south lot." I laugh and her face falls.

"Wait, what kind of animals are on the south lot?" she hurries out, nerves lacing her voice.

"You'll see."

We continue through to the E pasture, then D, then down the other side. When we exit through the A gate, she wipes the sweat from her brow and lets out a huff. "Where are all the animals? I thought they would be excited for food."

"They're up in the barns, we're headed there next."

I drive up to the East stables first. The three large, enclosed stables house the animals at night, and we lock the gates, so they aren't exposed to predators.

I walk up to Gambit first who already has his head sticking out of the stall door. The old red thoroughbred knickers as I walk up and I lay my forehead to his muzzle, inhaling the familiar scent of him. "Hey old man. Heard you got moved to the retired pasture."

He knickers again as his muzzle begins nibbling at my hair. I push him away with a laugh. "Alright don't be gettin' handsy, we have a lady with us."

Stepping aside I let him see Natasha and he whinnies. *Yeah, she's hot. I know. Horny old horse.*

"You can pet him," I encourage when I read the hesitancy all over her body. "Here," I say as I come up behind her. "Like this."

I take her small hand in mine, laying my palm against the back of her hand and straighten out her fingers. Then I lay our hands against his jaw and stroke downward.

"He's so soft," she whispers. Gambit uses his muzzle to play with the sleeve of her hoodie and she pulls her hand away quickly, spooking him a bit as he throws his head back.

I laugh and she slaps my chest. "It's not funny! He tried to bite me!"

"He wasn't trying to bite. That's his way of giving kisses."

She looks back at my favorite horse and reaches out again. "Oh. I'm sorry, I didn't mean to scare you. You scared me." She talks to him with the gentleness of a mother, and it makes my fucking chest hurt.

I walk her through the steps of feeding the seven older horses their grain and then show her how to unlatch the gates that lead to the pastures and all the animals scurry out, racing for their grain and fresh alfalfa.

She leans against the white fencing, gazing upon them as they eat the food we set out. "Do you guys breed them for the racetrack?"

"The horses? Fuck no. We save them from the track. Revival Ranch is a place for them to come and heal when the world discarded them as broken."

"So, all these animals are broken?"

"They were," I answer, taking in her perfect profile. Her nose has a slight upturn at the end, her full lips naturally part slightly in the center and there's a small dimple right where her lips meet at the corner. She doesn't even know how stunning she is, even covered in alfalfa and dirt, her braid half undone now. She's perfect.

As she looks out to the animals, her delicate face hardens, and she turns her burning gaze to meet my own. "Broken like me, right?"

My brows scrunch as I look at her. What the hell is she talking about?

"Is that why you brought me here, Hale. To fix me?"

She stomps back toward the 4x4, and I grab her by the elbow, turning her toward me. "I didn't want to bring you here, remember? It's the only place I could trust would keep you safe."

"So, I'm not worth fixing, is that it then?" She tries to pull her arm from my grip, but I hold on tighter.

"No, that's not... you're putting words in my mouth."

"Let me go, Hale. I don't want to be saved. Not by you, not by anyone." I release her arm because I don't want to hurt her and she turns from me, stomping down the road.

"You don't even know what you want!" I shout at her, and she spins around with a wildness in her eyes and I don't know if it makes me want to fight *with* her or *for* her more. No one has eyes with such vicious poison unless they have a reason to protect themselves.

"Screw you," she grits out and her response makes my decision easy. I want to fight with her. Every broken soul needs to learn that healing isn't about losing your fight but learning what to fight for.

She spins again but I reach out and grab her by the nape of her neck as I turn her to face me, clutching her to my chest as she pants like a raging bull. "Been there, done that. But I'm up for round two if you think it will help curb your attitude."

"Leave me," she whispers, like that night. I see the same fear, the same hurt, the same determination to release her pain.

"I can't do that."

"Then let me help you," she says before taking her knee and shoving it upward straight into my dick and I curl forward with a groan.

Max chooses this time to make an appearance as he trots right past me and settles in next to her side. He keeps pace with her as they both leave me behind.

The damn woman stole my fucking heart, my sanity and now my fucking dog.

natasha

My muscles ache as I silently slip downstairs to grab a snack. I'll never admit it to Hale, but lifting those bales of itchy, green straw and lifting the buckets of grain has my whole body sore and I don't even have my Epsom salts to soak in.

The best I can do is find a protein snack to help aid in recovery. After we fed this morning, I went straight to the shower and then hid like a hermit crab for the rest of the day. Mrs. Knight came up and brought me a turkey sandwich, some fruit and a little brownie but I only ate the turkey from the sandwich and the fruit. I put the rest under the bed so I could throw it away later.

The last wooden stair creaks and my body freezes. I wait, and wait, but I don't hear anyone coming so I take the last step and round the banister into the kitchen.

My hand flies to my chest and I gasp as Hale's mother spooks me. Perched on a stool at the kitchen island, the only light a soft glow of a candle in the windowsill.

"Natasha. I thought that might be you dear."

"I'm sorry, I didn't think anyone would be up at this hour," I say, coming further into the kitchen with the plate behind my back. I try to hide it but I see her eyes look down at it.

"I don't sleep well these days." She reaches her hand out. "Let me take that for you."

"It's okay. I can do it." I quickly dump the contents into the trash and then put the plate in the sink. But I know she saw all the leftover food.

"I... I just." God, what do I say? I've never had to explain this to anyone else. My mother encouraged it, my father never cared either way how much I did or didn't eat, and I hid it from everyone else easily. I always had an excuse for why I never ate much, blaming it on cheer or dance. But the knowing look in this kind woman's eyes tells me that I need to say something. Anything. "I—"

"Come sit, sweetie." She pats the stool next to her and as I sit, she gets up and gets a teacup from the antique hutch. The warm, brown tea fills the cup, and she sets it down in front of me, the ceramic making a small clink against the countertop.

"Why don't you eat?" she asks as she sits next to me again.

A bit intrusive...

"I do." My eyes drop to the cup of tea, as if it could save me from this encounter.

"I may be old, but I'm not blind." The stern look she pins me with has me feeling like a kid caught in a candy shop. "Now, I don't expect you to spill your entire life story in my lap, but I do expect the truth. If you aren't ready to give that to me, don't give me lies. Just know, when you're ready, I'm here to listen. Understand?"

"Yes ma'am." I nod as a small smile slips from my lips, one that confuses even me.

We hold each other's gaze for a minute, something trusting and sure crossing between us in that moment and I get the odd feeling that one day, I'll be able to open up to this strange woman. Something entirely pure and motherly emanates from her, it almost makes me want to spill everything onto her right now. To let her take it all away.

My eyes catch on a picture on the counter behind her and I get up to get a closer look. Hale stands in a Navy uniform, smiling as he holds onto his mother.

"Hmm, handsome, isn't he? That was taken the day he became a SEAL."

"Hale was a Navy SEAL?" I say, shocked as I turn to face her.

Immeasurable pride shimmers in her aged eyes. He mentioned being in the military, but I never would have thought he was a Navy SEAL. That level of dedication and training must have been incredibly challenging.

"Oh yes. He had always wanted to be one. He saw this movie in high school about the Navy SEALs and from that moment on, that was his dream. I always prayed he would choose something different. But alas, that wasn't God's plan for him. Not that being an FBI agent is much better; he's still always putting himself in harm's way for others. Always the hero, that one." She shakes her head before sipping from her cup.

"Why did he leave then?" Setting the photo down, I come sit next to her again.

"Hmm. I suppose it was because of his sister."

"His sister?"

She closes her eyes for a moment then continues. "Yes, she went missing when she was sixteen. Her and Hale were at a concert in the city when he went to the bathroom, he came back, and she was gone. Hale was beside himself. Always blaming himself for her disappearance."

"That's awful. I'm so sorry." Laying my hand over hers, her glassy eyes meet mine.

"She was found six months later. She had been trafficked and the only reason she was found was because she was taken to an ER, all the way in Seattle, after a pretty bad car accident. She was able to get alone with a nurse and told them that she was being trafficked."

What would I have done in her situation? In a years' time I could be exactly where she was. "That was incredibly brave of her."

"It was, but not surprising," Grace scoffs as if recalling a funny memory. "She was always the brave one. Her brother, despite how brave he became was the kid afraid of his own shadow."

"Now that is surprising. I think Hale is incredibly brave. Becoming a Navy SEAL, joining the FBI." ... Stepping onto the ledge of a rooftop with a stranger.

Grace's smile softens her face as she speaks of her son. "I knew he was always brave. I think it takes more courage to look after the wild souls, to bear that responsibility."

The tea warms my throat, filling my chest with the chamomile taste. "What happened to her? After she told the nurse?"

"She was brought home, but she never came home, not truly." Grace wipes a tear from her cheek with the sleeve of her robe. "I'm sorry. I–" She tries to continue but I stop her.

"No. Please don't apologize. I can't imagine how hard that must have been for you all as a family. It seems you love her tremendously. She's lucky to have a mom like you."

"I'll love her...both of them, till the day I die, and even after death. They are my children. I am their mother."

The familiar burn behind my eyes begins at the idea of being a mother. The idea of *never* being a mother. I jerk back when a thumb brushes my cheek. "Don't cry, child," she soothes which only brings more tears.

"Do you have children? Hale didn't say anything about any but..."

I'm not sure what compels me to share, but I can't stop the words when they come. "I lost my baby. Aurora, I...had a miscarriage in April."

"I knew you were a mother. There's something about you."

"I'm not a mother." My voice has an unintentional bite of anger. Anger that I wish I could control. Didn't she hear me? Didn't she hear that I lost my baby? I wipe my face with the backs of my hands and straighten my spine. *Pull yourself together, Natasha.*

"Did you carry that baby girl in your womb? Did you begin to knit her together with your flesh and blood? Did a piece of your soul shatter when you lost her? If so, then you are a mother. Whether you lose her at four weeks or 22 years old, you are her mother."

My baby isn't with me. Not like hers are. Every time I see a woman holding a baby or with a swollen, pregnant belly, a painful, debilitating jealousy thrums through my body. It rains over me, drowning me in a shower of everything I should but don't have. And now, I'm being forced to try and carry again. What if I lose another? What will my father do? What will Dante do?

What will I do?

Her gentle voice brings me back to her dimly lit kitchen. "You can't let what you went through destroy your life, Natasha. I know you're hurting. I know your pain is heavy. I know that each day feels like you're pulling concrete blocks through sand and some days, you might think, 'what's the point? Better to let the concrete take me to the bottom of the ocean than struggle through the sand.' But you are so young, child. You have so much left ahead of you."

Why is she saying this? Did Hale tell her about the rooftop? Is this pity? Is this her trying to fix me? Make me less broken? I don't need her. I've lived this long on my own and I'm fine. I don't need anyone, because no one needs me.

Standing, I set my cup on the counter, straighten my cardigan and tilt my chin up. I thought I could give her a piece of myself but all she wants to do, like Hale, is put my pieces back together. But if I'm all put back together, that means I'll have to face all the terrible things I've done with the excuse of being broken. And I'm not strong enough for that.

I'm a coward, so I do what I do best, and I let her see the worst part of myself.

"You don't know me. You don't know my pain. Don't think you can even begin to know what I've experienced," I snark as I let my lip curl. "I don't need anything from you or anyone else and I sure as hell don't need you trying to be my mother. Go be a mother to your two children who clearly have some issues of their own they need to deal with."

With that I walk away and not for the first time in my life, a bitter taste fills my mouth, and a darkness inks my heart at the vicious words I wield to protect myself.

Right as my foot hits the bottom step, her voice calls to me. "Natasha."

I turn to see her still sitting at the stool. "Your words don't hurt me. They won't push me away. And they won't push my son away either. We are in the business of healing the hurt done by others. You are no different. So, if you're going to fight this, be ready, because we fight back, and guess what, honey. We always win." With that she stands and heads down the hall and I am left speechless.

I've never had anyone fight for me and I... I don't know if I'm ready for it. If they are fighting for me, that means I must also choose to fight for myself and I don't know if I'm strong enough for that.

I'm content now. Yes, at one point, in the peak of my grief, when I had lost Aurora and knew the twins were coming for me, I knew questioned if my life was worth living. But then Hale gave me a piece of heaven. He showed me that there can still be laughter and light in this world, and he gave me something to fight for.

And I did. For months, I trained with Sabrina, and I taught lessons at the ballet studio. The twins owned me so I wouldn't say I was happy, but I was trying. I had been fine with trying, with getting by on mere fumes of happiness.

I've been here one day, and I'm tortured with a brighter future. Staying here, caring for the animals, soaking in the wild, quiet freedom that I've already experienced has my imagination dreaming up a fantasy. But that's it, it's all lies. And when you realize that it's all a mirage, created by a broken, sick mind in an attempt to get you through *one more day*, everything comes crashing down.

That's the difference between him and I, I know what goes up must come down. He's soaring in the clouds and I'm on the ground with broken wings.

natasha

The early morning sun made me drag my eyes open, making me nauseated. Don't they know about blackout curtains? Normally, I wake up easily in the morning, but after my late-night heart-to-heart with Mrs. Knight, I hoped to sleep in today. Mostly to avoid all interaction with her but partly because my body feels utterly spent. However, the bright sun and tweeting birds have other plans for me it would seem.

I roll to the side of the bed and go to lower my feet to the floor but a large weight over them has me pinned. Max sprawls out, snoring with one ear flopped back at the end of the bed.

"Max." I wiggle my toes but nothing. The dog is dead weight. "Max!" I say a little louder and he shoots up like a gun went off then hops down and trots out the door.

The satisfying scratch at my eyes makes me moan as I make my way to the bathroom door, half asleep and with my eyes only twenty-five percent the way open I walk right through the door and slam against a solid form.

"What the hell?" I bounce off said form and begin to fall backwards, until large arms wrap around my waist and pull me forward. The smell of citrus and wood invade my nose, and my heartbeat quickens when my palms touch heated skin.

"Jesus," I whisper.

"Not quite, sweetheart." Hale's voice radiates through the bathroom, echoing off the tile in a way that makes my heart do silly things.

Coming to my senses as I fully awaken at his touch, I notice the way his arms completely envelop my body, his hot skin pressed into mine... he's holding me close, practically glued to him and suddenly I have a thrumming pulse down below.

I look up into his deep blue gaze and notice a lightness that wasn't there yesterday. My eyes travel down his straight nose, his sharp jaw framed by a perfectly trimmed beard, then down his neck where small water droplets drip along the columns of his muscles, finally resting on his bare chest. My body begins to vibrate with need in response to the slow-motion perusal my eyes took down this man's body. I bite at my bottom lip to try and reign in the raging horny bitch lurking under my skin, but it's hard...

It's. Hard.

And even harder to ignore as it presses into me, and I try to wiggle away. "Why are you naked?" I manage to say, although I would consider it more of a squeak than the confident voice I had intended.

"I'm not naked, your eyes didn't look further than my chest to see I have pants on."

At the comment, my gaze drops to see that he does in fact have pants on. Jeans. This man stands naked from the waist up, sporting a dark pair of Wrangler jeans and the pulse in my pussy goes from a steady thrum to a downright physical pain at the little heart attack I'm having in my boy shorts right now.

Damn. Get it together, Natasha.

"Why are you in my shirt?" His brows scrunch as he lets me go, looking me up and down.

"It's yours?"

He turns back to the vanity, finishing up putting something in his beard, probably oil, and I take a moment to appreciate that he actually cares for it like a man should.

"It is. Where did you get it?" he asks further.

"I... uh," I stutter out before regaining my composure. "It was in one of the dresser drawers."

"I always wondered where that one went; she never could wear her own damn clothes." He shakes his head and finishes combing his beard before stepping out the other side of the bathroom into his own room.

I make a safe assumption and conclude that his sister borrows a lot of his things. Which seems a bit odd. I mean typically boyfriends and girlfriends share clothes, but I guess if siblings are close enough it could make sense. I wouldn't know since I don't have any.

"Hurry up. We have to feed in ten minutes," he says as he steps back into his room, throwing a shirt on and then a flannel over that, leaving it unbuttoned. I tilt my whole body to watch the entire ordeal and wonder how one man can make getting dressed look so sexy. My equilibrium fails me, and I stumble over, barely catching myself on the doorframe. As I clear my throat, the bastard chuckles to himself.

Smooth, Natasha. Real fucking smooth.

After a quick pee, I brush through my hair, adding a little curl to the ends and rifle through the closet. I find a pair of jeans and a long-sleeved white top. Throwing on the same hoodie Hale gave me yesterday, I make my way down to the kitchen.

"She's not ready," he whispers as I begin to round the steps. "Don't push her, mother."

"You baby her. She's perfectly capa—" Mrs. Knight spots me and my gaze falls to the floor. "Oh, there you are. Did you sleep well?"

"Fine," I say, making my way over to grab the cup of coffee that waits for me on the counter. I pray she doesn't say anything about last night and look at Hale, his eyes tracking my every step. I know that she must have talked to him. She must have. What else would they have been talking about?

"We have the South lot this morning. You'll want to cover your hair; these animals can get a bit frisky," Hale comments as his eyes flick up to my loose, long waves.

I instinctively run my hand through it and then begin braiding it back. "Frisky? Are they going to pull my hair?" I joke.

"They might bite at it. Better if it's back and tucked away. Here." He throws a ball cap at me, and I barely manage to catch it as my hands shoot from the braid I secured. "Might want to take those earrings out too."

My mouth drops open as I hurriedly remove my diamond studs. "Jesus, what kind of animals do you keep on the South lot?" I meant it as a rhetorical question but Mrs. Knight chimes in as she hands me a protein bar then picks up a large bucket of scrap food and hands it to Hale. "The wild ones, dear." She smiles innocently.

After tucking the bar into my jacket pocket and rushing into the boots I left at the front door yesterday, I slip out the screen door after Hale and follow him to the south end of the property.

His feet move far too quickly as I speed walk to catch up. He turns to look at me over his shoulder and gives me a smirk that I both love and hate. "This lot has everything we need right inside the enclosures, so there's no need to prep beforehand. We'll hit the furthest enclosure and work our way back toward the house."

I stay silent as I take in the surroundings, my mind racing as to what kind of wild animals they could keep in enclosures. The trees that line the grassy hills are tall and ominous in the morning light, as if they hide some deep dark secrets. We pass by the brick building I saw when we came in and then continue past another barn, this one smaller than the one that housed the horses.

After about ten minutes, we come to a large pasture, Hale bends down and slips through the white fence and I do the same. "This pasture houses our deer and elk that can support themselves. It helps provide them with some protection. All we do for this pasture is make sure the water is filled. Sometimes we throw out our scrap food for them, but we try not to make them too reliant on us, we want them to be able to transition back into the wild easily." I follow him as he shows me the water tank and how to refill it, then he tosses out a handful of the scraps.

After, he leads me to the small barn. "Here is where the injured animals stay. We keep them here until they can return to the wild." Like yesterday, he walks me through all the steps to feed and care for the animals.

The first stall houses two large dog crates. A hiss coming from inside makes me jump backwards. Hale kneels next to one of them and laughs as he slides some of the scrap food through the bars. "This is Rocky, our male raccoon. He's a bit grumpy until you give him a treat. Then he will let you fill his food dish."

The metal door creaks as he opens it and slides two tin bowls out. Closing the door, he goes over to the next. "And this is Roo, our female raccoon. Both were found on the side of the road, barely alive. A little rest, hydration, and patience and they should be good to set free in the next few days."

Following Hale to a feeding room, I watch carefully which bins he pulls out, scooping the feed into the bowls and then he takes the hose and fills the water bowls. He hands me Roo's and we walk back toward the stall.

I'm hesitant to open the raccoon's door but one look at Hale, one reassuring nod and my nerves settle. I slide the metal latch and slowly open the door. When I peek inside, I find the little raccoon curled in a ball in the far corner. Her glassy black eyes blink at me and her little nose wiggles as she smells the food. "Hold on, if the boy gets a treat for being a dick, you get two for being so sweet," I whisper to her and pick out the best-looking strawberry top and juiciest apple core, placing them in her food bowl and sliding it in toward her. "There you go."

Hale tries to hide a grin as he dips his head, but I see it and it makes my heart do that strange, silly thing again. Next, he takes me two stalls down where I find a bright orange-red fox curled up in a fleece blanket. "This sweet girl was found in a trap. Had been eating Miss Carole's chickens. Although she loves her chickens, she couldn't bring herself to kill the fox. So, she brought her here. She was severely malnourished and had an infected paw."

The fox picks her head up at the sound of Hale's voice and I can't help but fawn over her. "She's adorable."

"Yeah, don't let your guard down. Though she be but little, she is fierce."

My shoulder bumps into Hales as I look up at him. "Shakespeare."

He simply hums and walks toward the feed room again. Instead of following, I stay and watch the fox. "Stay fierce, little one. Someone might look at you and want to use you for that beautiful fur you have. But it's yours, do you understand me, *yours*."

Hale returns only a minute later with a bucket of raw meat and berries. "She loves strawberries, and I picked some of the wild berries from out in the forest around our house, something she would find in the wild."

He holds the bucket out to me, and I stare at it. "You want me to feed her?" I scoff.

"Stay fierce," he mocks with a smile and my eyes narrow.

Taking the bucket, I unlatch the door and slowly step inside. I assume if she's scared, she won't want to be approached quickly, even if I'm carrying her breakfast, so instead I sit on the straw in her stall and toss a berry toward her. She jumps away from the thrown berry but then her little nose sniffs at it and she greedily gobbles it up. It doesn't take her but a moment to bound over to me. My muscles tense thinking she may attack but then her bottom sits in my lap and her head disappears into the bucket.

"One ounce of kindness and you're already trusting of me? You have many lessons to learn, little fox," I say as my hand strokes her back. "How do you find the wild ones?" I ask as I scratch behind her large ears. She has settled in my lap as I sit with her in the stall. I'm covered in straw and smell like a literal rat's ass... or fox's ass would be more appropriate to say. This otherwise dangerous and wild little thing has decided my lap's the perfect spot for a nap now that her belly is full.

Hale stands at the stall entrance, his arms folded over the half door that leads into the stall. "People find them and call us or bring them in."

"Why do you guys help the wild animals? Isn't it better to let nature take its course? Survival of the fittest and all that?"

He shrugs with nonchalance. "We are part of nature, right? If we can help, shouldn't we?"

His blue eyes are soft as they look upon me and I can't help but blush. "You seem to love it here so much. Why the job in Boston? Why not help your family with the ranch?"

As I slide the fox off slowly, she stirs a touch but settles back into the fleece blanket I made a little nest for her in. I walk over to him, leaning my own arms on the door next to his.

He takes a few moments, possibly considering why the interrogation or what his answer will be. I'm not sure, so I allow the silence to stretch on.

Finally, he looks from the small fox to my eyes. "I don't know."

I'm struck by his honesty and not sure what to say, but I don't have the chance to think of a reply as he continues, "It started as a way to help victims who had been trafficked. But lately, it's been draining. I'm not the man I used to be when I took that job. It's rewarding when we're able to rescue the victims. But those cases are so few and far between, it constantly feels like..." His throat catches and he dips his head, swallowing hard.

"It feels like what?" I gently coax him to give me his vulnerability.

"It feels like I'm constantly failing. Like nothing I do matters." He continues to look down, not making eye contact and I can understand that. The hardest thing to do in this world isn't about strength, but vulnerability. To give someone the opportunity to hurt you, manipulate and use you based on something so close to your heart. It's terrifying. But it's the only real thing we can give in this world.

My mind goes back to what his mom told me. *Hale was beside himself. Always blaming himself for her disappearance.*

Reaching my hand out, I place it on his cheek and bring his gaze back to mine. "I'm sure you are making a difference. You're a hero to the lives you do save, like someone was your sister's hero when she was saved."

He straightens his spine and steps away. "What do you know of my sister?"

I unlatch the half door separating us and step through, latching it again so the fox doesn't get out. Taking a step toward him, I decide that the man in front of me is as scared as I am, the only difference are the monsters we face. "Your mom told me a little bit. I'd like to know more about her though. If you'll tell me."

His shoulders relax slightly, and his eyes soften. "I'll make you a deal. You eat, I'll share."

My chest freezes and a nervous pressure builds in my stomach, but I'm always up for a challenge. "Fine." I pull out the protein bar in my pocket, rip it open and take a large bite.

He chuckles to himself and then turns, motioning me to follow. "Come on. We have one more stop."

I munch on the peanut butter bar as we walk to the brick building. Once inside, a musical of birds greet me and when I look up, I notice a large aviary. The indoor portion, where we stand, has a small section blocked off by a wire fence that extends to the ceiling but then there are three large open windows that allow the birds to go from indoor to outdoor easily.

Hale unlatches a door in the wire fence, and we step through. I'm surrounded by small birds flitting about. They don't land on me, but they get close as they swoop down and fly over my head. Old branches fill the inside, wooden toys hang from the ceiling and there are multiple bowls scattered throughout.

"Stay here," he commands and I do as I'm told. Honestly, I don't know if I could leave if I wanted to. It's mesmerizing, striking and justifiably captivating here. "Here's their food and then this gallon has their water. Just refill the bowls as needed."

He comes back in with the water jug and a bucket of food and I try and watch him, but I can't take my eyes off all the small, feathered creatures around me.

"Where did they all come from?" I whisper more to myself, but he hears me all the same.

"Most come from people bringing them to us, like the others. They usually are dropped off when they fall out of the nest too young, some of their mothers abandoned them for whatever reason, some are even family pets that the owners couldn't care for, so they bring them to us."

He puts the food and water away after filling all the bowls and then motions for me to follow outside. I climb through one of the large open windows, the base only about two feet off the ground and extending easily six feet up.

When I step into the outdoor section, my breath escapes me.

"Oh my god," I whisper.

Lavender fills the outdoor aviary and ivy climbs the walls of the brick and parts of the fencing that keeps the birds enclosed. A large, three-tiered circular stone fountain sits in the center, many of the birds drinking or bathing in the water. In front of it, sits a stone bench, big enough for two people.

"This is..." I don't even have the words. The smell of the lavender and the sound of the running water calms not only my body and mind, but my soul. A safe haven no one could ever hurt me in. A space to hurt and heal because I'm finding that you cannot do one without the other.

Hale's calloused hand slips into my own, as his fingers intertwine with mine, he pulls me to the bench and we both sit. "This was my sister and I's favorite place. Anytime one of us was upset we would come here. Sometimes alone, sometimes together. Spending time with the birds was always the cure to everything..." His saddened gaze drops to our linked hands. Then he pulls his hand from mine as if he remembered he shouldn't be. "Almost everything," he finishes softly.

"Where–"

I go to ask where his sister is, but he interrupts. "Look there." He points to a small bird on the top of the fountain. "You see the one with the red band around her leg?" I focus on the legs of the birds surrounding the fountain and notice they all have different colored bands.

"Yes. I see her." She's tiny, small enough she could easily fit in my hand. She stretches her wings out and then tucks them back in as she dips her beak into the water.

"Don't tell me you don't recognize her. You're the one who saved her."

My heart thrashes against my ribs, making my breath catch in my throat. She can't be... "She's..." My eyes turn to Hale who's already looking at me with a gentle smile across his lips.

"She's your sparrow."

As my eyes go back to the small, once broken and desperate little bird, she stretches her wings and takes flight and the darkness inside my heart cracks. Just enough for a ray of light to shine through.

natasha

The next morning, I creep down the stairs in an expensive camisole and matching pants. This set my own this time. The way the expensive fabric brushes against my skin fills me with the confidence only my silken armor can provide.

I'm going to need my armor with Mrs. Knight this morning. Seeing that small bird yesterday altered my outlook on my time here. It made me want to be like her. To grow and heal like she did. If a fragile creature like her can carry such strength, why can't I? I don't know how or if I will be able to, my injuries are much worse than a broken wing, but if she can heal, I can try.

Hale told me how he brought her here that morning and how they kept her in the house, feeding and keeping her warm and safe until she was ready to move to the aviary the other birds.

After that, my mind was overwhelmed with everything, I retreated to my room again. I read some poetry, napped, and face-timed with Sabrina. She was shocked that I was living on a ranch now and honestly, seeing her made me even more homesick for the city. The car horns blaring in the background and sirens going off made me realize how quiet the ranch is.

I used to hate the noise, but I'd grown to find comfort in it, now to be launched back into silence. The small town I grew up in was quiet too. I enjoyed it. I found peace in being still. Although, due to the fact my parents always had me working toward something, there wasn't much time for peace. There was always something. Cheer, ballet, chess and piano lessons, social events my father paraded me around, trying to attract the men he wanted to talk business with. Always something. The only time I was able to sit in the silence and read was when I was with Everett.

The last step creaks, like it always does, and Grace turns to greet me, like she has the previous two mornings I've woken here. She slides the already steaming cup of coffee over to one of the bar stools and I sit, thanking her quietly.

A shyness fills me as I think about the apology I need to make, but I don't know where to start.

"What's on your mind this morning, child?" she speaks softly as she leans against the counter, a warm mug of coffee grasped between her hands. She's wearing a deep plum colored chunky knit sweater, wrapped tight around her chest and I get the unfamiliar urge to beg for her to wrap me up in her embrace and give me all her warmth.

"I... wanted to apologize for what I said to you. It wasn't fair of me." My eyes meet hers and she gives a sweet grin.

"You are forgiven."

"I was awful."

"You are healing. Lashing out is natural when people are confronted with something as profound as the changes you're going through. This will not be the last time you apologize to me." My stare casts downward because she's right. Her hand covers my own and my eyes meet her warm ones again. "And this will not be the last time I forgive you."

I release a breath, feeling a weight drop from my shackled ankles. What a feeling to know I have the freedom to make mistakes and will be met with love and understanding, not that I intentionally want to harm her or anyone... not anymore anyway. "It still wasn't fair."

"I will never treat anyone with fairness and neither should you."

She easily reads my confused expression because she continues. "Let's say two children come to you, one has a paper cut and one has a broken arm. What would be *fair* would be to give both a Band-Aid. But what's a Band-Aid going to do for the child with a broken arm?"

"Nothing."

"Exactly. I don't believe in fairness. I believe in giving what's needed and teaching others to do the same. There are grave injustices in this world, Natasha. As I'm sure you know, bad things happen to good people and good things happen to the worst of humanity. Sometimes, certain people need more help than others and it's okay to give them more. It's not and never should be about doing what's fair, it's about doing what's right." Leaning up off the counter, she rounds the kitchen island and swipes a piece of hair away from my face. "You remind me of my daughter."

"I do?" I ask, hoping she will tell me more.

"Yes. Looks wise you are a bit different. She was shorter than you and her hair was a darker blonde, like her brother's. But your attitudes, oh boy... you two are cut from the same cloth."

"Who?" Hale comes up behind me and I jump at his voice.

"How are you that quiet? I didn't even hear that damn bottom step."

His mother gives him a scowl and Hale curls his lips in, holding back a smile. "Oh, that boy knows every place in this old house that makes noise, he also knows how to avoid them all. Isn't that right, son?" she reprimands, and I'm transported back in time where I can practically see teenage Hale being scolded for sneaking out. He scratches at the back of his head, not able to make eye contact with his mother.

"Your favorite child was the one who taught me," he replies as his mother hands him a cup of coffee.

"I only have favorites on days that end in Y." She winks at him, and he places a kiss on her cheek.

"Thanks for the coffee, Ma."

"You're welcome." She nods and then turns to look at me. "I was telling Natasha here how she reminds me of your sister. Don't you think?"

Hale's eyes widen briefly before he comes to sit next to me at the kitchen island, both of us facing his mom now. His comforting scent washes over me like warm water soothing my cold heart. "No. I'd rather not think of Natasha as resembling my sister in any way shape or form. Thank you."

"Oh, that's right. I forgot you two had sex. That would be quite inappropriate I suppose."

Hale spits out the coffee that he had sipped, and I try and fail to hold back a laugh.

"Jesus, mother. Really?" he says as he wipes the dribbling coffee off his beard.

"What? We're all adults here. Not like I'm some Virgin Mary. Your old man and I—"

"Oh my god. Stop. Please stop," Hale huffs, then gets up and makes his way to the pantry.

Grace winks at me and I giggle. "Watch this," she whispers next.

"Hale, honey, you know your father and I enjoy making whoopee, I enjoy—"

"Oh my God! Mother. Stop. I beg of you," he grumbles from the pantry and his mom and I both try to hide our laughter and fail epically. "He hates that word," she snickers and I pull my lips in as he exits the pantry.

"And why are you laughing? Huh? Something funny?" Hale narrows his eyes on me as he approaches with a granola bar and a banana that he retrieved.

"Nothing," I lie as I try to cease the giggles that continue to escape me. My stomach muscles begin to ache, and I realize for the first time in a long time it's from laughter and not fear.

"What's everyone laughing at in here?" James comments as he steps into the kitchen from outside. He takes off his hat and coat, then his boots before slipping on his house shoes. Walking over to

Grace, he embraces her with an arm around her waist and a kiss to her cheek.

"Natasha thinks I'm hilarious," the antagonizing woman comments and Hale's father grins.

"You are, my dear."

"She's not." Hale says, rubbing his hand down his face. "Here. Eat these."

"I'm not hung—"

"It's either these or mom's famous cinnamon rolls she makes on Sunday mornings. Your choice, sweetheart."

I grab the granola bar and banana with narrowed eyes as he leans down close to me. His scent invades my nose, and I'm half tempted to pull him in and kiss him.

"Good girl," he whispers and I cross my legs to keep from wiggling in my seat at his praise.

Holy shit.

Breathe.

"Hale, I need your help moving some equipment in the barn. I want to get it done before breakfast," James says and Hale walks away from me but not before ruffling my hair like I'm a child. I glare at him as the front screen slams and then it's just Grace and I again.

"Come now. Let's get to making those rolls."

"You... want my help?" I say with trepidation.

"Well of course, child. It's a rare day when I get help in the kitchen and I'm going to take full advantage. Now grab an apron from right over there." She points to a set of hooks on the wall next to the walk-in pantry and I grab one.

Before we cook, she puts old country on the radio and begins walking me through all the steps. Before I know it, I'm humming along to songs that I have no idea what the words are. The only words spoken between us are the ones she uses to give me my next instruction and there's something in the way she allows me space and companionship all at the same time.

The warm, sweet scent of cinnamon and sugar fill the house as the rolls finish cooking. A song with a beautiful melody and even more beautiful lyrics comes on. "What's the name of this song? I like it."

"Oh yes. Me too. This is James and I's wedding song. It's called *I Can Love You Like That* by John Michael Montgomery."

As Hale and his father enter the house, the older man swoops in and begins dancing with Grace, right in the middle of the kitchen. My arms wrap around my stomach, the moment much too intimate for me to witness freely. It's strange to see a love like theirs. One that has lasted, I'm sure has been tested but remains incredibly pure.

As I admire their love, imagining what it would take to find something as profound as theirs, an arm wraps around my waist from behind, and I gasp as Hale pulls me close. My body melts into his strong and steady hold as his large hand splays out over my stomach and his other hand runs down my arm gently from shoulder to fingertip. He begins to sway behind me to the slow music.

"Hale..." I protest. But he silences my fears as he begins singing the chorus softly in my ear. His breath tickles my hair. His whispered lyrics fracture my heart.

I close my eyes as he continues to sing the song his mother and father were married to. The soft, romantic melody of the music,

Hale's deep voice, his mother's laughter... a symphony of heartbreak. All the sounds are soft, yet the firm touch he holds me with overwhelms me because I'll never experience that kind of love. This is all temporary. I don't, and never could, belong to a man like Hale Knight. He's meant for a kind, gentle, flawless woman. And I'm none of those things.

The tears behind my eyes build, my chest getting heavy. *This is all temporary*. It will never last. I'll have to go back to the twins sooner or later, be forced to carry their child or be forced into...

He'll leave you, Natasha. They all do. You don't deserve a love like this. A man like this.

A sob rips from my chest, my ability to hold everything in, gone in a split second. Why am I acting this way? Why am I weak?

Get it together, Natasha. Compose yourself.

I can't. I'm crumbling, all my pieces are falling, shattering and my hands can't catch them fast enough. My chest hurts, oh God. I can't breathe.

"Natasha?" Hale questions from behind me and I realize he's holding me up now. Both arms wrapped around my waist as I curl forward, shielding my heart. The song has changed and when I open my eyes, everyone looks at me.

"I'm sorry... I..." I can't catch my breath. The room begins to close in around me and I...

"Oh, my child," Grace says as she approaches. My head shakes, warning her away. I'll hurt her. Like I do everyone when I'm hurting. Hale backs off as his mother takes his spot, her arms replace his from behind me.

"Come, child. It's alright." She doesn't guide me to the couch or even a chair. She sinks to the floor with me and I sit between her legs as she continues to hold me from behind, her arms now wrapped around my shoulders.

"Shhh. It's alright. It's alright. I want you to feel everything, child. Live boldly in your pain. Don't hide from it. Feel your sorrow and then let it go. Let it all go."

Her words evoke a tidal wave of tears as they stream down my face and my chest racks with the grief that tears through me. What is happening to me?

Hale stays close, kneeling in front of me, his hand never releasing mine. The gentle stroke of his thumb against the back of my hand slowly calms my breathing, but my mind continues to race.

When glass falls, no one ever sees all the tiny cracks that form. It happens in a split second. One moment the spotless glass sits whole and the next it's in a million pieces. When did I shatter? And why has nobody seen me, lying on the floor in a million pieces, why has no one cared to pick me up? For once, I don't want to do it! I want someone to care enough.

I want someone to look past the perfect exterior and see that shattered soul. I'm screaming on the inside. My body my own hell, a false appearance of perfection hiding who I truthfully am.

Eventually, my sobs quiet down and my muscles quiver. I didn't know how long I had let myself fall apart, long enough to exhaust me mentally and physically. Grace rises from behind me and then his masculine scent comes to me as his arms scoop me up from the floor.

"Take her to bed, dear." A cold, small hand runs over my forehead, but I keep my eyes closed, tucking my head into Hale's chest, feeling more embarrassed than anything at my behavior. My fingers curl into his soft shirt as he takes me up the stairs. When I finally open my eyes and look up at him, his eyes are focused, a small dimple rests between his brows, but he hasn't looked down at me yet.

When he lays me on his bed, he tucks the covers over me and leans down, so we are face to face.

"Just rest. Okay?" he says gently.

"I'm sorry." My voice breaks as I release the words. The tears threatening to fall again.

"You don't need to apologize for crying, sweetheart." His fingers brush a piece of hair from my face and his eyes soften.

"That's not what I'm apologizing for." His brows furrow and I continue, "I'm sorry for everything. I wasn't always this way."

Once I was as pretty as glass... until someone tipped me over the edge.

"You are my angel that was forged in hell," his deep voice recites the sweet line of poetry and a smile blooms across my face as I close my eyes.

"I don't know that poet."

"I think you know him better than he knows himself."

He told me he cared,
He said he loved me.
The lying,
The name calling,
Everything.
You hurt me,
You made me do things that I didn't want to do,
I wanted you gone,
I wanted you out of my head,
It didn't work.
You're still there.
I cry.
-MP

natasha

The week had come and gone in what seemed like a day. Hale left the morning of my breakdown, and I haven't heard from him since. I don't blame him though; I'm a mess of emotions with a side of bitch. The logical side of me knows he couldn't stay, he had to return to work in the city, but my heart can't help but bleed at the thought that he left because of what happened.

I've been tending to the animals each morning, cooking and helping around the house during the day. In the afternoons, I spend most of my time in the bird house and lavender garden. Their home feels like my own.

Grace hasn't mentioned anything about the scene I made in the kitchen, and I appreciate it more than I could say. I don't even know what came over me. Containing my vulnerability in that moment felt like trying to hold back an avalanche—completely terrifying and hopelessly impossible. She has also been making me eat each meal with her. It's funny how sitting down at the table with someone naturally brings out the conversational side of people. Some days we can't stop talking about Hale as a child, her and James, the ranch. Other days we sit in peaceful silence.

She never pushes me or demands anything from me, she listens and I'm in awe of how she knows when I need space and when I need her to distract my mind.

After I eat with her, she always sends me out to the animals and when I'm here with them, whether it's with the birds or the horses, I never feel the need to be anything except quiet. It's obvious she knows I struggle with what I eat and how much, I'm not naive and as she said, she's not blind. I know she does it on purpose, but I like that she hasn't allowed me to not eat. It's a tough kind of love.

First, she put down healthy foods that my mind told me were good. Then she would sneak on something sweet, a piece of bread or even a piece of bacon once. My mind revolted as the grease dripped off the piece of fat.

But I ate it, like I would eat pizza when B and I would get together. Except this time, I found I didn't want to throw it up.

She consistently kept me busy. Caring for the animals distracted my mind enough that by the time I thought about what I had eaten or about the twins and that whole situation, my body was exhausted to the point that I slept.

"Natasha?"

"Here!" I call from the lavender garden. She gave me a journal as well and I've been writing things down as I sit with the birds, mostly simple lines of poetry. The sound of the fountain, the lavender scent and the noises the birds make as they flit about make me want to pour my soul into something and writing has been it.

"I figured I'd find you here." She comes and sits next to me on the stone bench. "It's been years since I've been out here." A somber tone fills her voice, and I can see the gloss of tears filter over her eyes.

"Why don't you come here more often?" I ask, closing my journal.

"This was my daughter's favorite spot. It reminds me too much of her."

"Do you still talk to her?" I look over and see her watching a particular bird in the fountain bathing itself.

"All the time," she whispers before standing once again. "Come now, I'd like you to help me prepare dinner."

I stand and follow her out, wondering if she talks to her daughter all the time, how she could miss her so much.

We come into the house, and she has everything for dinner already laid out. Looks like a roast tonight. "I'll need you to peel the potatoes, dear. Then chop the veggies. I'll get the roast seasoned."

I nod and rifle through the drawer till I find the potato peeler. I know this kitchen like the back of my hand now after helping prepare three meals a day for the past week. The ranch often has visitors for lunch or dinner. Ranch hands that help, people bringing in new animals, Mr. Jennings as he does a lot of work on the ranch with James. I mostly stay quiet as they visit but it's been comfortable, and they've all been polite.

As I begin to peel the skin away from the potatoes, I look up and notice that she isn't putting on the radio like she usually does.

My gaze meets hers and I know from the look in those stern but gentle eyes that I'm not going to like what's next.

"Tell me about your parents?" she asks, not a command but an opportunity to open myself up. Maybe someone who temporarily resides in my life is who I should tell my story to. Someone who won't be in my life long, someone I can give all my secrets to and then leave, never having to face them again.

"My mother and father are still married. But they don't have a marriage like yours. Theirs is... more of a business deal. My father owns a chain of hotels and resorts down the entire West Coast and now some even on the East." I don't mention that he's also in business with one of the largest sex trafficking organizations in the nation. "My mother's a socialite. Organizing parties, fundraisers and events to bring in more business deals for my father."

I finish peeling the potato and place it in the strainer to be washed. Then grab the next one.

"That sounds like a privileged upbringing," she comments as she spreads butter all over the roast.

"It was. I had all the clothes, shoes, cars, and make-up a girl could ask for. All I had to do was ask." She stays silent, now sprinkling seasonings all over the meat. "But... my parents had expectations of me. Ones I could never meet. My father always wanted a son. His father and his father before him have always carried on the Baldwin name and with it, the empire they've created, and it would be unheard of for the business to be passed to a woman."

I finish with the next potato and place it in the strainer.

"Would you even want the business?" she asks, peeking over at me and I pause. I never considered it an option because it wasn't one. I've always resented my father for doubting I was good enough to run his empire, but... would I even want to? I guess I only ever did to prove him wrong and when I think about it...

"No. I wouldn't. I want nothing to do with his business and the men he deals with to keep it running."

Thinking of Dante Alessi, who funds a large portion of the Baldwin resorts and knowing what kind of business he runs, I know now that he pays my father to use the hotels as a place of transport for the women he traffics.

"What about your mother?" Grace asks when more time than I intended passes. She probably assumes I grew up with a kind and loving mother.

"She tried to raise me to do what she does." I try to keep it simple but alas, Mrs. Grace's in the mood to push boundaries. Boundaries that I know need to be challenged.

"Be a socialite?" she asks.

"Amongst other things. I was expected to always look my best, attract men so that my father could interrupt and start a conversation, and when I was old enough..." I pause, wondering what she would think of me if I told her the truth.

"Old enough to what?"

My heart beats hard against my sternum at the judgment I know must be coming. Maybe it's not judgment from her, but from myself. I finish with the last potato and walk over to the sink to begin washing them along with the carrots.

"Natasha, child." She comes up next to me and begins washing the vegetables with me. "You are safe."

My eyes burn and I swallow my pride. I've never told anyone this and I fear what she will do with this information, but I don't want to die carrying this secret. I need to release it so that maybe I can move on.

"You can't tell anyone. Please," I beg and she tilts her head. I know I'm asking a lot of her, but after a small twist of her lips, she nods.

"When I got my first period... my father brought in a man. I didn't know who he was, I'd never seen him before. But he... he taught me how to please a man. From the time I was ten to thirteen I met with him a few times a week for lessons. They made sure I stayed... a virgin, but when I got my first boyfriend in seventh grade, I knew exactly what to do and how to treat him. But Everett... he was innocent. He didn't want to do anything that I'd been taught. I thought something was wrong with me... wasn't I doing everything right?"

A tear falls from my eye and rolls down my cheek. I realize I've stopped washing the vegetables completely, standing there with my hands in the water, body frozen, while my mind races, trying to run away as it always does when I think of those lessons.

"My parents and Everett's had an arrangement, a business deal as all things are in my father's world. I was supposed to get pregnant and carry Everett's baby. Joining my family and his. His father was the town mayor, who was set on climbing the political ladder, so a marriage and child between us would only benefit both families. But I couldn't get Everett to have sex with me. The lessons continued. More and more and more until I felt like my body wasn't even my own. It was the tutors."

The saltiness of my tears hits my lips as I lick them away. Now that I'm finally releasing my truth, it's like I can't stop. It keeps coming from my mouth as Grace stands there, the vegetables all but forgotten as she listens.

"Finally, Everett and I did have sex. Our junior year of high school but he always wore a condom. My mother showed me how to tamper with them, but I... couldn't do it. I couldn't trick Everett like that. I knew that after we started having sex, the clock was ticking and when I continued to not get pregnant... my father told me he would bring in help. He wanted his heir, and he would do anything to get him."

"He didn't..." Her voice breaks as her green eyes brim with tears and then overflow down her cheeks.

I try to hide it... but all truths surface at some point. "Everett broke up with me senior year and..."

"He did," she confirms, pulling me in and wrapping me in her arms.

My body has not been mine to control since I was a little girl. It's a fact I've come to accept. She holds me in her arms as I continue to tell my story, releasing all my sorrow. "At that time in my life, I didn't even fight him. I knew it was coming. But I did everything I could to not get pregnant despite the man doing all he could to get me pregnant, as he was paid to do. When he would finish, I would run to the bathroom and wash out all I could, I would drink as much alcohol as I could at parties, and I would have my friends buy me the plan B pill. They thought I was carelessly sleeping around and I never denied it. I felt dirty. My so-called friends called me a whore... and honestly, I felt like one."

She pulls back and wipes the tears from my eyes with her cold hands. "And when you finally got pregnant? Was it by Everett or..."

"It was Everett's. He didn't know about any of what was going on in my life. It wasn't his fault. My father had given me a choice when we graduated high school, get pregnant by Everett or by the man of his choosing and trust me, Everett was a much better option at the time. I knew if I had to choose a man to be the father of my child, I wanted it to be him. So, when I found out his girlfriend left him, I pursued him relentlessly. I didn't want..." I pause, catching my thoughts up to my words so I don't lose control. "I don't know how I did it, but I managed to convince my father to keep giving me time. I wanted to live life a little before I brought a child into this world, so I stayed on birth control, although my father never knew that. He thought I was unlucky; something was wrong with me. But finally, I couldn't placate him any longer, I got off the shot and almost immediately got pregnant."

Her brows pull in and I see her connect the dots. "But it was a girl," she says and then the last piece falls into place. "What did your father do..."

My chest feels like it breaks open. My last secret. I nod my head.

"I didn't know it at the time, but after I lost her, he told me that he had put pills in my drink to force a miscarriage. I... I know he's an awful man but I never thought he would... I thought he would let me try again but he said it had taken too long the first time... he couldn't wait..." I try to get everything out in between sobs but my lungs burn. "It's my fault. If I wouldn't have told him the gender... She would still be here."

Grace wraps me in her arms again and lets my soul shatter. I've carried this truth silently without breaking for years but speaking it aloud makes it entirely too heavy to bear. Maybe that's how healing strengthens us.

"None of this is your fault, child. None of it."

She runs her hands down my hair, stroking it like any consoling mother would. One more weight falls to the ocean floor and I rise closer to the surface as I tell my truth. I never knew it would be a woman I've only known a week but as she rocks me slowly, I know I chose right. For the first time in my life, someone knows everything about me and they chose to stay.

After what feels like hours, she pulls back and kisses my forehead. "You go and rest. I'll call you down when dinner is ready. Okay?"

I wipe away my tears and nod. The step squeaks as I place my slippered foot on it and I smile, thinking of Hale knowing where to avoid on this step. But as I go to take another step, a cramping in my lower belly hits and I almost double over, clutching my stomach and letting out a small grunt.

"You okay, Natasha?" Grace asks and I rush upstairs as warm liquid drips into my underwear.

"Fine. I just... I think I'll skip dinner tonight. Feeling a bit over-whelmed with everything."

I rush up the stairs before she can reply and run straight into the bathroom, locking the door behind me.

hale

One more meeting, then I can head back to Natasha, back home. This week has gone by slower than my mother when she's trying to get to the point, like it knows that I'm not meant to be here in this city, but with her. But I had to, I still have a job and people who depend on me to get my shit done.

On top of that, I couldn't miss this meeting. Rafael gave me the name of one of the top traffickers in Boston and I fudged some files and conveniently dropped some evidence against him in the current case we are working. To make it more believable, I let one of my agents come across the evidence and make the connection to avoid suspicion. Hence why I'm stuck in an emergency meeting at seven o'clock at night to go over everything.

Felix, one of my best agents, feels incredibly proud, and honestly, he deserves it. The man works harder than I do, gunning for my position and most days I'm ready to give it to him. I'm not even sure what keeps me here anymore. I know the work we do is important, but I can't help but feel like I'm not the right man for the job.

"Hey dipshit, focus." Gage nudges my elbow. I must have zoned out and the little hacker from hell can always tell when I'm not fully here.

"I am," I lie and pull my stare away from the pen I twirl in my fingers back to Felix who briefs the team on the new evidence. They're about to talk about a plan to bring him in and blah blah blah. I'm numb to it all.

The blonde, broken beauty crying in my bed occupies my every waking moment. Begging me with her eyes to stay but pushing me away with her words. She doesn't know that I see her. I see far deeper than her surface level bullshit, the façade she puts on to meet society's expectations.

I see her fragments and I'd happily cut myself, willingly bleeding out to put her back together.

And fuck if I understand it all myself, seems like I just met her but damn, she's fucking intertwined into my psyche, sometimes I can't tell her apart from myself.

She knows it too. She knows we were made for each other.

She's afraid. Afraid to heal, afraid to let me help her heal.

I get it. Healing fucking sucks. It hurts. It forces you to face the pain. I've seen it over and over again. Yet, I'm a fucking hypocrite because I have yet to face my own pain. But that's beside the point. We're talking about her here...

My phone vibrating in my pocket pulls my attention even further from the meeting and I look at my watch to see my mom calling and even though we speak over the phone often, something feels off. An instinct lighting my mind on fire.

I slide out of my chair and out into the hallway, answering on the third ring. "Ma? What's wrong?"

Her panicked voice fills my ear. "She's in the bathroom, Hale. She's not answering. She's in the bathroom." Her breaths fill my ears as she hyperventilates and I fucking hate it.

"Slow down Ma, breathe. What happened?"

"We had a moment, and I... I told her to go rest. I came to get her for dinner and she's in the bathroom. The doors are locked, Hale. She... she's not answering."

"Where is dad? Can he break in the door?"

"He's at your uncle's."

Fuck. My uncle has shit reception, she won't be able to get ahold of him till he comes home. Dammit! Why did she do this?

"Call the Sheriff, Ma. I'm on my way. Stay outside her door. I'll be there as soon as I can. She'll be okay."

She'll be okay.

Shooting Gage a quick text and cursing myself for walking to work, I run back to my apartment and grab my keys to my truck. The fear in my mind threatens to paralyze me, but I force those fears to the edges of my psyche and press down further on the gas pedal, pushing Rosey as fast as she'll go. I can't think about all the what if's running rampant, I can only focus on getting to her in time.

Because I didn't get to Ivy in time.

"Hale! Hale!" my mother screams from somewhere in the house. The morning sun peaks through my curtains as I shoot up in bed at the sound of my mother's panicked voice. I'm in town for a short visit

and it's been a trip from hell. All my stubborn sister and I have done is fight.

"Open the door, sweetie! Just open it for me please. Hale!" she shouts again, and I try to cut through the bathroom, but the door's locked. Not unusual since we share a Jack and Jill bathroom, she always locks it after I accidentally walked in on her naked one time.

I rush out of my room and down the hall, mom's wiggling the handle on the door as dad tries to shoulder it open. "What's going on?"

"She's locked herself in and she isn't answering. Hale, something's wrong. I can feel it."

What the hell? I step up and bang my fist against the white wooden door. "Open the door!"

Nothing.

I try one more time.

Nothing.

"Stand back," I tell my parents as I take a few steps back and then shoulder my way in with force, breaking the door in the process.

Red takes over my vision.

Red.

Red.

Red.

"No, no, no, no." My mother pushes through as she lets out a blood curdling scream, collapsing to the floor as my father catches her. Her broken sobs echo off the cold tile as he holds her, and my mind goes numb. My feet move on autopilot as I climb into the bathtub behind my sister and hold her to my chest as silent tears roll down my cheeks and cold water soaks into my clothes, my skin... my heart.

Cold.

Cold.

Everything's cold. Even her skin.

I hold her and kiss the top of her honey blonde hair, now tinted to look strawberry blonde.

I know it's too late.

I was too late.

Too late.

"Why would you do this? Why, Ivy?" I whisper in her ear as if she could hear me.

The gravel sprays the front of the house as I come to an abrupt halt in front of the porch, next to the Sheriff's car, the red and blue lights illuminating our home. More memories try to invade the walls of my mind as I race out of the truck, not even closing my door. My steps thunder through the house as I fly up the stairs to find Ma sitting down at the kitchen island, her face in her hands as Sheriff Michaels pats her back.

I don't pause to ask what's happened, instead I rush up the stairs, taking them two at a time. I need to get to her. Its all that matters, *she's* all that matters. I push the cracked door open slowly as the moist air from the shower fills my nostrils. Max lays on the bathmat outside the tub. His head perking up when I enter but then resting again when he sees me.

The water runs behind the closed shower door. When I pull it open, my eyes focus on the red color washing down the drain. Natasha lies at the bottom of the tub, her back leaning against the wall. Her broken eyes look up at me, red rims them as if she'd been crying but she isn't anymore. Instead, I'm met with a vacancy I remember too well. Her body is with me, but she isn't.

My sparrow is wanting to take flight, I can see it. The same haunting eyes from the rooftop.

I climb in behind her and when I'm settled close to her naked body, I close my eyes at the feel of her warm skin.

She's warm, but the water runs cold over her body.

"Hale." Her voice breaks as her chest begins to pump up and down with the impending tears that I know are coming. Sliding my hands down her wet arms, I lift each wrist, visualizing them clearly and my thumbs trace small lines along the smooth, intact skin.

"Sweetheart?" I finally answer her when I know I can trust my voice to not break.

"The mind is its own place, and in itself can make a Haven of Hell, a Hell of Heaven," she whispers as I link my fingers with hers and wrap her in my arms. The water runs down her naked body and I realize where the blood pours from.

"Milton," I whisper in her ear, and her body relaxes into my touch. Her weight a comfort, like the warmth of the sun's rays on the first day of summer.

"What happened, baby?"

"My mind plays tricks on me, Hale." She pauses as she takes a breath. "I saw her. My daughter. She was standing in front of me, as real as you are. She was real for a moment."

"I'm not following," I reply, trying with everything to recall any little piece of information she might have given me since I have known her. But nothing I researched of her mentions a daughter.

"A few months ago, I had a miscarriage. I lost my daughter. I haven't had a period—" She releases a small sob and pulls both our hands to her lower abdomen. "God, it hurts, Hale."

"Shh, it's alright," I soothe her and when her muscles relax again, I know the cramping must be over. My sister had painful cramps with her period too and I would be there, getting her a heating pad, chocolate, water. Anything she needed while she rode out the cramps.

"I haven't had a period since I lost Aurora. I guess in my mind... she was still with me. I could trick my brain into thinking that because I didn't have a period, she was still in my belly, happy and at peace."

I pull in a sharp breath and release it as it hits me. This is the first period she's had since she lost her baby. But that still doesn't answer what she means by she saw her.

"What do you mean you saw her?"

Her sniffles and the sound of the shower running fill the space as I wait for her. My head rests against her wet hair and I take in how grateful I am that it's still a beautiful blonde.

"When I was crying, I closed my eyes, and she was there. Four, maybe five years old and she had long blonde hair like mine. Green eyes like Everett and pink, rosy cheeks that matched her little lips. She was in a white cotton dress..." She pauses as she curls in again. Groaning a little as another cramp comes and I see a little more blood wash down the drain. "God, Hale. It felt real. I thought I could reach out and touch her and I tried. But then I opened my eyes, and she disappeared. It was a trick of my mind. Heaven and hell all wrapped into one."

I don't know what to say, instead I wait there in silence. Letting her take control, guiding me because I am beyond my element. As the time passes, I stay there, laying in the tub, still clothed in my suit as her weight melts into my body and her breathing slows. When I look down, her eyes move behind closed lids, and I wonder what she sees when she dreams.

Slowly, I climb out of the bathtub, then scoop her up with only a small moan escaping her lips and lay her in my bed. I do my best to dry her off with a towel and then wrap her in the sheets. Pulling the covers over her, I tuck her in and do something I haven't done in a long, long time.

"Thank you, God," I whisper before placing a kiss on her fore-head and walking out the door. Leaving it cracked.

After I change, I head downstairs and hit the creak on the last step and my mother's gaze turns to me. Her green eyes are glossy and the skin under, puffy from crying. She stands still as I step up and wrap my arms around her shoulders, holding her close.

"I'm so sorry, honey. I thought…"

"It's okay, Ma. I know. You did the right thing calling me."

She pulls back and sits down at the island, her hot tea long for-gotten. "Is she okay?"

I shake my head, not even knowing how to answer that. "I don't know. I told you; she's hurting. Like Ivy and I don't know what to do. I want to help her but…"

"But what, sweetie?"

I let out a breath, feeling more defeated than I ever have been. At least with my sister, I knew how to talk to her. I could tell when something was off. With Natasha, one moment I see the fight in her eyes, the fire to claw her way back to the surface and then other times, like the rooftop and tonight... her eyes are numb.

"I don't want to fail. I can't lose her like I lost Ivy. I don't know what it is about her, I mean the woman drives me up a fucking wall but... I can't get enough of her."

Ma pats the stool next to her, she could always tell when I needed to vent. Something in my eyes she used to say. But hell, she was and is always right.

"She's like a puzzle, as soon as I start to see the image clearly, I can't find the piece I need. Every time I think I have it figured out, she goes and flips the narrative, changing everything I thought I knew. I don't know what she's been through... well now I know a little more but... there's something still missing. I know it and by the time I figure it out I'm afraid I'll be too late."

My mother and I sit in silence for a moment while she waits to see if I have more to say. But I don't. I'm fucking exhausted. And not just my body but my mind, my emotions. Everything feels drained.

"She's not Ivy." Looking at her, I see the confidence in her eyes as she makes that statement.

"Natasha's not like your sister. I thought she was too, but she isn't. Ivy... Well, she was never able to open up. Ivy didn't want to get better. Natasha does. I can see it. And that's all you need to heal, honey, the desire to. Natasha *can* be saved."

Is she right? About Ivy? I always thought that Ivy was doing better. It had been years since she had been taken and it took time but she seemed happy. But then, I guess that's always how it goes, right? The most broken people put on the most convincing performance. Whether because they have always had to, or it's the only way they can look in the mirror, I'm not sure, but it doesn't change the outcome. If they don't want to get better, they never will.

"What do I do, Ma?"

"One minute at a time. One day at a time..."

"One life at a time," I say, finishing the slogan we use for Revival Ranch.

"So, what does she need right now?" the wise woman asks, and I think about it. What is one thing I can do at this moment? How can I love her the way she needs in this minute we are in?

As it comes to me, I stand and pull my keys out of my pocket. "I'll be back."

natasha

When I wake, naked and in Hale's bed, my brain feels foggy. My face feels swollen, and my eyes burn with how much I cried yesterday... Or today? I don't even know right now. I roll over and glance at the alarm clock on his nightstand. Eleven at night.

Okay, I only slept for maybe an hour or two at the most, but my body molds to the mattress like I slept for twelve hours. Funny how the best sleep you get comes after a complete psycho meltdown. Yay me...

A familiar weight at my feet has me looking down to find Max staring at me. As if he had been watching me the entire time I slept. As soon as I wiggle my toes, he hops off and trots out of the room.

Stepping out of Hale's bed, I pull the sheet with me and begin to walk back toward my room but then I stop and turn to face his closet. I don't know what it is, but I don't want to be in my clothes.

I want to be surrounded by him.

Opening his closet door, I pull down a gray shirt with the Budweiser logo on it and then slip into a pair of his boxers. Then I walk back to my room and pull on a pair of fluffy socks and put a tampon in. Thank God I had the forethought to pack some. The doctors told me that sometimes it could take months for the body to regulate again so I always kept a few tampons with me. I brush out my tangled hair and go to braid it but then decide to leave it down and wild.

As I come down the steps, the last one creaks, and I wince. I don't know if I hoped to be alone or not. But either way, it doesn't matter now. That damn step gave me away.

"Natasha?" Grace calls out then emerges from down the hall, stepping into the kitchen as she wraps a shawl around her shoulders.

"Hi," I say and then immediately feel like an idiot for doing so.

"Come, sweetie. Sit by the fire, I'll make you some tea."

I do as I'm told and wrap myself in a blanket as she delivers the warm cup to my cold hands. "Thank you."

She nods as she sits on the wingback chair next to me. "Are you okay?" she asks, concern heavy in her eyes.

"No. But this makes it a little better." I look at the tea and she smiles kindly.

"Where is Hale?" I can't hide the shakiness of my voice, nervous for her answer for some reason. My biggest fear at the forefront of my mind. Overwhelmed with the mess that I am, he's gone back to the city, needing distance and space from me.

"He should be—" as she says it, the screen door swings open with a creak and Hale walks in carrying two brown paper bags.

"Hey, I got—" His pretty eyes meet mine and my heart stutters with a relief so monumental tears come to my eyes. "You're awake." He finishes as he sets the bags on the counter.

My feet carry me to him, acting seemingly of their own accord, like they know where I belong. Watching his eyes as they rake up my body, heating when they see me in his shirt and boxers, I can't help but add a little extra sway to my hips when I notice. A reflex to a man assessing me.

When I stop inches from him, his mom's soft scuffles of her slippers against the hardwood tell me she has gone back to her room. I take in his tired eyes that swim with worry and I hate that I did this to him. He's in a gray Henley and jeans, his brown Carhartt jacket dusted with a light layer of frost as he comes in from the icy night. But I don't care. I step into him, tucking my hands between his jacket and the soft knit of his shirt, bathing in his scent and warmth. His arms wrap around me and his cheek rest on top of my head.

"Where did you go?" I ask, feeling incredibly weak that I care but dammit, I do. Even if I don't want to, even if I know it doesn't matter. I care where he goes. I care what he does. I care about him... and that terrifies me.

"I thought you could use some things..." He trails off as he pulls away and I practically whine at the loss of contact. He smirks like he knows exactly why I'm pouting, and I want to punch him in that perfect face of his.

Damn, I forgot how hormonal my period makes me.

"I didn't know what you use... my sister used pads and tampons, so I got both. All sizes too. And I picked up some Midol..." He begins removing item after item as he lists everything he went forty-five minutes away to get this late at night. "Heating pad, Gatorade..." He looks at me as he pulls out the last two items and I can't help but laugh. "Chocolate and a chick flick?"

Tears build in my eyes and his eyes grow with worry. "Shit, I didn't think... are you... I thought..."

"Hale. Stop." I step into him and take the chocolate from his hands. "Thank you."

"But you're crying..."

"Yes, and I'd rather not talk about the weakness that is currently leaking from my eyes. So can we dive into this chocolate and go watch..." I look at the movie he picked out and laugh. "...*Hot Chicks*, please?"

He turns to hang his coat up and I make my way to the couch. Once I settle in, tucked back under my blanket, I look at the nutrition label on the bag of peanut M&Ms and my stomach turns. 140 calories for 12 pieces, 7 grams of fat, 15 grams of sugar...

"Give me that." Hale snatches the bag from my hands, goes into the kitchen and then scratches out something on the bag. When he brings it back, I notice he took a Sharpie to the nutrition label. I roll my eyes as he tucks himself next to me under the blanket and rips the bag open.

"You know, I read it already," I say and repeat all the facts out to him.

"You forgot one thing..." He smiles as he pops a handful in his mouth.

"And what is that?" I cross my arms, knowing damn well I didn't forget a single thing.

He holds one out to me and I stare at it like it's going to jump out and bite me. "1000 grams of pure... chocolatey... happiness. Open, sweetheart."

I hesitate but as my eyes meet his, my body has no choice but to listen, my mouth falls open. "Tongue out." His voice deepens as his eyes move to my open mouth. He places the single M&M on my tongue, and I pull it in. My mouth waters as the sweet chocolate mixes with the saltiness of the peanuts.

"Oh my god," I moan and Hale chuckles.

"If all it takes to make you come is a single M&M, then I'm going to have you coming every single night, sweetheart."

I slap his shoulder, and it only makes him laugh harder. "Stop! I've never had one before. It's unlike anything I've tasted. I couldn't help it."

His head snaps my way. "Wait, you haven't had peanut M&M's before?"

"No, I haven't had chocolate before," I correct him and his face falls in horror.

"That's shameful," he mocks with a shake of his head and a sideways grin.

I fiddle with my fingers but finally get the courage to ask. "Can... Can I have another?"

He leans into me, and I turn my body without thought to allow him to lay one on my tongue, his head resting on my chest, my legs naturally wrap around his waist and my arms drape over his shoulders. It should be awkward; this position we are in since technically we aren't together.

But ever since the night on the rooftop, it's almost like him and I are doing things backwards. The sex and physical comfort coming before the emotional conversations that most people have first. Maybe that's exactly what I need though. To know that the body I've never been allowed to give freely, is safe to give to whomever I choose, and he has done nothing but care for it.

He lifts his hand, chocolate in tow and I pull his fingers into my mouth as I suck on them and in turn the M&M.

His eyes darken as he looks at my lips sucking on his fingers. "Sweetheart, I'm trying to be a gentleman and respect your boundaries, but if you suck on my fingers like that one more time, I can't promise I'll be able to control myself."

I giggle and his head moves with my chest, which makes me laugh even more. The movie plays in the background but neither of us watch it. Instead, we fall into a comfortable silence after our giggling fit. He continues to feed me the sweet candy and after we finish the bag, I decide to give him something not as sweet.

"Can I tell you something and you promise not to judge me?"

"I'd never judge you," he replies as he lays his hands over mine which are resting over his heart.

"I want to throw up right now. My mind races with how many calories I ate. I've never told anyone about my eating disorder... I mean I'm not stupid. I know I have one. But... it's how I grew up. I don't know anything else."

"What do you mean?" he says, rubbing small circles over the backs of my hands.

"My mom restricted my diet... since... well I guess as long as I can remember. No candy or sweets. Minimal carbohydrates. And what I was served was portioned out and if I was still hungry, I was given water to fill my stomach. I got used to eating so little. Then when I became an adult and had the choice to eat more, any time I did I felt sick. I weighed myself one day and saw I had gained three pounds and that crushed me. That's when I began purging and then throwing it all back up."

I brace myself for him to tell me I'm sick and I need help and what I'm doing to my body isn't healthy. Like I don't already know that... but he doesn't. The sound of the movie fills the space as I wait for his words and the air surrounding me becomes suffocating. The longer I wait, the heavier it gets.

"What do you see when you look in the mirror?" he finally asks and I close my eyes. Partly because I don't know if I can tell him. What if he sees the same thing? However, how am I supposed to heal and grow if I'm not honest with those around me.

I've been trying to do that more often... being vulnerable and honest. It's a bitch.

My silence must stretch on too long for his liking because he sits up and pulls me up with him. "Let me show you what I see."

I follow him up the stairs, our hands interlocked and then he pulls me into the bathroom, shuts the door and faces me so I'm looking in the full-length mirror. He stands behind me, towering over me. Even though I am taller than most girls, he's taller than most guys.

"What do you see?" I ask, my voice dripping with fear.

Bending down behind me, he wraps his large hands around my ankles and lifts one foot and thanks to my dancing history, I'm able to keep my balance. "I see the feet of a dancer. The delicate lines and curves when you point your toes…" And I do that as he says it, seeing the same lines of my muscles. "So elegant," he praises.

He drops my foot and runs his hands over my calves, still on his knees behind me. "Your legs are toned, but feminine. They are long and perfect, made to wrap around my waist and drape over my shoulders…" He kisses the back of my thigh under my butt and shivers race up my body. His hands caress the skin around my thighs then up my hips and to my stomach.

"Your hips move with a fluidity that takes my breath away, Natasha. No other woman I have seen moves like you do. You are grace and power, and you don't even see it."

He grips my hips and turns me toward him. His hands sneak up my shirt as he pushes it up and then places a kiss on my lower stomach. His heated, deep blue gaze meets mine and I thread my fingers through his course dirty blond hair.

"You are the most perfect thing I've ever laid eyes on and the only woman I would ever get on my knees for."

My breath catches in my chest at his assessment of me. I don't see what he does and maybe that doesn't matter as much as I thought it did. Lowering myself in his lap, his hands come down around my ass as he holds me against him.

The desire coursing through me pulls me into him but I hesitate. I don't want him making a mistake again, regretting being with me. He must see something in my expression, his grip around my waist tightens as he demands a truth from me. "Tell me what you're thinking. I can't read what's in that complicatedly beautiful head of yours. You have to talk to me, baby."

"I overheard you talking to your mom while we were at your apartment in Boston. You said you made a mistake sleeping with me and I don't want you to feel that again."

His brows pinch in and a hard, determined expression washes over his face. "Natasha, my mistake wasn't sleeping with you—it was letting you walk out that door. It was not holding you close enough, not binding you to me so you could never fly away. I let you go, foolishly believing you were one night, when what I should have told you that night was that I want every night, for the rest of my life, with you."

All words and coherent thoughts temporarily leave me at his confession.

"Please say something, because I made a pretty bold confession and I'm freaking out a little that you're going to bolt again."

The vulnerability in his eyes draws a smile out of me and I'm finally able to find my words again. "Can you do what you did for me on our first night together?" I ask as I stare into those perfect Neptune eyes.

"What's that?" he says as he leans in, our lips brushing.

"Show me what heaven looks like."

Without a single moment of hesitation, his lips slam to mine and I open for him, allowing his angels to consume my demons.

hale

Her lips taste as divine as I remember. Her skin and the way she moves make me want to light anyone who has ever put those false thoughts in her head on fire. If she wants me to show her heaven, I'll do that as she drags me to hell. Because that's exactly what she is—pure sin, and I'll face the fires of hell to have a taste of her sweet heart. She's my greatest weakness, the one person who takes my self-control and throws it out of a fucking window.

And the crazy thing is? There's no question. No hesitation. Nothing matters but her. I knew it that night on the rooftop. I know it now. If she would have jumped that night, I would have gone with her. If she jumps tomorrow, she'll find me as a broken bloody mess laying on the pavement holding her tight as we take our last breaths.

I spent my childhood looking after my sister, then my teenage years trying to save her, and the last eleven years trying to feel something again. Then this broken little sparrow comes into my life and with her—my purpose and my freedom come flooding back into my fucking veins.

Her tongue caresses mine and I moan into her mouth. Her gasps fill the space as I move my lips to her delicate neck and bite into her paper-thin skin. I can't keep my hands in one place as they roam her back, into her long hair, then back down to her ass again.

"Fuck, sweetheart. If you don't want me to fuck you right here and now, then you need to stop because I sure as shit can't," I say as she begins to lift at my shirt, clawing at the cotton that separates our skin.

I don't know how she feels about sex while on her period. I've been with some women who are turned off by it or embarrassed. Personally, I don't give a fuck. It doesn't bother me at all, in fact, it's a fucking honor to be the one person a woman feels safe and comfortable with enough to allow inside her while she bleeds the blood that gives life. But if she's self-conscious about it then I'll respect that.

"Don't stop. Fuck me in the shower," she whispers before her lips find mine again and she bites down on my bottom lip.

Shit. Don't have to tell me twice.

I stand, lifting us both as I fumble around with my free hand and turn the shower on. I pull open the door and take both of us in, not even undressing beforehand.

With our lips still chasing each other, I let her down and unbuckle my pants as she pulls down the boxer briefs of mine that she had on. Soon both of us are naked.

My hands trail up her thighs then my fingers find the little string hanging between them. Grasping it, I slightly tug and tilt my head, leaving the question unspoken. Her head nods with permission and

I pull her tampon out all the way, discarding it in the trash outside the shower door. "Are you going to be my good girl tonight, sweetheart?"

"Yes," she whines as she takes my cock in her hand and strokes me up and down. One thing I do remember from our first night together is that she doesn't mind taking control, but she also doesn't mind being my good girl either.

"Turn around," I command as I twist her hips and push her into the cold tile. She gasps as her breasts and stomach come into contact with it and I see the goosebumps rise on her pretty skin.

I slide one hand down her wet body to play with her pussy, the other gripping her hair at the base of her skull. Pulling her head back, I lick the droplets of water off that had accumulated on her full lips "So *fucking* perfect." Slowly, I begin to rub around her clit, making her writhe beneath me as I press her body further into the shower wall.

"No matter what, Natasha. You're in control. You control me. You control your body. It's all about you, baby. Do you understand?"

She moans out an unintelligible response.

"Words, sweetheart." I stop my fingers and her eyes shoot open.

"Yes. Jesus, yes," she rushes out and I can't help but smirk at her eagerness. I continue with my fingers as her eyes close again, her whole body melting into my hands. Her body practically vibrates under me, and I relish the feel of it pressed against mine.

"I need you, Knight. Please." My heart leaps out of my chest at the use of the name I gave her the night we were strangers relinquishing everything to the other through our bodies. In a way, it's no different now.

"Such a greedy little thing aren't you, love?"

"Yes, yes, yes," she whimpers with each roll of my fingers over her clit. I slow down enough to drive her mad. The need to see her lose all sense makes me fucking excited. Teasing her to utter oblivion, making her mind temporarily forget all the fucked up shit she overthinks about is my singular goal when I have her naked.

Letting her hair go, I slap her ass. "Lift."

She goes up on her toes and I line myself up. As I push into her, her pussy clenches around me and fuck... I'm home. There's no other way to describe the way she fits me and I her. Like coming home from war, she's peace personified. My sweet sanctuary.

She lets out a long, slow moan, filling the space with my favorite sound.

"God, beautiful, you are my heaven." I growl into her ear.

A whimper leaves her perfect lips as I circle her throat with my hand. My hips move in tandem with her breathing, but she's holding back. Her muscles shake violently but she isn't there yet.

"You're such a good *fucking* girl, Natasha. Taking me so deep, begging me to fuck you. You're my dream. Every breath, every word, all that makes you, you... is mine. And I am equally yours. Now... I want you to focus on me and come for me."

"I can't," she cries out with her eyes closed. Looking down on her as the warm water washes away her tears, I almost stop at the sight of them... but I don't. She would stop me if she wanted to. I know she would.

"Do you want to come, baby?"

"Yes. Please," she whimpers, and I bring my lips to her. She opens for me as I taste her sweet tongue, kissing away her fears as she begs me to provide something only she can give. It's my job to make her feel safe enough to relinquish it.

When I pull back and open my eyes, she's panting, and I can see she wants to... but she can't let go. I'm buried deep inside of this tortured woman and I'm wondering what she has experience that makes this difficult for her.

"Look at me, Natasha." Her whiskey brown eyes open, glassy with tears. I cease my hips, staying buried inside her and focus on the slow circles I make over her clit.

Her muscles tense again and her eyes close before I think she'll come.

"Open your eyes. Look. At. Me." I throw every ounce of command into my voice, knowing as much as she wants to be in control, right now she needs to surrender. Some people find safety in taking control, while others find safety in giving up control to someone they trust. My sparrow simply needs someone she knows will care for her through her vulnerability.

Her eyes open again.

"Don't take your eyes off mine, baby. Do you feel that? Feel what I'm doing to your body. Listen to it. What does it want?"

She blinks, long and slow and when she answers, her voice breaks. "I want you..."

I continue my slow assault of my fingers on her pussy, not changing pace. Not moving my hips. One sensation for her to focus on.

She lifts even more on her toes, her breathing stops, her eyes plead with mine.

"Let go, Natasha. Come for me."

She cries out as her body fully relaxes back against me and her muscles shake. "Such a good, good girl, Natasha. You did so good, baby. I'm so fucking proud of you," I praise her as I begin to move inside her again, riding out her orgasm and I follow quickly behind her as I hold her in my arms. She has gone completely limp, her chest rising and falling rapidly.

"Hale?" she whines.

"Yeah, sweetheart?"

"I needed to say your name." She turns her head to look up at me, her back still pressed to my chest and I lean forward and kiss her. "What does this make us?"

She lets out on a small laugh, and I kiss her again, not being able to satiate my thirst for her.

"It makes you mine."

She's silent for a moment as her eyes roam over my face. I know what she's thinking, she can't be mine because of the twins and the arrangement they have with her. But I don't care. I'll do anything to keep her.

"Then you're mine too," She confesses.

***

Early the next morning, Natasha lays with her arm across my chest, her body curled up to my side and at peace. I reluctantly slip out from under her warmth, placing a kiss on her cheek and after I get dressed, I leave a note for her.

I'll be back, baby.

Stay for me.

-Your Knight

I sneak down the stairs, but it doesn't matter, my mother's always up this early. Already brewing the coffee. "Good morning, Ma."

"Good morning, son. Did you have a good night?" She has a mischievous smile on her face.

"You know, it's creepy how you know these things."

"Thin walls, honey," she replies right before she sips from her ceramic coffee mug.

"Like I said. Creepy."

She shrugs and goes to her chair, picking up her book. I throw my coat on, and she catches me with a look that says *don't you dare*.

"I'll be back."

"Hale James Knight, you are not leaving that girl at a time like this!" she whisper-yells at me.

"I'll be back. I need to take care of some things in the city and with work. It's important," I plead with her, hoping she will trust me on this.

"*She's* important." She stands as she points her finger toward my room upstairs.

"I know that."

She tilts her head and gives me that mom look of hers that usually has me tucking my tail but not this time. I need to do this.

"Hale, she's not broken like you said. But she *is* fragile right now. You don't know—" She catches herself and I tilt my head, feeling a fuckton of confusion. What does she know that I don't? "This better be important."

"It is. Give me... two days. Max. I promise."

She shakes her head and sits back down. "I love you."

"I love you, too," I say before softly closing the screen door and making my way to the truck.

On the drive back to Boston, I make as many calls as I can this early. My last one being to my one and only friend.

"Why are you calling me this fucking late, asshole." Gage's rough voice reminds me that probably I woke him since he's in Japan with his new girlfriend, Colette.

"It's early for me and it's urgent," I say as I place him on speaker and set the phone on my lap.

"It always fucking is."

"I mean it," I reply as I get on the highway, only twenty more minutes till I get to the city now.

"Did your phone call have a point or are you wasting my time for fun?" he grumbles as his girlfriend mumbles something in the background.

"Pissing you off is my favorite hobby. But yes, I have a point to this delightful conversation. I need you to pull everything you have on Natasha Baldwin."

"You have everything I pulled on her."

"No, I need the underground shit that I know you also pulled but kept to yourself."

"I did no such thing." I stay silent this time. Letting him think about it. "Why the fuck do you want to know more about Natasha?" I continue my silence, letting that twisted head of his put it all together. "No. Are you fucking her? Seriously, Knight. You're a fucking dumbass." More grumbling from Cole. "I gotta go, baby girl. I'll be right back. Go back to sleep."

"So sweet," I chuckle.

"Shut the fuck up and give me a minute." The door shuts and then the click of his keyboard tells me he's working his magic. "Alright. What do you want to know?"

"Is there any record of her being assaulted?" Silence and some more clicks.

"No. No reports were made, no medical records indicating an assault."

"And from your own personal experience with her? What do you know?" I inquire further because I now know that Gage and Natasha grew up together.

He lets out a sigh. "If you're fucking her, you don't want to know what I think of her." I can practically see him running his hand down the back of his neck like he does when he's annoyed.

"Nothing you say will change my opinion of her. Give me your worst."

"Fine. No, from what I knew of her in high school, she was never assaulted. She was with my best friend, Everett, from middle school till senior year when they broke up. They fucked around in college a bit too but nothing serious. He would never assault her. She was a privileged little princess who got everything she wanted.

A royal bitch who could never let Everett go and attacked anyone who threatened their relationship."

That may have been how she acted, but that wasn't who she was. I know it. There's more to the story and I'm going to figure it out. "I need you to dig deeper. Go into her childhood. Look at her parents' records. I want to know who was in and out of her house. Everything. I want it all."

"Don't you think if she wanted to, she would tell you her secrets? Maybe you need to let her share when she's ready."

"Would you have ever shared your secrets with Cole if she hadn't pushed?"

A long silence fills the car. "I'll let you know what I find."

Hale: 2 Gage: 0

Bitch.

natasha

Two days ago, when I woke and Hale was gone, my panic took hold of me and wouldn't let go. After everything that had happened between us, I felt his absence like a knife to my chest, reaffirming everything I had been telling myself would happen.

I would give a piece of myself away, he would leave.

But his own mother assured me he would be back. She has kept my mind and body busy with work around the ranch and be- sides being with the birds and watching my little sparrow from the rooftop get stronger and stronger, I've attached myself to a particu- larly stubborn horse.

But what this mare, which I've learned is what they call a girl horse, doesn't know... I'm as stubborn as her. Each morning, after- noon and even sometimes late into the night when I can't sleep, I come to her stall, Max usually following faithfully by my side. The mare isn't allowed out in the pasture yet from the injury to her leg, so she's stuck in the small ten-by-ten-foot stall and boy do I understand why she acts like such a bitch.

One thing I know from my time in a cage, sometimes we bite the hand that feeds us because all we've ever been fed is poison.

Matilda and I are kindred spirits. Don't ask me why I've named her Matilda, she seemed like one.

"Come on, take the damn carrot. You'll like it," I say as I hold the carrot out to her over the stall door. I haven't been able to get in there yet; every time I try, she pins her ears back and gives me a look that says she's two steps away from murdering me in cold blood. So, I keep the barn door between us.

She takes a small step forward, now only three feet from me. She tries to stretch her neck out to reach with her muzzle, but I pull the carrot back. "No, no. The vet said you need to start putting weight on that leg." She broke her right front leg and the now healed bone needs to build strength again, she needs to start putting weight on it, then she can start walking again. But the vet said she'll probably never run on it again and definitely no riders.

She sets the leg down as she eyes the carrot but then lifts it again.

"I know it hurts, but sometimes we have to hurt in order to heal. You can do it. One step at a time."

Her eyes move from the carrot to mine, and she lets out a snort of hot air that ghosts over my face. I huff also, mimicking her attitude.

I turn and grab the bucket of grain. "You can have a bucket of grain, but the vet said to start cutting back. If you gain too much weight, it will hurt even more on that leg. But we can keep this between us."

I shake the bucket and the sweet scent of the grain wafts up filling my nose and based on the perk of her ears, I would say she caught the scent also. She lifts her neck and eyes the bucket. "This is a bigger prize, Matilda. I'm going to need you to come all the way to the door for this. Think you can do that? It's only three steps."

She puts her front leg down and bears the weight then lifts it again. I give the bucket another shake and she repeats the same move. Finally, she puts her full weight down and limps one step toward the door.

"Yes! Just like that. Two more!" I encourage her. Tears fill my eyes at how proud I am of her taking that first step. Why on Earth I am crying over a damn horse, I can't fathom but here I am.

She takes two more steps and hangs her all-black head out the door. The hair between her ears covering her eyes and her nostrils flare with the exertion she put herself through.

I offer her the grain, and she throws her head in, the weight making me catch the bucket with both hands but once she's steadily eating, I'm able to hold it with one hand and use my other to gently stroke between her eyes.

Her soft hair and warm body make me want to cuddle close to her in this cold December winter.

My forehead meets hers, the warmth of her filling my heart, a misunderstood gentle giant. "You need some time huh, girl? You're stubborn and want to do it on your own. I get that. I do. Probably more than anyone here. But you'll get there."

And so will I.

"Looks like you've made a friend." Hale's deep voice echoes through the barn and I turn my head, finding him standing in the entrance, the morning sun rising at his back. He looks delicious in his dark jeans, gray hoodie and tan Carhartt jacket. He has a beanie covering his dirty blond locks and gloves covering his hands. His arms are crossed over his broad chest, and I practically begin to drool.

"She only likes me because I give her grain," I respond, looking back down at Matilda as she lifts her head, the crumbles of grain falling out of her mouth.

Hale walks up and his body heat radiates off him, warming me up a little more. "Isn't she supposed to be on a diet?"

Matilda pins her ears back and reaches out to Hale with her muzzle threatening to bite him but then returns her head back to the bucket. I giggle as Hale steps back with his hands up.

"Shh. We don't talk about the D word in front of her. She needed some encouragement this morning, it's all about balance."

"You won't hear another word from me, I rather like my fingers and would like to keep them."

I look into his deep blue eyes as he steps up to me again. "I rather like them, also," I say with a flirty grin.

"Greedy, greedy woman." He leans in, hand wrapping around the base of my neck where my braid rests and kisses me softly. "I'm sorry I had to leave. I needed to make some arrangements. Forgive me?"

"Only if you tell me what you had to do." Matilda nudges my shoulder when her bucket runs dry, and I give her some scratches under her chin. "Ma'am, that's all you get right now. You can have a carrot later, remember. Balance," I say as I point my finger in her face. She snorts and turns away to give me her butt. "Oh, so you move fine when you want to give me attitude. You faker."

Hale grabs my hips and pulls me in after I set the bucket down. "Now that your hands are free, I can give you a proper hello." He dips down as I lift my arms around his neck, and he takes my lips with his. Opening up for him, I let him heal any small wounds his departure left with each stroke of his tongue. I didn't realize how much I missed him until this moment. He feels like coming home. He feels safe.

"I wanted to show you something. You up for a little trip?" he says, after pulling away from me, already heading toward his truck with my hand in his.

"Of course."

I'm afraid, Mr. Knight, I'd follow you anywhere.

After getting into Rosey, who's still nice and warm, he begins driving out onto the property, following a bumpy dirt road.

"Can we play a game?" I ask as I turn down the music.

"What kind of game?"

"Well, I realized while you were away that I don't know some of the simple things about you. I figured I could ask you something and then you could ask me something?"

He gives a sideways smile and glances over to me, his eyes meeting mine then running down my body buried beneath jeans and boots, a hoodie and jacket and beanie covering my head. I don't think I've ever looked as unattractive as I do now, but this man looks at me like I'm his entire world.

"Alright. You first."

There are many things I want to know but decide to start simple. "What's your favorite color?"

"Purple."

"Purple?" I question with a small smile.

"Don't give me that. Men can like girly colors. Y'all don't own them," he says jokingly.

"It's not that. I'm surprised. I would have guessed blue."

"And yours?" His hand comes to rest on my thigh as the truck bumps down the road. We can only go maybe five miles per hour on this old road. Forest and fields surround us, with no building in sight.

"Pink. But a light pink, not a bright pink. When's your birthday?"

"December 25th, 1992."

I look at him and see on his face that he already knows what I'm about to say. "You're—"

"A Christmas baby. Yes," he finishes for me. "And yours is April 18th, 1998."

"How did you know?" I narrow my eyes at him and he smirks.

"I did some research on you."

"Stalker," I joke.

"FBI agent," he corrects.

"Basically the same thing. . . So, then I would assume you know my full name?"

"Natasha Parker Baldwin," he says with confidence "And mine is Hale James Knight. We have time for maybe one more. So, make it good, sweetheart."

"Okay..." I look out the window and bite my inner cheek, think-ing about what I want to know most at this moment. "Do you want children?"

He's silent for a minute, staring off at the road. My heart beats faster and faster because I'm terrified to know his answer. I want him, but I also want to be a mother. If he doesn't want kids...

"I do. Three, maybe four." He glances at me for only a moment but doesn't ask a question.

"It's your turn," I encourage as he rubs small circles with his thumb on my thigh.

"I know." His voice changes, making me think he's unsure or maybe nervous. "Do you... do you want to try for another child? I mean... is that what *you* want?"

I know that he's referring to the fact that I'm under some weird contract to conceive a child for the Alessi and Baldwin empires to merge but... "Yes. I do want more children. But I would be lying if I said I wasn't scared. I don't know if I could go through losing another one." I give him an honest answer because I'm tired of hiding. Tired of keeping everything in. It's exhausting and it turns me into someone I'm not proud of.

"We're here." He pulls up on top of a small hill overlooking the ranch. Before us sits an unfinished house with a giant weeping willow tree about fifty yards from the skeleton home.

"Come on." His voice pulls me from my dazed state. The stunning property has me dreaming up another life, an impossible one.

He steps up onto the gray slab of concrete with unfinished walls and roof and then takes my hand as I step up. I look at it more closely and see the wood beams define different rooms but it's still unfinished enough that I can't imagine the layout yet.

"You are standing in what will be the kitchen." I look at my feet as if I could see the hardwood beneath it. "Over there the living room." He points to a large rectangular section. Then he begins to walk to the other side, and I follow him.

"One. Two. Three. Four." He points out four square areas, two on each side of what I would assume would be a hallway. "For the children."

I look up at him and my eyes begin to water. "This is going to be your house?"

"I started it eleven years ago but then..."

That must be when his ex and him split. He was building it for her and what would be their family.

"Ivy left," I finish for him.

"In other words, I guess. I could never bring myself to finish it. God, for years I couldn't even come up here. It hurt too much. She helped me design it when we were kids. I always knew I wanted to live on my parent's ranch, take it over one day. But... things happen, and plans change."

They knew each other since they were kids? That's incredibly romantic and . . . hard to compete with.

"I'd love to see it finished one day," I say, imagining all the wonderful things he could do with a home like this. He's got bare bones here; he could create such a beautiful and magical place if he could bring himself to finish it.

He takes my hand and kisses my knuckles then pulls me into him. "I can see it now." His arm wraps around my waist, the other lifting my hand as he begins to sway me back and forth. "Dancing with my wife, our children running around at our feet. Can you see it, Natasha?"

My head rests against his chest, a tear falling and soaking into his jacket. "I'd want nothing more, Hale. But..."

"Shh. Don't. Not now." His chest begins to vibrate and I realize he's humming a song. One I don't know the lyrics to, but I recognize the melody. The same one we danced to in his mom's kitchen.

When the song finishes, his hand grasps my cheek, and his lips meet mine in a gentle caress. A promise.

Then he's pulling me along with his arm around my shoulders and we step out of the skeleton house, outside again and toward the willow tree. "One more thing I want to show you."

"Did you love Ivy?" I ask even though I know the answer. She holds so much of his heart, I can see how he hurts without her and there's a jealousy in my heart at the idea that, if she was still with him, I wouldn't even be considered. Always a second choice. And what would happen if she came back? What if she realizes what she lost out on and wants him back. Would he leave me?

"How could I not? I loved her more than anyone on the fucking planet. She was a part of me. Two halves of one soul."

A tear falls down my face and my chest aches. I'm such a fool, falling for a man who could never fully belong to me. But what makes it even worse, I would still take him. I'm that weak that I'll take any part of him, even if he'll never truly be mine.

He leads me under the tree and a stark white gravestone stands alone. When I come up closer, I read the engraving and my heart sinks.

Ivy Carter Knight

December 25th, 1992 - April 30th, 2013

Beloved daughter, sister, and friend.

She *died*. She didn't leave him, she... died. God, I never asked. I assumed that she had left him. Ivy Knight, his last name. But the engraving doesn't say wife...

"Wait, who is Ivy?" I ask as my eyes frantically find his.

"My sister. Who did you think she was?"

Every moment he mentioned his sister rushes through my mind. Hale's defensiveness at me wearing his sister's clothes, his mother talking about how she left, how she still talks to her all the time, the painting of the ivy in her room and...

My hands come up to cover my mouth as I gasp. "Oh my god, I-I assumed she was your ex. Your mother...what I said to her. Oh god."

The tears fall from my eyes and Hale wraps his arms around my shoulders while I cry. "I'm so sorry, I didn't know. I thought she left home, I didn't know she died."

"It's alright, sweetheart."

"She wasn't your wife. Ivy was your sister."

He pulls back and looks at me, the dimple between his brows ever present. "You thought Ivy was my wife?"

"Well, no one ever told me your sister's name and I overheard you on the phone saying I was broken like Ivy, and you couldn't go through that again... I assumed... I'm sorry, Hale."

His hands come up and hold my face, pulling my eyes to his. "It's okay."

"Can you tell me about her?" I whisper and his eyes hold mine. I see the wheels turning behind his head.

"I...Yeah. I'll try."

He walks over to a stone bench, like the one in the lavender garden and brushes the snow off it. As he sits, I do as well, and he pulls me close to him.

I look at her headstone and read it once more. "You guys have the same birthday,"

He scoffs and begins to fiddling with my fingers. "She was my twin. But every bit the opposite of me."

My eyes turn to him and notice he's looking out over the ranch. You can see all the pastures and the roof of his parent's house from atop this hill. It's breathtaking.

"She was wild, carefree. Always witty and never following the rules. I was cautious and scared to do anything. I always felt like I was following her around, trying to keep her out of trouble. When we were teenagers...we went to a concert and..."

"If you don't want to say, your mom told me what happened."

His chest deflates, thankful to not have to talk about it I assume. "When she did come home, our roles had reversed. I was lost without her, acting out. Being a complete asshole to my parents. The guilt ate away at me. I drank too much, began failing my classes. I became a rollercoaster of emotions, one step away from flying off the rails. And Ivy... fuck, Ivy became numb. She rarely smiled, never joked around anymore. My parents put her in support groups and therapy. And after a year or so, we started seeing the old Ivy again. After five years she seemed completely back to herself, but sometimes I could still see her eyes go vacant. I mean, I knew why. I thought her being happy most of the time was enough. But in the end, the light didn't outweigh the dark."

He swallows hard, choking back tears and I squeeze his hand. Lending any comfort I can as I let him tell his story.

"When I was eighteen, I joined the Navy and left home. It was hard on her, I could tell. But I couldn't stay home forever. I needed to do something for myself. I wanted to see the world and I tried to encourage her to do the same, move away, live her life. She said she was happy at the ranch."

The whisper of the tree above us fills the silence as Hale collects himself.

"I was visiting home when she...We had a fight the night before. She wanted me to come home for good, saying she felt lost without me. She didn't understand that you can't quit the military. I said things I didn't mean. And... the next morning I found... but and it was too late to apologize."

A drop hits my hand, and I look up to find Hale's eyes now brimmed with tears. The wetness appearing like glass, making those deep blue eyes burn brighter.

"How did she..." I pause because it doesn't matter.

"She slit her wrists... in the bathtub. By the time we realized... it was morning, and I was too late. I should have known. I should have felt it. We always had a connection to one another, that twin telepathy people called it. I could feel every emotion she felt as if it were my own. But I missed this."

"Hale." He leans into me, tucking his face into my neck as much as he can as his sobs grow harder.

"It's my fault, Natasha. I left her at the concert. I left her at home because I selfishly wanted to see the world, but she needed me. I should have known she was hurting. I wasn't there when she needed me. I failed her over and over again. I couldn't save her."

"It's not your fault," I whisper as I cling to him, my arm wrapped around his shoulders and the other gripping the back of his neck. I run my thumb back and forth, doing whatever I can to show him I'm here.

"It's not your fault," I say again and again as he breaks in my arms. "It's not your fault, Hale."

After what feels like hours, he pulls away from me and rests his forehead to mine. "Why couldn't she see the light in the world? Why couldn't she know there was more for her? More on the other side of healing."

"Maybe she couldn't see the light in the world, because she was the light."

His eyes soften and he leans in, our lips connecting, I taste the saltiness of his tears that have coated his lips and try as much as I can to take the pain away from him. As if through our kiss, I could siphon all his pain away. He doesn't deserve it, so give it to someone who does.

"She was the light in my life... until you."

hale

The light hits her face, amplifying the freckles dotting her cheeks. I've never noticed them before—they're faint, barely noticeable unless you're close. A nervous energy fills my chest because this, us... we're happy right now and I can't help but feel the weight of impending change.

Her and I are starting something. That something remains unknown but there's a spark. But I know the call from the twins will come. They will take her from me as our deal outlines. If I could have known then what I know now, I would have...

What would I have done? As much as I hate to admit it, she's intertwined with the Alessis as much as she's tangled with me, maybe even more since technically they are engaged.

I need to figure something out. There has to be some way to make a new deal. Free her from the chains of Dante Alessi.

All I know for sure is that Natasha Baldwin is the most important person in my life. It would be juvenile to define us as boyfriend and girlfriend when she feels spiritual in my life.

And if I lose her...

"Knight?" her moaning my name in her sleep pulls me from my thoughts and has me and my dick more than awake.

I pull her back to my chest, whispering in her ear, "Yes, love?"

"Hmmm." Her perfect lips turn up in a grin, but her eyes stay closed as she wiggles her ass against me. "I wanted to know you were here," she mumbles, still half asleep.

"I'm here," I reassure her as I grip her face in my hand and turn her so I can place a kiss to those lips that haunt my dreams.

Turning fully toward me, she takes control, letting her tongue mix with mine. Her leg swings over my hip and she pushes me to my back as she straddles me. Her strong thighs grip my waist as her fingers run through my beard and she tugs slightly.

"Fuck, sweetheart," I whisper as her long blonde hair cascades down like a waterfall around us. "You're stunning," I praise as I look into her whiskey-glass eyes. Eyes that look like they're ready to own me.

Who am I kidding, they already do.

Her hips grind down on me and she whimpers, "Hale, I need you to fuck me."

"You need me to fuck *you*... or do you need to fuck *me*, baby." When she doesn't answer, I simplify it. Brushing her hair out of her face and tucking it behind her ear, I look into those eyes so I can read her. "Do you need control, Natasha, or do you want to lose control?"

Her eyes drift back and forth between mine, and I can see the indecision.

"I want to lose control," she whispers, and I need nothing more from her.

Thank fuck we sleep naked, no need to mess with clothing this morning, I can go right home. I grasp her hips and begin pushing her back and forth over the length of my cock. Her wet pussy moves seamlessly over it and when my tip hits her clit, her thighs tense against my sides.

"So fucking wet, sweetheart. Is this all for me?"

"Yes," She whines as her nails dig into my chest and her head falls back. When she's on the edge of her orgasm, I slow my hands and lift her hips, notching myself at her opening, I push her down slowly, teasingly and her eyes roll back in her head with a long moan.

"Shit," I say. "You're such a good girl, Natasha. Taking all of me with such fucking grace. I wish you could see yourself the way I see you. My greatest sin, my perfect angel."

When her eyes meet mine, I bring her in for a harsh kiss then pull away, tucking her face into my neck as I begin to thrust in and out of her, slow at first to let her adjust. "Can you be quiet, baby?"

She nods her head up and down before biting down on my neck. The bite of pain makes me hiss, but I don't care. Let her mark me, I need her to know she can put me through any pain, and I'll still be here.

Moving one hand to her clit, I begin circling it. She tries to ride me, but I halt her with a squeeze to her hips. "Stay still and hold on." Her hands grip the sheets above our heads as I play with her pussy, thrusting up into her. She reacts precisely how I knew she would.

Loudly.

Her moans fill the space, releasing from her throat with each thrust I deliver. I can't hold in my chuckle at her blatant failure and disregard for my orders, or maybe it's more of an inability to follow my rules but either way, she needs to quiet down.

Bringing her head down by a grip on the back of her neck, our foreheads touching, I place my other hand over her mouth, keeping her nostrils uncovered so she can breathe. Through it all, I keep fucking her like I know she needs right now.

"Shh, baby," I laugh again as her moans grow even louder, her eyes rolling back as I fuck her hard and fast.

"Hale! Natasha!" My mother's voice rings out before a knock sounds on my door and I am once again a seventeen-year-old horny teenager.

"Fuck, we need our own space," I hiss as Nat's eyes blow wide.

"It's time to decorate the tree, when you finish… *come* on down," Mom giggles at her own little pun and now that Natasha is silent as a fucking mouse, I can even hear mom's footsteps down the hall.

"Bad, bad girl." I shake my head as my goddess slowly rides me since I've stopped. Giggles cease from behind my hand, so I remove it. I begin to play with her again and it doesn't take long before her muscles are tight, and her eyes close as I see her struggling to release.

"Eyes on me, baby. You can do it."

She opens those wicked eyes and as they meet mine, her pussy pulse around me as she releases. She rides out her orgasm, nails digging into my chest and as her head goes back, her whole body relaxes as she lets go and it's the most beautiful thing I've ever seen.

I push her hips up as my release covers my abs. Grabbing a tissue from beside my bed, I quickly clean up my mess before she collapses forward. She pants on top of me as I run my fingers through her thick golden hair. "You did good, sweetheart."

"Do you think your mom knows what we were doing?" she shyly mumbles into my chest.

"She's not dumb... or deaf."

She sits up abruptly and smacks my chest. "I was not that loud!"

Landing a firm slap to her ass, I push her gently off me and stand, making my way to the bathroom. "Quiet as a mouse, sweetheart."

***

Mom has Christmas songs playing on the TV while she unpacks the ornaments. The tree's already up, that's always been dad's job, then mom, me, and Ivy used to do the decorating. Natasha sits on the floor, her oversized cream knit sweater hangs off her shoulder and her hair tossed up in a messy bun, my dog laying right next to her with his head resting in her lap.

Fucking traitor.

But I can't blame him, she's stunning. Who needs all these Christmas lights when her smile lights up the entire room. Correction, my *life*.

The image of her in this way will forever be imprinted into my brain because at her core, this is who she is. Not the bitchy-mouthed, defensive, princess that she displays as a coping mechanism, but this woman sitting before me.

Natural.

Transcendent.

Happy to be needed and loved.

That's *my* Natasha and I'm incredibly fucking honored to have this part of her.

Fuck everyone else, this woman is *mine*. Doesn't matter who puts a rock on her finger, her heart, her fucking *soul* belongs to me. And mine hers.

Mom smiles as she shows off all of mine and Ivy's handmade ornaments from when we were kids. "Ivy never paid much attention to detail when we would make these, gluing and throwing glitter wherever, but that one right there..." she nods over to me as I sit back on the couch, untangling the lights, "...he took his time. Even asked for a pair of tweezers one time so he could get the glitter right where he wanted it. He was adorable; his little tongue would stick out and the look of concentration on his face would always make his sister tease him."

The lights tangle up again in my hands even though I spent ten fucking minutes untangling this section. "Yeah, well, look whose ornaments still look spectacular and whose look like they went through the garbage disposal."

Mom tosses one of the pillows at me and I block it with my hand.

"They're all perfect." The old woman rolls her eyes and Nat holds one that has a picture of Ivy and I when we were about ten. "You guys are almost identical."

"Well, we are twins, love," I tease.

A second pillow hits me right in the face, my hands too occupied with the lights to block it. But honestly, hearing Natasha's laughter makes it worth it.

Holy fuck. That's a beautiful sound. It's a laugh I've never heard before. It's free and unrestrained and all I want to here it again and again. My eyes eat her up and when she stops laughing, straightening her head to look at me, her cheeks flush at my appraisal of her.

Just before I get up to kiss her, my phone vibrates in my pocket. Pulling it out, I see the last name I wanted.

Rafael Alessi.

I get up and hand the lights to dad who rolls his eyes but begins working on them anyway. "I gotta take this, be right back."

Stepping out on the front porch, the snow hits me, and I curse myself for not grabbing my jacket. The dark green Henley and sweats I'm wearing does nothing against the Massachusetts winter.

"Agent Knight speaking."

"Happy Holidays, Agent." His voice recognizable to the point that even if I didn't have his number saved, I'd know who spoke.

"When do you need her?" I cut straight to the point, already anticipating this call.

"She needs to be at the airport in two days, our flight leaves at nine am sharp."

"Sabrina will be joining her again?" I ask, making sure she has some layer of protection.

"No. Sabrina is unavailable."

"Then I'll be accompanying her."

Rafael laughs, thinking I'm in any way joking. "Do you think that's a good idea, Agent?"

"Does your father or any of his men know who I am?"

"Your name, yes. But not your face, however it takes nothing more than a Google search to find out who you are."

"So, we use a fake name. Tell them you hired me as her body-guard."

Silence on the other end has my heart pounding. There's no way I'm leaving Natasha alone in that house so he either lets me come along, or I'm sneaking in. Either way, I'm going.

"I can agree to play along, but Agent, you do understand that while there, Natasha will be ours. We will play the part we need, and you will have to stand on the sidelines, watching us with the woman you love."

My back teeth grind together at the image he painted, but it doesn't matter. Even if keeping her safe means giving her away for a time to the devils of Seattle.

natasha

"Here, sweetie. Let me help you." James comes up and hooks the lights onto a branch of the tree I couldn't reach.

"Thank you," I reply sheepishly. I'm not sure what has come over me but the simple help he lends touches my heart deeply. Like it heals a small part of me. The fact he noticed my struggle and helped me, it's... What a father should do.

The screen door creaking draws my eyes to the front as Hale walks in. I can see in his face he's stressed about something. His jaw tenses, and his eyes hard but as soon as they meet mine, they soften a touch. He comes up behind me and wraps his arms around my waist and I lean back into him. I see his mom try and fail to hide a smile.

"Oh yay, I was hoping that you all wouldn't put up all the ornaments in my absence," he says sarcastically. His mom rolls her eyes and his dad snickers. I push my hips back into him in a teasing way.

"Yes, we wouldn't want you to miss out on the festivities," I joke.

We begin placing the ornaments while the music plays. Grace goes to the kitchen and pulls out the cinnamon rolls she had placed in the oven earlier and his dad sits on the couch, directing what spots on the tree look bare.

As Grace sets the steaming rolls on the coffee table, Hale sprints to the kitchen, shuffling through a drawer and comes back with a single candle and lighter. "Alright. Here we go."

"Oh please, Hale. We can skip this part." His now bashful mother protests as she sits in James's lap.

"No ma'am, we cannot and will not skip this."

I look between Hale and his mom, waiting for someone to explain and Hale must read the confusion on my face.

"Oh. Right. Okay, today is Ma's birthday. And every year, all she wants and has ever wanted for her birthday is for us to decorate the Christmas tree as a family. She always tries to slide by without us singing but have we ever forgotten?" Hale looks to his mom with a sly grin.

"Unfortunately, y'all have not."

Hale lights the candle that he stuck into a single cinnamon roll and hands it to his mom. "Ready?"

I nod and we break out in song. Grace's smile infects me as she blows out her candle and Hale kisses the top of her head. "Happy birthday, Ma."

"Thank you, sweetie," she says as a tear runs down her face.

"Now for the last and most important part..." James hands me a white and gold Santa hat and the corner of his mouth lifts slightly.

"It's... a tradition that we haven't been able to do in eleven years and we would be honored if you would..." He sniffles as his voice breaks. Unable to finish the sentence, he pinches the bridge of his nose as Grace comes up and wraps her arms around him.

"What dad can't say is that Ivy always topped the tree with the hat. We..." Hale fails to finish the sentence also and I look to Grace.

"We haven't had a daughter in the house in a while, the treetop has sat empty all these years and we would be honored if you would... well, do the honors."

A tear falls down my face as I look down at the simple hat that holds profound meaning. "I would love to but... I can't reach."

"I'll take care of that," Hale says, wrapping his arms under my butt and lifting as he walks us over to the tree. His eyes never leave mine until he nods to the tree, and I turn slightly, hooking the Santa hat atop the tree.

He steps back and lowers me, my hands coming to rest on his shoulders and his lips capture mine. "Thank you," he whispers when he pulls back.

Hale steps into the kitchen and when he returns, he hands me my plate as he winks. One cinnamon roll with glistening white icing dripping down the sides sits there. I wait for my inner voice to warn me off, but it doesn't. Instead, my stomach rumbles and my mouth waters.

I want to eat every bite.

I want to lick the plate clean.

I want to savor every sweet moment of eating this cinnamon roll. And I do.

We sit around the coffee table, drinking our coffee and snacking on treats as the music plays and the surrounding candles light the space, giving the room a warm glow. The winter sun lights up the frosted corners of the windows.

But as I look at Hale, I see his burdened mind. My hand reaches out to him, and he takes it, not even questioning what I am doing. "Dance with me?"

"Of course," he replies without hesitation.

Standing, he pulls me up and right off my feet as he spins me one time and sets me down.

The song that filtered through the house stops and I look at Grace who holds the remote, the song "Surrender" by Natalie Taylor plays, and she winks, walking out of the room with her husband following.

Hale's arm wraps around my waist, and I place my hand in his as we begin to sway. My head falls to his chest, and I close my eyes. The lyrics fill the room and my heart.

"What's wrong?" I finally ask.

"Rafael called. You're going back to Seattle in two days." His voice hardens. I know this isn't easy for him. It's not easy on me either.

"I'll come back to you. You know that right?" I ask as I look into his eyes.

His forehead rests against mine. "No need. I'm going with you."

I stop in my tracks and pull away from him. "You can't." Fear grips my heart, making it hard to breathe.

"You can't stop me," he says as he steps into me, his hands holding my jaw, fingers wrapping in the hair at the nape of my neck.

"It's too dangerous for you. They'll know who you are. They'll kill you on sight, Hale. I can't—"

His lips meet mine as he halts all my fears. "They will not take me from you. Raf and I have a plan."

"You have to let me do this alone." I close my eyes and send a prayer to I don't even know who anymore, whoever will listen, I guess. At this point in my life, I'd happily make a deal with the devil to keep Hale safe.

"I can't do that. Don't you see? I can't leave you. I won't."

"You won't leave me," I repeat, trying to convince myself more than him. He kisses my forehead as my head dips. How can he be so stupid? They will know.

"I will protect you, at all costs. I promise."

"I will protect you," I whisper. As I say the words, a resolve comes over me because I will protect him. No matter what, they won't take him from me. He is my one piece of happiness in this world, and I will do whatever I have to, to keep him. I'll be who they want me to be, the princess, the whore... I'll embrace it all to protect him.

hale

The next morning, Natasha wakes in my arms, her soft skin like velvet brushes against mine as she snuggles closer, and I hold tighter to her.

Inhaling her lavender scent has my cock throbbing and I know she can feel it as a giggle escapes her. "Already excited this morning?" she asks with a lit to her voice.

Squeezing her waist in my large hands, I release the laughter from her fully as I attack her with tickles. "I'm always ready for you, sweetheart." Then I kiss her, her heart pounding against my chest.

"I have something for you."

At my words, her eyes slowly lift from my chest, where her fingernail had been gently tracing soft circles. "You do?"

I stand and walk over to my dresser, pulling the black box from my drawer. When I turn, she's sitting up in bed, holding the sheet up to cover her body. Her blonde hair falls over her shoulder and it's perfectly mussed from sleeping. My favorite version of this complex woman.

I round the bed and come behind her, lifting the gold necklace from the box, I reach over and hold it out in front of her.

A gasp leaves her mouth at the sight of the necklace. An oval pendant hangs on a delicate gold chain. She doesn't know that I had Gage install a tracker in the pendant.

"A sparrow," she whispers as her fingers run over the pendant.

"For my sparrow," I say before kissing the crook between her neck and shoulder. She tilts her head and lets out a soft moan as my lips taste her skin.

Placing it around her neck, I lock the clasp and lift her hair so it hangs as it should around her neck, the pendant landing right at the dip in her throat between her collar bones.

"It's perfect. Thank you," she says as she turns and reaches up to hold my face.

"I'll be right back," I say as I slip out from the bed and head downstairs. I make two cups of coffee and bring them back to our bed.

She greedily eats me up in a pair of gray sweats and then her eyes glow even more when she sees the coffee in my hands. "You're a saint."

Her hands wrap around the warm mug and a hum leaves her throat as she sips it. "You know I've never been much of a coffee person but hearing you when you drink coffee... I might become one," I confess as I lay on the bed.

As if it's instinct to her, she straddles me and settles her body on my hips. While I was downstairs, she slipped on one of my shirts and even though she's average height for a woman, it still drowns her. The soft cotton settles on her hips and hangs loosely around her neck.

Fucking perfection.

Her boy shorts ride up the creases of her thighs and I can see the shape of her pussy through the thin material...

Fuck. Focus, Knight.

"Can I ask you a question?" I say after sipping from my mug.

She shrugs, "You can. Do I have to give an honest answer?"

I tilt my head and narrow my eyes. "Brat," I snide and she gives a sideways smile.

"What's your fascination with birds?" I ask and her eyes drop to her mug that's grasped in her hands.

A few moments pass and I can see a vulnerability in her that wants to come out but I also know she isn't used to letting herself be honest, be raw. I can only hope that when it comes to us, to me, she knows that she's safe.

"When I was a little girl, I felt like I couldn't escape the life I was living. I used to climb to the top of our roof and watch the birds fly around. I was always jealous of them, being able to fly away from anything and everything. I wanted to fly away but I knew I never could."

"Do you still want to fly?"

"I think I'm too scared now," she admits.

"Why?"

Her eyes meet mine. "I'm afraid to fall."

My fingers reach up and brush her hair off her shoulder, then thread to the base of her skull and I bring her close for a kiss. I move slowly to not disrupt the coffee in our mugs but she easily balances the cup as our tongues mix.

When we pull away, her eyes are a bit glassy, and I know how to make her feel better. "Get dressed, sweetheart."

"What? Can't we lay in bed all day?" she protests with a pout, and I shake my head at her.

"Not today."

After we get dressed, I bundle her up, making sure she will be warm enough and I do the same. A beanie covering her braided back hair, a long sleeve shirt, sweatshirt and jean jacket keep her torso warm. Jeans with long stockings underneath and boots for her bottom half. I can't help but admire her ass in a pair of Wranglers. I bite my lip as she bends forward to slip into her boots.

Control, Knight. Find it.

I don't in fact find it as I come up and palm her ass. She shoots up with a giggle and smacks at my chest.

"Excuse you, sir. You're the one who missed his chance on having this ass, naked and in bed with you all day. So, paws off."

Spinning her, I tuck both of my hands into her back pockets and grab her, her ass filling my palms. Her hands come to my chest and her cheeks warm as her eyes dart to my lips. "You're mine, sweetheart, and I don't like being told I can't touch what's mine," I growl at her and although she tries to hold back a smile, she fails.

"I love that I'm yours," she whispers against my lips as she rises on her toes to kiss me.

"Good, cause that's never going to change. Now, let's go. We'll be out for a while."

I hand her a pair of leather work gloves and she puts them on as I do the same. Then, hand in hand, we walk to the horse stables. I go to the last stall and put the halter around Chance, the one horse we can ride here on the ranch.

"What are you doing?" Natasha asks as I clip Chance to the stable ties.

"Will you help me get him ready?" I say, holding a brush out to her. I've seen her brush the horses before, so I know she knows how to do this part and while she brushes him, I check his feet and clean out any rocks.

"What's his story?" she asks as she kisses his muzzle, running the brush down his forehead, between his eyes. His eyes close as he breathes her in with loud, full breaths. All our animals connect with her—it's like her superpower. Maybe they recognize in her the wildness and brokenness that they all have, but either way, these animals care for her as much as she does them.

"Chance didn't come to us for rehab, he was Ivy's. She was a barrel racer, competed in local rodeos and this big guy was her partner. They even won a few competitions but after Ivy came back, she distanced herself from the sport. She still took him out every once in a while but never competed again."

Nat's eyes grow with sadness. "So he sits here and does nothing?"

"There is a little girl who competes on him during the gymkhana season. But mostly, he enjoys his time with the other horses, and I take him out riding each time I visit."

"Is that what you're doing today?" She leans over as I throw the saddle pad onto his back.

"That's what *we're* doing today," I correct her with a smirk on my face.

I swear on my Ma that all the color drains from her face as she looks to the saddle I flung onto Chance's back. As I begin tightening the girth, she stutters out something unintelligible as she collects herself.

Finally, as I take his head from her hands to put his bridle on, she finds her words. "I'm not getting on his back. There's no way."

I laugh at my brave girl being scared of little ol' Chance here. "I promise he's well behaved. I'll ride with you."

She stays quiet as I lead him out of the barn and onto the dirt road. The sun shines directly above us, providing some warmth on this December day. The snow crunches beneath Chance's hooves, yet I don't hear her footsteps following. Turning back to the barn, the stubborn woman stands under the awning. Her arms crossed in defiance.

Tilting my head, I hold my hand to her. "Do you trust me?"

She huffs but then comes out, patting the horse's hind end as she approaches from the back, like I taught her. I trust this bomb-proof quarter horse with her, and he trusts me so he doesn't move a muscle as I guide her foot into the stirrup and then lift her by the waist. She grabs the saddle horn and swings her leg over him like a natural and I can't help but grin.

She looks good up there.

"Slide your foot out, while I get up." She does and I slip my foot into the stirrup as she did and swing my leg over.

For any other horse, I would worry about the weight of us, but Chance is stocky, he can easily take us both. But only for this one short ride. If she enjoys riding, I'll buy me a different horse and she can have Chance.

Shit, why am I thinking as if she will live with me here? I haven't even asked yet...

"What now?" Her voice shakes as I wrap my arms around her, picking up the reins. I squeeze my legs slightly and Chance steps forward.

She gasps and I can't help but chuckle. "I've got you."

The sound of his hooves meeting snow fills the silence as we go up the trail that I usually take him on. There's an open field on top of the hill and that's where I plan to go but I barely have to move Chance in that direction, he loves this trail and knows exactly where we're going.

"Did you grow up riding?" she asks, and I nod. "You're a real cowboy, huh?"

"Nah, we don't herd cattle, and I never did any rodeo, so I don't see myself as a true-blooded cowboy, but I love riding."

"You're good with the animals," she remarks, and I dip my head a bit shyly.

"You are too."

Her laughter fills the cold air. "You think so?"

"Considering my own dog, that I bottle raised from birth has all but forgotten me, I'd say yeah. You're great with the animals. Does ranch life suit the Princess of Boston?"

Her scoff tells me she hates that nickname, and I make a mental note to never use it again.

"I'm not a princess. But I do love being here. I didn't think I would, but I do. It's quiet and makes me feel like I'm not alone."

Chance comes up over the ridge and the flat plain of grass covered in a soft layer of snow comes into view. "You'll never be alone again, Natasha. Are you ready?" I whisper in her ear.

"For what?" Her body tenses a little in anticipation of what's to come.

"To fly," I say, squeezing her tighter between my arms, my hands reaching forward to give Chance more slack and then squeeze my legs tighter. I release him and he takes off in a gallop.

Nat screams initially but then bursts out in laughter as the cold wind hits our face. Chance soars through the field, letting his legs stretch out and as his gait smooths out when he reaches his top speed, Natasha lets go of the saddle horn and stretches her arms out like wings. Her head falls back and laughter like I've never heard bursts from her chest.

I'm amazed by her. At this moment her heart soars, her mind eases, her soul brightens. I hear it in the vibrance of her laugh, see it in the light of her eyes as she looks to the sky.

When I sit back, slowing Chance down, he trots then comes back to a walk. His deep breaths huff out, making clouds of breath leave his nose.

"You don't need to leave the ground to fly, sweetheart."

natasha

T he day has come to leave the ranch, but I know I'll be back. I've found a home at that ranch. It's ingrained into my bones at this point. The amount of growth and healing I've done there in such a short amount of time astounds me.

Now as I step out of the old Ford truck that I once despised, I fight the urge to claw my way back inside and haul ass back down those old roads and never look back.

"Raf." I nod at the always stiff and ever intimidating Italian hit man standing on the tarmac, hands tucked into his pockets per usual.

"Natasha, I trust you have been cared for in our absence?"

"Yes." I look over my shoulder as Hale lifts my suitcase from the bed of his truck. My cheeks heat as he smiles at me. Turning back to Raf, I scold him. "You know this isn't safe."

"Agent Knight... or should I say ex-agent, knows the risks."

Ex-agent? What is he talking about?

"Good morning, Mr. Knight. Leave the baggage, our assistant will get it. Follow me, we have much to discuss." Raf takes the steps up to the private jet as I halt Hale in his tracks with a hand around his bicep.

"Raf said ex-agent, what does he mean?"

He runs his hand down the back of his head, down his neck. "I uh—took a leave of absence. Technically I'm still employed, simply taking an extended break."

"Why would you do that?"

"You needed me more." He grips my face between his hands and leans into me. "I wanted this. Have been wanting it for a long time. Trust me," he encourages but the knot in my chest ladens with guilt. He can't do this for me, he's sacrificing too much.

"What about the deal? Are the twins still willing to give up names if you're not working for the bureau anymore? I know that information was important to you."

Hale places a kiss to my forehead before pulling back and leading me up the steps. "A new deal has been made. Names are still being provided, only to a different man. One we can trust."

I don't acknowledge his answer because honestly it all seems like too much. I'm overwhelmed with the ever changing and moving parts. And to add onto my aggravation, we step onto the aircraft and Enzo greets us with a wicked smile.

"Mr. Knight, a pleasure to see that handsome face again. Principessa, did you enjoy your little fantasy away from the nightmare that is your fiancé?" He turns to the side, letting us by.

The brothers sit across from one another, Hale and I across the aisle, our swivel chairs turned, sitting us in a circle. The waitress delivers two whiskeys to the twins and two waters for Hale and me.

Not a moment later, the jet moves and Hale's hand comes to rest on my leg.

His white button up shirt and black slacks are striking, his over the shoulder gun holsters hold two pistols and I can only hope he won't need to draw them. "Sweetheart, when we get off this plane, to you and everyone else, I'll be your bodyguard. Nothing more. The story's that the twins hired me to keep you safe. You'll need to call me Ace."

"Ace," I repeat, trying it out but it tastes foul coming out. He's my Knight.

"For this to work, *Ace,*" Enzo sneers, "you need to remember your place. You are her bodyguard." His eyes drop to Hale's hand on my leg. "You'll have to keep your hands off what's ours. She stays in either mine or Raf's bed. Understood?"

Hale's jaw clenches and I can see the animal inside him fighting to remain tame. "Understood," he grits out.

Great. This should go well.

"What should I know about your father and his men?" Like the SEAL and agent he was trained to be, he wants to know all the details. But I'm not sure how much the twins are willing to give him. I guess we'll find out.

Enzo looks to Raf who has his ankle resting on his knee, leaning back in his chair, the most relaxed I have seen him to date. "Your call, brother," Enzo remarks.

"Our father is getting impatient. He is under the impression that we've been fucking Natasha since May and he's questioning why she's still not pregnant."

"Why the urgency with a pregnancy?" Hale asks as he looks nervously at me. I can see he hates talking about all this in front of me but on a small plane and with little time left, he must know and it's now or never.

"Sparing all the boring details of the contract between our father and hers, there are two roads for her to go down, but the destination is the same."

"Stop speaking in riddles, Rafael. Speak plainly," Hale says, aggravation pouring from his sharp words.

"Natasha will become an Angel at Cloud Nine. That's our fathers' plans for her. The contract states that once she does, her father will get a quarter of her earnings. If she's unable to give us a son within one year, she becomes an Angel. If she gives us a son, once he is born, she will be sent to Cloud Nine."

"What's Cloud Nine and what's an 'Angel'?" I say quietly, not even sure which question in my mind to ask first.

"Cloud Nine's the underground club that the Alessi family operates. It's where men, women, and children go to be auctioned off. We have been trying to bust it for decades," Hale informs me as his fists clench and his jaw becomes stone.

"And the 'Angels'?"

Raf answers this time. "Angels are girls that are not sold to anyone but kept at Cloud Nine. They are the most sought-after men and women that our clients come to see. When a product is sold, it's a onetime purchase. Angel's, however, bring clients back again and again, creating a steady inflow of money."

"So, I would be an Angel?"

Hale grabs my chin, forcing me to meet his eyes. "I will never allow that," he growls.

"Neither will we, principessa," Enzo confirms, and I can't help but let my eyes bounce back and forth between all three of these men who seem to think they have any control over what happens to me. If I know anything about Dante, it's that he does not take well to having his belongings stolen.

"He isn't going to let me go, even if I give him a grandson?"

Enzo's eyes fall to his drink for a moment then meet mine again. "No, principessa. He isn't."

"In our world, women are used for nothing more than pleasure or reproduction. To our father, all he sees when he looks at you, or anyone for that matter, is what kind of money they can bring him," Raf confirms.

"My father would never allow that. He needs me to give him an heir," I chime in.

Raf draws his eyes from Hale to me. "Natasha, once you are at Cloud Nine, you will get pregnant."

"But Dante wants me to bear your son..."

"Just like with us, our father doesn't care who births the child, only that the Alessi name continues. He will find us a new bride; your father will take your child. That's the deal." Raf takes a sip of the whiskey in his hand.

"Then why me in the first place?" I can't help but ask, to wonder if Dante doesn't care then why did he sell me to the twins?

"Our fathers have a long-standing business relationship. Your father presented the idea to ours and it was a smart choice for them both. The Baldwin name merges with the Alessis', and you know how money works, the more of it, the more power. Through our son, our fathers would live a rich life. Merging a large hotel empire with an underground trafficking operation is all but guaranteed to thrive. If you don't provide us with an heir, our father still gains you as an Angel."

"Fuck." Hale's head turns sharply, drawing his gaze away and out the small window of the plane.

"It gets worse. Unbeknownst to Natasha's father, he will not live past this year. On a drunken night, your father revealed to Dante that if he passes before his heir is born, the business transfers to Natasha."

"That's why Dante wants us married so soon," I chime in as it all begins to come together. "Because if I'm married, the business goes to my husband." Hale looks at me, his brows furrowed. "I've read the marriage contract. Everything I have is Rafael's as soon as I say I do."

"But how are you sure her father won't live past this year?" Hale asks.

"Because our father is going to send us to kill Mr. Baldwin as soon as we marry Natasha."

I can see the wheels turning in Hale's beautiful head, cataloging all this information, trying to piece the puzzle together. "You would allow your father to send Natasha to Cloud Nine?" he asks after a moment.

"Dante is still under the impression that he has us under his thumb. He still believes us to be the dogs that obey any command he gives. To keep his suspicions of our true goals down, we have agreed to send Natasha away once we have a son or once we are married. But," Raf looks to me with a striking seriousness in his eyes, "that's not true, Natasha. We would never allow you to become an Angel. You have our word."

"We play our part well," Enzo adds with a wink.

All this information has my thoughts flying through my mind like a caged bird set free. I knew about the deal with me having to bear a son for both the Alessi and Baldwin line to continue but I didn't know anything about Cloud Nine or the plan to have my father killed.

Could they honestly believe I would willingly go to Cloud Nine? Although, what have I ever done to make them think I would fight? I've laid down like a dog my whole life for my father.

But I'm not that same girl.

The news that the twins plan to kill my father following our nuptials doesn't frighten me, doesn't fill me with sorrow. It's a relief.

One I wish would come sooner rather than later.

"I have already given you more information than you need, however, I will give you one more thing. Enzo and I have been working for years, slowly taking over our father's empire. We have shifted the power to favor us, but we need to be sure that when we strike, we will not miss. Our father is powerful, his reach wide, but trust us when we say, soon, Dante Alessi will be no more."

hale

As we step off the plane, my phone notifies me of a few missed calls – all from Gage. The asshat never bothers me this much, which tells me he found something.

"I have a call I need to return, give me a few?" I ask Raf before he steps into the SUV.

"Enzo." Raf nods and his twin follows me.

"No privacy I take it?"

"Not a chance," Enzo says with a smirk as he nods to my phone. "Make your call. On speaker."

I shake my head and dial Gage; he picks up on the first ring. "Gage, I have Enzo with me, you're on speaker. Seems like they don't trust us."

"Fucking dicks," Gage growls.

"I heard that."

"Obviously, you fucking cunt. I know what speaker phone means."

I shake my head at the size of Gage's fucking balls. "What did you call about?"

"I dug around into Natasha's childhood like you asked and although I didn't find anything obvious, which isn't a surprise considering who her father is, I did find something odd. Her father has high dollar amounts going to a man named Ethan Knowls from around the time Natasha was ten to thirteen. Then again when she was eighteen, in fact it was right around the time her and Everett broke up when we were seniors."

"What stuck out as odd? I'm sure he had many men on his payroll at those times." It's not that I'm questioning Gage, his intuition has never led us wrong, so I trust him, but I want to know what's going on in his head.

"The transactions are written off as tutoring. I've known Natasha since elementary school. She has always been a straight-A student. I think a tutor would be odd for someone like her."

"Maybe that's why she was a straight-A student, good tutor," Enzo remarks.

"No. I don't believe that. Looking into Ethan a bit more, I did a few not technically legal things and found that this Ethan guy, whose real name is Antonio Ricci, works for none other than…"

"Fuck," Enzo says at the same time that Gage says, "The Alessi family."

My eyes fly to Enzo who pinches the bridge of his nose. Looks like I don't need Gage anymore, all my answers are right here in front of me. "Thanks man, talk to you soon."

"Hope not," Gage says before he hangs up.

"Who the fuck is Antonio Ricci?" I say as I grab Enzo by the collar and shove him against the car behind him.

He grabs my wrists and forces me back. "First of all, pretty boy. Don't fucking touch me. Remember we are on the same team."

"Oh, I highly doubt that." I shove him off me and even though I know he could stop me, he allows me to get my anger out. "Explain."

"You're lucky I see that girl you're in love with as a sister or I'd put a bullet between those eyes of yours." He points his finger in my face, and I swat it away. I pace a few feet before finally he answers my question.

"Antonio Ricci, or Ricci as we always called him, was a tutor. But not in academics. He trained our girls."

"Trained them how?" I stop and tilt my head, my muscles bind up.

"To bring in the highest paying clients, you have to have skilled talent. At Cloud Nine, he teaches the men and women how to fuck and be fucked. Simple as that."

"So why the fuck was he going to Natasha's—"

"He was her tutor, I assume," Enzo interrupts.

It hits me like fucking train. Her father paid a man to train her... at ten fucking years old how to... "I'm going to be sick."

"Welcome to our world, *Ace*." Enzo claps his hand on my shoulder and walks back toward the SUV while I hurl up the fucking peanuts I had on the plane. In my time as unit chief, I've seen some fucked up shit, worse than what I now know happened with Nat, but it hits harder knowing it happened to the woman I care for.

I wipe my mouth with my sleeve then walk back to the SUV, once inside, Natasha's eyes catch mine and they are filled with worry. My sweetheart worried for me after everything she has been through.

Fuck.

She's incredible.

"Are you okay?" she mouths and I nod my head.

Enzo was right in welcoming me to his world... because now that I'm on the inside, I'm going to burn it all to the fucking ground.

natasha

The Alessi house, or mansion would be a more accurate term, remains unchanged from the last time I was here a month ago. Except now it's decorated in extravagant Christmas trees and wreaths, and I have to laugh a little at the big, bad mafia boss having his home decorated for such a jolly holiday.

Although, said Christmas trees are black and gold with deep red tinsel dripping down like blood.

This time when we walk through the front doors, Dante awaits us. Clad in an all-gray suit, his eyes lock onto me. When I approach, he takes my hand and kisses the back of it. "Natasha, I hope my sons are treating you well?"

The underlying message clear in the sly tone of his silky voice.

"They are," I reply, never letting my eyes leave his. I will not show weakness in front of this predator.

He stands to his full height, still dwarfing compared to his sons. "Rafael. Enzo," he greets with a cold tone.

"Father," they say in unison and then Dante's narrowed eyes glance over my shoulder to my Knight.

"Who have you have brought into my home?"

Hale doesn't move behind me; his body pressed into mine from behind and he makes no noise or attempt at pleasantries.

"This is Ace. He'll be watching over Natasha. Due to the events last time she was in *your* home, we felt it acceptable to hire someone to be with her in case we are called to other matters."

"Hmm." Dante's eyes narrow with suspicion. "Very well." Dante steps to the side and motions us all in further. "Make yourselves comfortable. Dinner is at eight per usual. Boys, we will meet following dinner to discuss Natasha's future."

We all nod our acceptance and then Rafael comes up and takes my hand, leading me to his room.

After settling in, we meet for dinner which is mostly silent outside of the occasional remark from Dante and one of the twins' responses. None of his men joined us tonight. If there's a God, this would be my time to thank him. I don't think I could sit here with all their eyes on me.

As I pick at my chicken parmesan, my stomach revolts. Not necessarily from the food but from being here in this room again. The red sauce reminds me of all the blood I saw that night.

"Natasha, how are you liking Boston? We didn't get to speak much last time you were here."

"It's a nice city. I enjoy it." I keep my answer short but my eyes steady as I stare into Dante's brown ones.

"I would like to visit you and the boys after the holidays. I'm thinking of venturing further East and with family in Boston, it only seems fitting."

"Your right hand... or should I say left hand man... going to join you, Father?" Enzo smirks and the mafia leader narrows his eyes.

"Thank you for your concern, son," he sneers. "Lorenzo is recovering fine. In fact, I should thank you. He speaks much less often now that he has half a tongue. My right hand was getting a bit too overzealous for my empire."

"I'd be happy to put him in his place anytime, Father, just say the word," Enzo sneers as he forks the entire chicken breast and rips a bite off. Not even using his knife to cut it. "And where is the offender?" he continues.

"On business, currently. I figured with my sons coming home I would have enough protection." Dante's eyes bounce between the twins and they both nod.

"We will always protect you father, you know this." Rafael's replies with confidence.

The rest of dinner consists of small talk about Boston, but I get the feeling this small talk is simply a way to try and trip me or the twins up. Hale stays silent the entire time, assessing the entire dinner with his hands grasped in front of him.

After dinner, I head to my room and change into a sports bra and biker shorts. I haven't boxed in a while, not since I've been on the ranch and my body craves the exercise. I know from last time I was here that Dante has a full gym, including mats on the level below the main one. Hale changes also, following me down when the twins go to their meeting with their father.

Hale stays back as I stretch out first. His eyes slowly peruse my body and said body heats with the look of praise in his gaze. I've put on some weight living at the ranch the last month, but I'm beginning to see that it's a healthy weight. I'm beginning to learn to love my new shape, the fullness of my hips, the strength in my arms and legs from lifting the bales.

Once I'm stretched out, I motion Hale... or Ace toward me. "Care to join? I need a sparring partner."

"You spar?" he questions with a quirk to his brow.

"I know some things." I shrug. "Sabrina had been teaching me before..." My eyes glance to the camera in the corner. Unsure if they have audio or not. "...everything." Hale glances up to the corner of the gym following my gaze.

"If we weren't being watched, I'd put that bratty mouth to use, Natasha," he whispers and I have to curl my lips in to keep my expression neutral.

"Does that mean I have free reign to be as bratty as I want?" I smirk and his eyes darken.

"Let's see what you can do, sweetheart." Hale throws his hands up and I throw a few jabs to get my muscles familiar with the stance and impact. "You're strong and you have good form, but you're too mechanical. Fighting is a dance, you need to flow, be malleable and ready to improvise as your opponent does as well."

When I throw my next hit, Hale bends down and grabs me by the waist, digging his shoulder into my stomach. He takes me down to the mats and settles between my legs. "Gotcha." He smirks and I use the maneuver B showed me to get out of this position.

I scramble to my feet while he gets up just as fast. Now that he's seen I'm not as weak as I seem, his eyes sparkle with mischief. "Oh, this is going to be fun, baby."

With that, he comes at me, and I block each jab and kick he throws at me. I know he isn't throwing all his power behind them or even moving as fast as I know he can, he's going easy on me, and I hate it. Throwing all my strength into my own hits, he easily swats me away as if I'm an annoying little kitten. I'm panting and screaming out my pain and he chuckles.

Black spots filter into my vision when he captures me in a head-lock, his strong arms wrapped around my neck and his hard chest pressed to my back. My own chest heaves whereas his moves easily and slowly, he hasn't even broken a sweat against me.

"Damn you," I grit out.

From behind, he kicks the back of my knee, collapsing my leg and I fall to one knee in front of him as he releases my throat. He stalks around me slowly before standing in front of me and gripping my chin with one hand, he tilts my head up to meet his eyes. "So pretty on your knees for me, baby."

"Screw. You." I narrow my eyes and throw all my remaining fight into my voice.

The door slamming behind me draws my attention to the man who walked in. Enzo walks with a confidence that engulfs the entire room as he approaches us and stands next to Hale, both these men looking down on me fills me with rage even though I know neither would ever hurt me.

I stand on shaking legs and lift my hands. "Two on one? Let's go," I challenge, and Enzo laughs while Hale shakes his head.

"Easy tiger. Let's take a break," he chuckles as he makes his way over to the bench to sit. My gaze moves to Enzo who has a fire inside his eyes.

"I've been watching you two. Ace is holding back, and you..." He steps up to me and places his hands on my wrists, lowering them to get a better look at my eyes. "You're relying too much on your sight. You need to listen to your gut. Your instincts."

He spins me quickly, his arms crossing and pinning me to his chest. "Time to fight like an Alessi, principessa," he whispers in my ear then releases me.

Pulling a handkerchief from his pocket then stripping his jacket off, he rolls his shirt sleeves then steps behind me. I stand still, my heart pounding in my chest but I won't let him see my fear. He wraps the piece of cloth around my head, covering my eyes and relinquishing me of my sight.

"Enzo...what are you—"

"Shh. You're watching your opponent too much, you need to learn to anticipate their moves based on feeling. Not sight."

"How am I supposed to know—" My voice halts when a presence comes up behind me. He isn't touching me, but I know he's still there.

"Just like that," Hale whispers from behind me and goosebumps race up my spine. "Listen to the sounds around you. Feel the shift in the air. What do you hear?"

Even though I have the cloth over my eyes, I close them and listen. "Heavy breathing. In front and behind me. Yours is a bit faster." I turn my head, directing my voice toward Hale.

"Good girl. What else?" As he says it, their footsteps move, circling me. The mats squish beneath their feet. It's almost quiet enough I don't hear it and if I had my sight, I probably wouldn't have.

"You're moving."

"Who is?" Enzo says, now from behind me but Hale's body heat seeps into my skin from my front now.

"Both of you."

They both remain silent, and I know I've answered correctly when I feel them step closer, I let my instincts guide me as I step to the side to avoid being pinned between them. Hale chuckles and then his smooth voice fills my ears. "She's a fast learner."

"That she is," Enzo says and I swear I hear a bit of pride in his voice.

I smirk at their praise, feeling more confident in this exercise. But before I can get too cocky, hands grab me from behind and I curse myself for getting distracted because I didn't hear who moved or from where. I'm pushed into a chest as a different set of large hands wrap around my waist. Then a hand comes up and cups my cheek, warm breath hits my lips...

"Enzo," I whisper and then his chest vibrates with a chuckle. I would know Hale's touch even in death. Enzo backs away and Hale comes up behind me but it's not slow, he's moving with intention as the air shift and before he takes me down, I spin to the side and his arm catches my waist. I elbow him in the stomach which he takes easily, only a slight grunt leaving his lips behind me. I maneuver myself behind him and take his knees out, as he did to me earlier. Slowly, I lift my hands to his shoulders and follow them around, before I remove the blindfold, I know I'm standing in front of him.

Pulling it from my head, I look down into his blue eyes and run my fingers through his beard, resting my hand on his cheek. "So pretty on your knees for me, baby," I whisper.

"Only for you."

hale

The days have been quiet since we arrived, but tonight the Alessis' Christmas Eve Gala will bring in all the dirty fuckers who work for Dante as well as his top clients.

Throwing my gun holster over my shoulders, I slip into it and make sure both my Sigs are loaded. Habit and paranoia make me check my back holster to ensure my extra clips are secure. Then I throw on the black suit jacket and fix my tie in the mirror before heading to Rafael's door to collect Natasha. Rafael and Enzo are already downstairs because being the devils of Seattle requires their full attention at these events, but I'm not complaining. That means I get Natasha to myself.

I knock on Rafael's bedroom door, knowing she's inside getting ready.

"One minute," she calls and I wait patiently.

My heart races. Something's going to go down tonight, given the party and its guest list of psychopaths. I'm on edge and some would call it nerves but I know better. My instincts4 are talking to me and I'd be stupid not to listen.

The door opens and my jaw clenches at the fucking world-shattering woman standing in front of me. Her long black dress hugs her breasts and waist then spills down her hips. A slit in the dress comes up to her mid-thigh, giving me a peek at her perfect, long legs. Her shoulders are bare despite the long sleeves of the black gown and crystals that look like diamonds line the neck of the dress. With each breath she takes, her breasts push against the restricting fabric and all I want nothing more than to lean down and kiss her flesh.

"You... Fuck. You're going to make me kill someone tonight, sweetheart."

She giggles like I'm kidding.

I'm not kidding.

Her blonde hair has a soft wave to it, both sides tucked behind her ears and large diamond studs bringing out the sparkle in her eyes. Her lips are painted red, and I can only imagine that they must taste as delicious as they look.

In fact, fuck my imagination, I want a real taste. But not of those delicious lips, of another...

Stepping into the room, my body pushes hers back and the look of what-the-fuck-are-you-doing crosses her face as I smirk. "You forgot to buckle your shoe," I lie and kneel, unlatching the silver clasp of her red-bottom heels.

"No, I didn—" She pauses when she sees me unbuckle it then smiles. "Hale..."

"Yes?" My hands run slowly up her calf then up to the back of her thigh, as I leave small kisses on her skin. Her head tilts back as she begins to pant, a small gasp leaving her as I kiss her inner thigh.

I tuck my head under her dress and run my nose up her center.

"We're going to be late," she protests, but I don't care.

"They can wait," I growl as I lift one of her legs and place it over my shoulder. Her standing leg doesn't even wobble in the high heels. Pushing her panties to the side with my nose, I run my tongue up her center, parting her and finally tasting what I've been craving.

Her.

"Hale." Her breathy moan makes my cock twitch. Fingers dig into my hair as she begins to move against my mouth. She's in control right now, riding my face like the good fucking girl I know she is.

Her muscles tense and I know she's close. Sliding two fingers into her pussy, she clenches around them as my tongue sucks her clit. So fucking delicious.

Pulling back to watch her, her brows furrow and her perfect mouth pops open as she tries to reach heaven. My fingers curl and my thumb circles her clit, "Eyes on me baby."

Her lust filled gaze meet mine and because I know she needs this; I encourage her with my words to let go. "Whose fingers are you riding?"

"Yours."

"Whose tongue did you fuck?"

"Yours," she whispers again, keeping those siren irises on me.

"Who do you belong to?"

"You!" she screams as her pussy grips my fingers and she throws her head back. My mouth finds her once again and I happily suck down her release. She tastes as sweet and sharp as her attitude and I fucking love it.

The fact she stood through all of that, on one leg no less, has me impressed but that's nothing new, I'm always impressed with her. She's unlike anything I've ever come across.

Wiping my face with my shirt sleeve, I lower the leg draped over my shoulder. She's catching her breath, looking down on me with burning eyes. When I go to stand, she stops me with her heel to my chest and her perfectly arched brow lifts. "My shoe, *Ace*."

Looking down, I realize I never re-clasped her heel and so I do, then leave a kiss on the top of her foot.

"Such a good boy for me," she praises with a flirtatious smile, and I swear my heart stops.

Fuck, I love to see her take control. To watch her take what's hers, the "what" in question being my heart. Standing, our arms link together as I lead her out of the room. Her lavender scent fills my lungs, and I contemplate running away with her right now, but I know we wouldn't get far. Dante would never give up his prize Angel. Little does he know, I'd die before she became an Angel, and I know my girl's wild enough that she would follow me into the afterlife to keep from letting another man use her like that again.

Winding down the staircase, Enzo and Raf meet us at the bottom. Raf remains silent but Enzo whistles and bows in a formal way to her. "Our queen." He smiles at her, and she rolls her eyes.

"Let's get this night over with, shall we?" Rafael holds his arm out and I reluctantly place her hand around his arm.

I walk behind them, never letting my eyes leave my woman who's attached to another man's arm.

When we enter the space, everyone looks toward us... No, toward her. I can't blame them; she could captivate a city. Their eyes don't deserve to look upon her. A sudden urge to kill every person in this room washes over me and I clear my throat and shake my head in an attempt to rein in my violence.

Standing against the wall of the grand ballroom housed inside this mansion, Nat picks at her food. The dirty eyes of multiple men trail up and down her body and I fight to restrain the animal inside me that wants to tear them limb from limb. Funny, I've never been a possessive man but with her, all cards are off the table. I find myself, for the second time this evening, barely holding onto my control.

When dinner ends, the tables are cleared, and people begin mingling and continuing to drink. It doesn't go unnoticed by me or the other men in this room that Natasha's the only woman here and I have to wonder to what end?

Enzo walks up, standing next to me, whiskey in hand as he watches her while she dances with his brother. He slowly sways her, one hand on her waist, the other holding her hand. She occasionally smiles at something he says.

"Where are the other women, Enzo?"

"They will be coming. My father never hosts a party without pussy. He needs to show his most recent possession off first."

"I don't like it," I grit out.

"I don't either but there's a fine line we must walk. He has to believe he's still in control." The ice in Enzo's drink clinks as he finishes off the whiskey.

"How many men in this room are aligned with your father?"

"None of them," he confirms. "None of these men will touch Natasha. She's been claimed by Raf. That was established the last time she was here."

"What does that mean? Claimed? And how can you blindly trust that these men will honor that?"

"I do. Because they're our men. Our father doesn't know it, but he's a little rabbit amongst wolves right now. Our wolves."

I sneer as Rafael leans in and kisses Natasha softly. A growl releases from my chest and Enzo's hand finds my shoulder.

"Easy, Ace. We all have a part to play, remember?"

"Let me get this straight, none of these men belong to your father. Have you and Raf completely taken over his empire from underneath him?"

"Not yet. Dante still has some powerful contacts who are loyal. But none of them are here tonight."

Before I can say more, Dante walks up to Rafael and Natasha, a man in a black suit in tow, taking her hand, he stands in the middle of the room. Rafael stays firmly rooted to the hardwood floor behind her, watching the crowd that has now silenced in anticipation of their don speaking.

"Gentleman, for those of you who have yet to be introduced, I wanted to let your eyes feast on my son's fiancée, I would like to formally welcome you... to their wedding." Enzo and Rafael's spines both straighten, and Rafael's eyes meet his brother's. A slight narrowing of his eyes tells me this announcement came unexpectedly. A palpable shift occurs in the room and that one word hangs in the air.

Wedding.

"What did Dante do?" I seethe at Enzo whose eyes have turned murderous.

"He moved up our timeline."

natasha

Dante's sly smile makes me want to retch but I hold back my gag reflex, something I've been trained well to do. "Wedding?" I ask.

"Ah yes, I'm tired of waiting. I want what is owed to me and yet, you enter my home with a flat stomach. If I must put a baby in you myself, Natasha, I will. The next time you enter my home; your whore body better be swollen with my grandchild. Until then, I'll take your daddy's empire."

"Rafael would never allow you to rape me."

"My sons will do as they're told. And so will you. You will marry my son tonight, but it will be me you find in your bed, sweet Natasha."

My stomach turns and I focus on breathing in through my nose, holding back the vomit that threatens to rise. I must maintain my mask, if I show any indication I'm scared, I know that Hale will die to protect me and that I cannot have. I'm put in a position where I must bow down enough to seem malleable and meek but keep my eyes high enough for the dogs surrounding me to know that I will fight when pushed.

"Rafael, take your bride's hands," Dante commands and Rafael listens. His large hands hold mine in a punishing grip, but his eyes are gentle as they promise everything will be okay.

The priest comes to stand next to us, ironically, he flips open a bible and before he can begin, Raf speaks up. "We are set to marry in June, father."

"You marry her now or my men will use her till the day you do marry, Rafael. Your choice."

Raf looks at me, his jaw tightening and his eyes begging for forgiveness. "Fine. But once she's my wife, I say when I'm done with her. Understood?"

Dante smiles, knowing he got what he wanted, manipulating Rafael with my body to force the marriage sooner. My heart beats out of my chest and my stomach twists. Is this happening?

A loud clap sounds as Dante smiles. "Very well then."

My mind clouds as the man in the black suit says something but it all sounds like I'm listening from underwater. My vision tries to focus on Rafael, but it's going in and out. I only seem to come to my senses when Rafael's hand holds my cheek and he leans in, kissing me slowly. I meet his kiss with tears running down my face because I'm officially an Alessi.

After the kiss, Raf wipes the tears from my cheeks as he whispers in my ear, "It will be okay. I promise."

"A dance! To celebrate the newlyweds," Dante exclaims as music plays and Rafael pulls me close. He spins me around the dance floor, eyes of all the men staring at me. My body wants to crawl out of its skin.

"Rafael."

Before I can finish, Enzo steps in. "May I have the next dance, my lady." He bows and I nod my head.

"Of course."

When Enzo takes me by the waist, he's closer than Rafael and when he looks at a fuming Hale and winks, I know it's simply to piss him off. "Can you not antagonize him? I'm sure this is already difficult for him."

"Hey, he wanted to join our threesome, not my fault if he can't handle all the love."

"Enzo," I chide and he chuckles.

"But in all seriousness, principessa. Raf and I will fix this. You won't be married to my less-handsome brother for long."

"I don't know what to do. How are we going to get out of this—"

"Son," Dante's deep voice interrupts and my blood runs cold. "I believe it's my turn. Come Natasha, dance with your father-in-law. It thrills me to finally have you part of the family."

That sick bastard. He gets off on this, doesn't he? Wanting to fuck me and call me family. I swallow hard, choking back tears and vomit as I play my part and take his hand.

Dante's hold is tighter than Enzo's. "I'm looking forward to finally getting a piece of what I've been looking at since you were little, Natasha. But you're going to be such a good girl for me, aren't you? Ricci trained you well, his reports back to me were always so... detailed."

Ricci? Who the hell is Ricci? The only person who comes to mind would be the tutor my father hired all those years... he worked for Dante?

The monster before me leans in as if he's going to kiss me and I close my eyes and turn my head. His lips meet my neck, and my mind and body go numb. I block out every touch against my skin like I used to.

But when my eyes open, my gaze lands on Hale and my heart sinks.

hale

If a single man in this room lays a hand on her, their life is mine. I will sell my soul to the devils before I allow her to be touched against her will ever again. Dante's dancing with her now, Enzo back at my side, holding me back from tearing that vile man limb from limb as he holds my woman.

But then his lips meet her neck.

Her broken eyes, the same vacant ones I've come to know too well meet mine.

A mask of numbness she wears to separate her mind and her body.

No. More.

Never. Again.

Not for her.

"Ace. Control yourself—" the twin to my side reminds me, but then Dante's hand grabs her jaw and turns her lips toward his. His fingers dig into her flawless skin, claws that have captured my stunning sparrow.

"Fuck it," I say as I stride toward her. I pull my Sig from my holster and rest it against Dante's temple before his lips meet hers. "Your lips touch her skin one more time, your brain meets the fucking wall," I grit through closed teeth.

Ten men surround me, all guns pointed but I couldn't give two fucks. He will not touch her. Dante smiles down at her, pausing. He leans in and Nat's eyes flash toward me and the fear I see in them burns the last remaining feathers of my wings to ash.

I pull the trigger.

Blood covers her face as Dante Alessi's body hits the floor and I push her back into Rafael's arms, ready for my life to end by one of the guns pointed at me.

"Hale!" Her scream fills my ears as I take my last look at my girl.

But nothing happens. No guns fire.

"Fucking shit. Do you know how long I've been dreaming of doing that." Enzo walks up to me, hands tucked into his pockets as he looks down at his father's body. With a wave of his hand, all the men back off, lowering their guns. "You've surely made a mess, Ace."

Natasha runs forward and I catch her in my arms, her tears are falling fast as she begins to hyperventilate. "It's okay. It's okay," I reassure her as I stroke her hair.

"You're—" she hiccups, "such a fucking idiot!"

Looking around the room, all the men are gathered, Rafael speaking with them, already doing damage control. Enzo was right, all these men are loyal to the twins. Thank fuck, because although I was ready to die for this woman, I still want a life with her.

"Idiot for sure. But he's an idiot I respect the hell out of," Enzo says as he claps my shoulder. "But now you're an idiot I have to hide because word of this will reach my father's loyal men, and they'll want revenge. Ready to go into hiding?"

"I'll go back to the ranch, stay out of Boston. They don't know who I really am. I'll be fine."

"You willing to risk your family, Ace? Because I wouldn't be so sure these men won't find out who you are."

Contemplating his question, I can't say I am willing to risk it. If it were me alone, sure but I can't risk my parents. "Where will I go? And for how long?"

Rafael comes up to us now, toeing his father's cold fingers before signaling for one of his men to remove the body.

"Ace, you killed the leader of the Alessi Mafia. In order to protect you, Enzo will be taking you to one of our safe houses. You will hear from us shortly. When we have eliminated the last remaining loyalist to my father, we will let you go. But until then…"

"I won't leave Natasha," I protest. They'd have to be fucking crazy if they think I'll leave her with them.

Okay, they are fucking crazy but—

"Hale. I need you. Therefore, I need you to be safe," Her hand holds my cheek, and her brown eyes beg me to give in. "Please."

"She'll be safe?" I ask Enzo and Raf, knowing they live by their word.

"We would never let any harm come to her, you have my word, Ace," Rafael confirms and I look back to Natasha one more time. She nods and I let go of my sparrow yet again.

natasha

After Enzo took Hale, Raf led me upstairs to his bed where he helped me out of my dress, and I showered. My face and chest were covered with blood splatter and for the second time, I sat in a tub with red running down the drain.

When I finish, a soft, cream cashmere set of pajamas sits on the counter. After brushing my hair and braiding it, I open the door to find Rafael sitting on the bed. He looks defeated and tired. Does he ever get any rest?

"Rafael, what happens now?" I ask as I sit next to him on the bed and he turns his head, looking at me with a steady gaze.

"Now, we head to Oregon. We need to meet with your father. Notify him of the power change and terminate the contract him and our father made. We set you free, Natasha."

Silence fills the room as I take in his words. "You're going to... terminate the contract. I won't..."

"You will be free to be who you want to be. And to be with who you want. I already have my lawyers working on divorce papers."

He talks about freedom, but I'll never be truly free. Not if my father lives. He will always demand an heir.

"Hold on the papers. If my father dies, since we are married, you get his empire. Right?"

Raf's brows furrow. "That's correct."

"Then let's go to Oregon, but I don't want you to terminate the contract. I want you to terminate him. I want his empire to belong to you and I want you to tear it to shreds. I want my mother to be left with nothing and then I want to marry Hale and live in peace on the ranch. Can you make that happen, Rafael?"

A slow grin spreads over his rugged face. "Look at you, spoken like a true Alessi."

***

The next morning, Enzo, Rafael and I boarded their private jet and took a short flight to Portland. My body and mind were exhausted, and I slept the entire flight but now that we are in a car heading to my parents, my stomach clenches.

But I'm not nervous about what I asked Rafael to do. After everything my parents put me through, death is a mercy for my father and my mother will suffer for the role she played. She was not naive to all my father put me through.

I don't want any of this drug out. I want it to be over, I want to move on, I want to be with Hale, I want to have his children, I want to be his wife. For the first time in my life, I know exactly what I want. But I wonder if Hale could ever feel that sense of peace.

He's lost more than anyone should have to... he lost his twin sister to the same world I'm part of.

I capture Rafael's eyes with mine, asking him the question I want to know most. "If Enzo ever died, what would you do?"

Without hesitation, his deep voice reverberates through the small, enclosed space. "Find the person responsible, slowly skin them alive and remove every digit and extremity from their body with a dull saw blade, cauterizing each wound, ensuring they wouldn't bleed out, then burn their body with acid down to the bone, but only a little at a time to drag it out. After I burned through their sternum, I'd take their heart in my hands and squeeze till it no longer beat. Then I'd take a gun and put a bullet through my own head. Why?"

"Jesus." I didn't expect that... "I... just wondering."

"Planning on killing me, principessa?" Enzo leans in and gives me one of his famous playboy smirks and I swat him away.

"No. I just..." I hesitate, wondering if I should share Hale's story but I know they could easily look all this up themselves if they haven't already. "Hale had a twin, and she died. I was curious, I guess, if all twins felt that strongly for one another."

The brothers make no comment about what I shared with them; they only look at one another. A silent conversation occurring between them.

Rafael answers again, "I can't speak for Hale and his twin, but if I ever lost my brother, it would be worse than hell. If anyone ever hurt Enzo, I would delight in their misery and personally hand deliver not only their torture but their death as well."

"What is it with you and Hale? Is this a sweet little fuck-fest or are you in love with him?" Enzo asks, leaning back casually in the black leather seat across from me.

The answer to his question doesn't come easily though... it feels deeper than love but it's also new. I never expected to feel as taken by the man as I am and I'm not sure how to process it all. I feel more for him than I have anyone else. He's made me realize that what I had with Everett wasn't love.

"It's... undefinable," I settle on and Enzo nods.

"And what about you and Sabrina?" I smirk but his face grows hard. He loses the jovial, sarcastic air about him. In an instant, Raf's eyes flick up from his iPad, acutely tuned in to the new topic of discussion.

"I don't know a Sabrina," Enzo grits out and my eyes roll.

"Oh stop. Five foot nothing little red head that can put you on your ass with her attitude alone? Ring a bell?"

"If I ever met a woman like that, I'd lock her in my basement and never let her leave."

What in the hell is he saying? There's no way he has forgotten her, the two were electric.

"Oh, come on, you have to—"

"Natasha." Raf's harsh tone stops my protestations. "Leave it," he warns, and I do.

Whatever, it's not in me to keep up with Enzo and his crazy ass. I'll leave it for now and check in with B to see if she knows why he's being weird.

No one speaks the remainder of the drive, Rafael on his phone, Enzo passed out, snoring next to me and me, looking out the window, watching the Oregon trees pass by. A light layer of sleet covers the streets.

Raf and Enzo are staying with my father, our true intentions unbeknownst to him, who has plenty of space in our home. Although it's not as extravagant as the Alessi mansion, it still has eight bedrooms, a formal dining, sitting, and living room, an indoor pool and gym, and of course ten bathrooms and a kitchen larger than most Boston apartments.

When we arrive, my mother and father greet me with fake pleasantries, and I don't have the stomach to conform.

"Please, don't pretend you care. Either of you." I bounce my eyes back and forth between my parents and then look back to Raf. "Can I show you where you'll be staying?"

He nods and both twins follow me through the front doors. I lead them to the two vacant rooms that bracket my own on the East side of the house. Luckily, my parents stay in the west wing.

The boys go into the room I showed Raf to have some meeting I'm sure and I make my way to the kitchen to see if Darla, our cook, is still in.

Even though it's Christmas day, she's busy in the kitchen preparing dinner. "Darla, my father didn't give you today off?"

The robust, short woman with curled auburn hair neatly tucked back and in a clip, spins as she hears my voice. "Oh, my sweet girl. Welcome home." She wraps me in a hug, keeping her flour covered hands away from my body. "And no, has he ever given me a day off?"

"I suppose not. Can I help you?"

Her eyes blow wide and a smile graces her elderly face. "Of course. I'm breading the chicken. Can you chop the vegetables?" Her head nods to the carrots and green beans on the counter and I begin without further instruction.

I wasn't grateful enough growing up in this house for Darla. Yet despite my sour attitude, she always greeted me with a smile. She always asked with genuine interest how I was. I think deep down she knew a small portion of what my parents were forcing me to do and maybe if I wasn't such an awful human back then, I could have opened up to her. Seen her for what she was always trying to be for me—a safe space.

Before I can finish chopping a single carrot, my phone rings and I pull it out to see an unknown number flash across the screen. My heart jumps into my throat.

I answer quickly as I step away from the kitchen, giving Darla an apologetic smile and Hale's voice fills my ear. If I wasn't already about to sit on one of the stairs, I would have fallen to my knees at the relief my mind and body experienced.

"Hale. Are you okay?"

"I'm good, sweetheart. I was more worried about you."

I glance around and although I'm alone, I don't trust my father to have cameras or listening ears. "Can I call you back in ten minutes. I... can't talk here."

"If you don't, I'll be blowing up Rafael's phone which I don't think he will appreciate. You're on a timer, baby."

I hang up and head to the garage where I can borrow one of my father's cars. Shooting a quick text to Enzo, I tell him where I'm going and head out before he responds. I know I'll be safe where I'm headed, there's no need for them to worry. No one will touch me in this town; they all know who my father is and who his friends are.

I pull up into the small parking lot of Mill's Coffee House. The little coffee shop is a local favorite, but I haven't been here since middle school when the old man kicked me out after me and my girlfriends were picking on Leora Laney.

I remember that day vividly. I had seen Everett watching her in class, a smile on his face that he never had with me, and I was jealous. I was also a kid, a kid whose only safe space was on the verge of being ripped from under her feet. My young mind thought that tearing her down would make me feel more secure.

I was wrong.

So many times, I was wrong.

As I walk through the door, a bell rings out and I look around to find it's empty. I guess most people would be home with their families on Christmas. Why isn't he?

"Be out in a minute," his deep voice calls from the back and I find a seat at one of the back tables. He stands at the counter, leaning over and raises a brow. "You order at the counter, miss. I'm no waiter."

I dial Hale on my phone as I approach the counter and order while it rings. "A coffee, black. Please."

I slide my card over, but he places his hand atop mine, "On the house. Merry Christmas." I nod as Hale answers.

"Nine minutes and thirty-six seconds. Cutting it close, sweet-heart."

A smile blooms across my face at the sound of his voice and then take my mug from the old man, walking it back to the booth. "I love to keep you on your toes."

The first sip of the coffee makes me let out a small moan, it's incredibly sweet for being straight black and it's smooth. It goes down with no bitter aftertaste. "Jesus, that's good."

"What the hell's making you moan?" His voice carries an edge, and I giggle at his jealousy.

"Coffee. Calm down, cowboy."

"Better be."

I take one more sip and then explain what happened after he left. He tells me that Enzo took him to a safe house in Boston and gave him a phone to use so he could call me. I can't believe Enzo delivered Hale to Boston and made it back in time this morning to be here. But who knows, maybe the man doesn't sleep.

"And now you're in Portland. They are going to kill your father, aren't they?"

"They weren't but... I suggested it. I'll never be at peace with him alive, Hale. Does that make me a bad person?"

"I think he's getting exactly what's owed to him, baby. Don't you dare feel an ounce of guilt. You understand me?"

"Yes." Ready to ask him about me moving to live on the ranch, my gaze draws to the bell dinging above the coffee shop door.

A man in a dark coat and dress slacks comes into the shop and the old man greets him. But the mystery man ignores the owner and locks eyes with me.

My instincts tell me something's wrong. That I need to run. "Hale."

"Yeah, baby?"

"Stay on the phone." As I pull the phone from my ear, the soft murmur of Hale asking 'why' drowns out when I shove the phone under my thigh as the man comes and sits in front of me.

"Are you Natasha Baldwin?" His eyes are bright blue and his hair a platinum blond, skin porcelain. He would be quite beautiful if his eyes didn't spell danger. My heart pounds in my chest, urging my muscles to move but I'm frozen.

Looking over the man's shoulder, I see the owner watching, his eyes wary. He must see something in my own because he begins to walk toward us.

"I asked you a question," the mystery man persists.

"I... I don't know who Natasha is," I lie through my teeth but he smirks. Before I can blink, he pulls a gun from his jacket and the cold tip of the muzzle meets my forehead and as it does, the muzzle of a pistol meets the stranger's temple from the side.

I follow with my eyes from the gun to the old man holding it. "You best be going, son. I don't take kindly to bullies in my shop," the owner says with a calmness that feels impossible.

"This business doesn't concern you, old-timer. Go to the back and you won't get hurt," the man with the icy eyes warns and my eyes meet a similar set of blue eyes as I look at the owner. I don't want him hurt but I'm at an utter loss. What should I do? What can I do?

"It's been a while since I've killed a man, but make no mistake, I won't hesitate."

The mystery guy turns his head, guns still trained on me as he stares down the owner of the shop. Damn, I wish I knew his name... "I've got a job to do here, don't waste my time. You're not my target so I suggest you back the fuck up before I end your miserable life."

"If I go, I'm taking you with me." The two men are in a standoff and his gun still rests against my forehead, but I have no doubt he could easily turn it on the old man.

I don't know why he's willing to risk his life on someone who happened into his shop, a stranger, but he is. My eyes fill with tears as I'm suspended, frozen in the moment and feeling completely useless. Hale screams but I can't clearly make out what he's saying.

"I'll see you in hell, old man." The mystery man smirks, knowing that when he kills me, he'll also get a bullet to the head, and I know he's seconds from pulling the trigger. He doesn't care about his own life, as long as he takes his target down with him.

"Don't save me a seat, I'll be in Valhalla."

Bang.

I close my eyes as warm liquid splatters my face for the second time in less than twenty-four hours. My ears ring and my entire body shakes as I open my eyes to see the old man standing stock still.

The man who threatened my life falls forward onto the table and I...

I...

I...

"NATASHA!" Hale's voice pulls me from my trance, but I can't make my body move.

Someone pulls the phone from under my leg and the old man's says something. He's right next to me but his words don't translate in my head. I can't take my eyes off the pool of blood reaching toward me as it grows. Closer and closer. I don't move my fingers as the warmth seeps between them as if I were dipping them into a jar of warm honey.

The jingle of the bell.

Enzo's mischievous timber.

Rafael's calm vibrato.

My paralyzed body screams for release as my mind vibrates with fear. I can't move no matter how many signals I send to my muscles.

The shopkeeper presses his warm, large hand to my cheek, guiding my head to turn. "Natasha." I meet glacial blue eyes framed by wrinkles, and I suck in a breath like I've broken the surface after drowning. In a single second, all the voices rush in.

"Principessa, what the fuck did you do?" Enzo kicks the dead man's leg.

"It wasn't me... he... he was going to kill me."

Rafael and Enzo begin speaking at the same time, both asking me different questions and I find myself drifting again. Rafael scolds me for leaving without one of them, Enzo asks me what the man said when he showed up. It's all too much.

"What is it about you? This is the second man to kill for you in a span of twelve hours."

"I think she needs to rest, gentleman." The old man's deep, gravelly voice settles me.

"Who the fuck are you, anyway?" Enzo asks.

"You can call me Ski." With not a single ounce of fear in his voice, he stands and faces the twins. His old, battered yet strong frame acting as a barricade between me and them.

Silence hangs in the air a moment, then Rafael extends his hand and Ski eyes it carefully before deciding to shake it.

"Thank you, Ski. We'll handle this mess. Do you have a shower she could use perhaps?"

Ski simply nods before extending his hand to me and I take it, following him to the back. I don't know why, but my heart instantly trusts the shop owner and it goes deeper than the fact that he saved my life... it's an instinct I choose to listen to.

natasha

S ki leads me to a back room and up a narrow set of steps. I enter a cozy and quaint studio apartment. It's funny how much detail I notice about the small studio considering everything still feels a bit numb. Like I'm floating outside my body.

Two men have died mere inches from me. Their blood soaked my hair. Their lives gone, because of me.

But strangely, that's not what twists my stomach in knots and constricts my heart with fear.

No. It's the fact that a man tried to kill *me*.

Even though I've been treated like a whore my entire life, I was needed at least. My life had never been in danger because if I was dead how would my father use my body?

But this stranger, he held a gun to my head, ready to put a bullet in my brain...

There have been two times in my entire life I've felt scared of death. Once when I stood on the rooftop of a historic hotel and a man stood next to me. I looked into his eyes and knew if I went over, he would follow.

And the second, a few minutes ago.

"Natasha, the shower's ready for you. Why don't you go get that blood off. I'll get you something else to wear," Ski says as he motions me toward the small bathroom to the left of the door. I blindly follow his orders and when the warm water hits my skin, I turn it hotter, and the red-stained water washes down the drain.

After my shower, I find a gray crewneck and sweatpants on the bathroom vanity. I roll the sweatpants and pull the string so tight, almost breaking it. My fingers run through my hair and I take a quick glance in the mirror, then exit and make my way down to the coffee shop.

When I round the corner from the back office, a deep red stain on the tile is all that remains of the mess I created.

Enzo and Rafael are speaking with someone in a blacked-out SUV outside of the front door and Ski sits in a booth at the back, sipping a cup of hazelnut coffee based on the warm aroma. I decide to go sit with him, but I couldn't say why my feet drew me to him. I guess there's something comforting about the old man.

"Feel better?" he asks as I slid into the booth, placing myself in front of him. My eyes meet the old wood table, seeing the names Everett and Leora carved into the wood and a small laugh escapes me at the irony.

"I do. Thank you for the shower."

He nods, takes a sip and stares out the window again.

"Why..." I fiddle with my fingers, nervous to ask. "Why did you do that for me?"

He shrugs. "I don't like bullies. And I sure as hell wasn't going to let an innocent woman be killed in my shop."

Another little laugh escapes me. "I'm not innocent."

"None of us are, I suppose," he says, still not looking at me.

"Do you know who I am?"

He nods and I let the silence fill the space between us. "You're Natasha Baldwin. I kicked you out of my shop many years ago for bullying my Leo."

He does remember me. Letting out a small sigh, my eyes meet the table again, feeling a sickening amount of shame for how I acted back then. "Yeah, that's me."

He finally turns to look at me and his eyes are full of understanding. "No, I don't think it is. That *was* you, it's not who you are today."

I'm not sure what to say, choosing instead to hold his stare.

When a small smirk graces his aged face, I can't help but mimic that same smirk. "You know, I fell in love with a girl like you once, a long time ago. She was always worried about pleasing her friends and family, always worried about what others thought of her. She put on a fake identity to keep artificial friends close."

"But you still fell in love with her?"

He chuckles, his wide shoulders shaking. "She didn't give me much of a choice. When she realized what was real, she fought hard as hell to keep it. All those years ago, your eyes told me you hated how you were acting. I always waited to see the day you decided to take control of your own life."

"I don't know how to do that," I confess as a tear rolls down my cheek. I look at his hands, a light coating of espresso grinds on the tips of his fingers.

His thumb comes up and swipes my cheek in a comforting way, the same way a father might comfort a daughter. The grinds roughly stain my cheek, mixing with my wet tears. "Find what's real, Natasha. And fight like hell to keep it."

"Principessa." Enzo's voice pulls my attention away from Ski and I turn to see him approaching. "We need to head home."

"To my father?"

I don't want to go back there. I don't want to be anywhere except for where my heart longs to be. To the ranch, with the horses and the birds. To the skeleton house on the hill. To Hale.

"No, we won't be going back there. We're going back to Boston."

Looking back at Ski, he gives me a small smile and nods his head. "It's okay to forgive yourself, Natasha. I hope to see you again." He stands and I follow and without an invitation, I wrap my arms around him. After a second of shock, he envelops me with large, warm arms.

"Thank you, Ski."

***

Boarding the twins' private jet has me feeling emotional whiplash. It's late in the night and all this back and forth has me more than exhausted. I could sleep for several days straight at this point.

Enzo comes up and sits next to me, whiskey in hand and a tired look in his eyes. "You'll be going to stay with Hale in the safe house."

"What? Why?"

Raf settles into the seat across from Enzo, typing away on his iPad. "We need to eliminate whoever tried to kill you tonight, Natasha. Until then, we need to keep you safe, and we can't have you in the way."

"No. If someone's after me, Hale needs to stay far away."

"Try telling him that, principessa. The bastard's disgustingly obsessed with you. There's no way in hell he will let you out of his sight."

Enzo sips his whiskey and closes his eyes, clearly done with this conversation. Rafael nods in agreement to his statement and my hands fist with my frustrations.

"He's in danger if he stays close to me. You must realize this?" My eyes plead with Rafael. They have to talk to him, make him see reason. He needs to lay low, away from me and the twins.

Rafael scoffs, his fingers tapping on the arm rest with annoyance. "The fool is in love, Natasha. What would you have me do, chain him in a basement until we can ensure your and his safety? I have enough problems with you Boston women, I don't need to add Hale, who I might add is a perfectly capable and well-trained ex-navy SEAL and federal agent, to my list of problems."

My head jerks back slightly and I straighten my spine. "So that's all I am to you, a problem to be dealt with?"

Rafael's hard eyes snap to mine. "Currently, yes. You're to stay in the safe house. Hale will protect you until I can deal with the

Romanovas. No more questions. I'm tired. You have had a long day; you should rest before we land."

"Who are the Romanovas? Are they who sent that man after me? Why do they want me dead, I don't even—"

"Natasha. No more questions." Rafael's sharp tone silences me, but my mind runs on.

Huffing out a childish sigh, I cross my arms and look out the window as the plane begins to speed up, preparing to take off.

Stubborn men. Raf and Enzo seem to be throwing little tantrums over who the hell knows what, probably this other Boston woman they mentioned, and Hale isn't going to let me be, not like he should. He thinks himself invincible, or rather thinks that if he dies for me, that I'll be okay. But he couldn't be more wrong. He has become every good and heavenly thing in my life, the light at the end of my healing and if I lose him there will be no healing from that pain.

hale

The electronic noise of the door unlocking has me springing up from the small bed in this even smaller underground safe house. Enzo walks through a second later carrying two cups of coffee from Henry Leo's. "Where's Natasha? Is she okay?"

"Chill your tits, Casanova. Natasha's fine. Rafael is taking her to her apartment to grab a few things. Then we're bringing her here."

Honestly, I didn't think when I killed Dante Alessi that they would go to such extremes to hide me. I hate it. I'm like a caged fucking beast, pacing the floor till they let me out. But that's the thing, when I saw her vacant eyes, his lips on her... I didn't think. I reacted.

That's what she does to me, makes me completely reckless. But I'd do it again, in a heartbeat I'd kill whoever touches her against her will.

Rafael was right, how the angel has fallen.

"The new plan then?" I say, raising a brow because I'm not going to argue that I fucked up.

Enzo and I sit at the small kitchenette table, and he hands me a lavender latte.

"Really? Lavender latte?"

"You seemed like the latte type, big pussy. And pussy whipped by a little devil who happens to smell like lavender. I thought it was pretty clever on my part actually."

"I hate you."

But as I sip the coffee, the small hint of lavender fills my mouth and damn, the bastard's right. It's a bold coffee flavor with a hint of my Natasha. "So, the plan?"

"We find who tried to kill her. We kill them. Then you two are—"

"You mean you haven't figured out who tried to murder her? Aren't you all supposed to be some big bad hounds of the underworld?"

"Let me finish," Enzo says with a quirk of his own brow. "We know who he works for but going after his boss would be a larger operation than we can handle at the moment. Thanks to you, we're also dealing with the stupidly powerful men who were still aligned with our father, the men who are not pleased right now. For the time being, you both will lay low here."

The rage that had built up in me simmered down at their plan for me to stay with my girl. Even if they had tried to keep me away, they would have failed.

"I want to help in taking whoever this boss is out. I have skills that would be useful."

"That's great." Enzo's rolls his eyes, sarcasm dripping from him. "Our little knight in shining armor. Currently, the best way to help us is to stay the fuck out of it. We do, however, need you to step down from your position at the bureau," he says as he hands me my work phone, the one he confiscated before he locked me in here.

"Easy. I was planning on it anyway; I've already been training my replacement, and he's been in a temporary position while I was on leave."

"One more thing, no contacts outside of Raf or myself until further notice. We don't know exactly where Ilya has eyes and ears, we can't trust anyone right now."

"Who is Ilya?"

"None of your business."

Rolling my eyes, I rephrase to try and get it through his thick fucking skull the importance of keeping me in the loop. "If I'm to protect her, I need to know who I am protecting her from, you dipshit."

Enzo smirks at my nickname for him, recognizing it as what it is, an offering of peace, a dare I say, brotherly teasing.

"Touché. Alright." Enzo stands, goes into the kitchen and pulls a coffee mug out of the cupboard. He then pours the coffee out of the to-go cup and into the mug. "I fucking hate the feel of plastic on my lips. I need the real fucking thing. You know?"

I don't know actually... that seems like such an odd thing to hate. But who am I to questions the definable serial killer sitting in front of me. Suppressing a laugh, I shake my head at the gaudy, ceramic mug with a rainbow shooting out a unicorn's ass, the words "I'm a delight" above the happy creature.

He looks down at the mug, following my own stare. "The accuracy is astounding. I am a fucking delight. I'm taking this when I'm done. I'll give it to Raf for Christmas. He'll hate it. It'll be perfect." The devious twin smirks and I shake my head.

"Back on track. Who's Ilya?"

"Ah yes. Ilya Romanova. We run the empire on the West, he runs it on the East. They are Russian, much less handsome and clever than us Italians, it didn't take long to track down the identity of the man who tried to kill Natasha, leading us to the Romanovas."

"If they run the sex trade in the East, why haven't I heard of them?"

"According to your information, who heads the East?" Enzo asks with a smirk.

"We don't know. Mostly a cluster of small gangs, nothing as organized or proud as your business."

"Exactly. They seem small and unorganized but it's only their tactic to keep the Romanova name and family out of the light. Where my father thrives on you squeaky-clean do-gooders knowing who he is and being unable to pin him down, Alexey, Ilya's father and previous head douchebag, thrived on remaining a ghost. Ilya has continued with the same cowardly approach. But trust me when I say, the Romanova family is larger than ours and more powerful. They have spread their wings wide and yet they remain hidden and under your radar."

"Why would such a powerful and large organization target Natasha?"

"Alexey has a bone to pick with my father. He doesn't want to see the Alessi line continue. It seems he's been informed of Natasha's role in continuing our line. Which means we have a spy among our ranks."

"Any idea who the spy might be?"

Enzo waves his hand dismissively. "We have our theories, but we prefer to be sure before we pull the trigger."

"I see. So, we will stay in the safe house until you settle things with the Romanovas. Will you kill Ilya?"

"Nah. He's untouchable right now, but in time. We're going to attempt to make a deal, at least until we have the forces to take him out. Until we do, you two need to stay out of sight."

"And how safe is this bunker you have for us?"

"No one will get in." His eyes move away from mine, as if he's remembering something. He takes a sip of his coffee and then his brows furrow. All his small little micro expressions tell me he's hiding something.

"What is it?"

"Well, I can think of only one who could access our safe house, who's good enough to do so but no one has heard from her in a long time. It's not likely. I wouldn't worry yourself over it."

"Well, that's comforting, now I'm definitely going to worry about it." I roll my eyes and let out a sigh.

"Yeah, you should worry. If Ilya or Alexey want Natasha gone that bad, he will send his best assassin after her. They call them White Owls, silent in their kills, but they always leave a signature. They are the Romanovas' best and only one is active at a time. She was better than any of them until one day she disappeared. Never made a kill again."

"Sounds like an urban legend. What happened to her? Do you think she would come out of retirement for Natasha?"

Enzo's phone vibrates and he pulls it out looking quickly at the screen. "Look at that, time for me to go."

"Enzo. What happened to her?"

"No one knows, but we've been searching. She disappeared ten years ago, without a trace."

"Why have you been looking for her?"

"She killed the woman who raised us, the closest thing we had to a mother, and she... it doesn't matter. Let's just say I'd love to use her head as my Christmas tree topper."

My stomach rolls at the image and I shake my head to clear it. "You're a sick son-of-a-bitch, you know that?"

The maniac laughs as he gets up and heads for the door.

"How did things go with Natasha's father?" I ask as I meet him at the door.

"Let's say he met the devils, prayed for mercy and was found wanting."

"That's vague," I remark.

"I'm in the presence of an FBI agent, Mr. Knight. You think I'm stupid?"

"I think we both know I don't give a fuck what happens to that man, in fact I'd love to have been in on this meeting. How about the next time you meet with someone who has hurt Natasha, you give me a call." Enzo eyes me and then grins. "And that's ex-FBI agent, as of... now." I press send on the email containing my official resignation letter and hold up the phone to Enzo. He snatches it and then hands me a new one.

"Welcome to hell, Mr. Knight. Glad to have another devil amongst Angels."

natasha

The twins bring me to the basement of a massive apartment complex which they have converted into a safe house. They allowed me to pack a few simple essentials, a sketchpad and notebook, some pencils and pens and that's it. No cellphone, no laptop, tablet, nothing.

The electronic door opens as Enzo types in a code. "The door needs a code to get in but not out. I'll trust that you will be good and stay where you are put until we tell you?" Enzo smirks as he looks down at me.

"I'm always good."

"Fucking liar," he whispers as the door fully opens and I see the only man who's made my heart do silly things.

"Hale!"

I run, jumping into his arms as his hands come up under my ass to support me. My heart feels sporadic at the sight of him again, in one piece, here. My soul calms and this prison doesn't seem as dark anymore.

Initially, I didn't want him with me, worried I would put him in danger. But now that I'm with him, I can't imagine not having him here, and I must put my faith in the twins that they have a plan. I pull my face out of his neck, kissing him until I am completely and utterly at home.

"Sweetheart." His forehead rests against mine. "You're here."

"Alright love birds, break it up. I like to watch but not with you two..." Enzo leans against the door frame, arms crossed over his chest. He would never admit it, but I see the smirk. I would say that deep down... way deep down inside, Enzo Alessi roots for love.

"Whatever will we do all by ourselves... without interruption... for the foreseeable future?" Hale's devious and delicious tone make my heat.

"Yeah, I'm out of here. Don't knock her up, Casanova. Condoms are in the bedside drawer."

"I make no promises, there is nothing I would love more, actually."

Enzo rolls his eyes and exits as Hale scoops me up again and sets me on his lap as he sits on the end of the bed, which happens to be in the living area since we are in a studio.

"I've missed you." He kisses the tip of my nose, then brushes my lips. I want to be utterly consumed by him at this moment, but my fear still sits heavy in my chest.

"How long do you think we'll be here for?" I ask, unable to hide the trepidation in my voice.

"Hopefully forever." He smirks and I smack his shoulder.

"Be serious for a moment. I feel like a ball rolling down a hill, things are picking up speed and it's like I can see the end. I'm anxious for everything to finally be over with. How long do you think?"

"You're scared," he says, tilting my chin up to look at his eyes.

"Of course I am. I feel like for the first time I have a small morsel of happiness and it's about to be taken from me."

"We have to trust the twins, baby."

"And once they take care of these Romanova people, then what?"

Enzo and Raf filled me in on their long-standing beef with the Russian mafia on the East coast. All about Alexey and his sister who abandoned her family because she fell in love with an Alessi. About Ilya, Alexey's son who now rules and has carried on his father's plan for revenge. Apparently as the woman meant to carry Rafael's child, Alexey and Ilya have decided the best way to stick a knife in the heart of an Alessi is by killing little ol' me.

Yay me.

His fingers brush down my cheek and I lean into them. "One minute at a time. One day at a time. You have me for life, I'm not going anywhere."

"You better promise me, Hale Knight," I challenge as tears brim my eyes.

"I promise," he whispers and my hand finds his throat. I tighten and his eyes flare with desire.

"You want control, sweetheart?" My smirk answers him. "Then take it."

I give his throat a squeeze and he pulls his sweater off. Admiring the golden skin and rippled muscles of my Knight, I lean into him to whisper in his ear. His citrus and oak scent fill my senses, and I know my panties are soaked.

"Did you bring your handcuffs, Agent Knight?"

His cock jumps in his pants at the sultry tone of my voice.

"Back left pocket."

Reaching in, I find them and the small key and cuff his hands in front of him. I slide off his lap and pull down the leggings I wore under my large crewneck sweater before yanking that off too, standing in front of him completely naked.

His mouth falls open slightly and his eyes rake up and down my body. Appreciating every curve I've hated and when his eyes meet mine again, they beg me to come closer.

I reach for his belt, unclasping the metal buckle and sliding the leather out of his jeans. Then I slowly begin to drop his zipper. His body leans in, his lips only a moment from meeting mine when I pull back. "No, no."

"Fuck, baby." His head falls back when I grasp his cock and pull him out, stroking him up and down slowly. "Hands above your head, Knight."

His cuffed hands go up immediately, resting on top of his head as he looks up at me.

"Such a good boy," I praise as I run my finger over his lips. He tries to bite it but I pull back. Quirking a brow at him, he understands my meaning and I do it again, he keeps still this time, and I drag my finger down, over his bottom lip, over his chin and down the column of his throat. I continue down his chest as I drop to my knees between his legs.

"I want you to try and not come for me, can you do that?" I ask in a sweet, innocent voice. His eyes are burning with barely contained control. "And no touching, you keep your hands up. Understand?"

"Yes," he grits out and I smile before licking the underside of his cock from base to tip. "Shit," he hisses.

I smile at the way I'm making him feel before taking him fully into my mouth. I know exactly how to take him down my throat without gagging and I do that. His head falls back again as he lets out a long, rumbling moan. I move up and down in slow, languid strokes, tasting the salty pre-cum that leaks from his tip.

When my mouth leaves him, my hand continues to slide up and down and his head jerks forward, his eyes flying to mine as I lick my lips, "Fuck baby, I'm going to..."

I remove my hand, and he groans. "Shit."

"I told you not to come." I bat my lashes, feeling incredibly sexy, powerful and... in control.

"Hard not to with that wicked mouth wrapped around me, love," he pants out and I rise, pushing him back onto the bed as I climb atop him and reach between my thighs, grasping him and lining him up.

"Condom?" he questions and I shake my head.

"Not right now. I need to feel you," I say, slowly lowering myself onto him. He fills me perfectly, not too large but he presses against every wall inside me. I never understood when people talked about how a woman was made from the rib of a man, but being with Hale, I understand. He is part of me, as much as I was made for him. My hair curtains us, only him and I under a waterfall of blonde.

Just him and I.

"You were made for me, Hale." I begin grinding against him, feeling the most delicious pressure against my clit.

"We were made for each other, Natasha."

My eyes close of their own accord as my orgasm builds, it races all over my body, piquing in my lower stomach but like every time I try to release, I can't.

Come for me like the whore I've trained you to be. Your mind may hate me, but your body loves it. Watch...

"Baby?" Hale's voice pushes my tutor's words out of my mind and I open my eyes to see his blue ones. "It's me. You and me. No one else. You can do it baby, look at me and let go. You're safe. I've got you."

As he encourages me, my body releases and my muscles spasm, my legs shake as I collapse onto his chest and I cry out, letting my tears fall onto his skin. His cuffed wrists land on my lower back as he holds me.

"Good girl, sweetheart. You belong to *me*, you come for *me*," he emphasizes the last word, and I take a deep breath, my chest shaking as I try to settle my tears. When my mind catches up and the euphoria of my orgasm fades, I perk up, resting my chin on his chest. "Did you come?"

"You told me not to..."

I laugh and then try to hide it as guilt filters in. "Such a good boy, aren't you?" I tease and he glares at me.

"If you're offering, I'd very much like to. It's fucking killing me. For fuck's sake, sweetheart, I'm still inside you."

Lifting my hips off him, he slides out and I scoot down on the bed, taking him into my mouth once again. I taste myself on him and it only takes moments before our combined tastes fill my mouth.

"God, you're fucking incredible." He groans out, his abs flexing as his body reacts to his orgasm and I swallow his release before pulling back and licking my lips.

"The key, baby?"

"What key?" I say as I stand.

His face falls. "Don't mess with me, my love. Un-cuff me."

"Oh yes, there was a key, wasn't there? I must have lost it," I tease as I turn around, throwing an extra sway in my hips as I make my way toward the bathroom.

Hale stands, tucking himself back into his jeans. "Natasha," he warns, and I look over my shoulder, dangling the key on my finger as I tease him.

He lunges for me, and I jump, running off down the narrow hallway. I get only a few feet before his cuffed wrists come over my head and he traps me against his chest.

"Uncuff me, you little brat."

"Beg," I reply before turning my head and placing a kiss to his neck.

He brings up his hands, releasing me, then circles to my front and drops to his knees.

"So pretty on your knees for me," I tease with the saying that's become ours.

Holding his wrists up to me, his eyes go from silly to serious in a breath. "Unbind my wrists, baby. But I beg of you, never unbind your heart from mine."

Slipping the key into the small hole, the cuff releases and before I can reach for the other one, Hale wraps his arms around my waist and pulls me into his lap. His forehead meets mine and I close my eyes, taking in this moment.

"My heart is bound to yours, Natasha. It could not survive without you. Please, never leave me. I beg of you."

My heart sinks with the fear in his voice. "I'm afraid it is you who will leave me, Knight."

"How do I love thee? Let me count the ways," he whispers against my lips and my heart stutters inside my chest. Is this an admission, a confession? Or simply a fitting poem to our little game?

"Elizabeth Barrett Browning," I say and kiss him before I can find if he does in fact truly love me as I do him.

natasha

"What are you drawing, my love?" Hale comes up behind me, placing a kiss to my shoulder as he peers over it. "Wait..."

I let him pick up the drawing pad as I spin in my chair to see his full reaction. "Is this the house on the hill?"

I nod.

"You're designing it?"

My heart rate picks up and a nervous flutter happens in my stomach, I might have overstepped somehow. Did he have his own visions for it? Did he not imagine us living there?

"Is... that alright?" My fingers play with the sleeves of my oversized sweater, well, Hale's sweater.

"It's perfect. You dream it, I'll build it," he says as he kneels in front of me, flipping through all the pages. "Did you do every room?"

"Yes," I whisper as he looks up at me. "Do you like it?"

"I love it." He kisses my inner thigh, then stands again and collapses onto the bed. He had finished in the shower, his skin still hot from the water, only wearing a pair of grey sweatpants.

We've been here almost a week now. Enzo dropped off some groceries this morning and told us that a meeting with the Romanova leader, Ilya, is scheduled for tonight. Hopefully they will be able to come to some agreement and Hale and I can get out of here.

As much as I love being in our own little world, I need fresh air, the sound of the birds, the smell of the fields at the ranch. And speaking of the ranch. "Does your mom know where we are?"

His eyes are worried as his hands come up to rest behind his head. "No, I told her we were going on a little vacation where there wouldn't be service. I do my best to keep her in the dark about my work and what's going on with the twins. I did tell her I stepped down from my position at the bureau which she was actually pretty happy about."

"Yeah, she didn't like you in that position. I know that."

He crooks his finger at me, calling me to him and my feet lead me to my home in human form, settling in next to his side.

"She always wanted me at the ranch, taking it over for them. They deserve it, to simply retire there and not have to worry about it anymore."

Looking up, I see the love in his eyes for his parents. "You love them so much," I comment without meaning to.

"Of course I do." A heaviness fills my chest as I see a hopefulness in his eyes. A dream of us living in the house on the hill, taking over Revival Ranch and I must admit that would be my dream but I'm a realist. I know we have many, many obstacles to navigate before that dream could ever be a reality.

"If anything happens to me, promise me that you'll go home to the ranch. Finish our house and heal. Don't look for revenge."

His fingers find my chin as he tilts my face to meet his. "Nothing is going to happen to you. I promise."

"You don't know that. Just... don't follow Ivy. I'm saying this right now, Hale, if I'm gone, I want you to find out what's on the other side of healing. And one day, when we meet again, you can tell me what that is. Promise?"

His lips meet my forehead as a tear rolls down my cheek. Seems lately all I do is cry, whether from happiness or utter sorrow, but he's always there to catch them all. "I will promise but only because I know that you will be safe. I will always protect you."

"And I you," I whisper. As I reach up and kiss him, his tongue dives into my mouth, colliding with my own and my heart comes alive again. Beating wildly for this man.

When he pulls away, his eyes meet mine. "What do you want to do today?"

"Enzo dropped off a chess board. Want to play?" I suggest and he laughs.

"You are so on."

I hop up quickly and pull the board and pieces from the bag, making my way back to the bed and set it up. "White for the lady."

"You take white," I offer, and he tilts his head. "White has the first move advantage and I like to beat the odds. I'm always black."

"Fine," Hale concedes and makes his first move. In a predictable fashion, he picks up his E4 and moves it two spaces forward. I roll my eyes and move my pawn to C5.

We go about, moving our pieces around, both concentrating on the board. We both make necessary sacrifices and finally I have him.

"Checkmate."

"You little sneak." He grins as he looks at the board. I give him a moment to read and try to counter, but the moment he realizes there's nowhere to go, he shakes his head.

"Don't be a sore loser, I can let you win next time if it will appease your ego." I shrug flirtatiously and the next thing I know the board flies from the bed as he tackles me around the waist, and I fall back against the pillows with a burst of laughter.

"Why don't we play my version?" he growls as he holds up the white queen.

His head levels with my breasts, and I gasp when he places the cold marble piece against my lower stomach, lifting my shirt slightly and it brushes my skin, forcing goosebumps to race up my abdomen.

"Queen to navel," he whispers as he slowly runs the piece up my skin, then kisses my belly before placing the piece over my navel.

"Your move." His eyes peer up at me with a burning intensity.

"Queen to left rib," I say on an exhale, and he drags the piece up, my shirt riding up even more and the cool air hits my skin, eliciting goosebumps everywhere. He kisses my ribcage on the left side and circles the chest piece around before holding it still.

"Queen to right breast." His breath on my ribs tickles and makes me squirm but he simply chuckles and keeps me pinned with his arm laying across my hips as he drags the piece to my breast. His mouth covers my nipple as he sucks it into his mouth, a sharp yet pleasurable sensation shoots down my spine as my back arches.

"Fuck," I moan.

"Your move, sweetheart," he says when he releases my breast.

"Queen to right hip," I say, leading him where I want his mouth, and he complies moving torturously slow.

My body writhes, the languid strokes of the chest piece with his mouth following have me barely able to control myself let alone think clearly.

After he leaves small nips and kisses on the sensitive skin of my inner hip, he dips the piece under my panties and circles the marble against my clit. Pleasure rips up my stomach and makes me moan out his name.

"Checkmate," he says before ripping my panties off and devouring me. His tongue like magic as it circles and consumes. My fingers thread through his thick hair as he settles between my thighs. My panties are long gone, and his hand pushes up my shirt as he grabs my breast and squeezes. All the sensations running through me fill my blood with pure, unrestrained pleasure.

"Hale!" I cry as my body tries to release but can't.

His large hands reach under my thighs, then to my hips as he flips us, so I am now hovering over his face.

"Take control, baby."

I'm panting uncontrollably fast. I can barely speak as I look down into his deep-sea eyes. Slowly sinking down, his mouth meets my pussy once again and I begin to move my hips, taking control as he commanded and before I know it, with his large hands on my ass and my own hands gripping the headboard, my orgasm crashes into me with an unexpected intensity.

My thighs clamp shut and my whole body shakes as he finishes his meal and then slides out from under me. My body falls forward into the pillows as my legs remain open and my ass in the air.

He notches himself behind me and his grip on my hips has me whining with pleasure. My eyes open to look at him behind me. "That's it, sweetheart, eyes on me when I make you fly."

He slams into me, pushing me forward slightly and I can't help but gasp. He continues to relentlessly pound into me, pulling out almost completely before ruining me over and over again.

One of his hands comes to the small of my back as he pushes down, making me arch more and I admire the view of him as his abs tense and his head falls back.

"Fuck," he draws out as his hips slow, and pulses inside me.

His cum fills me up and when he least expects it, I move my hips back and forth again, teasing out a longer orgasm from him.

"Shit. Fuck. You can't do that to me, sweetheart. It's too much." He grins as his hands run over my skin. I do it again and am rewarded with a smack to my ass cheek. "Brat." He smirks.

I wiggle one more time and he pulls out of me, collapsing to the side of the bed. Snuggling up against him, I wait for his breathing to even out. Then I sneak away, clean up in the bathroom and then come back, tucking us both in for our little afternoon cat nap.

natasha

A rattling of noises draws me from sleep, and I open my eyes to see the most breathtaking sight. Hale Knight, shirtless and in a pair of black sweatpants. The golden skin of his back practically glows, small freckles lining his shoulders flicker as his muscles flex while he cooks up something that has my stomach growling.

"Well, hello there," I say, my voice a bit hoarser than I meant. I clear my throat, and he chuckles.

"Dinner?" he says, peeking over his shoulder.

"Yes please," I squeak out. I slip off the side of the bed, grabbing his shirt and slipping it over my head before pulling on a pair of leggings. I make my way over to the small, simple kitchen, only containing the necessary appliances and a little island that fits two bar stools.

"I have for you, my lady, a chicken piccata."

"Fancy," I remark as I raise a brow at him. "Did you learn to cook from your mom?" I ask, even though I already know the answer.

"I did indeed. I also learned how to sew, iron clothes, and properly sort laundry. Even though I was a guy, Ma never let me use that as an excuse. She always harped on how important it was that I knew how to do these things. Ivy had to learn to change oil in the truck and change a tire."

"You know how to sew?" I say with a giggle as I lift myself onto the granite countertop of the island.

"Don't you laugh at me." He pinches at my waist and I attempt, and fail, to swat him away. "It came in handy in the military. The guys might have laughed at first but then who do you think came knocking when they tore their uniform or needed their patches sewn on? Huh?"

He leans in and kisses me, my face squished between his large, calloused hands. His tongue dances with mine in a slow recital. I love the way he moves, he never rushes me, isn't hasty or demanding. Scratch that, he is demanding but it's in a way that makes it feel like my choice.

When he pulls away, I pout, and he kisses my nose. "Greedy, greedy girl." Turning away from me, he dishes up two plates and sets them at the island.

Sitting next to him, I dig in and moan at the taste. "So good," I say with a mouthful, and he chuckles. "Do you think it will be much longer?" I ask between bites.

He shakes his head. "No, while you were asleep Enzo called on the burner phone he gave me. He said we should be out of here in a few days. I guess the meeting went well with Ilya, some kind of deal was made, and they have agreed to leave you be. The twins want us here a few more days to be safe."

"I see." I can't hide the sadness in my voice and of course he picks up on it.

"You don't want to leave?"

I take a sip of water to clear my throat. "I mean I do. I just... don't know what happens next. The Romanova issue is dealt with but what's next?"

Hale plays with his food a moment, the rise and fall of his chest exaggerated by the sigh he

releases. "You finally get your happy ending. You've been through enough." He stands and pushes between my thighs.

"What do you mean?" I know he's done his research on me but the way he said that makes me think he knows more than what a background check would show. Did his mom tell him about my past? My gut twists, no, she wouldn't. I know she wouldn't.

"I know about your tutor."

Those words make my world stop on its axis. My body freezes, my breath stills in my chest, and I push at his chest to scramble away from him. "How do you..."

"It's okay. I think I already know but I want to hear it from you. I don't want to make any assumptions..."

"Assumptions? You've already made them it seems. How did you find out?"

"I knew you were hiding something from me, I needed to know."

I back away even more, right into the wall. He looked into me? Like I was some suspect? "You had no business looking into my past."

He tilts his head and gives me a look that he did actually have the right to. "You were involved with the Alessis, Natasha. I had to dig. I told you I looked into you. That's not what you're honestly upset about..."

"My tutor had nothing to do with the Alessis, Hale. You had no right to go that far back! How did you even..." I know my father would have covered up the dealings with the tutor. How did Hale know? Then it hits me.

Gage.

He must have used his super nerd skills to dig further than what he typically would for a case. Which means not only does Hale know how much of a whore I am... so does Gage.

Hale gets up and walks toward me. "Baby, please. You have to see it from my side. I met a ghost of a woman on a rooftop. Then she left me and months later, I found her involved with the same people I was building a case on. And when I met you again, you were nothing like the woman I had started to fall for. You were challenging and stubborn, you were hiding, and I had to know why."

He's closer now, crowding me and I can't breathe. "Get away from me."

"Natasha."

"Get away!" He takes a single step back and the pressure in my chest releases, but only a fraction. "You could have asked me."

"You wouldn't have told me."

He took the minuscule amount of control I had over my past and ripped it away from me. I could always control who knew about that time in my life but no more. I wanted all of this to stay buried, but he had to dig it up. He had to bring my worst shame to the surface, ask me to share it before I was ready. My heart cracks open and everything comes spilling out, I can't hold it in.

"So instead, you force memories of what they did to me to the surface. You force me to see it again? I want to forget it all!" My fingers thread through my hair and grip my scalp. I probably look like a crazy person, but I don't care. My throat tightens and my voice breaks. "The way he forced my body to respond in ways I couldn't control. The way he forced my mouth around him, gagging me until I learned to swallow like the good whore he trained me to be. The way he would use his fingers and mouth to pull from me an orgasm that wasn't his to take! The way he would bring in his friends to test me. They would tell me all the ways I could be better, sloppier, cleaner, skinnier, fuller, too tight, not tight enough!" Pausing, I watch his eyes fill with remorse. "Is that what you wanted to know?" I whisper.

"Natasha." He steps toward me again and I push against him.

"Don't touch me! Leave me!" I scream at him as the tears fall faster and my vision blurs.

"I can't do that, sweetheart."

I beat against his chest as he keeps his hold around me. "I'm not your sweetheart! You broke my trust, Hale!"

"I know," he whispers.

"I trusted you!" I cry.

"I know. I'm sorry, but I'm still here."

"I don't want you to be," I admit as my knees collapse and he catches me in his arms.

"I won't leave you alone with this, Natasha. I'm here, whether you want me to be or not. I'm not leaving you."

I'm already alone. He'll never see it. I'm beyond repair. I thought that maybe, being at the ranch, in the peace and quiet, I could find what awaited me on the other side of healing, but the past haunts me. It's always going to be there.

He doesn't deserve my fury, because he's right. I never would have told him about my past. I could never give him every dirty part of who I am. I could never fully belong to him, not when I don't even belong to myself.

He's an angel, pure and good. He deserves heaven, I only bring hell.

"Take me to bed. Please," I whisper into his chest, and he tucks us both in. I lay there pretending, like I do best and when his breathing evens out, I continue to wait. For hours I lay in his arms, then I slip from beneath them.

I step into my boots and wrap his jacket around me. Packing a small bag of clothes and my wallet, I leave my notepad as I unlock the door and slip out in the night. Leaving my heart behind for the second time.

natasha

The Boston sky rolls with storm clouds, but the rain has yet to fall. Still, the threat remains. I'm not sure where I'm going or what I'm even doing. I knew I had to get away. The walls were closing in, reality invading my heaven.

Hale broke my trust; he betrayed me in a way that hurt like a bullet to my chest, but I forgave him the instant his arms encircled me. Because I love him more than I love myself. And that's the bitter truth that I didn't see before.

I couldn't stand the thought of losing him, but right now, in my life, there are too many moving variables. Too much risk. Because I love him more than myself, I need to let him go.

If I make it out of my situation, I'll go back to him. If he still wants me that is. But for now, he needs to let me go.

Just leave me.

Finding a payphone, I slip a few quarters in and dial his mom. It's early in the morning, still dark but I know she wakes at three each morning. She should be up by now, if not I'll leave a message.

"Hello?" Her sweet voice fills my ear, and I smile. A comfort invading my chest.

"It's Natasha."

"Oh hello, child. Are you and my son back in the states? How was your trip?" I can't force myself to lie to her, she told me once to never do that. I have too much respect for the woman to do it now, choosing to evade the questions entirely.

"Grace, I... I don't know when I'll be able to come back to the ranch, but I wanted to thank you, for everything you did for me. You saw something in me that I never saw, a strength to fight for myself. I love your son; I love him so much that it hurts, and I wanted you to know that. No matter what comes, please know that I love him, more than I ever loved myself."

"Natasha, where is Hale?" The urgency in her voice makes me smile. She's worried but she doesn't need to be. For the first time in my life, I know I'm doing the right thing. It's strange, the peace that has washed over me, like a storm cleansing the Earth of its impurities. I feel the weight of the water, but also the serenity and quietness that follows.

"He's sleeping. He'll be okay. He'll come home to you, make sure he heals for me, okay?"

"Natasha, where are you?" Her voice breaks and I hang up the phone. He will be okay. He promised me and Hale is many things, one of them being a man of his word. This I know in my core. He will be okay.

I dial Raf next and he picks up on the first ring, "Hello?" his deep voice rumbles, still rough from the early morning.

"It's Nat. I had to leave the safe house."

"What the fuck, Natasha? Get your ass back there, now." His calm command makes me hesitate. But only for a moment.

"I can't. Hale's there and I can't be around him right now. I needed to breathe, Raf. I'll be on the rooftop of the Copley; I need some time to myself. Give me an hour and then come find me."

He begins to say something, but I hang up.

I want to dial Sabrina, but I don't remember her number off the top of my head, not like I had Raf, Grace's and Hale's memorized. She probably wouldn't answer anyway, not this early. The woman usually sleeps till at least ten.

The Copley's only a few blocks from here, so I begin my walk. The occasional car passes on the quiet Boston street and I see shop workers milling about inside their stores, preparing to open for the morning.

I pass an old man, sitting on his front steps, smoking a cigarette and nod my head at him, he returns it and there's a sense of belonging knowing I'm not the only one who enjoys the night in this way.

When I get to the Copley, I show the attendant my access card and he lets me in. I go straight to the rooftop, my key card programmed to access the private space. I leave the door propped open for Raf or Enzo since I'm not sure if they have access, although it wouldn't surprise me if they did.

I set my bag down and step up to the edge of the rooftop. The peaceful breeze lifts my air. The city in the night, black with the glow of the lights. The soft illumination of city lights in the dark night makes me think of when I met Hale.

How close I was to flying.

The little sparrow flew past me, flying right into the brick wall that supports the entrance door. I remember picking the bird up and knowing without a doubt, she would die.

But she didn't.

That night seems like forever ago and like tonight, it's not that I necessarily wanted to die but I wanted control. I wanted to feel like I had control over one fucking thing in my life, even if that one thing was my life.

In all honesty, I wasn't sure if I was going to jump. Could have gone either way until that little sparrow flew past me. I remember holding her, wishing I could show her how beautiful life could be, willing her to live.

That little sparrow saved me in that way. Because pouring my hopes and dreams into her made me realize that I still had hopes and dreams of my own. I needed someone to share them with... and then he spoke.

He pulled me from the edge and into his arms and I hated him for it because as soon as I looked into those blue eyes, I knew I would never belong to anyone the way I did him.

"Natasha." I turn to a voice I don't recognize and find a man, not much different from the one who tried to kill me in the coffee shop, standing behind me. Blond hair, ice blue eyes. A Romanova.

My heart picks up speed inside my chest. "Yes," I reply, not denying this time who I am. I know who I am now.

"Do you know why I'm here?" he asks as he steps closer to me, hands in his pockets. My heart feels like a jackhammer against my sternum, my throat tightens with tears. I didn't come up here to die, but if they try, I won't go down easily. Not anymore.

My footsteps slowly inch to the side, I have no weapon on me but if I can turn us so that I'm closer to the door, I can make a run for it.

The man mimics my steps until we're both perpendicular to the door. He pulls out the gun from his pocket and I tilt my chin up, swallowing hard as tears come to my eyes. I'm not close enough yet. I need to keep him talking.

"Before you kill me, can you at least tell me why? I deserve that, don't you think?"

He smirks and shrugs. "Alexey Romanova wants you dead. He can't get to the twins... yet. Rafael Alessi's wife is the next best thing."

Did he not hear about the deal that the twins made with Ilya? "A deal was made."

"It was," He confirms.

"So why are you here?"

"Ilya's a fool. A brother willing to do anything for a lost sister. But Alexey's judgement is not clouded. The Alessi line dies with you."

"I mean nothing to them; they will find another woman. Killing me won't matter." I take a few more steps to the side and the man's eyes move to the door; he sees my plan now.

"You matter enough."

"Natasha!" Hale bursts through the door and in a split second he sees the man with the gun pointed at me, he steps in front of me, pushing me behind him.

No. No. No. Hale Knight, you idiot!

"Move," the man says.

"Never," Hale growls. My hands search the back of his waistband but of course he didn't bring his gun. I peer around his shoulder and see the decision in the man's ice blue eyes. A pressure in my chest, an instinct has me reacting faster than my thoughts can comprehend as I take out Hales' knees from behind and my body spins to block him.

"No!" he screams as his hands find my waist.

The shaking of tree's fills my ears, a flock of birds bursting from the leaves.

The shock in his eyes has me smiling down at him. His blue eyes are my heaven, like an ocean I want to drown in.

"So pretty on your knees... for..." I start to say as I cup his face in my hands, but my breath leaves me on the last word. A warmth drips down my back then my front. Like warm honey, it drips down my sides.

My legs go numb, and I can't... breathe.

His mouth screams my name, his lips form the syllables. But I can't hear his beautiful, deep voice. Why is there no sound? I want to hear his voice. *Talk to me, Knight.*

My eyes close and his face fades.

A warm, wet hand to my face wakes me, the smell of iron fills my nose. He's bleeding. Why is he bleeding?

Hale's lips continue to move, tears stream down his face but there's still no noise. I study his lips closely—*I love you.*

I love you. I try to say but my chest feels heavy. The words don't come out.

It's all silent.

Quiet.

Peaceful.

A small bird flies over us.

I always wanted to fly.

But the view from his arms is what I've always dreamed of.

hale

A faint buzz filters into my dream. I ignore it but then realize there's a weight missing in the bed next to me. Opening my eyes, I find it empty. The buzzing starts up again and I realize it's the burner phone I bought. I told Enzo I would not be without any communication in case something happened. I only gave the number to one person and told her only to call for emergencies.

I look down the hall, not seeing any lights on, as I answer the phone. "Ma? Everything okay?"

"Is Natasha with you?" She sounds fearful and my instincts light on fire.

I stand from the bed, pinching the phone between my shoulder and ear as I slip on a shirt. It's a studio style apartment, the only two doors are a closet and bathroom. I check both. Both empty.

"No. What's going on Ma?"

I place the phone on speaker while I throw a jacket on. "She called me from a number I didn't recognize. Hale, she spoke as if I'd never see her again. As if *you* would never see her again. I'm worried."

What the fuck? Where the hell could she have gone and where are the twins? The security measures set in this apartment are supposed to alert them anytime the door opens. She could easily disable the alarm, but the twins should have known something was up.

"I'll find her, Ma. Don't worry." I hang up and dial Rafael.

"We're already headed to her," he says before I even say who it is. With that sentence he confirms that he does know she left and where she is.

"Where is she?"

"The Copley."

The rooftop. Of course. I race out of the apartment, forgetting everything except the clothes on my back and my badge. They haven't had me return it yet since my official termination doesn't go into effect until Anderson's fully trained.

"What the fuck happened between you two?" Enzo says and I assume I'm on speaker or connected through their car.

"We had a fight. She must have snuck out in the night."

"What a special agent you are..." Enzo quips but I'm not in the mood.

"Fuck you. Where are you?" I'm only a few blocks from the Copley and at the pace I'm moving, I should be there in less than ten minutes.

"About ten minutes," Raf replies.

"See you soon," I say before hanging up. I pick up my speed and make it to the hotel in seven minutes. I show the attendant my badge and he lets me right in, taking the elevator up to the top level then taking the roof access stairs the rest of the way, I see the door propped open.

That's a good sign, if she meant to jump, she would have locked the door.

I rush through it, calling her name and see her six feet to my right, almost to the door. My heart stops when I see what she's facing– a gun, pointed at her chest.

I catch her waist and shove her behind me as the man smirks. "Move."

I brace for what I know will be the bullet that kills me, but hopefully the twins will be here before he can get to Natasha. She pats my back and I curse myself for not grabbing my gun.

"Never," I reply and in a split second, my knees come out from under me, colliding with the cement. Nat rounds me and puts her fragile body between me and the bullet. "No!"

Bang.

Her hands find my face as she looks down on me with those eyes I'd like to die in. "So pretty on your knees... for..." Her breath leaves her as her eyes flutter and her knees collapse.

Her chest fills with red, too much red.

"Natasha!" I scream.

Raf and Enzo burst through the door and the echo of a gun travels straight to my heart, but I can't see past the red.

Her eyes close and my blood-soaked hand grips her beautiful face as it drains of color. Her eyes open once again but they aren't there. Not really. She isn't even looking at me, watching my lips.

"No. Baby? I love you! Okay? Stay awake for me! Natasha!"

They close again.

And they don't open.

"Natasha! Sweetheart? You can't leave me!" I shake her face again, but she's limp in my arms. "Baby? Wake up!" I cry over and over.

"Hale!" Rafael shouts and grips my shoulder, pulling me back enough for Enzo to scoop her up, pulling her from my arms. "She's alive, but her pulse is thready. We need to take her to Doc."

Enzo looks at Raf who nods.

They are taking her from me.

"No!" I don't know where I find the strength, but I stand and Raf blocks me as Enzo disappears out the door, carrying my whole world in his arms.

"Leave her with him."

"I can't! Get the fuck out of my way!"

I push but Raf pushes back. "You need to let her go!"

"I can't!" I scream back at him, my hands find my hair and pull, trying with everything to pull me from this nightmare. I rush him one more time, but his gun comes up and a pain in the side of my head has the world fading as my body hits the ground and I drift off.

hale

I wake in my apartment with a raging migraine. Reaching up, my fingertips brush over a stitched up cut to my temple and it's all fuzzy, but it begins filtering back in slowly. Rafael knocking me out... red... Natasha...

No. No. No.

I fly out of bed, still in the same blood-soaked clothes and I don't even bother changing. I reach for my phone, dialing Rafael. He doesn't pick up. I try Enzo. Still nothing. I try both again and am met with nothing.

"Fuck!"

I begin calling to all the local hospitals, asking about any Jane Does who match Natasha's description and might have been brought in with a gunshot wound to the back. But nothing. I know Raf and Enzo wouldn't have brought her to a hospital, most likely taking her to their private doctor. Of course, the rich bastards have one on standby in every city they frequent. But I had to try.

I'm going out of my mind, pacing my apartment. I don't know where to look, where to go...

"Her locket." I stop in my tracks, calling Gage, he picks up immediately.

"Gage! I need you to trace Natasha's locket."

"It's fucki—"

"Shut the fuck up Gage! I don't have time for your bitch ass comments! Natasha's locket. Now!"

He's silent but his keys clack. "Got her. Sending it to you now."

A moment later I get the text with her coordinates, and I rush out the door. Coming to a warehouse thirty minutes outside the city, I see Rafael's SUV and know I'm in the right place. I bang on the steel door and it rolls aside a moment later, Enzo blocking my path.

"Where is she?"

"Go home, Hale." His eyes have bags under them, his face fallen. No sarcastic smirk or devious mirth in his eyes.

"Where is she?" I demand, my heart beating wildly in my chest. Like a raging storm that needs release. Why won't he tell me?

"Go. Home. We will come by later." He stands a little taller, readying for a fight and I'm willing to give one for her. I'll take on the fucking world to get to her.

"She is my home!" I scream out, pointing behind him where I know she is.

Rafael comes up behind Enzo. The same look in his eyes. "Not anymore, Hale. I'm sorry."

My heart feels like it's skipping beats. Stuttering inside my chest. They aren't saying what I think they are...

"No."

Both their heads dip. "Doc did what he could, but the bullet punctured her lung, made a small tear in her aorta. He couldn't save her."

"No." I step back, the world collapsing beneath my feet. "I don't believe you. I want to see her."

"Her body's already on a plane headed for Oregon; she'll be buried in her hometown," Enzo says as he steps closer to me. His hand comes to my shoulder, an attempt at comfort.

"Get the fuck off me!" I push him back, but he doesn't fight me like I want. I want someone to hit me. Someone to kill me. Someone to take this pain in my fucking heart away!

I clutch my chest, God it hurts. It fucking hurts. It's a visceral pain, like I've never felt before. Am I having a heart attack? God, please tell me I am because I can't fucking live without her.

"Here." Rafael hands out a plastic baggie, inside it the locket I gave her still coated in her blood. "I'm sorry, Hale. We loved her too. And we will have our revenge."

For a split moment, the thought of killing the man responsible eases the pain in my chest. "I want in."

"Go home, Hale. To the ranch. You know that's where she would want you to be right now. Live a good life, away from this hell," Rafael says as he turns back to the warehouse.

Hale, if I am gone, I want you to find out what's on the other side of healing. And one day, when we meet again, you can tell me what that is. Promise?

The promise I made her filters into my mind, the sound of her voice calming my heart. Damn that promise. Damn her for asking me to live without her. Damn her.

Taking her locket out from the baggie, I place it around my neck. Knowing I'll never heal from her. "When you kill the bastard who took her from me, you call me."

Enzo nods his head, and I turn back for my truck. Slamming the door, I see her sitting next to me, complaining about the old truck. God, I'd give anything to hear her voice again. Feel her skin. Be in her presence because she was my heaven and without her in my arms, I'm in hell. Those wings I had been trying to repair?

Obliterated in the ashes of her loss.

***

Seven days later, I find myself standing over a freshly filled grave, the musky scent of the new dirt filling my nose. The placeholder tombstone mocks me, I never thought I would see her name on one. I never thought I would see my sisters on one either, but the universe seems to enjoy taking the people I love the most away from me.

"Hale?" My mom comes up, placing her tired hand into the crook of my elbow. "Honey, everyone's gone now, it's starting to rain. We should..." She hesitates.

Running my hand down my face, I turn into her and wrap her in my arms. "Yeah. Let's head out."

Our plane departs tomorrow morning, we were only here a few days, long enough to see the woman I love laid six feet deep. I tried to reason with Rafael, her fucking husband, to have her buried at the ranch but he wouldn't budge. A simple 'the arrangements have already been made' as he mindlessly scribbled something on a piece of paper was the only answer I received. I punched him in the face, and he didn't fight back.

It's like he knows I'm off my fucking rocker, losing her made me lose my sanity and he won't punish me for it, like he knows I want him to. I made her a promise I wouldn't end up like Ivy, doesn't mean I can't make someone else deal the final blow.

That's how I found myself in bumfuck Aurora, Oregon, saying my last goodbye to my fucking soulmate, laying her in the soil her father owns. My stomach turned at the idea, but the twins refused to see anything wrong with it. "It's just her body, Hale" they had said.

But it's so much more than that.

"I can't believe she is gone." My mother's voice breaks as I walk her to the rental car. I want to break too. I want to dig my hands into that dirt and open her white casket. I want to see her body for myself, I want to lay with her, hold her as they close me inside too.

I didn't even get to see her perfect face one last time. They chose a closed casket due to the injury to her chest. Bullshit to me, the wound would have been easily covered with her clothing but again... I had no say in any of it.

She wasn't *my* wife.

The twins were present at the burial, as somber as they were the day they told me she was never coming home to me. My instincts told me something was off—they seemed too calm and collected but then again, they aren't novices when it comes to handling death. And I guess they could say the same for me. I've been holding myself together but only for my Ma. She doesn't need to worry about me, she doesn't need to shoulder my grief. She doesn't need to know I've downed a bottle of Jack each night since the woman I was madly and deeply in love with took a fucking bullet for me.

Once I drop her off at the ranch, I know I'll break. Alone, because that's what I deserve. I couldn't save her. She used my own move against me to sacrifice herself and I hate that I didn't see it coming. I hate that I didn't react fast enough. I hate that I didn't wake up when she slipped out of my sheets. I hate that she felt she had to leave in the first place.

I regret more than anything bringing her tutor up, asking her to confess her past to me when it was never my right to do so. If I wouldn't have pushed, she would be in my arms.

Instead, she's six feet in the ground and I'm a walking corpse without her.

Shutting my Ma's door, I walk to the driver side and plug in the address for the Baldwin Inn into the GPS. The fucking irony... but it's the only place for lodging in this small town.

Ma turns the radio down, preparing to make me talk about everything, but I'm too numb to want to do anything.

"Hale, honey, are you going to be coming back to the ranch?"

"I need some time, Ma," I say as I pull out of the iron cemetery gates and onto the black, slick pavement.

"But you are... right? Coming home I mean?"

"Yeah. Once I get my apartment packed and settled. Maybe in about a week." My numb voice blares loudly in my mind and I hate it, but I can't find the point in trying to sound any different than the way I feel.

Silence hangs in the cab of the SUV for a minute, then five, then her hand finds mine. She gives it a squeeze, but I don't look at her. I can't.

"This wasn't your fault," she whispers and my eyes close, willing the tears to stay behind the flood gates a little while longer.

"Don't, Ma." I pull my hand from hers and get out of the car then take our bags from the trunk. When we got in, we went straight to the funeral, not even having time to check in beforehand.

She remains silent while we get our room keys, while we walk up to our rooms and even when I place a kiss on her forehead. Her body utterly deflates, my vibrant mother, once again defeated by the loss of a daughter.

I imagine she's processing in the only way she knows how as well. Both of us have always been the type to want space when we are handling anything larger than we feel prepared to carry.

I place my key card into the lock and the light turns green, but I can't go in. I can't function. I need her.

Fuck do I need her.

I close my eyes and an image of her appears in my head, she's lounging in my bed, my shirt hanging off her shoulder, a steaming cup of coffee in her hand as she smiles at me with those brown eyes and perfect lips.

Pulling out my phone, I google the closest coffee shop. Mill's Coffee House. Less than a mile from here. I shoot Ma a text to let her know to call if she needs me and begin the short walk to the coffee house.

When I enter, a bell rings out above, announcing my arrival and an elderly but built man wipes down the counter with an old white rag.

"Welcome in," he says in a deep, rumbling voice. "What can I get you?"

I approach the counter and order. "A latte, please. Do you by chance have lavender syrup?"

He nods and I slide him over my card. "You look like you've been through hell, it's on the house."

"I'm not through it yet, still currently residing there," I mumble, and he scoffs as if he knows exactly what I mean.

I sit down at the little bar across from him as he slides my cup toward me. "You passing through?" he asks, leaning onto his forearms.

"Yeah." I take a sip of the smooth latte, the lavender flavor making my throat constrict as I fight back tears.

"Here for the funeral?"

"Yeah."

"How did you know her?" My eyes meet his and before I say anything he nods. "Yeah. I know that look."

"What look?" I snarl but quickly give him a remorseful dip of my head. I didn't mean to be defensive toward the intrusive old man but I'm afraid I don't have the energy to hold my attitude back.

"I see it in the mirror every day, son. The look of a man who has lost the wind beneath his wings. I hate to break it to you, but it doesn't get better."

"Yet you're still here?" I raise a brow. If he thinks he knows how I'm feeling, that he knows how I struggle everyday not to put a bullet into my fucking skull.

"You find other people to live for. The pain never ends, but on the other side of that pain are people who still need you."

"I don't have anyone who needs me, not the way she did," I confess.

"Natasha would think differently." He turns, pulling the towel from over his shoulder to begin drying some mugs.

I sit up straighter at the sound of her name. "How did you know her?" I repeat his question back at him.

"I didn't. Met her only twice. But she had spirit, each time I met her I knew she had a fight in her that was rare, and I imagine if she loved you like you loved her, that fight lives in you too. Hang on, stay. Not for yourself, but for her."

I finish sipping my coffee and slide the mug back toward him, thinking of his words. He's right. She did have a fight in her that was feral and beautiful. A fight that made her sacrifice too much for people who never deserved it.

I think about all the things she wanted in life.

To be seen. To be loved. To be a mother. I can't give her any of that anymore. In fact, there may be only one dream of hers I can bring into reality.

Sliding off the stool, I look back at the old man. "Thanks for the coffee."

"Come back if you need another. My doors are always open to those who need them to be."

We both nod and I exit, the bell dinging once again.

hale

T he buzzing of my phone wakes me and I squint my eyes as the bright light burns my retinas. Gage. Although I want everyone and their mother to fuck off, we're riding to the airport together this morning.

Reluctantly, I swipe the green circle over. "Hello?"

"I've got coffee and a crying elderly woman in the lobby. *Help. Me,*" he grits out and for the first time in seven days I actually let out a small laugh.

"Be down in a minute," I say as I hang up.

I meet him downstairs, dragging my luggage behind me as we head for the rental car. Everyone stays silent as we pack the car and head out. My mom wanted to take the back seat, saying she felt like she wanted to take a nap on the way to the airport, so Gage rides passenger.

"How are you doing?" he finally asks, staring at the dash like it might bite him and I know it comes from an unfamiliarity and an outstanding hatred for confronting people.

"You don't have to do this, you know?" I say as I tap my fingers on the steering wheel.

"What?"

"Ask how I'm doing. Comfort me."

"Thank fuck," he whispers as he runs his hand down his face. "You'll be okay. Give it time."

I let out a sarcastic chuckle. "Yeah, how long do you think it will take before I stop missing the other half of me?"

He shrugs. "Fuck if I know. A year maybe?"

I shake my head at him. Fucking dick.

***

Silence fills the cab of the truck on our drive to the ranch. No complaints of bumpy roads, the way Rosey has little to no suspension left in her old frame, no amazement at the beauty of the ranch.

Just.

Silence.

Of fucking course they delayed our flight, instead of landing around two in the afternoon like we were supposed to, we're getting in closer to nine at night. "You shouldn't drive home this late, honey. Stay tonight and then head to the city tomorrow." She pats my cheek and heads to her reading room, where she always escapes when she needs time alone.

As much as I want to be in my own solitude right now, she's right. I'm fucking exhausted from the funeral, the traveling, and... life, so

I head up the stairs to my room but pause before I open my door. Glancing over to what was Ivy's then Natasha's white wood door.

I open her door instead and step inside. Her notebook lays on her bedside table, her lotions on the dresser, her robe still lays on the end of the bed. Like she meant to return shortly.

I grab the leather-bound notebook and sit on the edge of her bed. I hesitate a moment feeling as if I'm invading her privacy, peeking into the place she sought sanctuary feels wrong, but everything's already fucked, what would it matter now?

Cracking it open, I see her gentle handwriting, the soft cursive that exposes her deepest thoughts and emotions. All written out in poems. Each one signed with MP.

My brows dig in, why MP? I remember her telling me one time that she hated her name, would rather have been named Mae because it means spring growth and that was always her favorite time of year, seeing all the beauty that arose after a harsh winter. And I make the safe assumption that the P stands for Parker, her middle name.

Flipping through the poems, I find the last one she wrote and my eyes water with her brutal but beautiful words.

I keep fighting
Thinking I'm alone
As I've always deserved to be.
I was vicious
Cruel
Unlovable
I wanted to fly into the light

But my angel wings were broken

By a man I loved for a night.

He ruined me and saved my life.

Grounded me

Forced me to grow.

Showed me the view from below

How could I see the stars

If I refused to look up?

In the night

I was seen

Brave

Real

Him and I are one

The knight and I.

-MP

A wetness begins to smear the ink, and I realize it's the tears falling from my eyes. It's funny, earlier at the coffee shop and in the car with Gage, for a split second I felt a light, a glimpse at healing but then one moment of her, one simple reminder of her absence and the world darkens again. The anger that radiates through me finally boils over and I throw the journal across the room, needing her away from me, but with me simultaneously.

Why did she do that? Why did she leave me?

Why did she think that I could live on this fucking planet without her and why the fuck did she make me promise to? Why did I make that promise?

She was everything and now only her memory remains. In the shivers that race up my spine, the whisper of the trees, the warmth of my bed before I wake full, my ghost calls me to her.

She's everywhere and nowhere at the same time.

She's in me and gone from me.

She's my heaven and my hell.

The poem she once recited to me invades my mind and I finally realize what she was feeling in that moment.

"The mind is its own place, and in itself can make a Haven of Hell, a Hell of Heaven"

"Hale?" My mom comes into the room, and I pause, not even realizing that in my rage I had knocked over the dresser and busted a hole in the wall. Looking down at my knuckles, they drip a bright red blood onto the hardwood floor.

"I'm sorry, Ma. I... I didn't..."

She rushes to me and wraps me in her arms as I collapse to my knees. "Don't apologize, honey. Feel that pain because it's the only thing that's going to get you through. Don't go numb. She wouldn't want that."

"How do I move forward without her, Ma?"

"Who says you have to? Find something that is wholly her and keep it with you. Surround yourself in the love she left with you because she did love you, Hale. She loved this ranch; she loved the life you gave her after the life she had lived before. She may be gone, but don't think for a single second that you didn't save her. You did."

My chest heaves as I try to control my breathing. But pulling in oxygen burns my lungs.

"I don't want to live without her."

"You may not want to, but...." My mother releases a sob as she holds me. "You need to, Hale. I need you. I can't lose you like I did your sister."

And there it is, like the old man from the coffee shop had said. The ones who need me.

I didn't think about what would happen to my parents if I left this world. Even after seeing it with Ivy, I was too lost in my own grief to think about anyone else. But I feel it now, how strong my mother and father have been and how easy it would be to break them if I left too.

Adjusting our position, I wrap my arms around her. "I'm here, Ma. I won't leave you. Okay. I promise."

Another fucking promise.

But one I know I will keep, like I said I would for Natasha. I harden my heart and resolve myself to live a life she would want for me. When alcohol calls me to the bottom of the bottle, like it did when Ivy died, I won't drown. When her memory haunts me, calling me to an early grave, I won't. When grief consumes me and makes my soul ache for her, I'll stay.

I'll stay because Natasha asked me to.

I'll stay because my mother needs me to.

But I will never be the same after her.

gage

Six Months Later

Abuzzing wakes from sleep and I reluctantly roll to the side, an unknown number flashes across the screen. What the fuck?

"Hello?"

"Is this Gage?"

"Who the fuck's asking?" I grumble as I sit in bed. Colette's hand falling from my chest.

"I found this number in an emergency contact list for a Hale Knight? You know him?"

I repeat... what the fuck? I stand, already jumping into my jeans. "Yeah, I know him. Is he okay?"

"He's down here at Luke's Bar, completely hammered. He's cut off and needs a ride."

Fuck. Hale has been struggling since Natasha died six months ago. I know he had been fighting the demons who called him to the bottle. Looks like he finally lost...

"What's the address? I'll be there as soon as I can."

He lists off an address forty fucking minutes away in bum fuck nowhere Massachusetts. He fucking owes me.

I pull up to the old hole in the wall bar and lock my car, the large wood door creaks as I swing it open, and I'm presented with an almost empty bar. Hale sits at the bar top, well, sitting would be giving him more credit than he deserves, it's more like slumped over the bar.

I walk up to him as the bartender, probably the one who called me nods. Slapping his back, he moans and then falls off the stool.

"For fucks sake." I lean down and pull him up by the collar of his jean jacket. "Hale!" His eyes stay closed, but his lips mumble out an almost incomprehensible "Natasha."

"Not quite. I'm much prettier," I say as he opens an eye.

"Gage?" he slurs.

"The one and only. Come on big guy. Let's get you home." I begin to drag him away, but he pushes me off him with his forearm. He's surprisingly strong despite his inebriated state.

"I have no home without her," he slurs as he stumbles toward me, and I catch him.

"This isn't you, man. Get yourself together."

"What would you do if you lost Colette?" My jaw tenses and my skin bristles at the thought.

"I'd put a fucking bullet in my head but that can't be you."

"Why not?" He has dark circles under his eyes and his pale, sweaty skin glistens in the low light of the bar.

"Because you're better than I am. Than this," I say as I drag him fully upright again. I see the numbness in his eyes. He needs to stay.

He can't leave this fucking planet. I made her a promise to keep him here.

"Fuck you. I'm tired." I know he doesn't mean that a good nap would fix his exhaustion. This man's on the hunt for a dirt nap six feet under, but I won't let him have it. He's my brother, as much as Everett is and I won't let his demons have him.

I pull his forehead to mine by the back of his neck. "You have to hang on. You'll be home soon. I promise."

hale

Six Months Later

I 've officially been able to retire my parents. They enjoy the ranch but don't have to lift a finger if they don't want to. I hired a ranch hand to help me, a young man who had struggled a bit with the law. He's turning out to be a respectable and reliable man who, when ready, will be on the right path to live a good life.

Adoptions of our horses are happening faster than we can rehabilitate which I'm not complaining about. Our animals deserve the best. We've had anonymous donations flowing in steadily, although if I had to guess I would say they're from the twins. Rafael and I haven't spoken more than a handful of times but surprisingly, Enzo and I talk at least once a week. He kept me updated on taking down the Russian bastard responsible for Natasha's death and just a couple months ago told me that Alexey Romanova was dead.

Gage has been pestering me about coming back to the city, if I were to guess, the bastard misses me, but he would never admit it. It's okay, I can read him like an open book. I told him I would come in soon. I haven't been back since I left a year ago. I have no desire to see Boston anymore. I don't have a desire for much anymore, her absence from my life has resulted in a grief I've never known.

Even in moments of laughter and when I'm smiling, I'm still fucking sad. In of happiness and pure joy, I'm still fucking sad. But that's what grief is, a deeply rooted sadness that always lingers. It's how I felt when I lost Ivy, until my broken little sparrow came along and consumed my grief as if it were hers to claim; she consumed enough of it that I stopped surviving and began living again. She consumed so much of it, that somewhere along the way she began to feel like her life was worth less than mine. But that's where she was wrong, her life became mine. My heart beat with hers and now that hers has stopped, I wonder each day how mine still functions.

Still, it beats in my broken fucking chest and wakes me each morning. Like this morning, as I throw on my beanie and gloves and head out to feed, I drink my black cup of coffee that brings me closer to her and brace myself for another fucking day. Going through the routine settles my mind, staying busy has been the only thing saving me from being with my girl, from drowning my liver in alcohol. That and the stupid fucking promise I made to her and then my mother. I promised I would find out what was on the other side of healing.

Shocker... I still don't fucking know because I will never heal without her but at least I'm not drinking a bottle a night anymore. I sobered up at Gage's that night he found me at the bar and he helped me over the next few weeks, detoxing from alcohol and I could never thank him enough.

Finishing up at the pastures, I give Matilda an extra treat. She's become one of my favorite horses and even though many have offered to adopt her, the rude mare was Nat's favorite, and I can't bear to let her go, even though she still tries to bite my fingers off.

I stop in and check on Ma and we eat breakfast together as she rambles on about Uncle Jenkins. Something about his tractor again and I tell her I'll take a look at it... again.

When I'm all done, I park the 4x4 back in the barn and then hop into ol' reliable Rosey to head back home. I drop the tailgate and the dogs hop in the back then head back to my house.

As I pull up to my house, a red pickup sits in the drive to the left of the porch and a woman stands at the steps. Her short, dark curled hair reaches the edge of her jean jacket collar.

Getting out of the truck, Max hops over the tailgate and rushes to her, he sits in front of her, tail wagging and she leans down to scratch his head.

Dropping the tailgate, Gracie the not-so-graceful Great Dane miscalculates the proximity of the ground and face plants when she jumps down from the bed of the truck. My head shakes when she looks up at me with a grass stain across her white face. "You're a mess, Gracie."

The Great Dane runs over, looking like a baby giraffe toward the woman and sits next to her, tail wagging and tongue lolling out the side of her mouth.

I remember that I'm meeting someone this afternoon about an adoption, maybe I wrote down the wrong time... but either way, this must be her.

"Sorry, Ma'am. I thought our meeting wasn't until this afternoon. I can take you down to meet—"

She turns and my heart stops.

"You finished it." That voice. That smile.

The force of her beauty physically knocks me back, taking a step to catch myself. "Natasha?"

I can't move. I can't take my eyes off her as she walks up to me, her graceful steps as breathtaking as I remember. Inches from me, her head tilts and I'd know those eyes anywhere. They haunt my dreams every night. Except the eyes I see in my dreams are dull, lifeless.

These whiskey eyes are filled with that fire I love.

"Knight," she says as her eyes go glassy with tears, and I know it's her. I'm not dreaming. But you know, to be sure, I grab her face in my hands and kiss the living shit out of her. Her tongue wraps around mine as she brings me back to life.

It takes every bit of my strength to pull away from her, but I do, leaning my forehead to hers, she tucks her arms between my Carhartt jacket and sweater. "You have some serious explaining to do, sweetheart."

"I know. I'm sorry, Hale. But I had to. It was the only way. Please, hear me out."

"You're already forgiven," I say as she steps away from me, but I grab her wrist and haul her into my chest, my hands finding her ass, that perfect ass in those tight Wranglers and I hoist her up. Her legs naturally wrap around my waist. She's home. I'm home.

Once inside I set her on the kitchen counter, the island the exact cabinetry color she chose, and I look into those dark eyes once again.

"What the fuck, baby?"

Her small hands scratch through my beard before wrapping to the nape of my neck.

Her little giggle goes straight to my cock, and I mentally will it to calm the fuck down so she can talk, and I can pay attention.

Her silky voice begins to explain everything. "After I was shot, Enzo took me to their doctor. I was in an induced coma for two weeks. When I woke, I had a chest tube and needed three more surgeries to repair the damage that the bullet had done. The twins had come up with a plan while I was in my initial surgery, the perfect solution to the Romanova problem."

It clicks then and my head falls to her chest as she begins to run her fingers through my hair. My hands grip her thighs to ensure her presences remains, my mind not fully believing it yet.

"Your death," I whisper.

"Exactly. With me dead, the Romanovas would believe their hit on me was successful. They wouldn't come for me any longer."

"It was the perfect plan. Why *the fuck* couldn't I have been included?" I look up at her and try to show my anger at their deceit but fuck, I can't. She's here.

She smirks, knowing she's got me, and I slap her ass with a playful smirk.

"I couldn't risk you knowing, Hale. Dante's few remaining men were on the hunt for you and the first place they'd look was through me. Plus, I couldn't put you on the Romanovas' radar. I would rather lose you for a year than for a lifetime."

Her fingers link together at the nape of my neck. Fuck, she's too smart and too damn brave for her own good.

"The first six months I was recovering in Doc's warehouse, therapists were brought in to help me. I was in PT and OT for a while and when I was finally strong enough, I began boxing again. But I was still stuck in that warehouse until the twins took out Alexey and ensured my safety. After about ten months, Alexey was finally dead and Illya agreed to a truce. We decided that it would be best to hold off from me coming home to you for another couple of months to be safe. And when I did, I needed all new... well everything. New look, new name."

My head tilts. "So that explains the dark hair. I like it by the way."

She reaches up and fluffs her new short hair. "I like it too." A mischievous grin grows across her supply lips. "Well, aren't you going to ask me my new name?"

"Okay. Who do I have the pleasure of loving then?"

She holds up her left hand and I'm not sure how I missed it before but now I see a simple gold band wrapped around her ring finger. "Mae Knight. Previously Parker and we, my dear husband, have been married for one month."

I can't help but let out a roaring laugh. "I missed my own proposal and wedding?"

"I had some help from this nerdy tech guy, he fudged up some good documents. Sorry to steal your thunder."

Pulling her to the edge of the counter, I slide my hands around her waist and lift her up. "Well, I'm sure as fuck not going to miss my honeymoon, Mrs. Knight."

The weight of her body pressed into mine entrances me, a euphoria I thought I would never know again. Her curves meld into mine like a puzzle that's found its last missing piece and I relish the fact she's mine.

Only mine.

Her eyes leave mine as we enter our bedroom. I painted it in the same lavender purple she picked out with a white shiplap ceiling and bronze fixtures. I always thought it a bit too feminine for my tastes alone but every time I saw the color, I thought of her.

"Lavender."

"Like you." I place a kiss on her jaw as I lay her on the bed, my body resting between her thighs. I'm finally fucking home.

"Hale." She lets out on a breathy moan that makes my cock jump to attention.

"I'm here, baby," I remind her as I place kiss after kiss to her jaw, then down her neck. The damn jean jacket and knit sweater she wears prevents me from going any lower.

I bite at the collar of her sweater and give it a playful tug which elicits a laugh from her and... fuck. My chest physically hurts at the sound, but it's a welcomed pain. The kind of pain you grow to appreciate and even crave. The pain that pulls you from the numb abyss your mind was once consumed by.

"I need these off. Now," I command, and she sits up with a smirk.

"Yes, sir." The saccharine smile that graces her lips makes me fucking melt. God, how did I live a year without this woman?

The slow slide of the jean jacket down her arms teases me and when she reaches for the knit of her sweater ever so slowly, I lose my patience. Leaning over her, I rip the clothing off and earn myself another small giggle.

"Don't want to take this slow?" she says as I hurriedly rip off my own jacket and shirt.

"One year ago, I kneeled on the grave of the woman I love." I drop to my knees beside the bed and grip the waistband of her jeans, sliding them and her panties down. "Now, I kneel in between her perfect thighs, having been denied the one and only thing that can bring me to heaven and I will wait no more. I have forever to take it slow, right now I'm a man deprived, and I need you."

"So pretty on your knees for me." She cups her hands around my jaw. "Such a good boy."

"Is that what you want tonight, baby? You want your good boy?" I smirk up at her, asking the question I do every time because even if she gives me control, both of us know that it's always been hers. Control over her life, over her body, over me, she has it all in her hands, all she has to do is ask for it and I'll fucking give it to her.

"No. Right now I want my knight." Her body lays back on the bed and I drag her ass to the edge with a growl of appreciation for her answer.

Sliding my tongue over her pussy, she inhales sharply, and my eyes catch the expansion of her ribs, the soft curves of her skin over her bones that turn sharp as she inhales. "God, Hale." She moans as I suck her clit into my mouth, soaking in the scent and taste of her. She's heaven and hell all in one. The one who saved me and ruined me.

I continue to run my tongue over her, lapping at her juices as she fills the room with her moans and her hips wiggle beneath my hold, she never could be quiet or sit still. Scooting my arm up higher so

I can wrap it over her stomach, I pin her down with my forearm, releasing one hand and pushing my fingers inside her. Curling them slowly, I feel that spot that makes her detonate and wait for my beauty to hold back.

But she doesn't.

Her release fills my mouth, and I take it in with surprise. She has never been able to come without some encouragement but here she is, defying my expectations yet again.

Her muscles quiver as I lift my head, placing a kiss to her inner thigh then wiping my beard with my hand.

As I stand, I slide my pants down then brace myself over her. Her body beneath mine again makes my chest seize up. Am I in another dream?

Before I know it, her hand wipes a tear from my cheek. "I'm here, Hale. I'm here."

"Are you sure?" I say as I continue to stare at her chest, right at the almost perfect round scar, right where the bullet left her body.

"I love you," she whispers the words I had never heard her say before and my eyes fly to hers.

"Fuck, baby. I love you. If this is another dream, don't wake me. Please. I beg of you. I can't survive waking again without you next to me."

"I'm here, Hale. It's real. I promise."

I sit back on my heels, bringing her small body up with me, her thighs straddle mine as I slowly slide her down onto me. Her warmth suffocates me, and I can't breathe.

"Shit," I hiss out as she releases a decadent moan. When our eyes open again, hers are brimmed with tears, tears of happiness, I hope. My hands brush a scar on her back, under her left shoulder blade where the bullet entered.

I look down at her chest again, running my hands over her rib cage. The pads of my fingers trace a long, jagged scar along the left side, and she must see the confusion on my face. "They had to cut my ribs open there to stop the bleeding. The bullet nicked my aorta. Any higher and I would have bled out in minutes."

I'm inside her but both of us are unmoving. I almost fucking lost her. I *did* lose her. The reality of her injuries all floods in. I've seen men with lesser wounds succumb to the grim reaper but my beautiful, soft, incredible little sparrow, survived against all odds.

"You should have died," I whisper, not meaning to say it but I'm in utter disbelief.

"I did die," she says as her hands scoop my face and lift it to hers. Her lips meet mine in a soft kiss, our tongues slowly colliding as we both relish in the feel of one another. "But you saved me."

I shake my head and rest it against her chest.

"You did. Dying never scared me. I never had anything to live for. But the thought of never seeing you again, holding you... I thought I wanted to fly but in the end all I want is to stay grounded with you."

"Baby..."

Her hips lift slowly and come down just as slow, cutting off what I meant to say as my head rolls back and I release a long groan. She continues to ride me as I hold her hip with one hand, the other wrapped in the now short, dark hair at the nape of her neck.

Her pace picks up and I use my grip on her hair to push and pull her kiss where I crave it, we are driving each other mad as we share control.

Her muscles tighten and the tension in her body coils like a spring needing release. "Let go, sweetheart, cover me with that sweet come I've been denied a whole fucking year."

And with my command, she does. Her pussy strangles my cock, and I follow right after. I fill her with my release as I pulse inside of her, her panting breath mixes with mine as a smile breaks out across her face.

"I hope you don't mind but... I'm not on birth control."

My heart races with excitement. "Fuck me. Let's go again." Her fit of laughter forces her to squeeze tighter around me since I'm still inside her and I can't help but curse at how good it feels.

With her in my arms.

I'm home.

mae

His body's warmth soothes a part of my soul that was desperately calling out to him. While I was healing from my injury, I struggled with lying to him but I knew I had to. I couldn't risk him for my own selfish needs, and I had to hope that he would keep his promise to me.

Of course, I recruited Gage to help look after him since the grumpy hacker from hell not only knew about our plan but helped see it through. Without him, we may not have been able to pull this off like we did. He ensured all the documents were believable, well at least looked legit enough for people to believe. He helped me with my new identity, even giving Mae Parker, turned Mae Knight physical records dating all the way back to her made up birth.

I breathe a sigh of relief thinking of the Romanovas, knowing that they are no longer a threat. With Dante and my father gone and with the new deal they have with the Romanovas, the Devils of Seattle are taking care of their Angels.

"What has your mind turning?" Hale's gruff voice makes me jump as he wraps himself around me.

"Nothing," I lie.

"Don't lie to me. Not anymore," he says and though I know he isn't truly angry with me, the crack in his voice fills me with guilt.

Turning my body to face him, I run my hand down his cheek. "I'm sorry that I had to lie to you. That so many of us had to."

His eyes are vacant until they meet mine. "Who all knew?"

I hate that I'm about to hurt him but no more lies. "The twins... and Gage." The smallest quiver of muscles between his brows tells me that stung. "Don't be mad at him."

His jaw tenses. "How long did he know?"

"Rafael called him in during my first surgery, he was part of the plan from the beginning and there is no way we would have succeeded had he not helped us."

Hale's eyes roll and then close. "Fine. But I'm punching him in the face, once. To get it out of my system."

I giggle and smack at his chest. "Play nice."

"Trust me, if you knew Gage, you'd know punching him in the face is nice. It's practically a declaration of love. Actually, I should probably give him a nice long hug instead."

"You're not being nice at all," I scold him and then we fall into each other's eyes, lost in the reality that our dreams have come to fruition. I'm home with him again, we are free to begin our lives.

"What about Sabrina? She didn't know?"

I let out a sigh. "Actually, I haven't heard from her in... a while. After I died," I say with air quotes around the last word, "I couldn't reach out to anyone, it was too risky. But when I got the clear, I called her and even stopped by the gym, but no answer and the gym had a

S. E. EMORY

closed sign up." My fingers pick at the edge of the sheet. "I'm a little worried about her."

"Well, have you talked to Gage? I know they are pretty close or were at least."

"Yeah, I called him on the drive here actually. He said that he hasn't had contact with her. But he's working on it. He was being vague which tells me he knows more than he's letting on."

"Yeah, sounds like him. I'm sure she's fine."

"Yeah..." I trail off as the doorbell rings and my head flies toward the door to our bedroom. My heart rate picks up and I begin breathing harder. Max's head perks up from where he laid at our feet and Gracie jumps up from the floor next to my bed, bounding out the bedroom door and into the kitchen.

"Hey." Hale pulls my face to his and kisses me softly. "It's okay. I've got you." I nod as he slips out of bed and puts a pair of sweats on. We've been in bed almost all day, he called and rescheduled the adoption appointment he had and now we're approaching dinner time.

"Mae!" he calls from the living room and I dress in one of his shirts and a pair of his sweatpants, rolling the waist to keep them up.

"Who's Mae?" My heart flutters at her voice.

I step out from around the hallway to see Hale's mother. She hasn't changed since I saw her last, still as welcoming. She sets down a casserole dish on the kitchen island and then her eyes turn toward me.

"Oh, my heavens..." She clutches her chest, and tears immediately brim her eyes. "Natasha?"

"I guess my disguise wasn't that deceiving if you both recognized me immediately." I let out a small laugh and walk toward her. She wraps me in her arms and my eyes close.

"I'd recognize you anywhere, child. How are you here?" Her voice breaks on the last sentence and Hale motions for us to sit.

"I'll make some coffee. Nat—Mae has quite the story for you, Ma."

Her small, wrinkled hands hold my face as tears run down her cheeks. "You're home?"

I nod, my cheeks as wet as hers. "I'm home."

mae

Ten Years Later

"**M**om?" Henry tugs on my black dress, looking down into his bright blue eyes, I wipe a tear from my own. "Can I go sit with Rune and Callahan?"

"Sure, honey," I say and he runs over and sits at a stone table sitting under a large tree.

Leo comes up next to me and I give her a small hug. "Henry will cheer Rune up; he's taking all this hard."

"Are you holding up okay?" I ask as we pull apart. Over the years, Leo has become a close friend. She loves to bring Rune, Callahan and Rory out to the ranch. Hale and I take them horseback riding while her and Everett spend time in the bird garden. Sometimes they even drag Gage and his wife Colette along but those two are always busy traveling.

They never settled down with kids like we did. Always saying they preferred to be the cool Aunt and Uncle. They're both close with our kids, it's like having their own in a way and between Leo and Everett and Hale and I we have seven kids to pour our love into.

Rory stands next to Leo, holding a single rose in her hand. She lays it down on the fresh dirt and looks up to her mom. "Can I go with Henry?" Leo nods and the little girl in her black flats trudges off to join the boys.

Leo looks at the already engraved headstone, the old man had one already prepared, the only thing missing was his date of death. "You know, as much as it hurts, I'm happy. He's with his girls now. Millie and Evangeline needed him."

Gage steps up with a sleeping Ivy on his shoulder. "She's out like a light," he says as he sways back and forth.

"Here, I can take her."

I hold out my arms, attempting to take the sleeping four-year-old from his arms but he shoots me a glare. "I've got her."

I give him a sideways smile. He enjoys the boys' company, Rune, Callahan, Henry, Levi, and Carter are the unruly boys of our group. Rune being the only one who can seem to keep them in line. But Rory and Ivy, those two girls have Uncle Gage wrapped around their little fingers. He would... and does, do anything to make them happy.

"What do you think he's doing up there right now?" Gage asks as he looks down on the headstone.

Leo scoffs, "Drinking a hazelnut coffee, probably looking down on us and preparing his next life altering speech."

"How many of those did you get over the years?" Gage raises a brow at Leo.

"Too many to count," she chuckles, and I can see in her eyes that she remembers each and every one. Embedded into her like ink. Ski, will forever be tattooed into our souls. Living on in who we are.

"He gave me one too," I add and their heads both turn to me. I never told them what Ski did for me all those years ago. I told them about almost everything else, the sexual abuse, the deal between my father and the Alessis, the fake death and new identity. But what Ski did for me, it felt too personal.

"What did he do for you?" Gage asks.

"He saved me."

I lay my sprig of lavender down on his grave, then Leo sets her rose down, finally Gage lays down a lily before walking over and laying a dahlia on his own mother's grave.

Funny how one simple man, who only ever wanted to live an easy and quiet life with the woman he loved ended up saving three completely broken souls.

He *chased* down our trust, *found* us in our sorrow, and *saved* our hearts.

"Yeah." Leo wipes a tear from her face. "That sounds like Ski."

The End

Acknowledgments

Thank you, thank you, thank you for reading Saving Sparrow and if you are like me, with tears in you eyes at the end of this series, then know that you are not alone. These characters and this world mean more to me than I could ever put into words and it physically hurts to let them go... but you never know... maybe some time down the road there will be a legacies series??

I must first thank my readers for allowing me to share the stories of Natasha and Hale and all the couples of this series. Without you taking a chance on a small indie author, my dreams would be lost and forgotten. You are what make these stories and characters a reality, you are what keep me opening my computer and writing, you are why I write. I couldn't thank you enough, my loves.

Second I have to shout out and thank my amazing beta readers, Emily Wendt, Hannah Small, Nichole LaShae, Alexis Brown, and last but not least the amazing CAS. Seriously, ladies, I could write the stories but you are the ones who give me the confidence to share them with the world. Not only do you catch all my silly typos and when I use the word beautiful too many times but you hype me up when I feel like my writing isn't good enough. You are irreplaceable and if you ever leave me, I'll hunt you down like Enzo (;

I of course have to mention my amazing editor Mallory Day. Holy cow woman, your insight is invaluable. You allow my creative voice to shine while also guiding my writing in the right direction.

I also have to throw in my wonderful husband who allows me to vent my crazy ideas. You encourage my writing and my love for romance and give me a safe space to be creative without judgement. You inspire me, you love me, and you keep me going. I lava you.

Lastly, I have to get a little deep here. I want to thank Maegan Parada, my sister. You're resilience inspired Natasha's bold, but caring personality, Mae Mae. I don't know what your past holds but I know that just like Natasha, you are not who you once were and you should be fucking proud of where you are now. When I was young, I never understood and maybe I still don't. But by writing Nat, I saw a piece of you. I saw a girl with a broken soul who only ever wanted to be loved and who coped in the only way she knew how. Never be ashamed of your past and the decisions you made, they made you into the strong, brave, caring, and beautiful woman you are today. I love you, I forgive you, and you are a part of me as much the ink on my skin. One minute at a time, one day at a time, one life at a time, Mae.

Till our next adventure.

-S

S. E. Emory is a contemporary romance author who enjoys writing heart-wrenching stories. She loves taking real life struggles and heartaches and creating the happily ever afters that we all deserve. S.E. enjoys playing with her two kiddos, watching anime with her husband, and sipping coffee in her rocking chair with a warm blanket and her latest all consuming read.

<u>Connect with S. E. Emory online</u>

www.seemorybooks.com

g

goodreads.com/seemorybooks

instagram.com/s.e.emory

tiktok.com/@s.e.emory

Website

www.seemorybooks.com

Instagram

www.instagram.com/s.e.emory

Goodreads

https://www.goodreads.com/seemorybooks

Pinterest

https://www.pinterest.com/seemorybooks/

TikTok

https://www.tiktok.com/@s.e.emory

www.ingramcontent.com/pod-product-compliance
Lightning Source LLC
Chambersburg PA
CBHW021125260626
47169CB00005B/1450